"I would like you to stay until Gideon is better," Becca said.

"But you must understand that we cannot afford to pay you for your help."

Tully leaned back in his chair. A wry smile curved his lips and showed a dimple in his right cheek. "A few days of your good cooking will be payment enough. You don't have to worry about putting me up. I can sleep in the barn if the animals don't mind my snoring."

"Why are you doing this?"

His smile disappeared. His eyes grew serious. He leaned forward and clasped his hands together on the tabletop. "I wasn't exaggerating when I said it had been a long time since I was somewhere that felt like a home. When I got out of the army two years ago, things didn't go well for me. Let's just say I messed up. Somebody gave me a helping hand when I needed it. I'd like to think I'm repaying that favor by helping you and your family. Just until Gideon is back on his feet."

After thirty-five years as a nurse, **Patricia Davids** hung up her stethoscope to become a full-time writer. She enjoys spending her free time visiting her grandchildren, doing some long-overdue yard work and traveling to research her story locations. She resides in Wichita, Kansas. Pat always enjoys hearing from her readers. You can visit her online at patriciadavids.com.

Emma Miller lives quietly in her old farmhouse in rural Delaware. Fortunate enough to have been born into a family of strong faith, she grew up on a dairy farm, surrounded by loving parents, siblings, grandparents, aunts, uncles and cousins. Emma was educated in local schools and once taught in an Amish schoolhouse. When she's not caring for her large family, reading and writing are her favorite pastimes.

USA TODAY Bestselling Author

PATRICIA DAVIDS

A Haven for Christmas

&

EMMA MILLER

An Amish Holiday Courtship

LOVE INSPIRED
INSPIRATIONAL ROMANCE

Recycling programs
for this product may
not exist in your area.

LOVE INSPIRED®
INSPIRATIONAL ROMANCE

ISBN-13: 978-1-335-41886-9

A Haven for Christmas and An Amish Holiday Courtship

Copyright © 2021 by Harlequin Books S.A.

A Haven for Christmas
First published in 2020. This edition published in 2021.
Copyright © 2020 by Patricia MacDonald

An Amish Holiday Courtship
First published in 2020. This edition published in 2021.
Copyright © 2020 by Emma Miller

All rights reserved. No part of this book may be used or reproduced in
any manner whatsoever without written permission except in the case of
brief quotations embodied in critical articles and reviews.

This is a work of fiction. Names, characters, places and incidents are either the
product of the author's imagination or are used fictitiously. Any resemblance
to actual persons, living or dead, businesses, companies, events or locales is
entirely coincidental.

This edition published by arrangement with Harlequin Books S.A.

For questions and comments about the quality of this book, please contact us
at CustomerService@Harlequin.com.

Harlequin Enterprises ULC
22 Adelaide St. West, 40th Floor
Toronto, Ontario M5H 4E3, Canada
www.Harlequin.com

Printed in U.S.A.

CONTENTS

A HAVEN FOR CHRISTMAS

Patricia Davids

This book is dedicated to the thousands of men and women who suffer from addiction and are working to overcome it. May you find strength, solace and peace in God's love.

Now the God of hope fill you with all joy and peace in believing, that ye may abound in hope, through the power of the Holy Ghost.
—*Romans* 15:13

Chapter One

"**D**id Rosie have her *bobbli* last night?"

Becca Beachy pinned her daughter's white *kapp* to her thick red hair, then tweaked the seven-year-old's nose. "*Nee*, she did not. Do you think I would keep it a secret if your new calf had arrived?"

Annabeth couldn't hide her disappointment. "*Daadi* thought she might, and he knows everything about cows."

Becca glanced over her daughter's head to where her father-in-law sat at the kitchen table enjoying his first cup of coffee. She met his eyes and arched her brow. "Your grandpa Gideon may think he knows everything about cows, but he doesn't know everything about Rosie. She will have her calf when she is ready. Not before. Sit down and eat your breakfast."

Annabeth's lower lip stuck out. "But I wanted to tell everyone at school about my new calf."

Becca gave her a small push toward the table. "When you have a new calf, you may share the story with your friends. Your impatience won't hurry the event."

Gideon coughed and put down his cup. "It might

be that your calf will be here when you get home from school today."

"Then I will have to wait until Monday to tell everyone." Annabeth plunked herself in her chair at the table with a pout on her face. She pulled her lower lip in when she caught her mother's frown and folded her hands waiting for grace to be said.

Becca dished up the scrambled eggs, sausage links and pancakes onto a plate and sat at the foot of the table. Gideon bowed his head and began the silent blessing. Becca added a plea for his improved health to her prayer of thankfulness for God's blessings. She needed his help to run the dairy. She couldn't do it alone. The last thing she wanted to face was failing at this new endeavor and having to uproot her daughter yet again. Her husband had never found the place where he wanted to put down roots. They had moved every year of their marriage, even after Annabeth was born, but Becca knew home wasn't a place to be found. It was a place to be made. Here in the north of Maine was where Becca was making a home.

When Gideon looked up, signaling the end of the prayer, Annabeth reached for the pancakes. Becca pushed the pitcher of syrup toward her, knowing her daughter's sweet tooth. She covertly studied Gideon's drawn features as they ate. He wasn't getting better, and that worried her. A cold was one thing, but his cough had hung on much longer than it should. She waited until he finished eating. "Gideon, why don't you drive Annabeth to school today? I'll take care of the milk for a change." She held her breath, waiting for his answer.

"You won't try to lift those heavy milk cans by yourself?"

Because their Amish religion didn't allow the use of

electricity, their cows were milked by hand. The milk was strained and poured into ten-gallon stainless steel milk cans. The cans were taken by wagon every morning and every night to the refrigeration facility two miles away. Ten gallons of milk in a steel can weighed nearly a hundred pounds. She had filled five of them that morning. They were still sitting in the milking parlor.

She sought to ease Gideon's mind and convince him to take the easier task of driving Annabeth to their Amish school in New Covenant. "I'll wait on you and get started on my baking. If you don't stop to gossip with the neighbors, we can get the milk to the collection point before the truck comes. If we miss it, nothing is lost. The milk won't spoil in this weather. We'll take a double load this evening."

"*Nee*, you take the child. I will see to the milk as usual."

"I want you to take me. Please, *Daadi*," Annabeth said with her mouth still full of her last bite of sausage.

Becca didn't scold her for her table manners. She hoped the child's pleading would sway Gideon. It usually did. This morning was no exception. He smiled and nodded. "All right, I'll take you. It will make a nice change for your mother."

Becca's tense shoulders relaxed. "*Goot*, now take the plates to the sink, Annabeth, and go wash your hands and face."

"*Daadi*, will you tell me another story about the little boys with red hair that you used to know?" the child asked as she gathered the plates.

"If you do as your mother tells you," he said softly.

"Okay." She put the dishes in the sink and ran to wash up.

He looked at Becca. "Do you think she knows they are stories about her father and his brother?"

Becca's heart contracted with pain. "Not yet, but one day she will realize the truth and thank you for it."

Among the Amish it was proper to grieve for a lost loved one, as Becca still grieved for her husband, but it wasn't considered proper to speak about them afterward. In doing so it might appear that a person was questioning God's will in calling their loved one home. Annabeth had only the vaguest memories of her father. He died when she was barely four. Gideon's stories of the little red-haired boys were his way of sharing his memories of his sons with her without naming them.

Annabeth came rushing back into the room, pulling on her coat. "I'm ready."

Becca handed her a blue plastic lunch box and held open the door for the pair. The cold late-November air rushed in. Gideon took Annabeth's hand and walked with her to the black buggy parked by the front gate. Cider, their buggy horse, stood waiting patiently, his warm breath rising in puffs of white mist from his nostrils.

Annabeth looked up at her grandfather. "Tell me the story about how the oldest red-haired boy saved his little brother in a runaway buggy."

"You have heard it many times."

"But it's my favorite."

Gideon coughed and pressed a hand to his chest for a moment before he lifted her into the buggy. "All right. I will tell it again."

"And many more times, I pray," Becca said softly. She watched them drive away and closed the door against the chill.

* * *

"I'm sorry to do this to you, Tully. I hope you know that."

Tully Lange stared at the eviction notice he had just been handed by the kid who managed the apartment building. His rent was two weeks past due, but he had hoped to get a month's extension. So much for hope.

Things weren't going his way. He'd lost his job as a night watchman on Monday when the owner of the corner pawnshop where he worked died. Tully hadn't found another job yet, but he was looking. The high point of his week had been a lukewarm Thanksgiving dinner at the local soup kitchen the day before yesterday. And now this. Happy holidays. It was enough to drive a sober man to drink.

He crumpled the paper in his hand. He wasn't going to be that man again. "It's okay, Reggie. I know you're just doing your job."

The skinny young man with spiked blond hair and thick glasses sagged with relief. "It's nothing personal. You know that. The super won't let me cut you any slack. I mean, I told him you just got out of rehab. I don't think he has any idea how tough that is. Don't let this bounce you off the wagon, Tully. I've seen how hard it is to quit drinking. My brother went through rehab. It was rough, but he stayed sober seven years."

"Tell me he is still sober." At the moment Tully needed to hear it could be done.

Reggie pressed his lips together and stared at his feet. "I wish I could. His wife left him. He couldn't handle it. But hey, seven years, that's a lot."

Tully turned away before Reggie could see how crushed he was. For every story about people who stayed sober, there were dozens more about people who had failed. "Yeah, seven years is a lot. I hope he finds his way back to sobriety."

"Thanks, man. I hope he does, too. What are you going to do?"

"I've got no job. It looks like I've only got two weeks left in this paradise." He let his gaze drift over the peeling paint, tattered carpet and water-stained ceiling in what passed for a lobby of the low-rent Philadelphia apartment complex the rehab center had located for him. What was he going to do? "I'll think of something."

"I can let you know if I hear about a job." The offer was half-hearted, but Tully nodded his thanks.

Too bad his Alcoholics Anonymous meeting wasn't tonight. He could still call his sponsor and…do what? Cry on the man's shoulder? Life was tough. Tully Lange, formerly Sergeant Lange of the United States Army, needed to be tougher.

At least no one was shooting at him.

He unlocked his mailbox and pulled out the usual junk mail along with one oversize red envelope. He smiled when he saw it was from Arnie Dawson, also formerly of the United States Army and a longtime friend. Arnie was among the few people Tully had told he was going into rehab.

He tore open the envelope. On the front of the card inside was a baby in a diaper wearing a black mortarboard cap with a gold tassel. Inside the card read, "Graduation is only the first step. Keep stepping."

Arnie had added a handwritten note.

Couldn't find a card that said "congrats on getting through rehab." Thought this one had pretty

much the same message. I'm real proud of you,
Cowboy. I wish I had half your guts. Pop up to
Maine and see me soon. We'll swap lies about
our good old army days. I might even convince
an Okie like you to stay in my slice of heaven.

Arnie loved teasing Tully about his Oklahoma roots,
boots and Midwestern drawl. He never called Tully anything except Cowboy. Tully turned the envelope over
and studied the return address. Caribou, Maine. The
place even sounded cold. Would there be snow already?
Tully almost chuckled. Wouldn't Arnie be shocked if
he took him up on his offer?

"Well, why not?" he muttered to himself. What did
he have to lose?

"Why not what?" Reggie asked.

Tully had forgotten the boy was still hovering nearby.
"A buddy has invited me to visit him in Maine. I guess
I've got the time. It'll be good to see him again."

"Maine? Nothing but lumberjacks and moose that far
north, unless he lives on the coast. I hear the seafood is
awesome, though. At least that's what they say on those
TV travel channels. I've never been there myself. I've
never been outside Philadelphia."

Tully stared at the envelope in his hand. If he spent
the rest of his last paycheck on gas, he could make it
in a day or two, provided his car had that many more
miles left in it. He didn't have much to pack. That was
the upside of being homeless and living out of his car
for a year. The only upside.

An unfamiliar sense of excitement began creeping in
to replace the despair that always hovered at the edge of
his consciousness. A road trip and a visit with a friend

he hadn't seen in more than two years. What better way to celebrate four months of sobriety and the upcoming Christmas season? He needed to go. He had to get away before his old life pulled him back down to the gutter. Maybe this was his chance to make a real change.

He tossed the junk mail in the trash can by the door and walked down the musty-smelling hall to his studio apartment. He would let his sponsor know where he was going so he didn't think Tully had relapsed. Other than his outpatient therapist, there was no one else to tell now that his old boss was gone.

He had burned a lot of bridges with the people in his life. This was his chance to save one of the few he had left.

Now that he had a plan, he rushed to get going before he changed his mind. Before he didn't make it past the bar on Clover Street.

How many times had his determination to get sober been derailed in the past? There had always been a bar or a liquor store between him and his commitment to quit drinking. There would be one in Caribou, Maine, too. But there would also be his friend Arnie and most likely an AA group nearby if he needed help.

He pulled himself up short. Not if. He would need help. It would never be easy.

If he had learned anything in rehab, it was that his alcoholism could be mastered but never cured.

Now that the first rush of enthusiasm was wearing off, Tully sat on the worn, lumpy gray sofa that served as his couch and bed. He pulled out his cell phone, grateful that the rehab facility had provided him with a prepaid one. It didn't have any bells and whistles, but a fellow couldn't get a job without a phone and an address. He punched in Arnie's number. His buddy picked up on the third ring.

"What did you think of the card?"

Not even a hello. Tully chuckled. "I think your taste is questionable."

"Give me the spiel."

Tully knew what he meant. It was the way AA members introduced themselves at his local meeting. "Hello. My name is Tully and I'm an alcoholic. I've been sober for four months and five days."

"Man, you don't know how good it is to hear from you, Cowboy. Have you heard from any of the other guys?" Arnie asked hopefully.

"I heard Mason reenlisted but only because O'Connor stopped by to visit me once in rehab. He didn't know where anyone else was, but he had heard about Brian." Saying his friend's name still choked him. He drew a shaky breath.

"It wasn't your fault," Arnie said firmly.

How Tully wished that was true. "I knew how drunk Brian was. I had his car keys. Why did I give them back to him?"

It had been the last straw. The last bad decision that cost his friend his life and the lives of two other people when Brian ran a red light. It had been rock bottom for Tully. It had been his wake-up call.

"You handed over the keys because you were drunk, too. You weren't thinking straight."

It was an easy excuse. One that he would never use again.

"You can't change the past, buddy," Arnie said.

"I know."

"Have you found a new job?"

"Not yet. I've been looking. I need to find one person to have faith in me and believe I'll stay sober. There don't seem to be many like that around here. The truth is, I'm on my way to see you."

"What? You're coming here? When?" Arnie's surprised excitement was what Tully hoped to hear.

"When? That depends. How long does it take to drive from Philadelphia to Reindeer?"

"Caribou."

"Right. Same thing." Tully knew his friend wouldn't let that slide.

"Caribou are not reindeer, my cowboy friend. While they may be the same species, reindeer have been domesticated for more than two thousand years. Caribou are wild. It's sort of like comparing a mustang to a Shetland pony."

Tully laughed. He should've called Arnie ages ago. "My grandpa bought a Shetland pony for us kids. That animal put any mustang to shame when it came to bucking off a rider. Billy was the meanest little horse that ever walked the earth."

"I've missed your Oklahoma ranch life stories."

"Look, I have to be stingy with my minutes. How long?"

"Twelve hours if you go straight through, but don't. You don't want to meet a moose when you're sleepy."

"Okay. You'll see me when you see me, and I will avoid meeting any and all moose." Tully hung up and sat back. This was a good decision. At least he hoped it was.

Fourteen hours later, dawn was only a faint light in the eastern sky when Tully rounded a bend on an isolated snow-covered stretch of Maine highway. That wasn't a moose in his headlights. It was a Holstein cow.

He hit his brakes and swerved to miss her. He didn't see the calf until it was too late.

"Can I help you milk this morning?" Annabeth asked, rubbing the sleep from her eyes as she came into the kitchen.

"You just want to check on Rosie. I'll come and get you if she has had her calf." Becca glanced at Gideon's door. He wasn't up yet. She didn't intend to wake him. It was Sunday, but there was no church service this week. It was a day of rest, and Gideon needed it. Hopefully she would have most of the milking done before he joined her.

She finished washing the milk pails and gathered the handles of two in each hand. "Open the door for me, daughter."

Annabeth pulled the kitchen door open and took a step back. "*Mamm*, there's a man stealing Rosie. He has a calf, too!"

Becca moved to stand behind her daughter. There was a stranger outside their front gate. It wasn't one of their Amish neighbors or anyone else she knew. He was *Englisch* by his dress. He was wearing jeans, a faded blue denim jacket and a battered gray cowboy hat. He didn't seem intent on fleeing with his armload of newborn calf. Rosie stood beside him, nosing the baby's face and licking her.

"I don't think he is stealing our cow, but I have no idea what he is doing."

She stepped outside the screen door and put her buckets on the porch floor. "Can we help you?"

"Ma'am, is this your cow?" His slow drawl was low and husky.

"That's my Rosie," Annabeth said peering around Becca.

"You have a new little heifer, but she is hurt. Where should I put her?"

Becca spoke quietly to her daughter in Pennsylvania Dutch, the language the Amish spoke at home. "Go wake your grandpa."

Annabeth darted down the hallway. Becca then walked down the steps of the porch and stopped with her hands on the gate. "Where did you find her?"

He gestured toward the cow with his head. "Mama was standing in the middle of the highway about a quarter mile from here. Her calf was off to the side of the road. I swerved to miss the cow and hit the calf. She's scraped up, and her front leg is broken. I'm real sorry, ma'am."

The loss of any animal was hard to bear, but Annabeth was going to be heartbroken if the calf couldn't be saved. "Bring her down to the barn."

Becca hurried ahead of him and was surprised to see the corral gate standing wide-open. She quickly closed it and held open the barn door for him. "That would explain how Rosie got out." How many others had found the opening?

The man followed her inside the barn. "I once had a horse that could open a barn door by himself. He just took the handle in his teeth and turned his head, but I've never heard of a cow doing it."

"I suspect my daughter left it unlatched when she came out to check on Rosie last night. She has been waiting eagerly for this calf to arrive."

"You might want to check the rest of your cattle. I saw a lot of tracks heading out your lane."

"I was just thinking that." She opened a stall door. He carried the calf inside and tenderly laid her down. She struggled to get up. He kept her down with one hand. "Easy, little one. You just take it easy. Everything's gonna be okay." The calf quieted at his gentle reassurances. "You might want to close that gate so Mama doesn't get in here with us."

It took a second for Becca to realize he was speaking to her in the same soothing tone. She quickly shut the stall door. Rosie tried to push her way in, but to no avail.

The first rays of the sun streamed through the small window and illuminated the pen. He pushed back the brim of his hat, and she got her first good look at the calf's rescuer. His eyes as he gazed up at her were such a deep brown they almost looked black. His hair—what she could see of it—was black as a crow's wing and cut short as a newly shorn sheep. His face was thin, as if he had recently lost weight. Her guess was borne out by the extra notches she noticed beside the silver buckle in the tooled leather belt he wore to hold up his loose jeans. He had on boots, but not the kind she was used to seeing. The pointed toes didn't look comfortable, but they were clearly well-worn. He didn't say anything. He just waited for her to finish her assessment.

"Thank you for stopping to care for my animals. I am Rebecca Beachy, but everyone calls me Becca."

He touched the brim of his hat. "Pleased to meet you. My name is Tully—"

She saw a flash of indecision in his eyes before his gaze fell away from hers. He turned back to the calf. "I can splint this leg until your veterinarian can get out here."

His quick change of topic had her wondering what else he had meant to say but didn't.

Chapter Two

Tully kept his gaze on the injured calf. He couldn't believe he'd almost introduced himself to this pretty Amish woman as an alcoholic. He was still embarrassed to admit that he was one, even though he knew accepting it was part of the process of coming to grips with his addiction, but it didn't feel right to tell her. She'd probably never dealt with a drunk in her life. He prayed she never would.

"What is this my granddaughter tells me? Has someone come to steal our *milch kuh*? Seems to me he should take her out of the barn, not bring her inside. But perhaps he's not a very good thief."

Tully glanced up to see a formidable-looking Amish man scowling at him from beside Rosie. The little red-headed girl he had seen earlier was peeking from behind him through the wooden slats of the gate. She and her mother shared the same intense green eyes. Where the child had bright red hair, her mother's was a deep auburn.

"Annabeth, you know that's not the truth," Becca said. "Gideon, this is Tully. Tully, this is my father-in-law, Gideon Beachy. Tully found Rosie and her calf out on the highway. He accidentally struck the calf with his car. She's hurt."

Gideon looked down at the child. "And how did Rosie find her way out to the highway?"

"I don't know," Annabeth said, trying hard to look like an innocent little girl. Tully struggled not to smile.

"Someone did not latch the gate properly when she came out to check on Rosie last night," Becca suggested with a pointed look at the child.

"I thought I latched it."

"Next time you will make sure." Her grandfather's stern tone caused the little one to nod and bow her head. He spoke with a thick accent that reminded Tully of the time he had been stationed in Germany. "Now we will see what must be done to help Rosie's baby."

Gideon pushed the big cow away from the gate and slipped inside. Annabeth climbed to the top and looked on.

"The right foreleg is broken," Tully said. "We should splint it until your veterinarian can examine her. I'm more concerned about her head. She seems pretty groggy."

He caught the look that passed between Gideon and Becca. He wasn't sure if the Amish used veterinarians. Maybe they would just put her down to keep her from suffering. "A simple break in a calf this young will heal fine if it's properly splinted and you can keep her from moving around too much."

Gideon nodded at Becca. "Go to the phone shack and call Doc Pike."

"Can we afford that?"

"We'll manage."

Tully wished he could offer to pay for the vet, but he had less than twenty dollars to his name.

"I will see if I can find something to make a splint." Becca left the stall and took Annabeth with her.

Gideon sank down beside the calf, keeping one leg extended in an awkward position. He patted his thigh. "I know something about broken bones. Let us see if she has other injuries."

The two men carefully examined the calf. "She seems okay," Tully said.

"You know something about cattle?" Gideon asked.

"Beef cattle. Angus, mostly. I grew up on a ranch in Oklahoma. I know next to nothing about dairy cattle except that your Holsteins are really big."

Gideon chuckled. "I have thought the same thing when one is standing on my foot."

"I noticed tracks in the snow leading away from the house. Any idea how many more cattle are missing?"

"It can't be many. I saw at least six waiting to be milked. We have eleven counting Rosie. I will check as soon as we take care of this one. A man can solve only one problem at a time, no matter how much he wants to do everything at once."

Tully smiled. "I like your philosophy."

Becca came back into the barn a short time later with several rolls of cloth tucked under her arm. She held a length of plastic pipe in her hand. "Doc Pike says he'll be here in an hour. Will this work to stabilize the leg if you cut it in half lengthwise? It was left over from when we put in the new water system."

Gideon got up and took the pipe from her. "It should. I'll be back in a bit."

Tully held the calf's leg straight, making it bawl in

protest. "Go ahead and pad it before we put the splint over it."

She had to lean close to him in order to bind the leg. She spoke gently to the calf with the same singsong German accent as Gideon. Her hands were small compared to Tully's, deft and gentle as she worked. Her auburn hair was parted in the middle and tucked beneath a white bonnet. He wasn't sure if it was her hair or bonnet that smelled fresh, like linen that had been dried in the sun. It reminded him of the way his grandmother's sheets used to smell when he had helped her gather them off the clothesline. It was a good memory. One that had been buried far too long beneath unhappy, painful ones.

It had been a while since he had spent time this close to a woman. "Your hair smells nice. Like sunshine."

She drew back. Her startled, wide-eyed expression told him he'd said something wrong. "I'm sorry. I meant that as a compliment."

She went back to work. "To say such things is not our way."

"Then I apologize. I meant no disrespect. I don't need an irate Amish husband coming after me."

She smoothed the end of the bandage into place. "My husband is dead, so you need not fear." She got to her feet and left without looking at him.

He closed his eyes and hung his head. "Nice going, Tully. Insult the first Amish lady you've ever met. Maybe keep your mouth shut from now on."

"Even a fool is counted wise if he says nothing," Gideon said as he came in with the cut piece of pipe in his hand.

Tully nodded. "Good advice given five minutes too late. I regret that I upset your daughter-in-law by mentioning her husband, your son, and I'm sorry for your loss."

"It was *Gott*'s will. My son is at peace. You had no way of knowing. Becca will not hold your words against you. For us forgiveness comes first." Gideon handed Tully the length of pipe. "See if this fits our patient's leg."

It did, and they used the rest of the cloth strips to secure it in place over the padding.

Rosie had been standing quietly outside the gate, but now she gave a low moo. The calf bawled pitifully.

Tully got up. "Maybe she's getting hungry. Let's see if she can stand."

He lifted the little heifer to her feet. She wobbled but couldn't stay upright without Tully holding her.

Gideon grimaced. "*Dat es* not *goot.*"

"Let Mama in and see what she does." Tully hated to get his hopes up. He wasn't used to having things work out for the best, but the little critter deserved a chance. Gideon opened the stall. Rosie came in and began to lick her baby. The calf made no effort to stand. Tully lifted her and positioned her at her mother's udder. With a little coaxing, he was able to get her to latch on and suckle, but she gave up after only a few minutes. Tully lowered her to the floor. It wasn't looking good.

"My granddaughter will gladly bottle-feed her. She feels bad about leaving the gate unlatched." Gideon started coughing and struggled to catch his breath.

Tully shot a sharp glance at the older man. "Are you okay?"

Gideon nodded. After a minute he cleared his throat. "I will be fine. I must go get the rest of my cows before the lumber trucks start coming down the highway. They don't slow down for anything smaller than another truck."

"I'll go round up your cattle. That's what cowboys do."

"Are you truly a cowboy like those from the wild West?" Gideon looked intrigued.

"Among other things."

Tully didn't bother to list the jobs he'd had and failed at since leaving the ranch at seventeen. The only place he'd truly fit in had been the army. He missed the camaraderie of his unit and the sense of belonging that had once bound them together. Loyalty to the men he'd fought beside had carried him through two tours of duty in some mean places, where losing those same friends came with a high cost. After a while it became easier not to have friends or to be one. The bottle had helped with that until it became his only friend.

He walked out of the barn into the sunshine of a new morning and drew a deep breath. Those days were behind him. He was sober. He was going to stay that way.

Becca walked toward him, carrying four shiny buckets. He gestured toward the lane. "I'm going to get the rest of your gals."

"Let me give these to Gideon so he can start milking and I'll help you."

He knew he could probably manage by himself, but he waited anyway. She came hurrying out of the barn a few moments later. "We are missing four."

Together they walked quickly to the end of the lane. She saw the tracks without him pointing them out. It was no surprise. She was a country girl used to being around cattle. She could probably track them better than he could.

She put her hand to her brow to block the bright sunlight glaring off the snow as she scanned the area to the east. "It looks like they are headed toward New Covenant. There's no telling how far they could've gotten."

"Why don't we take my car? We can use it to herd them back. I'd much rather use a good cowpony, but I can make do with a beat-up Ford."

She hesitated but then nodded.

"Wait here. I'll get it." He started jogging up the roadway to where he had been stopped by Rosie.

Becca didn't seem to be upset with him for his careless remark about her deceased husband. That was good. If he could get her cattle rounded up, it would even the score in his eyes. He reached his car and looked back. She was nowhere in sight.

A sharp stab of disappointment hit him. She must have decided she didn't want to ride with him after all. He couldn't blame her. He was a stranger. Not many women would willingly hop in a car with someone they didn't know. He got in, turned around and drove past her lane in the direction the cattle had gone. He rounded a shallow curve in the road and saw her walking with her head down. He pulled to a stop beside her and pushed open the passenger side door.

Becca had prayed that her cows would be just around the bend, but they weren't. She faced Tully in his car. She wasn't afraid of him, but she found him…disturbing. She was curious about him, and that was unusual. She rarely gave a stranger a second thought, especially an *Englisch* stranger, but there was something about this kindhearted man that appealed to her. She liked him.

That alone should be enough to make her refuse

his offer of a ride. Instead she got in the front seat beside him.

"You won't get in trouble for riding in a car, will you? I know the Amish use horses and buggies. I wouldn't want to get you shunned or whatever it is you call it."

She looked straight ahead. "Riding in a car is permitted. Owning one is not. To be shunned I would have to deliberately disobey the rules of my church. Shunning is a very serious matter and is never done lightly."

"Now I'm just feeling ignorant. I confess I know nothing about you folks."

She looked at him then. "You cannot be expected to know our ways. I appreciate your concern for me."

"Okay, since I don't have to worry about getting you in trouble, where do you think your cows might've gone?" He drove slowly, scanning both sides of the highway for any sign of the animals.

"Their tracks ended where they started walking on the highway. I was hoping they were in the neighbor's field, but something must have tempted them to move farther along."

"Who else has cattle near this road? I've never met a cow that didn't want to investigate another herd."

"We are the only dairy, but nearly all of our neighbors have at least one milk cow."

They came to an intersection. He stopped the car and got out. She bent her head to see him. "What are you doing?"

"I'm listening. I hear bellowing coming from that direction." He walked away from the car and examined the ground beside the road for a dozen yards. He gave her a thumbs-up sign and came jogging back. He climbed in and flashed her a boyish grin. "They went that way. A couple of them stepped off the roadway and left tracks."

They drove on until she spotted her four cows standing by a pasture fence where a dozen young steers were bawling at them.

Tully stopped the car. "Do those animals look familiar?"

"They look like Bessy, Flo, Dotty and Maude."

"Then let's see if we can convince them to leave their newfound babies. Those youngsters don't sound like they have been weaned very long by the way they are calling for their mamas." He cupped his hands around his mouth and gave a loud imitation of a bawling calf.

She grinned. "That's *goot*. Perhaps they will follow you if you talk to them sweetly."

"Ya think?" His dark eyes sparkled with mirth.

"I think it will take more persuasion." She got out of the car and walked toward the cattle.

Tully got out, too, circled around to the other side of them and raised his arms. "Ha, cow, ha. Move out. Let's go."

The group reluctantly left the fence and ambled toward the road as he encouraged them. It seemed they had tired of their adventure and were ready to go home and be milked. Once they were headed in the right direction, Becca walked behind them urging them along. Tully got back in his car and followed her with his flashers on to warn anyone coming up behind them.

He rolled down his window as he came up even with her. "I wish there was a way to get around them and make sure they turn the right direction at the intersection. Is there another road I can take?"

"*Nee*, there is not. They will go the right way."

"What makes you so sure?"

"Because I see one of our neighbors coming this way. He will lend us a helping hand." Up ahead she saw Michael Shetler wave at her from his buggy. She waved back.

He leaned out the window. "Are you driving them home?" he shouted.

"*Ja*, will you make sure they go the right way at the crossroads?" she yelled back.

"I will." He turned his buggy around and returned to the intersection to wait for them.

She looked at Tully. "We can manage them from here."

"Is that your way of saying 'get lost, Cowboy'?"

Before she could answer, one of the cows spun around and made a dash past her, galloping toward the calves still bawling in the distance.

"I'll get her." Tully put his car in Reverse and shot backward until he was ahead of the animal. He got out and raised his arms. "Whoa. Wrong way, darlin'."

Dotty stopped and lowered her head. Becca held her breath, afraid the big cow was going to charge him. The most obstinate one in the herd, Dotty could easily knock him aside. His confidence seemed to deter her, but only for a moment. She charged. He jumped out of her way. She went by him without pausing.

Tully dashed back to his car and overtook the cow once again. This time he used his car to block her path as he laid on the horn. She gave up and went trotting back to the group.

Tully pulled up beside Becca once more with a big grin on his face. "Now what were you saying?"

He was enjoying teasing her. She tipped her head in

resignation. "I was thinking perhaps you should follow us all the way home to prevent any more breakaways."

"That's what I thought you would be thinking."

Dotty stopped in the road and looked back. He honked his horn, and she kept walking. He held his arms wide. "See. I'm useful."

Becca smiled to herself as she walked on. He was much too charming for her peace of mind, but she was glad for the help and would find a way to repay him.

The cattle turned the right way at the intersection with Michael working as a blocker. Once the cattle were ambling toward her home, Tully rolled down the window of his car and doffed his hat to Michael. "Thanks for the help."

Michael was leaning out the window of his buggy. "Have you hired a cowboy to manage your herd now, Becca?" he asked with a chuckle.

"*Nee*, this is Tully Lange, who stopped to lend a hand." She didn't bother explaining how they had met. The cows were getting farther away from her.

"We are grateful for your kindness," Michael said.

"I hope they don't go past the lane. *Danki*, Michael." She hurried after her cows, but they were done wandering and turned toward home as if that had been their plan all along. Gideon held the corral gate open, and they filed into the corral and into the barn to be milked.

Annabeth was waiting for Becca on the front porch. "I'm sorry I let the cows out, *Mamm*."

"You are forgiven. I hope you have learned something."

"Not to be in a rush when I close the gate."

Becca patted her daughter's head. "Life gives the test first and then teaches you the lesson afterward."

"Doc Pike is here. He is going to put a cast on the calf's leg."

"Okay. Go on inside. Set the table for breakfast while I finish helping Gideon with the milking."

"Is that man going to eat with us?"

"Tully? I think that's a *goot* idea. It's the least we can do after all his help. He was kind to carry Rosie's baby home to us, don't you think?"

"I guess. Can I name the baby?"

"Of course. You have named all the others. Do you have one in mind?"

"I'll ponder it for a while." She rubbed her chin the way Gideon did when he was giving something extra thought.

Becca held back a grin and went into the barn. Gideon stood with Tully watching the vet work. After finishing the cast, the vet stood and shook his head. "I'm worried that she isn't more active. Let's let her rest for now. I've given her something for the pain. Hopefully she'll perk up soon. When she does, try to get some milk into her. If she'll stand, put her with her mother every three or four hours, but it's probably safest to keep them separated the rest of the time until the calf is more active. You can try bottle-feeding if she won't nurse. I'll check back with you folks tomorrow." He gathered up his supplies and left.

Becca turned to Tully. "Are you leaving us now, too?" For some reason she was reluctant to say goodbye.

Chapter Three

Tully touched the brim of his hat. "If it's all the same, I'd like to stick around for a while and see how she gets on."

"I'm sure that's fine." Becca glanced at Gideon. He nodded.

Tully smiled at her. "Thanks. I feel responsible for causing you folks so much trouble. As soon as I get a job, I'll repay you for the vet bill."

"That won't be necessary," Gideon said.

"All the same, that's what I intend to do."

"Breakfast will be ready soon. I hope you will join us," Becca said.

He started to refuse, but something in her eyes made him change his mind. "Breakfast sounds great. Thanks."

Becca grinned happily. "*Goot.* I will start cooking once we finish milking."

Gideon looked from Becca to Tully and back. "Tully will help me finish. He has been telling me he wants to learn to milk a cow."

"That's right, I do," Tully said, although this was the first that it had been mentioned. "A man can't really consider his education complete until he's milked at least one cow."

"Are you sure?" She was looking at Gideon.

"Go cook and leave this work to the men." Gideon dismissed her with a wave of his hand. She looked ready to argue but held her peace.

Tully watched her leave the barn. Gideon clapped a hand on his shoulder. "Come, I will show you what to do."

"That's good, because I'm pretty much clueless. We got our milk from the grocery store in town."

"They charge too much." He walked to the first cow who was standing in her stanchion patiently waiting. He took a three-legged stool off the wall and showed Tully how to place it beside the cow and sit down.

The first thing Tully noticed was that his hat was in the way. He pulled it off and looked for a place to put it. Gideon chuckled. "Not a milking hat?"

"Nope, but I'm partial to it." It was a reminder that he'd once had the right to call himself a cowboy. That ranch life and the open prairie were part of his DNA. Although that life was in the distant past, it would forever be a part of him. He handed his hat to Gideon, who hung it on a wooden peg on the wall along with his own.

He took a flat brimless hat off the wall and clapped it on his head. It was Tully's turn to laugh. "All you need is a red jacket and a hand organ."

"Are you saying I look like a monkey in my milking hat?"

"There is a vague resemblance."

"We will see who is the monkey when you can't fill your pail."

Gideon showed Tully how to brush the cow's back

legs, tail and udder to prevent any debris from dropping into the pail. Then he showed him how to wash and dry the teats. He stood behind Tully, giving him a few directions on how best to go about milking without hurting the cow before he moved to the adjacent animal and set to work.

It didn't take Tully long to get the rhythm. He was nowhere near as fast as Gideon, but he filled his bucket before the older man had filled his second one. Tully moved to the next cow. The muscles in his forearms were burning before he was done with her.

"Not bad for an *Englischer.*" Gideon stroked his long beard.

Tully glanced up at him. "What's an *Englischer*?"

"*Da Englisch* are those who are not Amish."

"I'm not English. I'm an Okie and proud of it."

"What is Okie?"

"Means I'm a cowboy from Oklahoma."

"Okie." Gideon grunted. "You are still *Englisch* to me."

Tully stood with the full pail of milk in his hand after finishing the last cow. "Now what?"

Gideon walked toward the back of the barn with two buckets in his hand. Tully followed him carrying the other two.

In the milk room, they poured the milk into a large strainer that emptied into one of the steel milk cans. They had enough milk to fill two of the large containers. Together they carried one of them out the door and placed it in the back of a cart, where there were already several more cans. Tully was surprised at how heavy they were.

Gideon was taken with another coughing fit. He had

to sit down on the back of the cart to catch his breath. Tully suspected something was seriously wrong. "Have you seen a doctor about that cough?"

"It's getting better."

Somehow Tully knew that wasn't the truth. He followed Gideon up to the house. The moment Tully opened the kitchen door, he was surrounded by delicious, mouthwatering aromas. Bacon frying, fresh baked bread and perking coffee. His stomach rumbled like an M2 Bradley fighting vehicle. Annabeth giggled, gave him a shy smile and retreated to stand beside her mother.

Gideon hung his hat and coat on one of several wooden pegs by the door. Tully did the same. Then Gideon showed Tully where to wash up. They might milk by hand, but the family had a modern bathroom with hot and cold running water. When he made his way back to the kitchen, he saw a refrigerator, but Becca was cooking on a wood-burning stove. He took a seat at the table and let his curiosity get the better of him.

"I've heard the Amish don't use electricity, so how is it that you have a fridge?"

"Our church allows members to use propane or natural gas for appliances."

"Then why are you cooking on a wood-burning stove?"

She carried a plate of bacon and sausage to the table. "Propane is expensive. Wood only costs our labor to cut and haul it. How do you like your eggs?"

"What are my choices?"

"Dippy, hard or scrambled."

He arched one eyebrow. "What is a dippy egg?"

"One that the yolk is runny enough to dip your bread

in. What do you call an egg cooked that way?" She tilted her head to the side. He found the gesture endearing.

"Over easy. The cook turns it over easy enough not to break the yolk."

"Isn't it funny that we have different names for the same things?"

"I never thought about it, but yes. I'll have my eggs scrambled, if it isn't too much trouble."

Annabeth sat down at the table across from him. "That's the way I cook mine."

He smiled at her. "Is that so?"

Gideon came in and took his place at the head of the table. He spoke to Annabeth in what sounded like German, but Tully recognized only about half the words. He was pretty sure *pride* was one of them. Annabeth looked chastised and remained silent.

When all the food was on the table, Becca sat at the foot of the table and bowed her head. Tully noticed they all did, but no one said grace out loud. He sat still, feeling ill at ease. Finally Gideon looked up and said, "Eggs."

Becca passed the plate to him. Annabeth helped herself to a generous portion and handed the rest to Tully. He took some but wanted to leave room for the toast and bacon. Once he started eating, he didn't want to stop. Everything tasted so much better than it had at the rehab facility or any army mess hall. The bacon was crisp. The eggs were fluffy. The toast was home-made bread the likes of which he hadn't tasted since his childhood, when his grandmother baked every Thursday. The strawberry jam was bursting with sweetness.

He caught Becca staring at him. He laid his fork down. "This is a mighty fine meal."

"I'm pleased that you like it," she said softly.

He tore his glance away from her pretty face flushed with the heat of the stove and looked at Annabeth. *"Wie geht es deinen eiern?"*

Annabeth's jaw dropped. "You speak *Deitsh*?"

"I speak a little. Did I get it right? What did I say?"

"You asked how are my…something. I didn't know the last word."

"I was trying to ask, how are your eggs?"

"*Oiyah* is eggs," Becca said.

"*Oiyah*, I'll have to remember that. I lived in Germany for two years. I knew a woman who taught the language to corporate big shots. She gave me lessons. I don't think it's the same German you people speak."

Gideon chuckled. "I've met a few tourists from Germany. I couldn't understand half of what they said, nor they me."

"I thought you folks spoke Pennsylvania Dutch."

"*Deitsh* isn't Dutch at all, but that's what folks call it," Becca said.

"We *Englisch*?" he asked.

She looked up and grinned. "*Ja*, you *Englisch*."

"*Nee*, he is Okie," Gideon said.

Annabeth's eyes grew round. "What's that?"

"*Das ist* the proper name for a cowboy from Oklahoma," Gideon said solemnly, as if he had known all along what the term meant.

Tully couldn't look at Gideon for fear he would burst out laughing. There was a brief conversation in *Deitsh* between all of them. Becca and Annabeth nodded in understanding, but they didn't fill him in. It was definitely not the German language he had learned.

"Are you a real cowboy?" Annabeth asked with wonder in her wide eyes.

"Yes, ma'am. I grew up on a working ranch that my family homesteaded in 1893 called the Diamond X. Can't get much more cowboy than that."

When everyone was finished eating, Becca stood and began to clear the table. Tully jumped to his feet and began to help. From the expression on everyone's faces, he figured he'd done something else wrong. "It's okay if I help with the dishes, isn't it?"

Becca handed him her plate. "More than okay. Take note of how it's done, Gideon."

"I'll never hear the end of this. I'm going to take the milk to the co-op." He pushed back in his chair.

Becca grinned at his gruff retort and turned to Annabeth. "You may go along with Gideon."

Annabeth grinned. "Okay, but I have to go say good-bye to little Diamond first."

"That's her name, is it?" Becca asked with a sidelong glance at Tully.

"Is that okay?" Annabeth frowned slightly.

"Maybe it's a bit fancy."

"But she has a white diamond-shaped spot on her forehead," Annabeth said.

"Okay, Diamond it is. Hurry and get your coat. Don't keep Gideon waiting."

Becca moved to stand beside Tully at the sink. She dried the plate he handed her and gave him a questioning smile. "Is it permitted to name a calf after your family's ranch?"

She had a dimple in each cheek when she smiled. He wanted her to smile more often.

"It's perfectly acceptable to me," he said. "I'm honored."

"All right. *Danki*. I mean, thank you."

"I should get out of your hair." He handed her the last plate. "I'll be down at the barn if you need anything."

"You don't have to watch over her. We can do that."

"I feel responsible. I can't leave without knowing that she'll be okay…or not."

"If you feel strongly about it, I won't try to discourage you."

He slipped on his coat and settled his hat on his head. He touched the brim as he nodded to her. "Thanks again for breakfast, ma'am. You're a mighty fine cook." He went out the door without waiting for her reply.

After Gideon and Annabeth returned, Becca tried to act as if it were any other Sunday without a church service. She listened as Gideon read from the Bible, but her mind kept drifting. How long was Tully going to stay? Where would he go when he left? Her eyes were drawn to the kitchen window, but she didn't get up to see if he had gone.

Gideon closed the Bible. "Why don't you sing for us, Annabeth? Perhaps some of the songs you are learning for your Christmas program."

Annabeth happily sang several carols. When she was done, Becca joined her in singing some of their favorite hymns. It forced Becca to stay away from the kitchen window. When they finished an old German hymn, Annabeth looked up at her with bright eyes. "Maybe Tully would like to sing with us. I can go ask him."

Gideon shook his head. Annabeth's smile faded. When noon rolled around, Becca fixed a light lunch for the family. Although it was normal to spend the off Sunday afternoon visiting neighbors or friends, she hadn't made plans to go out and had quietly asked members of the community not to visit. Becca wanted Gideon to rest.

He finished his sandwich and took a sip of his coffee. "Is the *Englischer* still here?"

"I don't know," she was able to answer honestly. She was dying to find out. She hadn't heard his car start up, so she was reasonably certain he was still watching over the calf.

"Annabeth, look out the door and see if the outsider has gone," he said.

The child jumped up, raced to the door and pulled it open. "His car is still here, but I don't see him."

Gideon nodded slowly. "I reckon that means the calf hasn't improved. Becca, why don't you take him something to eat? I believe I will lie down for a bit."

Although she was tempted to jump up as eagerly as Annabeth had done, Becca calmly fixed another sandwich and poured some coffee in a thermos.

"Can I come with you?" Annabeth asked hopefully.

"Not this time. You can start on the dishes and then I will help you learn your lines for the Christmas play."

"Teacher says I have the most lines of anybody. I hope I can remember them all."

"You will if you practice enough." Becca put on her coat and scarf and went out.

The sunshine was bright off the snow-covered ground, but it gave little warmth. Winter in their new home had arrived in mid-November and now had a firm grip on the land. She hurried across the yard, pulled open the barn door and stepped into the dim interior.

It was noticeably warmer inside the snug barn thanks to the body heat of eleven large cows contently munching on their hay.

Becca heard Tully before she saw him. "Come on, sweet stuff, you can do it. Your mama has all the nice milk you could ever want. All you have to do is latch on and help yourself. That's it. Now you're getting the hang of it."

"How is she?" Becca opened the stall door and slipped inside. Tully was on the other side of Rosie, holding the baby upright with a sling made from a burlap sack.

"She has made a little progress but not enough. I was about to come up and ask for a bottle to feed her with."

"I'll get one for you. In the meantime I brought you some lunch." She held out the plate and thermos. "Church spread and coffee."

"That was thoughtful, but I'm not hungry. Not after that huge breakfast. The coffee sounds good, though." He looked up from the calf he was holding. "What is church spread?"

"A sandwich made with peanut butter, marshmallow crème and corn syrup. It's really good."

"Sounds good. Okay, Diamond, I'm gonna let you rest now." He carried her to the far corner of the stall and settled her in a mound of hay. She bawled pitifully. He sank down on the bedding beside her and stroked her head. "This nice lady is going to get you a bottle. You won't have to try to stand on that sore leg."

Rosie moved restlessly back and forth. Tully had made a halter from a length of rope and had her secured to the manger. Becca handed him the coffee and the plate. "I'll milk Rosie. We can give that to the calf. It's better for the little one than the milk replacer."

Becca went to the milk room. Inside she found the clean bottles and nipples in a cabinet by the sink. Taking a bucket and a milking stool, she carried her supplies to the stall, where Tully was sipping coffee from the thermos lid.

She saw he had taken a bite of the sandwich. "How is it?"

"The coffee is great. The church spread is a little too sweet for me. I imagine the kids love it."

She chuckled. "They do. So do most adults, myself included."

"Must be an acquired taste. Have you ever tried fry bread?"

She put the stool beside Rosie, sat down with her head pressed to the cow's warm flank and began milking. "I haven't. What is it?"

"It's a type of dough that's deep-fried. I love mine covered with powdered sugar or cinnamon and sugar. Sometimes I dip it in honey. It works to make tacos, too."

"We have tacos once in a while."

"You should try using fry bread instead of taco shells."

She looked his way. "You must send me the recipe."

"I'll do that."

She finished milking Rosie and poured some of the milk into the bottle. "Where are you going when you leave here?"

"I'm on my way to visit a friend in Caribou."

She handed him the bottle as she sank to her knees

on the other side of the calf. "Will he or she be worried that you haven't arrived?"

Tully shook his head. "I wasn't sure how long it would take me to drive there from Philadelphia, so Arnie isn't expecting me just yet."

"Is Philadelphia your home?"

"It was temporarily. I'm sort of between residences right now." He gave the calf his attention as he tried to insert the nipple in her mouth. A lot leaked onto his hands before she figured out how it was supposed to work.

His face lit up with a bright smile of relief. "I think she's got it. Her chances of getting better just improved."

The words were barely out of his mouth before the calf let go of the nipple and began coughing. Her head sank to the hay. He rubbed the white patch on her forehead. "It's supposed to go suck, swallow, breathe. Don't be so greedy."

"How is she?" Annabeth asked from outside the stall.

Becca scowled at her. "I thought you were practicing for your school play."

"I got worried when you didn't come back in. You said you would help me."

Becca realized she had been gone much longer than she'd expected. "I guess I lost track of time."

She held out her hand, and Annabeth came into the stall. She sank to her knees beside Becca and stroked the calf's neck. "Is she getting better?"

"She's not feeling the best," Tully said. "I don't blame her. Having a broken leg can't be any fun."

"I had a splinter in my foot once. It wasn't any fun at all," Annabeth said solemnly.

Becca shared an amused glance with Tully. He managed to keep a straight face. "That must have been awful for you."

"*Mamm* got it out with her tweezers. *Daadi* said I hollered up a storm before it was over."

"I imagine I would holler, too," he said, letting a tiny smile slip out.

Annabeth didn't seem to notice as she continued to stroke the calf. "Is she going to get better?"

Becca slipped her arm around Annabeth's shoulders. "We will do what we can for Diamond. The rest is up to *Gott*."

"What if He's too busy looking after people to take care of a little calf?"

"*Gott* is never too busy. He cares for all creatures. We can't know His plan for Diamond or for any of us."

"Did He plan for her to get hurt?"

Becca had struggled with that same question when her husband died. How could such a thing be part of God's plan for her family? She hugged her daughter and closed her eyes to hold back the sting of tears. "He allowed it to happen. We must accept His will even if we don't understand why."

Annabeth sighed. "Okay. Are you coming in to help me practice my part for Christmas?"

Becca nodded. "You run along. I'll be in shortly."

Her child jumped up. "*Danki* for taking care of Diamond, Tully."

"I'm happy to do it," he said.

After Annabeth left Becca wiped her eyes, got to her feet and dusted the hay from her coat. "If you want to be on your way, Tully, we can look after her."

"I know that. I know it wasn't my fault she was in the road and that I hit her, but I feel guilty about it anyway.

I don't mind staying. I've missed being around cattle. I didn't realize how much until now."

"In that case, you are welcome to stay as long as you like. Come up to the house when you get hungry."

"Can I ask you a personal question?"

She nodded. "I may not answer, but you can ask."

"What happened to your husband?"

She stared at him intently and saw only compassion in his eyes. She crossed her arms and stared at her feet. She didn't have to tell him anything, but she felt compelled to share her story. "My husband, his parents and his brother were coming home from visiting some neighbors when their buggy was struck by a speeding pickup that ran a stop sign. I saw it. My husband and his brother died instantly. My mother-in-law died a short time later. Gideon spent many days in the hospital."

She opened her eyes and saw a stricken expression cross his face before he looked away. "I'm sorry."

"*Gott* allowed it. I have accepted it."

"What happened to the driver of the pickup?"

"He didn't have a scratch on him," she said, letting an edge of bitterness out with her words and regretting it instantly. "I have forgiven him."

Her throat closed with grief. She hurried out of the stall before Tully could see her tears.

Chapter Four

Tully cringed as Becca hurried away from him. He pulled his jacket tighter across his chest. He couldn't keep his curiosity about her in check, and he'd upset her again. He rubbed Diamond's soft ear. "You need to get better so I can leave these good people in peace."

The afternoon stretched into the evening. Gideon and Becca came in to do the second round of milking for the day, but they didn't linger. He was able to feed Diamond a little more the next time she showed signs of interest in the bottle. When it grew dark, he started wishing for a heavier coat and a flashlight. He hadn't exactly thought this plan through. He had his arms crossed and was stomping his booted feet when Becca came in carrying a kerosene lantern and a heavy quilt.

She hung the light from a nail high on the wall, bathing the area in a soft golden glow. "I thought the baby might be getting cold."

"I don't know about her, but I am."

"Then this will help, unless you have regained your senses and intend to come into the house with us." Becca's bundle was actually two quilts. She handed one to Tully.

"Can I bring the calf in with me?" Tully wrapped the blue-and-white quilt around his shoulders while Becca spread the other one over Diamond.

"I do not approve of having a cow in my kitchen, even a little cow."

He nodded. "That's what I figured."

"Her ears are up. Her eyes look brighter." She stroked the calf's neck.

"I gave her another dose of pain medication about half an hour ago. It seems to be helping. She took a little more from the bottle this time. Now if she would only stand and nurse on her mother, my job would be done."

"You have done more than enough. Go up to the house and get warm. I will be her *kinder heeda* for a while."

"*Kinder* means 'children,' but I don't know *heeda*."

She smiled. "The one who watches the children when the parents are gone."

"Babysitter?"

"*Ja*, I will be the babysitter." She sat on the milking stool she'd left earlier. "You can take the lamp with you. I don't mind the dark."

The calf put her head down and closed her eyes. Seeing Becca prepared to stay made him realize he was being foolish. The calf had eaten and was going to sleep for a few hours. He wasn't needed and neither was Becca. He could sit in a warm kitchen and come out to check on her every hour or so.

"I think she'll be fine on her own for a while. You don't need to stay with her."

Becca looked surprised. "You'll come in for a while?"

"I will." Tully hugged his quilt around his shoulders as he followed Becca out of the barn into the clear, cold night. The rising quarter moon illuminated the buildings, snow-covered fields, woods and pasture in stark black and white. He took in the beauty of the night, and something clicked inside him. God had created a stunningly beautiful world that Tully Lange had failed to appreciate for far too long.

He drew a deep breath of the clean air and slowly blew it out as a white mist that rose over his head. Maybe God's plan for little Diamond was simply to make one jaded cowboy stop long enough to appreciate the beauty of the world around him.

Becca looked back at him. "Is something wrong?"

"I was noticing how pretty the night is." And how lovely she was with her face bathed in the lantern light.

"It's a nice view, but the cold takes getting used to. It's much different from our last home."

"Where was that?"

"Pinecrest, Florida."

"Florida?" He burst out laughing. "You moved to Maine from Florida? Not just Maine but northern Maine?"

She giggled. "Sounds silly when you put it that way, but I have lived in many states. Ohio, Pennsylvania, Maryland. My husband had a restless streak."

"So why Maine?"

"My grandfather, Samuel Yoder, is one of the founders of this new Amish community. He wrote to us when he saw this dairy farm was for sale. The price was reasonable. Gideon had owned his own dairy before the accident. We sold what we didn't need and came here. This is where I intend to stay. This is where I want Annabeth to grow up. We don't get the tourists like the Amish settlements in Ohio and Pennsylvania do. Here we don't have to put up with outsiders gawking at us."

Her eyes widened, and she clapped her gloved hand over her mouth. "I didn't mean that the way it sounded."

"As an outsider, I take no offense. I'll try to keep my curiosity in check."

"I don't mind your curiosity." She started walking toward the house again.

"You don't? I thought I upset you earlier."

She stopped again to face him. "Grief is like that. Sometimes the least little thing will catch me off guard and remind me of the man I loved and lost. I was not upset with you."

"But my question brought it to mind."

"He is never far from my thoughts. If not you, then Annabeth or Gideon will do or say something that reminds me of him every day. Time heals the hurt, but it cannot make me forget. Come. It is too cold to have this discussion out here."

He marveled at her calm strength and acceptance as he followed her to the house. Inside he found the kitchen almost stifling after the chill of being outside. He laid his quilt aside and took off his fleece-lined jean jacket. He hung it next to his hat on the pegs by the door.

She was at the stove stirring something that smelled delicious. "I saved some chicken and rice for you. Sit."

"Yes, ma'am." He pulled out a chair and sat down as he yawned widely. The heat was making him sleepy. He'd driven all night the previous day, and he hadn't had so much as a nap today.

He blinked hard and found her staring at him. "You're tired."

"A mite. Where is everyone?"

"Gone to bed." She put a steaming bowl of chicken, rice and chopped vegetable in front of him. "Eat and then stretch out on the sofa. I will wake you in an hour."

He realized he was too tired to argue with her. He nodded mutely and dug into the food. A glass of milk appeared beside his plate. He looked up and caught her smiling at him. "I like to see someone enjoying my cooking."

He raised his spoon. "This is better than my grandma used to make. I didn't think that was possible."

"Danki."

He gazed into her pretty green eyes. "I'm the one that should be thanking you."

Becca looked away first. "It's only a little warmed-over chicken and rice."

"Your kindness is about the only thing that tops your cooking."

She knew she must be blushing. She turned away and busied herself at the sink. "Enough talk. Finish eating and get some sleep."

"Only if you promise not to let me sleep too long. I'm afraid Diamond will start missing me. I've been telling her cowpoke jokes all afternoon. Did you know in Oklahoma we use a crowbar to tell how hard the wind is blowing?"

"What?"

"Yes, ma'am. We got a hole in the side of the house. If we want to know how windy it is, we stick the crowbar out."

"And what does that tell you?"

"If the crowbar is bent when we pull it in, the wind is

about normal. If it's broke, it's best not to go out, 'cause our hats will end up in another state. I have at least six in Texas, I reckon."

Becca smiled. "Eat. Be funny later."

"Yes, ma'am."

He was quiet for a little while, but then she heard him push back from the table. "Thanks again for the grub."

After he went into the other room, she sat down at the table and opened her prayer book. After reading for a half hour, she got up to check on Tully. He was curled on his side on the sofa with her quilt snuggled underneath his chin. He reminded her of a little boy. She listened to his even breathing and then went upstairs to her bedroom. She laid down without undressing, knowing she wasn't going to get much sleep. She dozed off for a while and then jerked awake. The battery-operated clock on her bedside table showed it was just after midnight.

She crept downstairs and saw Tully hadn't needed her to wake him. He was already gone. She was tempted to go out to the barn just to visit with him again but realized she was being foolish. She went back upstairs and slept soundly until five thirty, her usual time for rising.

She put on the coffee and brought in the milk pails to scrub them with soapy water and bleach. She was just finishing up when Gideon came in.

"*Guder mariye*, Becca. Has our friend gone?"

"Good morning, Gideon. I looked out a little while ago, and his car was still here."

He got into his heavy coat and took several pails from her. "I reckon I'll see how his little patient is doing. The man sure has his heart set on seeing her get better."

"As does Annabeth." Becca put on her scarf and

heavy coat, picked up the rest of the pails, and followed him out to start the morning milking.

They met Tully coming in. He looked tired. "How is she?" Becca asked.

He smiled, and she realized how handsome he was with a grin on his face. "Standing on her own, nursing like a champ. It looks like she's gonna be just fine."

Gideon patted Tully's shoulder. "That's *wunderbar*."

"She came out of her slump about two in the morning. She hasn't slowed down since. She's even making a few attempts to run. Now I will say goodbye and get on the road."

She heard the reluctance to say that farewell in his voice—or maybe she only wanted to hear it. "You will not go anywhere until you've had your breakfast. No arguing. The coffee is ready. We will be back when the milking is done."

She couldn't be sure, but she thought he looked relieved. He tipped his hat to her. "You'll get no argument from me on that score. I have already tasted your cooking."

Becca rushed through the morning milking, getting a few protests from the cows for her hurried actions. She set the final bucket down in the milk room for Gideon to strain. "I'm going to go start breakfast."

Up at the house, she found Tully and Annabeth at the table. Annabeth was laughing. "You tell good stories, Tully. Tell me another one about your pony."

He leaned toward her. "My pony was so mean that I couldn't ride him barefoot because he would swing his head around and bite my toes to make me get off. If that didn't work, he would run under the clothesline and I would find myself sitting on the ground with Grandma's clean sheets over my head."

Annabeth grinned. "But your grandma wouldn't be mad at you, would she?"

"No, but she had a powerful lot of choice words for grandpa about his knowledge of horseflesh."

The child giggled. "My friend Maddie has a pony."

"I hope it's not a mean pony."

"Oh *nee*, she's a wonderful pony. *Daadi* says I can get a pony when I'm older so I can ride to school and *Mamm* won't have to drive me every day. Did you ride your pony to school?"

"Nope. The school bus came to pick me and my cousins up every day. It sure would've been more fun to ride the horse, but it was twenty-five miles to school."

Gideon came in and washed up. She heard him wheezing, and she glanced at him frequently. He turned to her as he dried his hands. "I'm getting old," he said in *Deitsh*. "I will let you help me load the milk cans." He spoke again in *Deitsh*, so she knew he didn't want Tully to understand.

"Of course." She watched him with concern but didn't want to say anything in front of Annabeth or Tully. After a few minutes, he seemed to recover and smiled at her. She dished up oatmeal loaded with raisins and pecans and put out the brown sugar for her daughter's sweet tooth. Tully didn't seem to have the same affliction, for he added only a sprinkling to his cereal.

The breakfast that morning was one of the most pleasant times she had enjoyed in her new home. Meals were normally a quiet time, but Tully had them all laughing with his tall tales of growing up in what he called the Wildest West. Becca wasn't sure how much was real and how much was embellished to make the story better. She was sorry when everyone finished eating.

She carried the dishes to the sink. "Annabeth, get ready for school."

"Okay." She headed to her room.

Gideon finished his coffee. "I'd better get the milk loaded."

"If you wait a minute, I'll help," she offered.

"*Nee*, I'm fine now. Tully, you have been an interesting guest. Come back and visit us someday soon." Gideon held out his hand.

Tully stood and shook it. "I'll do that."

After Gideon went out, Becca stacked the dishes in the sink and then laid her towel aside. She couldn't put off the moment any longer. "I'd better get the horse hitched or Annabeth will be late to school. I have enjoyed meeting you, Tully Lange. I will think of you kindly each time I see Rosie's new calf."

"I'll think fondly of you and your family." He looked around the kitchen. "It's been a long time since I've been in a place that feels like a real home."

Pity stirred in her chest at the sorrow in his voice. "What kind of places have you lived in if they haven't been homes?"

"Army bases—army housing, mostly. Apartments. Some good, some not so good."

"You were a soldier?" She recoiled in shock. Such a profession went against everything her religion stood for.

"You say that like it's a bad word."

She dropped her gaze, ashamed of her unkind reaction. "I didn't mean to criticize. We Amish believe in peace, in turning the other cheek. We are conscientious objectors to any kind of war."

"I see. Then I'm glad I didn't tell you until now."

She caught his arm before he turned away, stunned at her boldness, but she needed to make him understand. "If you had told me the minute we met, you would not have been treated differently by me or any Amish person."

"Sure. That's why your jaw dropped."

"I will admit you took me by surprise. I had a moment when I couldn't reconcile your tenderness for an injured baby calf to someone who could take a human life in war."

"And now you can?"

"Now I see the man in front of me. I see Tully Lange, a kind and helpful person. I cannot judge you, for only God knows what is in any man's heart."

"Thanks." He gazed into her eyes with such gentle longing…almost sadness.

What did he see? What was it that he wanted? He was about to walk out of her life forever. Would he find a place he could call home, or would he be like her departed husband, unable to settle anywhere? It saddened her that she would never know if he found peace.

She resisted the urge to lay her hand on his cheek and comfort him. Why was she drawn to this stranger?

He turned away and slipped into his coat, then took his hat from the peg by the door. He settled it on his head. When he looked at her from beneath the brim, his eyes were no longer sad. They held a glint of humor. "Becca Beachy, your cooking was worth all the trouble your cows gave me."

He opened the door and stepped outside. A second

later he turned to her. "Something has happened to Gideon." He took off down the steps at a run.

Becca looked out the door and saw Gideon lying on the ground beside the milk cart. She ran after Tully and was relieved to see Gideon trying to get up. He gripped his leg with both hands as he grimaced in pain.

She stepped around the spilled milk can. "What happened?"

Tully supported Gideon with an arm around his waist. "Did you hurt yourself?"

"My bad leg gave out on me. I tried to keep the milk from falling, but the can twisted, and that's when I fell."

"Is it broken?" Becca asked, feeling it gently.

"It hurts in my knee. I can't move my leg."

Tully looked at Becca. "Get Annabeth and get in my car. His knee is dislocated. He needs a doctor."

"I don't," Gideon protested.

Tully placed Gideon's arm around his shoulder. "I've seen this kind of thing before, and you do. Stubbornness is a form of pride, old man. Get in the car."

Becca was relieved to let Tully take over. If it had been only her, Gideon would not have sought treatment. She opened the front door of the house and called for Annabeth. Her daughter came running. "What's the matter, *Mamm*? You sound scared."

"Your grandfather has been hurt. Tully is taking us to the doctor."

She hurried Annabeth outside, and they got into the back seat of Tully's car.

He turned in the seat to look at her. "Where is the nearest ER?"

"Presque Isle. Head toward New Covenant, the same

way the cows went, only go straight at the crossroads where they turned."

They reached the city thirty minutes later, and Becca directed him to the emergency center. He helped Gideon hobble inside.

They were fortunate that the emergency room wasn't busy. A doctor was able to examine Gideon within fifteen minutes. After X-rays, the doctor finally came in to speak to them twenty minutes later.

"Your knee is dislocated. Some of your ligaments are torn. I can relocate the joint, but it isn't going to be pleasant. After that I'm going to put you in a brace that you'll need to wear for the next four weeks. Use ice to keep the swelling down. The cough is also a serious matter. You have pneumonia. I'm surprised you are out of bed. I'd like to put you in the hospital for some antibiotics, but I suspect you'll refuse."

"I will. I have a dairy herd to take care of," Gideon said firmly.

"Find someone else to do that. No heavy lifting. I don't want you picking up anything heavier than a five-pound sack of flour until Christmas." He wrote on a pad and handed Becca two prescriptions. "This is for the antibiotic. See that he takes them four times a day, and this one will help the pain. Someone will be in to fit him for a pair of crutches."

She nodded mutely. She didn't have the money to pay for the ER visit, let alone pain pills. They moved Gideon into a wheelchair. At the billing office, Becca explained that she would have to have their bishop raise the money to pay the bill.

The kindly woman behind the desk smiled. "We've learned the Amish pay their bills. Don't worry. I've

dealt with Bishop Schultz before. I'll send him a letter
by the end of the week. Take your prescriptions to the
hospital pharmacy. They will fill them and add them to
your bill. I'll let them know you are coming."

Becca nodded and turned back to Tully. "Can you
take us home after that?"

His eyes were troubled. "Of course. Anything you
need. You don't have insurance?"

She shook her head. "*Nee*, we do not."

"Let me guess. It's not your way."

"We take care of each other. Our congregation will
hold a collection for us." She didn't expect him to understand. Part of her wanted to lean on him for the support
he offered, but the other part knew she needed to avoid
becoming more involved with him. He was an outsider.

"What about the dairy?" he asked.

"Our neighbors will help. We will manage." She
hoped her tone closed the subject. She might insist they
would be fine, but she knew it would be a struggle to
get the work done and keep Gideon from trying to do
too much. The Lord was testing her once again. This
time she would be stronger, but was she strong enough?

Tully kept glancing at Becca's face in his rearview
mirror as he drove them home. She looked like she had
the weight of the world on her shoulders. It must seem
that way to her. Would the community help as much
as she predicted? What if they didn't? He could see her
trying to do it all by herself.

It wasn't like it was his concern. She wasn't part of
his family or even a military spouse. He had done all
he could to help by saving her calf and gathering her
strayed cattle. Arnie was expecting him. Not any certain

day, but soon. He needed to see the one buddy who'd showed he still cared. Arnie's occasional card or phone call had meant the world when there was no one else.

He turned in to the Beachy farm and pulled up in front of the house. Becca and Annabeth helped Gideon out of the car. Becca waved Tully away. "We have delayed you long enough. Do not worry about us. We are in God's hands. Our faith is in His mercy."

"Okay. Annabeth, I may stop in some day and see how Diamond is getting along. Take good care of her for me."

"I will."

Gideon moved slowly on his crutches with Becca and Annabeth hovering close beside him. They all went into the house.

Tully turned his car around and drove down the lane. He stopped and waited as two logging trucks blew past. Once the coast was clear, he still didn't move. He slipped the gearshift into Park. He looked into his rearview mirror and saw Becca walking to the barn. She came out a few minutes later leading a horse. She had milk to take to the co-op and a child to take to school. The young widow had had her hands full even before Gideon fell.

She wasn't his problem. She didn't want his help. He had more than enough trouble without borrowing some from an Amish family. He was broke, out of work and homeless again. He had a friend, maybe his only friend, waiting to see him. Becca and her family would be taken care of by the other Amish. She had made that plain. She didn't need him.

No one had ever really needed him.

He put his car in gear.

Chapter Five

Tully stepped on the brake. He couldn't do it. He couldn't just drive away. She was going to get his help if she wanted it or not. He had made a lot of bad decisions in his life, but this wasn't going to be one of them. This time he was making the right choice. Maybe it was because she had suffered so much at the hands of a reckless driver and he was somehow trying to make amends for that. It wasn't rational, but it was what he needed to do. He shoved the car in Park. Picking up his phone, he dialed Arnie's number.

His buddy answered on the second ring. "Are you in town already, or have you chickened out? Wait. Who is this?"

Tully knew the drill. "This is Tully Lange. I'm an alcoholic. I've been sober for four months and one week."

"It still gives me chills to hear you say that. I'm proud of you, Cowboy."

"Thanks, man. That means a lot."

"So where are you?"

"I had to take a small detour."

"Oh yeah?"

"It wasn't a moose. It was a cow."

"You hit a cow?" Arnie didn't even try to control his laughter. "'Cowboy Cow Collision in Northern Maine.' It could make the national news."

"I didn't hit the cow, but I hit her calf and broke the little thing's leg. I took her to the closest farm. Turned out to be a dairy run by an Amish family. It was their cow. Look, the family is in a bind right now. The old man that runs the place got hurt. He has only his widowed daughter-in-law and his granddaughter to help him. I'm going to stick around for a while and give them a hand."

"Ah, there is a woman involved, isn't there?"

"Nothing like that."

"Sure. Is she pretty? Is it the widow or the granddaughter?"

"The granddaughter is in the first grade."

"So it's the widow. Tully, you sly dog."

Tully grew annoyed. "I said it's not like that."

"Okay, my bad. Stay and help the family for as long as they need it. You aren't likely to find a drink on an Amish farm."

It was a good point. "Look, I'll see you at Christmas. I just need to make sure they're going to be okay."

"Don't forget me, Cowboy."

Tully caught a note of sadness in his friend's voice. "You know I can't forget you. You saved my life."

"Twice," Arnie added emphatically.

"And you'll never let me forget it."

"That's right. You owe me big-time. Someday I'm gonna call in that marker."

Tully chuckled. "Any time you need someone to save your life, I'm your guy. See you in a few days."

He might have made a joke out of it, but Tully was serious. He owed Arnie more than he could ever repay. After ending his call, Tully turned the car around and drove into the Beachy farmyard again. He saw Becca and Annabeth lifting the heavy milk cans onto the back of a wagon. He got out of his car and lifted the last two steel containers onto the wagon bed for them.

Becca brushed the snow from her gloves and frowned at him. "I could have managed those. I thought you were leaving?"

"Ma'am, if you know anything about cowboys, you should know that we have a powerful sense of right and wrong. It is just plain wrong to leave a woman in a lurch if a fellow can help."

"I thank you for your offer, but don't concern yourself with us. Annabeth, get up on the seat. We need to get going." Becca moved to the front of the wagon. She ignored the hand Tully held out to help her up.

He looked at Annabeth and rolled his eyes. "Your mama is a stubborn one."

"Sometimes." The child held out her arms. Tully lifted her up beside her mother.

He pushed his hat up with one finger. "I've decided to stick around for a while. No point in telling me to move along, because I'm not going to do it. I'll be here when you get back. If you have any chores that need doing, tell me now."

She stared straight ahead. "None that I can think of."

He held back a smile. "Annabeth, can you think of any?"

"*Daadi* was going to split some kindling for the stove this morning."

Becca scowled at her daughter. "That's enough. It

was kind of you to offer, but your help isn't needed." She lifted the reins, spoke to the horse and headed the wagon down the lane.

Tully watched them until they reached the highway. Annabeth looked back and waved. Becca did not. Her rejection hurt more than it should.

"I like the cowboy," Annabeth said. "I'm glad he's going to stay. Aren't you? He can help with lots of chores so *Daadi* can rest."

Becca glanced at her daughter's face. "He won't be staying. We will do our own chores and Gideon's, too. We will just have to work harder until Gideon is better."

It was going to be difficult, but Becca had never shied away from hard work. Tully's offer to stay and help was kind, but she couldn't afford to pay a hired hand even for a week, let alone for the month that the doctor had said Gideon needed to heal.

Annabeth tipped her head to gaze at Becca. "Don't you like Tully?"

She liked him a lot. That was the trouble, but she couldn't tell her child that. She barely knew the man. "He has shown us great kindness. For that I'm grateful, but don't expect him to be at the farm when you get home from school."

Among the Amish such acts of charity were common. She wasn't used to seeing the same behavior from the *Englisch*. She didn't know what to make of him.

"I hope he will be there," Annabeth said wistfully. "He makes me laugh."

When they arrived at the school, the children were outside for the morning recess. Their teacher, Eva Coblentz, waved from the schoolhouse steps. Her brother

Danny stood beside her. Eva planned to marry after Christmas. Her brother would take over her teaching job when she left. Danny was single and a nice fellow. He had asked Becca to walk out with him several times. She had politely refused. She wasn't interested in stepping out with him or anyone. She had no intention of marrying again. Loving someone else didn't seem possible.

Danny gave Becca a warm smile as he walked over. "We were wondering what had become of Annabeth this morning. I was just about to drive out and check on you and your family."

Becca tipped her head slightly and avoided meeting his gaze, not wanting to give him any encouragement. "I appreciate your concern."

"Rosie had her calf, but Tully hit her baby with his car and broke her leg. Then *Daadi* Gideon slipped in the snow and hurt his knee and the cowboy took us to the hospital," Annabeth said all in a rush.

Danny's eyes widened. "It sounds like you've had a busy morning. How serious is Gideon's injury?"

Becca sighed. Danny would find out soon enough. "He dislocated his knee."

"That's not *goot*," Danny said. "Is there anything I can do?"

"*Nee*, we are fine."

He shook his head. "Nonsense. My cousin dislocated his knee two years ago. He was laid up for weeks, and he is a lot younger than Gideon. I'll come out to help with the chores before and after school."

"That's not necessary." This was exactly what she had hoped to avoid. Becca didn't want to spend her mornings and afternoons working alongside Danny.

Nor did she wish to spend weeks resisting his persistent attempts to get her to go out with him. He was a fine man, but she wasn't interested in him romantically.

He leaned closer. "Don't be prideful, Becca. Let me help." He held out his arms to Annabeth, who went to him happily.

Becca looked away. "It isn't pride. We…we already have a man helping us. An *Englisch* fellow."

Danny lowered Annabeth to the ground. She gaped at Becca. "The cowboy is staying? Before you said—"

Becca cut her short. "Never mind what I said."

A faint frown appeared on Danny's face. "Is it someone I know?"

"*Nee*. He is new to this area. Would you ask Bishop Schultz to come out to the dairy when you see him? I need to get this milk to the collection station, or I would go see him myself."

"I'll take care of it," Danny said. "And I will bring Annabeth home this afternoon so you don't have to make the trip."

She couldn't see a way to refuse his kind offer. *"Danki."*

Annabeth waved to her friend Maddie on the swings. "Guess what? I have a new calf. Her name is Diamond, and we have a real cowboy staying with us."

Becca knew the whole community would be curious about their visitor once the children took home Annabeth's information. She was sure to have visitors as soon as word got out about Gideon's injury. She would need to have a suitable story ready to explain Tully's presence. If he hadn't already left.

She thanked Danny and turned her horse around. The collection station was at the farm of an *Englisch*

A Haven for Christmas

dairyman named LeBlanc some two miles past her own farm. He maintained refrigerated storage tanks that she and several other small dairies rented from him. The milk truck came three times a week to take the collected milk into the city to the processing plant. Thankfully he was in the building when she arrived. He emptied the milk cans for her.

Heading back to the farm, Becca kept her horse at a steady trot. A flutter of anticipation settled in her midsection as she turned into her lane. Would Tully be there?

As she drove into the farmyard, she saw his car was missing. She tried to ignore the letdown that seemed to sap her strength. She hadn't really expected him to stay. She wasn't sure why she was so disappointed.

She climbed down from the wagon stiffly. The cold seemed sharper than before. The sun slipped behind the clouds, making the morning gloomy. She unhitched the horse, checked on little Diamond, who seemed to be doing well with her cast, and then went into the house. She stopped on the threshold. Tully was down on one knee filling the kindling box beside her stove.

He rose to his feet and dusted off his gloves. "If that's not enough, I'll bring in another armload."

He was still here. "I thought you had gone. Your car isn't here."

"Gideon told me to put it in the shed because it is going to snow. He's doing okay. I had him take two of those pain pills, although he wasn't happy about it. I put an ice pack on his leg. He's a hard man to keep down." He shifted nervously from foot to foot. "I threatened to hog-tie him if he got up without help again. Is this enough wood?"

"That is fine for now. Tully, I appreciate all you have done."

"It's nothing."

She moved to take off her coat and thick woolen scarf and hung them up. "It is much more than nothing. Please sit down." She gestured toward the table.

He took a seat and waited for her to speak. She sat across from him with her hands folded on the table in front of her. She didn't like discussing their financial situation, but she didn't feel she had a choice. "I would like you to stay until Gideon is better, but you must understand that we cannot afford to pay you for your help."

He leaned back in his chair. A wry smile curved his lips and showed a dimple in his right cheek. "A few days of your good cooking will be payment enough. You don't have to worry about putting me up. I can sleep in the barn if the animals don't mind my snoring."

"Why are you doing this?"

His smile disappeared. His eyes grew serious. He leaned forward and clasped his hands together on the tabletop. "I wasn't exaggerating when I said it had been a long time since I was somewhere that felt like a home. When I got out of the army two years ago, things didn't go well for me. Let's just say I messed up. I ended up homeless and living out of my car. I know what it feels like to be down and out. You folks have hit a rough patch. Somebody gave me a helping hand when I needed it. I'd like to think I'm repaying that favor by helping you and your family. Just until Gideon is back on his feet. I'm serious about sleeping in the barn. I've slept in worse places."

What places and why? She longed to ask him, but she didn't. It was unlikely that she would ever know the answers, but the pain he tried to hide underneath his words touched her deeply. "That won't be necessary. We have a spare bedroom you can use, but I must talk this over with Gideon before I can give you an answer."

"Fair enough." It wasn't an outright no. Tully relaxed a fraction. He was prepared to leave if she insisted. He didn't want to stay if he made her uncomfortable.

"What do you need to discuss with me?" Gideon asked as he slowly made his way into the kitchen on his crutches.

Tully scowled at him. "What did I say would happen if you got up without help?"

"Tying the hog is not needed." Gideon lowered himself slowly onto a chair. "As you can see, I have managed on my own. What are the two of you talking about?"

Tully glanced at Becca. When she didn't explain, he did. "We were discussing my staying on to help with chores for a few days until you get back on your feet."

"I am on my feet."

Tully scoffed. "You're barely on one foot and two crutches. Explain to me how you are going to feed and milk your cows."

"He has a point," Becca said. "If he wants to help us, we should let him."

"We can't pay him. A laborer is worthy of his hire."

"Room and board will be sufficient payment for me. I don't know much about dairy cattle. I may end up being more trouble than I'm worth."

A smile tugged at the corner of Becca's mouth. "If that becomes the case, I will stop feeding you."

He grinned at her. "And I will be gone before nightfall. Now that you know how to get rid of me, what chores need to be done?"

"I will show you." Gideon attempted to rise, but he grimaced and sank back onto his chair. "Perhaps Becca should show you what you need to do."

"I will after we get you back into bed," Becca said, motioning for Tully to help her. Between the two of them, they were able to get Gideon up on his crutches and into his bedroom. Tully stood back and waited as she carefully propped Gideon's injured leg on a pair of pillows and pulled a quilt over him.

She stood beside the bed looking uncertain. "Is there anything you need? Do you want another pain pill?"

"I'm fine for now. Don't fuss over me."

She tucked the quilt around his shoulders. "I will fuss over whomever I please. Promise me you won't try to get up until we are back in the house."

"I promise. Now go away and let me sleep." He closed his eyes and turned his face away from them.

Tully stepped out into the hall. Becca followed him and closed the door. A second later she opened it a crack. "I want to be able to hear him if he calls out."

Tully longed to offer her some measure of comfort or reassurance, but he wasn't sure what to say. Comfort hadn't been a big part of his life. His grandfather had been fond of saying, "Be tough, boy, because life is tougher." The army hadn't been big on coddling, either. He cleared his throat and took a stab at it. "He's a strong man. He'll get over this."

"I pray you are right." She turned away from the door.

"What made you decide to let me stay?"

She wouldn't look at him. "Annabeth wants to hear more stories about your cowboy ways."

He sensed it wasn't the whole truth. "That's nice to hear, but I don't believe it's why you changed your mind."

"I have my reasons." She propped her fists on her hips. "Do you want to stay or don't you?"

He held both hands up. "I want to stay, but only if I won't make more trouble for you."

She rolled her eyes and shook her head. "All men do is make more trouble."

He had to laugh. It was the wrong thing to do.

She scowled at him and pointed to the end of the hall. "Your room is there. I have baking and laundry to do. Stay out of the kitchen."

She spun on her heels and walked away.

"You had better do as she says," Tully heard Gideon say.

He pushed open the door to make sure Gideon wasn't trying to get up again. "I know how to follow orders."

"That is *goot*. When Becca is in a mood, you had best avoid her. If you can't, do what she says. My wife was the same way. I blamed it on her red hair."

Tully stared toward the kitchen, where he could hear pots and pans being rattled about. "I seem to have a knack for upsetting Becca."

Gideon chuckled. "Don't feel bad. My son used to say the same thing."

Tully moved to stand beside the bed. He pushed his hands into the front pockets of his jeans. "Becca told me what happened to your family. I'm real sorry."

"They are with *Gott*. As we all shall be when He wills it." Gideon raised himself up in bed and scooted back to lean against the headboard. "Why didn't you go on your way?"

Tully couldn't admit the whole truth. "I like you folks. I couldn't leave without trying to help."

"Our community will take care of us." Gideon made a sour face.

"You don't sound thrilled about that."

"Charity is much harder to accept than to give. I sometimes suffer from the sin of pride." Gideon gestured to his leg up on pillows. "When I prayed *Gott* would help me overcome it, I wasn't expecting this to be His answer."

"I know what you mean. I don't want to add to Becca's workload. I hope you'll steer me in the right direction."

"Can you cook, clean, darn socks and do laundry?"

"I can do all that. My grandma made me learn to take care of myself on the ranch, but I'm a lousy cook."

Gideon chuckled. "When I see something that needs to be done, I will tell you. When Becca sees something that needs to be done, she does it herself. You will help best by getting out of her way."

"Got it. Thanks for the advice. What can I do for you?"

"How good are you at checkers?"

"Pretty good, if I do say so myself."

"There is a board and pieces in the desk in the living room. Bring it in here. We shall see if the Lord will help you overcome your sin of pride."

"If that's a convoluted way of saying you think you can beat me, I'll show you a thing or two."

Becca came to the door. "Gideon, you are supposed

to be resting. I'm going to take the trash out to the burn barrel."

"I'll do that," Tully said quickly.

She glanced at each of them and then went away.

Tully looked at Gideon. "Where is the burn barrel?"

"Behind the shed where I had you put your car."

"I'll be back with the checkers set in a bit." Tully went down the hall to the kitchen. Becca was at the table cracking an egg into a mixing bowl. She glanced up at him and tossed the shell into the overflowing trash can. It rolled out and hit the floor.

Tully jumped to pick it up as Becca bent to do the same. His hand closed over hers. He met her eyes, and they both straightened slowly. He still held her hand.

His heart started thudding heavily in his chest. His gaze swept over her face. What would it be like to kiss her?

Chapter Six

Becca's breath caught in her throat. She wanted to pull her hand away from Tully's grasp, but she didn't. She waited—for what, she wasn't sure. His eyes darkened and then softened as he gazed at her. She couldn't look away. She licked her dry lips and then pressed them tightly together. She wasn't a giddy teenage girl, but for a few seconds she felt like one again. Tully had put her completely off balance with the simple touch of his hand. Her head was reeling.

It wasn't supposed to be this way. He was an outsider. She barely knew him. Yet there was a connection between them that she couldn't explain. She was sure he felt it, too.

A shadow passed over his eyes. Regret? He looked away and took a step back. "Sorry."

So was she. Had their fragile friendship been damaged?

He pulled out the brown paper bag she used to line the trash can. "Shall I burn it, too?"

She dropped the eggshell on top of what he carried. "*Nee*, but make sure the lid is on tight so animals don't get into it."

"Okay." He didn't look at her as he gathered his jacket off the peg and went outside.

Becca sat down and drew a shaky breath. What had just happened? She replayed the charged moment in her head. Had it been real?

He wasn't Amish. There couldn't be anything between them other than friendship or business dealings. Any other relationship was forbidden.

Should she insist that he leave? How would she explain her sudden change of mind to Tully? To Gideon?

He accidentally touched my hand and my knees went weak?

Gideon would think she had lost her mind.

She gripped her hands tightly together. Maybe that was the answer. Perhaps the stress of managing the dairy, Gideon's failing health and his injury—not to mention the bills that were piling up—had all come together and rattled her enough that she mistook a simple bit of light-headedness for a romantic reaction to Tully's touch.

She took several deep breaths and started to relax. Nothing had happened that couldn't be explained. She was being silly to imagine a mountain when there wasn't even a molehill. She had been pushing herself too hard. Gideon was always telling her that. Maybe it was time she listened.

She looked at the pans she had lined up to make coffee cakes for the people she knew would come to visit. She didn't need five cakes. Two would do. That would give her more time to get started on the laundry.

The outside door opened, and she jumped. Tully looked in, and her heart started pounding. What did he think had passed between them? What should she say about it?

"The vet is here to look at the calf again. Do you want to hear what he has to say?"

"Of course." She was responsible for every aspect of the farm with Gideon confined to bed. She opened her mouth to tell him that and shut it again. She forced herself to let Tully handle this.

"On second thought, you can deal with him. Tell me later unless he needs to speak to me. I must get these cakes made before the bishop shows up. I'm sure he won't come alone."

"Sure. Happy to do that." He looked relieved and went out again.

"That wasn't so hard," she said aloud. Only it was. She cracked another egg into her bowl and resisted the urge to grab her coat and follow Tully outside. If he took her hand again, she would know for certain if her feelings were real or imagined. She closed her hands into fists and pushed them into her apron pockets. It would be better if a second touch never happened.

She was putting the filled pans in the oven when Tully came back in. "The vet just left."

"I hope he gave you good news."

"He did."

"Fine. I was about to go check on Gideon."

Tully took his coat off and hung up his hat. "I can do that. He wanted a game of checkers, unless you have something else I need to do."

"I can't think of anything." She found herself staring at the back of his head. He was avoiding her gaze. Was he uncomfortable with what had passed between them? She wanted to set his mind at ease and return things to the way they had been before.

"Okay." He scooted out of the kitchen without looking at her. She was about to follow him when she heard the whinny of a horse outside. She looked out the window. It wasn't the bishop. It was Danny with his sister Eva and Annabeth.

Her daughter jumped down from the buggy and came running into the house. "I don't see his car. Is Tully still here?" she asked with a worried expression.

"He's having a game of checkers with Gideon."

"Oh, *goot*." Annabeth sighed loudly with relief. "I was afraid he had gone. How is Diamond?"

"You should go and get a report from Tully. The vet was just here."

Eva and Danny came through the door as Annabeth went charging down the hall. Eva shook her head. "I have never seen that child so energetic. The whole school year she has been as shy as a mouse. I thought giving her a big part in the school play might bring her out of her shell, but I never expected her to pop out like a jack-in-the-box."

"All she has talked about all day long is her cowboy friend," Danny said. "I can't wait to meet him."

"He and Gideon are engaged in a game of checkers in Gideon's room." She kept her smile in place and tried to give the appearance of a calm, in-control woman.

Eva pulled off her gloves and traveling bonnet. She straightened her *kapp*. "I'm eager to meet this paragon, as well."

"Tully is hardly a paragon, but Annabeth has met so few outsiders that he seems larger-than-life to her. Danny, did you have a chance to tell the bishop we needed to see him?"

He hung up his hat. "I did. He should be here soon."

She couldn't think of another reason to stall. She

was going to have to face Tully sooner or later. "Well, come and visit with Gideon for a bit and cheer him up. He is depressed at being forced into bed rest, as you can imagine."

She led the way down the hall. As she reached for the doorknob, she heard an explosion of laughter from inside the room. She opened the door. Annabeth was giggling as she sat on the end of the bed clapping her hands. "He beat you, *Daadi*."

Gideon was howling with laughter. "You did not just do that!"

Tully chuckled as he leaned back in his chair with a wide grin on his face and crossed his arms. "I told you I was good at checkers."

"Twelve moves—that's all it took on his part. I can't believe it." Gideon guffawed and slapped his thigh. It happened to be his bad leg, and he grimaced. "Oh, look what you made me do."

Danny leaned close to Becca's ear. "So very depressed."

It wasn't the scene she had been expecting. She was sure Gideon would be grumping about having to stay in bed, but he sounded and looked more cheerful than he had in months.

"*Mamm*, you should have seen *Daadi*'s face when Tully took his last two kings. It was so funny."

"I heard."

Danny crossed the room and held out his hand to Tully. "I'm Danny Coblentz. This is my sister Eva. She is Annabeth's teacher, and I am a teacher in training."

Tully surged to his feet and shook Danny's hand. "Mighty pleased to meet you folks," he said in his thickest drawl.

"Annabeth has been telling us all day about the cowboy that is staying at her house."

"I grew up on a ranch in Oklahoma, but I don't do much cowboying these days."

"What do you do?" Danny asked.

"A little bit of everything. I'm between jobs right now, so you can imagine that I was plumb tickled pink when Becca and Gideon asked me to stay on and help the family. Especially since I'm responsible for injuring their new calf."

"What did the veterinarian have to say?" Becca asked, as if relying on Tully's information was something she was used to doing. She saw Gideon's eyebrows rise, but thankfully he held his tongue.

"He was happy with the way the cast is holding up. Much of the swelling has gone down in her leg. He was really pleased that she was up and nursing. He said he would be back in two weeks to replace the cast. If there's more swelling or discoloration of the skin below the cast, I'm to call him right away. I added his number to my phone."

"All good news, then. You must show me how to beat Gideon at checkers. I've never bested him."

He met her gaze and smiled. There was nothing in his expression to suggest he was shaken by their encounter. She relaxed and pushed the troubling episode to the back of her mind.

Tully had his emotions well in hand as he gazed at Becca. Although he had been surprised by the intensity of his reaction to holding her hand, he wasn't going to make her uncomfortable with unwanted attention. Yes, he'd thought about kissing her, but what right did he have to even think such a thing? She was way out of his league. It was best to pretend those few stunned moments had never happened.

He could manage to be the jovial cowboy for a few weeks. He was used to pretending things were okay even when they weren't. Just like he could deny he wanted a drink when he did. Like right now.

Except that would be more than a relapse on his part. It would be a betrayal of Becca's trust. He couldn't do that. So he was going to smile and pretend he was fine.

"Something smells *goot*," Gideon said.

"Oh! My cakes! I almost forgot them." Becca spun around and hurried out of the room with the ribbons of her white bonnet fluttering behind her.

Tully turned to Eva, knowing she was a teacher. He figured she wasn't likely to be upset by his questions. "I'm sorry to say I know next to nothing about the Amish, but I'd like to learn more. What's that thing you Amish women wear on your heads called?"

"It's simply called a *kapp* or prayer covering."

"I hope you don't mind my asking, but why do you wear it?"

"It is a mark of our faith, but also because the Bible tells us we should cover our heads when we pray, and we may want to pray many times during the day. So it's best to always wear something."

"I see." It made sense when she explained it that way.

"We also use them to cover our hair," she added, "We believe only God and our husband should see our unbound tresses."

"Amish women never cut their hair," Danny said.

Tully nodded as the image of his grandmother fixing her hair each morning came to mind. "My grandmother never cut her hair. She always wore it braided, folded up and pinned to the back of her head. She told me once that her hair represented her thoughts and wearing it loose would lead to scattered thinking."

If Becca had never cut her hair, it had to be past her knees by now. He tried to imagine how it would look if she wore it down. Would it be like a long, rippling cape of red and gold? Just as quickly he dismissed the thought. He wasn't her husband.

"I'm sure Gideon or Becca will be happy to answer your questions about our Amish faith," Eva said.

Gideon nodded. "Indeed I will, but only after a rematch. You won't take me so easily this time."

Annabeth sat up straight. "You can ask me, too."

Tully chuckled. "Thanks, kiddo. I appreciate that."

She grinned at him. "Tell Eva and Danny about your mean pony. Tully is a *goot* storyteller."

"Maybe you should go and see if your mother needs any help in the kitchen first," he suggested.

"Okay." She hopped off the bed and went running down the hall.

He looked at Gideon. "She is a sweet kid."

"She is like her mother."

Tully shook his head. "Maybe Becca used to be that sweet, but that was before she got bossy."

Danny laughed. "You are right about that."

Eva rolled her eyes at her brother. "A man who gives orders is in charge. A woman who gives the same orders is bossy."

Tully held his hands up in surrender. "I stand corrected by the teacher."

The door opened, and Becca came in with several plates in her hand. Each one held a generous slice of streusel coffee cake. Tully moved the checkerboard from the table beside Gideon's bed and accepted a plate from her. He held it close to his nose and sniffed the wonderful aroma of caramelized cinnamon and brown sugar. "Umm, this smells delicious." He looked at Danny and pointed to the cake. "This is why I'm staying here. The woman can cook."

Danny smiled at Becca. "A *goot* thing for a single man to know about a single woman."

Tully glanced quickly between Danny and Becca. Was Danny implying that he was interested in Becca? Was she interested in him? If she was, it made it that much more important for Tully to keep a lid on his feelings for her.

Becca smiled demurely and left the room. Tully saw it as his chance to gain a little more information about their relationship. "Are the two of you a couple?"

Danny shook his head. His sister grinned at him and then at Tully. "My brother has high hopes that the situation will change."

Gideon adjusted his position in the bed. "My daughter-in-law claims she's not ready to marry again, but it would be *goot* for her, and for Annabeth, to have a man around the house who isn't an old cripple."

"I'm not in any hurry," Danny said. "I can wait until she is ready."

Tully was glad to know the lay of the land. It would help him ignore his attraction to Becca now that he knew there was someone waiting to step up and take care of her. Someone who wasn't an alcoholic ex-soldier and down-and-out cowboy.

Danny fixed his eyes on Tully. "I offered to come

do the chores with her, but she said she already had a man to help."

Was that the reason Becca had suddenly changed her mind about letting him stay? "It's fortunate I was able to give her a hand."

Becca and Annabeth came back in with plates for Danny and Eva. "There is more if someone wants seconds."

Eva turned and looked out the window behind her. "I believe that is the bishop arriving."

Danny kept his attention on Tully. "I hope he approves of your staying here."

"You mean he might not?" Tully looked at Gideon. "I don't want to cause trouble for you and your family."

Gideon waved away his concern. "Elmer Schultz is a reasonable man. He will not object, but I would like to visit with him in private."

Eva and Danny nodded. Becca looked at her guests. "We can retreat to the kitchen."

"We should be leaving," Eva said. "We have so much work to do to get ready for our Christmas Eve production. I've never put on a school program before. I'm worried the parents will think I have done a poor job."

"Nonsense," Becca said. "From everything that Annabeth tells me, I'm sure your program will be a complete success."

"If the Yoder twins behave and don't shoot paper wads at the back of our heads like they did today," Annabeth said in disgust.

Danny patted her shoulder. "I will keep a closer eye on the twins from now on. They won't cause any more trouble."

"We hope and pray," Eva added.

The group followed Becca to the kitchen. Tully hung back as everyone greeted the bishop when he came in. He was an imposing man in his midfifties with a shaggy gray-and-black beard that reached to the middle of his chest. He wore a flat-topped felt hat that looked identical to the ones Gideon and Danny had hung on the pegs near the door. Tully's gray cowboy hat was the only one that wasn't black.

The bishop caught sight of Tully right away. His short haircut, Western-style shirt and blue jeans set him apart from the somber dress favored by the Amish.

Becca introduced him. "Bishop Schultz, this is Tully Lange. He has agreed to work for us until Gideon is recovered."

"Are you new to this area?" the bishop asked, looking Tully up and down.

"I'm just sort of passing through."

The bishop's eyebrows rose at that, but he didn't comment.

"Thank you for the coffee cake, Becca," Eva said. "Annabeth, did you tell your mother about the party?"

Annabeth shook her head. "I forgot. I'm sorry."

"That's all right," Eva said in a tender tone. "You have had a busy day. Becca, I am supposed to tell you that Dinah and Leroy Lapp are hosting a Christmas cookie exchange the Saturday before Christmas. You and your family are invited, of course."

"That sounds like fun. Annabeth and I will be there. I hope Gideon is up to coming by then." Becca went to the door.

Danny stopped beside her. "Don't worry about fetching Annabeth after school. Eva or I will be happy to bring her home this week."

"I would be grateful. *Danki.*" The brother and sister went out. Becca closed the door behind them.

Annabeth got her coat down. "May I go visit Diamond?"

Becca nodded. After the child left, the bishop looked at Becca. "Have you written to your grandfather about this? Samuel will want to return from Pennsylvania to help you."

"I will write soon, but his brother in Bird-in-Hand is dying. I don't want to burden Samuel with this news yet when I have all the help I need."

"I understand. I would see Gideon now."

She gave a slight bow of her head and went down the hall ahead of him. Tully was helping himself to coffee from the pot on the back stove when she returned.

He held out the cup he had just filled. "Would you like some?"

"I would, *danki.*" She took it from him and sat at the table.

He filled another cup for himself and sat across from her. "It's been quite a day."

She sighed heavily. "It has."

"I like Annabeth's teacher."

Becca smiled softly. "Eva is a good woman. She cares for the children as if they are her own. Three of them will be after the wedding. She is marrying our blacksmith, Willis Gingrich."

He hesitated but couldn't resist learning more about her relationship with Danny. "Her brother seems like a nice guy."

"He is." She stirred a small amount of sugar into her coffee.

Tully tried to read her expression, but she wouldn't look at him. "He seems to like you a lot."

"We are friends."

"Just friends? I get the feeling that he wants to be more than that."

She glared at Tully. "Then he will have to learn to live with disappointment."

"Sorry, didn't realize it was a touchy subject."

"It is a closed subject."

He held up one hand. "Got it. Now what?"

"We still have the evening milking to do."

He flexed his sore fingers, took a sip of coffee and started to rise. "I'll get started on that."

"Finish your coffee first."

He sank back onto the chair. "Are you worried about what your bishop will say?"

"A little."

"Can he refuse to help pay the hospital bill?"

"He won't. If Gideon had been hurt doing something that went against our *Ordnung*, he could, but not for a simple accident."

"*Ordnung*, that means 'order.' If he did something against the order?"

"*Ja*, the *Ordnung* is like the rules of our church."

"What would be against the rules?"

"If Gideon had been driving a car or a snowmobile, doing something that isn't permitted."

"Do you have a lot of rules?"

"We have exactly enough," she said with a little smile.

"Who makes them? The bishop?"

"They aren't a set of written rules. They are the way we are expected to live our lives. The way we dress, the way we treat each other, the way we worship. I think in the same manner you learned to be a cowboy, our children learn to be Amish. Certain things are understood and expected. We wear plain-colored clothing. We don't use electricity in our homes. Our women wear *kapps*, and the men wear black hats in the winter and to prayer services but straw hats for working in the summer."

"You mean like a cowboy has a hat for work and a better one to wear when he goes to church?"

"*Ja*, I think so. We do get more specific. Each church group decides things like the style of *kapp* the women will wear and the size of the band around the men's hats."

"Why does it matter how wide a man's hatband is?"

"It helps us identify each other. If I see a woman with a heart-shaped *kapp*, I know she is from Lancaster. The same goes for the men's hats."

"Do the rules ever change?"

"Most have been the same for generations, but twice each year the entire congregation of baptized members can agree to a change. This church voted to allow propane furnaces and appliances several years ago. Other Amish use only wood to heat their homes, while still others allow solar power. As I told you, I have lived in many different places. In Kansas the Amish farmers use tractors instead of horses as we do here. We may all be Amish, but we aren't the same."

"Interesting." It seemed the Amish were more diverse than he first thought.

She tipped her head slightly as she regarded him. "Is it?"

He nodded. "It is. I've never known much about the Amish. I'm happy to lessen my ignorance."

"I'm pleased by your desire to understand us. Not everyone wants to make the effort."

"Do you mean the locals?"

"Here?" She shook her head. "We have been welcomed in this community. This area has been home to family potato farms for generations, but many of their young people have moved away looking for what they believe are better opportunities. Older farmers know the land they have spent a lifetime caring for will pass out of the family when they are gone. But they see us, using horses to plant and harvest, holding tight to our faith, our families and community the way their parents and grandparents did, and they like what they see. Many have sold their land to us rather than see it gobbled up by big commercial farms who can pay more than we can afford."

"You make it sound like a slice of paradise."

"Paradise is what we strive to obtain after this life. What we seek here is hard work, food for our bodies, *goot* friends and a loving family."

"Still sounds a bit like paradise, except for the hard work part. Which I know is waiting in the barn for me, so I will take my leave of you."

"I will be out after the bishop leaves."

"I might be done by then."

"Ten cows milked by you alone?" She leaned back in her chair and crossed her arms. "I don't think so."

He put on his fleece-lined jean jacket and settled his cowboy hat on his head. "Be careful. Gideon didn't think I could beat him at checkers, either." He ran his fingers around the brim of his hat in a salute and went out the door.

Chapter Seven

Tully wasn't done milking by the time Becca came out that evening. Thankfully the bishop came to the barn with her to help finish the job. He even took the milk to the collection station in the back of his buggy.

Afterward, Tully climbed the steel ladder into the tall concrete block silo and pitchforked out several hundred pounds of silage to fill the waiting feed cart below. Annabeth then drove the docile draft horse down the center aisle of the barn while Becca and Tully shoveled the silage into the feed bunks on either side. By the time they finished the chores, it was dark and snowing heavily.

Tully collapsed onto a kitchen chair, feeling more worn out than he had been since boot camp. Becca got busy putting together their supper. He barely had enough energy to eat it. Afterward, he poked his head in to see how Gideon was getting along on his way to his own bed.

Gideon was reading by the light of an oil lamp. He closed the book. "How are my cows?"

"Milked and fed. That's all I can say."

"Are any of them off their feed? Did you check the

ones you milked for cracked teats or signs of infection? Never mind. I should go check them myself. Hand me my crutches." He pointed to them beside the door.

"Becca would know if there was anything wrong. She's bringing your supper. Ask her. I'm going to bed and I may never get up again."

"Not so easy to milk ten cows by hand, is it, Cowboy?"

"No comment."

Tully continued down the hall with the sound of Gideon's mirth following him. He pulled off his boots and crawled under the covers without taking off his clothes. It seemed like only a few minutes later that Annabeth was nudging his shoulder.

"Tully, *Mamm* says it's time to get up."

He opened one eye. It was still dark outside the window. "It can't be."

He closed his eye again. Everything hurt. His arms hurt, his shoulders hurt and especially his hands. They ached like he had broken bones.

Annabeth shook him once more. "*Mamm* says to get up or she will pour water on your head."

"She wouldn't dare," he muttered.

"Are you sure about that? I have a glass in my hand," Becca said from his doorway.

Merciless woman. "I'm up. I'm up. Go away."

"If you aren't in the kitchen in five minutes, I will be back. Come on, Annabeth. We will see if we have gotten a bargain in our hired man or not."

"I never said I was a bargain, I said I worked cheap. For room and board. Which means something to eat and a place to sleep!" he shouted at the closed door.

He sat up in the cold room and shivered. This was

too much like his unheated second-story bedroom back on the ranch when he was a kid. He used to scrape frost off the windows in the winter with his fingernails. He shot a glance at the window. Yup, lots of frost.

He grabbed his boots and hurried to the kitchen, where Becca had the wood-burning oven door open, beating back the chill. He stood in front of it slowly turning around to warm all sides.

"Your room was a little chilly this morning."

"A little?"

She chuckled softly. "You might want to open the heating vent."

"There's heat? Now you tell me."

"*Ja*, we have a propane furnace. I keep the room closed off when no one is using it. I forgot to open it yesterday. The coffee is ready. When you're done roasting yourself and have had some, meet me in the barn."

How could she be so chipper this early in the morning? She was putting him to shame. He couldn't let a little slip of a woman like Becca make him look bad. "No point thawing out if I'm going outside."

He glanced at her face. She was struggling not to laugh at him as she handed him a cup. "Wear Gideon's overcoat and muck boots. We had about six inches of snow last night."

"*Wunderbar!*" He poured himself a half cup of hot coffee, added enough water to cool it and downed it in two gulps. He set his cup on the table.

Annabeth balanced a full cup on a saucer as she walked toward the hall. "I'm taking this to *Daadi*."

"Tell him I hope he gets well real soon. Real soon."

"I will." She smiled brightly, not catching on to the sarcasm in his voice.

He saw it was still snowing when he opened the door. He pulled his hat low on his brow and trudged across the farmyard, following Becca's tracks to the barn. Inside, he saw the glow of her lantern by Rosie and Diamond's stall. He walked over to lean on the gate. She was checking the calf's leg.

"How is she?"

Becca looked up. "Fine, I think. The leg is warm. The swelling is a little better. She was nursing when I came in, so she seems to be getting around on it."

"That's good news."

The calf moved away from her. It came to reach between the boards and nuzzle Tully's knee. He scratched her head. "Did you miss me last night?"

Becca came to stand beside him and patted the calf's back. "I believe she did. She has bonded to you."

He crouched to rub the calf under her chin. "I'm the one who almost ran you over."

"I think she has forgiven you for that."

"I hope so." He stood up. "I should get started milking. You're twice as fast as I am, but I will do half of them even if it takes longer so you can get Annabeth to school."

"As you wish." She handed him two clean pails and went down to the milking stanchions, where she lit a second lantern.

Tully couldn't believe how sore the muscles in his forearms were. He hoped he could work the stiffness out of them, but it didn't take long to prove that wasn't going to happen. Becca finished her half of the cows and left. He was working on his third cow when someone blocked the light. "I'll take over, *Englisch*."

He looked up to see an unfamiliar Amish man holding out his hand for Tully's pail. The man was younger than he was, tall, blond and he didn't have a beard. "Who are you?"

"Gabriel Fisher, but most folks call me Gabe. These are my *brudders*, Asher and Seth." Two men walked past Tully, each with a milk pail in their hands. One looked identical to Gabe.

Tully might have sore muscles and aching hands, but he wasn't about to admit he couldn't do the job. "I'm fine. I'll finish here."

"We can't both milk the same cow," Gabe said, nudging Tully with his knee.

Tully stood. Gabe took the bucket out of his hands. *"Danki."*

Tully stepped back. The man sat down on the milking stool and got to work.

Tully frowned. "I'll go fill the feed cart."

"Moses is doing that," Gabe said without looking up.

"Who is Moses?"

"Our baby *brudder*," one of the others said.

Gabe looked up at Tully. "Go get your breakfast."

Tully couldn't think of an argument. He rubbed his aching arms and walked up to the house just as Becca drove in. She had done half the milking and taken her child to school before he had finished a quarter of the morning's work. He wasn't proving to be much help to her.

He held the horse's bridle as she got down from the buggy. "You didn't have to call in the cavalry. I would've gotten everything done."

"What are you talking about?"

"The Fisher brothers are in the barn doing the chores for me."

"Are they? How kind of them. The bishop must've told them we needed help."

"You didn't ask them to come this morning?"

"*Nee*, I took Annabeth to school and came straight home. I spoke to Danny but no one else."

"Oh."

"You sound disappointed that the brothers are here."

"I wanted to do it myself." To accomplish something that helped her.

She chuckled. "That was not the impression you gave me this morning."

He followed her into the house. "Maybe I'm a slow starter, but I can pull my weight. You hired me to do a job. I intend to do it."

She took off her coat and large black bonnet. "Do not worry, Tully Lange, there is much more work for you. Sit. I will fix your breakfast."

He reluctantly sat down. It was humiliating to realize how little help he had provided to the hardworking family.

Another failed job. All he had really done was give Becca one more mouth to feed. Maybe it would be better if he left.

He looked so much like a pouting little boy that Becca wanted to laugh and ruffle his hair. She didn't. She didn't want him to think she was making fun of him. It was easy to see he was feeling low. She patted his shoulder. "You will get faster."

"Sure." He didn't sound convinced.

"How do you want your eggs?"

"Scrambled. I can cook for myself if you have other things to do."

"Do not worry about making more work for me. I like to cook. Shall I mix some sausage in with your eggs?"

"That sounds good. How is Gideon this morning?"

"Fussy. Grumpy. Pretty much the same as he is every day except when Annabeth is around."

"It's easy to see that he dotes on her. She's a cute kid."

"Have you any children?" He had never said if he was married or not. Becca cracked the eggs into the skillet.

"Nope. No wife or kids."

She glanced at him over her shoulder. "Why not?"

He looked surprised. "Why haven't I married? Oh, all the usual excuses. Never found the right woman. It never seemed like the time for me to settle down."

"But you would like to have a family, wouldn't you?" She tried to imagine him as a father with a little dark-haired boy at his side wearing boots and a cowboy hat, standing with his hip cocked and his thumbs hooked in his belt.

"Someday, I guess. When I have my life in order. I'd need a job and a place to live, for starters."

"Do you still have family in Oklahoma?"

"My grandparents raised me. They are both gone. The ranch went to my uncle. He and I never got along. He's an attorney in Tulsa. He sold the place as quickly as he could."

"That must have been sad for you. What about your parents? Where are they?"

"I have no idea."

She turned away from the stove to gape at him. "You have no idea where your parents are?"

"My mother left me with her folks when I was a few days old. She never came back. I must have been one *ugly* baby," he said with a broad grin.

"I see no humor in your story."

"If I don't laugh about it, I'm liable to cry."

She sat down at the table across from him. "There is no shame in our tears."

He shrugged. "I don't normally talk about that part of my life. My grandmother thought the man my mother ran off with was my father but never knew for sure. It was hard growing up knowing my own mother didn't want me, but I got over it. I haven't thought about her in a long time." He fell silent again.

He seemed to be miles away. Becca waited for him to speak. Finally he drew a deep breath. "When I was a kid, I always hoped she would come back, you know. To see how I turned out, maybe even say she was sorry for dumping me with my grandparents, but she never did."

Becca went back to the stove and stirred the eggs. It was difficult to imagine a mother leaving her baby and never returning. While the tone of Tully's voice was casual, she knew his mother's actions must have caused him great pain. "Have you forgiven her?"

"I guess so. I can't know what her life was like. She might've had a good reason for doing what she did. I thought about trying to track her down. It would be nice to know if I had brothers and sisters somewhere."

"Family is very important to us. Many Amish families have three or four generations living on the same farm, even in the same house."

"That isn't the way most folks do it, but if it works for you, more power to ya."

He grimaced and rolled his shoulders back as she

dished the eggs and sausage onto his plate. "Who knew milking cows was such hard work?"

"Everyone who has milked them by hand." She pulled out a pan of biscuits she had kept warming in the oven and set them on the table. She sat down with a cup of coffee.

"It sure explains why getting your milk at the grocery store caught on." He began eating and soon cleaned his plate, plus three of her biscuits loaded with butter and her homemade peach jam.

He sat back with a satisfied sigh. "That was delicious. *Danki.*"

She inclined her head. *"Du bischt wilkumm."*

"That means 'you're welcome'?"

"It does."

She reached for his plate, but he held it away from her. "I will take care of this. It's the least I can do."

"Danki."

"Du bischt wilkumm, Frau Beachy," he said smugly and carried the plate to the sink.

"Sis kald heit, ja?"

He frowned slightly. "I understood 'cold' in that sentence, but what is cold?"

"Not so *goot* is your *Deitsh.*"

He turned around and leaned his arms on the counter behind him. "Then teach me."

Did he mean that? "I said it is cold today."

"Sis kald heit." He pointed to the coffeepot. "Coffee."

"Kaffee."

He pointed to the door. *"Tur."*

She shook her head. *"Nee,* is *deah."*

"That's crazy. I wonder why the difference if the Amish came from Germany originally?"

"I don't know."

He pointed to his waist. "What's this?"

"Belt."

"I know it's my belt. How do you say it in Deitsh?" She leaned toward him. "Watch my lips closely. Belt."

"Very funny." He patted his head. *"Kopf."*

"Ab en kopp," she said with a chuckle as the outside door opened. The Fisher brothers filed in with a blast of cold air.

The three eldest brothers were triplets, but only two of them, Gabe and Seth, were identical tall blond men with bright blue eyes. Asher had brown hair and dark eyes. He looked more like Moses, the youngest brother.

Gabe took off his hat. "We have finished the milking, fed the animals and cleaned the stalls. We have loaded the milk cans on your wagon. We'll deliver them for you."

"I appreciate that." Becca gestured to Tully. "This is Tully Lange, who is helping us until Gideon gets well. These are the Fishers. They are wheelwrights and buggy makers and new to the community, like us."

"Nice to meet you," Tully said without sounding sincere.

Gabe nodded to him. "If that's all, we'll be back this evening."

Tully straightened. "You don't need to do that. I can manage."

"Da Englisch ist ab en kopp right enough," Gabe said with a big grin. His brothers all chuckled.

Tully looked at her suspiciously. "What's wrong with my head?"

"Nothing." She tried to appear innocent.

Tully looked at Gabe. "What did she say earlier?"

"She said you are off in the head, *Englisch*. A fellow in his right mind wouldn't want to milk all those cows by himself. We will be back tonight and tomorrow, but not all of us. I'm afraid we won't be able to help for long. We have two cousins getting married in Pennsylvania, and we'll be attending the weddings next week. See you later." He held out his hand, only to jerk it away before Tully could shake it.

"I don't want to risk hurting those tender fingers. You will need them." Gabe chuckled as he put his hat on. His brothers followed him out the door.

"Funny man," Tully muttered, crossing his arms over his chest.

"Gabe is well-known for his sense of humor."

"You have the same problem, *Frau* Beachy. *Ab en kopp*," he muttered in mock disgust.

"It's not a problem, *Englisch*. It's a gift."

She caught the sparkle of mirth in his eyes and was happy his glumness had vanished. He tried to keep a straight face but started chuckling. It was contagious. Soon they were both doubled over with laughter.

He was a man who could take a joke and laugh at himself. She liked that about him. "I'm glad you decided to remain with us, Tully Lange," she said, realizing how much she meant it. He might not be the best farmhand, but there was something about him that made her want to smile.

"Thanks. I reckon I'll stay on a few more days and see if I can get the hang of being a dairyman."

She stopped smiling. "Were you thinking of leaving sooner?"

"It crossed my mind. I'm not exactly *goot* help."

"Do not be so hard on yourself."

"Guess it's a force of habit. I'll go see if Gideon is ready for our checkers rematch."

"He will enjoy that, but maybe let him win one game."

"Can't do that. It would make him mad if he thought I wasn't playing my best. He wants to win fair and square. I'm the same way. What other work do you have for me?"

"The milk room needs to be washed down and the equipment cleaned with hot water, soap and bleach. I'll get the water heating for that. The wood box outside is getting low. Oh, and the wheels on the buggy need to be greased."

"Got it. Anything else?"

"That's enough for one morning. Go enjoy your game with Gideon."

He flexed his fingers. "I hope I can pick up a checker. Gideon might have to move his pieces and mine."

"I have something that might help." She turned to the cabinet where she kept her ointments and medical supplies. She found the bottle she was looking for and carried it to him.

"Give me your hand."

He did, and she poured some of the oil into his palm. He sniffed. "What is it?"

"A little cayenne pepper in olive oil. Rub it in well, but be careful not to touch your mouth or your eyes." She realized how close she was standing to him and how natural it felt to look up and see him smiling at her. His smile faded, and his eyes darkened.

What did he see when he looked at her so intently? She wanted to ask, but she was afraid of the answer.

"I can't remember the last time someone wanted to

take care of me. You're a good woman, Becca," he said softly. "Thank you."

"You're welcome." Her voice sounded breathless to her own ears. He stirred her in ways she had thought she had buried with her husband.

The sound of Gideon's crutches thumping down the hallway caused them to move apart. She stepped to the stove, opened the firebox and started adding wood. Tully rubbed his hands together, spreading the oil over them. Gideon came slowly into the kitchen with a look of intense concentration on his face.

"You shouldn't be up yet," Becca said sharply.

"I can't stay in that bed another minute. What are the two of you doing?"

"Nothing," they said together and then exchanged guilty glances.

Gideon arched one eyebrow as he glanced between them. Becca closed the firebox and banged the lid back into place.

Tully flexed his fingers. "This is getting pretty hot."

"What is it?" Gideon asked.

"Some of the rub I make for your hip. You will have to wash that off before you milk tonight," she said, indicating Tully's hands.

A grin tugged at the corner of his mouth. "Or not. That might make for an interesting show."

She shook her head at his foolishness. "You mean seeing how far a cow can kick a grown man? It would only be funny for the onlookers."

Gideon chuckled. "Let me know when you try it so I can sell tickets."

"I may sell tickets to our next checkers game instead

so everyone can watch you getting whomped by me again. Are you up to a game today?"

"What is whomped?"

"Beaten, badly."

"There will be no whomping done by you. I know your tricks now."

"Ha! You know some of them."

"Go get the board. We will see your pride go before your fall."

"My fall? Not a chance." He walked down the hallway to get the game.

Gideon gave a little laugh. "I like that fellow even if he is a boaster."

"I like him, too. He makes me smile, thinking about the nonsense he utters."

"I will enjoy having him around for a few weeks." Gideon slanted a glance in her direction. "He will brighten our Christmas season, but he will be gone after that."

Was Gideon giving her a gentle reminder of that fact? He didn't need to. It was always in the back of her mind. She could like Tully, but not too much. He didn't belong among them. He was an outsider who was simply passing through their little corner of the world. He would get in his car and drive away, leaving her behind to resume her sad, lonely life.

She straightened her shoulders. That wasn't right. She had Annabeth, Gideon and many friends in New Covenant. She wasn't sad, but sometimes she did get lonely. A man like Tully Lange might ease that ache for a short time when he made her laugh, but he wasn't the answer for her. She must guard her heart against caring too much.

Chapter Eight

The following morning Tully opened his eyes when there was a knock on his door. "Tully, are you awake?" Becca asked.

"I'm up," he said, wishing there was some part of him that didn't hurt. If the cows had run over him one by one, he figured he would feel about the same. It was starting out to be a bad day. At least it wasn't as cold in the room with the small heating vent open.

He sat up on the side of the bed, rubbed his face and sighed heavily. He had a choice to make. Head on to Caribou and forget about the pretty Amish widow and her family or tough it out and become useful. It'd been a while since he had been useful even to himself.

He pushed to his feet, wondering if he could do it. Could he really make a difference and become something other than a liability for Becca?

In the kitchen she handed him the clean pails. "How are you?"

She barely looked at him. Her demeanor was cool. What was up? "It's too early to tell," he muttered, reaching for Gideon's overcoat.

Becca shook her head. "You do not need to stay with us. We can manage." She looked at him then. "I thank you for all you've done so far."

This was his chance to bow out gracefully. Except when he looked into her weary eyes, he realized he didn't want to leave. Not yet. "You can't get rid of me that easily."

"I'm not trying to get rid of you."

"Glad to hear it, because I surely do love your amazing cooking."

The smile he hoped to see tugged at the corner of her lips. "Flattery is not our way. I have told you this."

"Becca Beachy, your cooking is downright horrible. It could make a skunk gag." He leaned toward her and grinned. "Is that what you'd rather hear?"

She giggled as she stepped around him. It was a beautiful sound. "You know it is not, you foolish fellow." She flashed him a grin and reached for the doorknob.

In that instant he forgot about how much his arms ached and how tired he was. He could do one thing to brighten her day. He could make her laugh.

When she opened the door, the cold hit him full in the face, sending a shiver to the soles of his feet. As he followed her out into the dark and frigid morning, he called himself every kind of fool for choosing to stay for no other reason than to see her smile.

The barn was a welcome haven of warmth when he stepped inside out of the wind. They stopped to check on Diamond and Rosie first. He figured Annabeth would be waiting for a report when they came in. Rosie was lying down chewing her cud with her sleeping calf pressed close to her side. "They both look comfortable," he said.

"I agree. We won't disturb them until they are up."

Four of the cows had already moved from their bedding area to their milking stanchions on their own. Becca lit the second lantern hanging on the wall and took down her three-legged stool and a currycomb. "Don't try to rush just because the Fishers are coming. The cows will not appreciate it. They can sense your moods. A calm, happy cow gives more milk."

"In other words, I need to be a pleasant cowboy."

"Exactly." She walked back to the next cow in line.

Tully hung up his hat and took down his little seat and the remaining brush. "Which one is this?" he asked as he swept the loose dirt and bedding from the animal's back legs and udder.

"That is Dotty."

"I remember you, Dotty. You're the troublemaker."

The cow tossed her head and switched her tail. He patted her hip. "Prove me wrong and behave. There'll be an extra ration of grain for you if you do."

He heard a chuckle from Becca. "Bargaining with a cow? Is that how Oklahoma cowboys manage their herds?"

"We do whatever it takes." He sat down and got to work. In a few minutes, his stiff muscles began to limber up. Dotty shifted restlessly. He started singing to calm her. "Home, home on the range. Where Dotty and her friends can go play. Where never is heard a discouraging word and cowboys can sing songs all day."

He heard clapping from the front of the barn. He'd forgotten about the Fishers.

"*Goot* tune, *Englisch*. I can take over."

Tully thought it was Gabe looking over Dotty's back,

but he couldn't be sure. "It's Cowboy to you, mister. Go find your own cow. This one is mine. Better yet, take over from Becca and let her go start breakfast. I'm getting hungry." She deserved a break from the hard work more than he did.

Gabe laughed and moved to her side. "You heard the cowboy."

"I did. The man thinks of nothing but his stomach."

She walked past with two full pails in her hands. Tully had only filled one. He settled into his work once more.

Tully learned Gabe and Moses were the only two brothers to come that morning. Moses had filled the wagon with silage and was waiting to get started feeding when they finished milking. Moses drove while Gabe and Tully shoveled the feed into the long troughs on both sides of the center aisle.

"Do you feed cattle this way where you are from, Cowboy?" Moses called over his shoulder.

"My family raised beef cattle, not dairy cows. We fed silage in the winter but from a grain wagon pulled by a tractor. In the summer the cattle were out on grass in huge pastures. I spent a lot of hours checking cattle and fences on horseback."

Gabe grinned at Tully. "Did you ever ride wild bucking horses?"

"Not on purpose."

Gabe's brow furrowed, then just as quickly his confusion cleared. He slapped Tully on the back. "Not on purpose. Ha! That's a *goot* one. Once *Mamm* decided to plow her garden because *Daed* hadn't gotten around to it. The plow horse spooked and jumped the fence while he was still harnessed to the plow. He pulled down a ten-foot section around *Mamm*'s garden. *Daed* asked if she had torn down the fence on purpose. Quick as can be, she said she wanted to put a gate there all along."

The brothers shared funny stories about their own experiences with horses that didn't go as planned. Tully was grinning from ear to ear when they were finished with the chores. The two reminded him of the ranch hands who had worked for his grandfather. Hardworking, humor-loving, loyal, dependable men. Were other Amish the same, or were the Fishers unique?

The brothers waved goodbye as they drove the wagon loaded with milk to the collection station, leaving Tully feeling that he had managed to improve their opinion of him and make two new friends in the process. Which was good because they had promised to return and help with the milking, and he needed the help.

Becca was at the stove when he came in. She cocked her head to the side. "Why the big smile?"

"Those Fisher brothers are a hoot. Are all Amish so funny?"

"Are all cowboys as funny as you?"

"Some, not all."

"It is the same with the Amish."

He patted his stomach. "What's for breakfast? And lunch? And supper?"

Annabeth came running into the room. "Tully, you're still here. I was worried."

He caught her up and lifted her to straddle his hip. "I'm not gonna leave without telling you goodbye, so don't worry."

"To worry is to doubt *Gott*," Becca said.

Tully deposited Annabeth on her chair. "See. No worrying from now on."

"Okay. Tell me a story."

"Nope. I'm gonna go help your grandpa get up. Stories will have to wait until after school."

"Aw."

He leaned down and whispered in her ear loud enough so Becca could hear him, too. "What did the duck say to the dog?"

"I don't know. What?"

Tully tweaked her nose. "Nothing, silly. Ducks can't talk."

He left the room with the sound of their giggles gladdening his heart. It wasn't turning out to be such a bad day after all.

The following morning Tully was already in the kitchen getting the fire going when Becca entered the room. She stopped short at the sight of him and grinned. He liked the way her eyes lit up when she smiled.

She set her hands on her hips. "You are up before me. I am impressed."

"Don't be. I happened to be hungry and got up looking for something to eat."

She chuckled. "You are a glutton."

He realized how different his life had become. Only a few months ago, his first thoughts in the morning had been where to find his next drink. A week ago it had been how he would avoid taking a drink. Now the first thing he wanted was to see Becca's smiling face. He hadn't thought about taking a drink all week.

He handed her two of the pails he had already scrubbed. She handed them back. "You and the Fishers can do the milking. I have work to do in the house."

"As long as it involves cooking, I'm fine with that." He slapped his hat on his head and went out.

Becca's smile faded as she realized it was impossible to harden her heart against the man. Every minute she spent in Tully's company was a joy. She was wise enough to know the path she was on would only lead to heartache. She simply didn't know how to step off it. He was going to leave one day soon, taking this strange joy with him, and then it wouldn't matter.

She fixed breakfast and then took Annabeth to school. Danny was waiting on the school steps, but she let Annabeth out and quickly drove away. She didn't want to speak to him or anyone.

She worked the rest of the day doing mending and sewing Annabeth's costume for the Christmas play in the little alcove off her bedroom. That way she avoided Tully's company. He kept Gideon entertained. She could hear them laughing in Gideon's room down the hall, and that made her smile. Tully was surely a godsend for her father-in-law.

When it was time for school to be over, she came out of her room. She hoped Eva would bring Annabeth home, but she hoped in vain. She and Tully were in the living room with Gideon when Danny came in. He nodded to Gideon. Annabeth went straight to Tully. "How is Diamond?"

He grinned at her. "Why don't we go out and check on her, unless your mom has chores for you to do."

Becca shook her head. "They can wait until you've seen your calf."

"Okay, come on, Tully." She darted to the door.

He gathered his hat and coat. "Wish I had your energy."

"Tell me another cowboy story, Tully."

"Let's see. Have I told you about the time I roped a coyote?"

"Nope. Is it a funny story?"

Tully chuckled. "It is now. Not so much when it was happening, though." He went out with her and closed the door.

Danny turned to Becca. "The child is overly fond of him."

Becca shrugged. "She likes his stories. I don't see the harm in her listening to him."

"I worry that he is making the outside world seem too attractive to her."

Gideon chuckled. "I hardly think a few cowboy stories will entice Annabeth to leave the Amish. She's only seven."

"Her hero worship isn't healthy," Danny said, giving Becca a pointed look.

Becca didn't care for his tone. "I know my child. If I see something to be concerned about, I will deal with it."

"I hope so. If you need help dealing with him, let me know."

"*Danki*, Danny, but I'm sure Gideon and I can manage." She folded her arms across her middle. "Goodbye."

He seemed to sense he'd stepped over the line. "I'll bring Annabeth home again tomorrow."

"That will be fine." She walked to the kitchen door and opened it.

He looked as if he wanted to say something else.

Becca narrowed her eyes at him. He wisely held his peace and left.

She returned to Gideon. "The nerve of that man."

"His concern is as much for you as for Annabeth."

"I'm not suffering from hero worship any more than you are."

"Aren't you?"

"I'm not." She left the room and retreated to her bedroom. She didn't slam the door, although she wanted to. She dropped to sit on her bed and rubbed her forehead. Was Danny right? Was Tully a bad influence on Annabeth?

He is a bad influence on me.

She needed to put an end to their growing friendship, but how? Should she tell him to leave?

Tully finished the morning chores with the help of only Moses on Friday. After the young man left, Tully walked into the house and stopped short in the doorway. Annabeth was seated at the kitchen table, crying, as Gideon and Becca looked on.

"What's going on?" He closed the door.

"They won't let me take you to school," she said and sobbed harder.

"Annabeth, calm down. This is not how we behave," Becca said sternly. She looked at Tully. "She has told her friends about you, but none of them believe you are a real cowboy."

"Maddie's brother Otto told me there aren't any cowboys in Maine," Annabeth said between sobs.

He crossed to where she sat and crouched beside her. "I'm sorry if they upset you."

"She is upset with me," Becca said. "I told her she

can't take you to show-and-tell today. It would be rude to ask you to be on display."

"Oh, I see. Your mom is right, Annabeth. I wouldn't like to be your show-and-tell exhibit." The idea of standing up in front of a schoolroom full of kids was enough to make his palms sweat. Being in front of the group had been one of the hardest parts of his therapy.

"But Jenny brought *bobbli* Eli."

Tully looked to Becca for an explanation. "Her sister's new baby," Becca said.

"Well, Annabeth, I can see how that would give you the idea to bring me. Becca, do you suppose it would be okay if I rode to school with you this morning so I could meet her friend?" Meeting another first grader wasn't intimidating. He could manage that.

Annabeth turned pleading eyes to her mother. "Could he, *Mamm*?"

Becca looked to Gideon. He nodded once. "If Tully wishes to meet your friends, that is fine, but you are not to boast to others about having him stay with us."

Tully rose to his feet and held his hands out to his sides. "I'm not someone special. I'm just a man who grew up in a different place. Where I come from, there were lots of cowboys. You would've been the unusual one, because there were no Amish folks where I lived."

"None at all?" she asked, drying her tears with her hands.

"Not a one. Have you been practicing your part for the Christmas program?"

The change of topic brought out a hint of a smile. "I have. *Mamm* listens to me every night."

"I'd like to hear you recite your lines. Would that be okay?"

She nodded eagerly. "I'll tell them to you on the way to school."

Gideon folded his hands on the tabletop. "Now that this crisis is over, let us have our breakfast in peace."

Tully took his place across from Annabeth and bowed his head. He glanced up once to find Becca gazing at him. She looked down as soon as their eyes met, but he thought he detected gratitude in her expression. It could be that he was finally becoming something other than a burden.

Tully was being kind to her daughter. A spot of warmth settled in the center of Becca's chest. He had no idea how much she appreciated his compassionate understanding. Annabeth was a sensitive child. Perhaps because she was an only child. Becca sometimes wondered if she was doing her daughter a disservice by not seeking to marry again. Perhaps she was selfish, but she didn't want Annabeth to think of another man as her father.

After they finished eating, Tully helped Gideon to his favorite chair in the living room and settled him with the newspaper and a book close at hand. Becca took several bricks she'd had warming in the oven out to the buggy. Tully and Annabeth came out of the house as she drove the buggy up to the gate. Her daughter was smiling at Tully with something close to adoration in her eyes.

Becca opened the buggy door. "Hurry, or these bricks will be cold before we get to school."

Tully lifted Annabeth into the buggy, climbed in behind her and shut the door. "*Sis kald heit.* Did I get that right?" he asked.

Becca nodded. "*Ja*, it is cold today. I'm impressed you remembered."

"I've always been good with languages. I studied Spanish in high school, along with football and girls. Then I learned German when I was in the service. Not that speaking another language has ever done me much good. Annabeth, what do you want for Christmas?"

She scowled at him. "What do you mean?"

"You must have some special gift you are hoping to find under your Christmas tree. Maybe a doll, a new dress or a game you like."

Becca cleared her throat. "We don't give our children presents at Christmas the way the *Englisch* do, and we don't decorate trees. We may add a few pine branches to the mantel, and we will hang the Christmas cards we receive on ribbons, but nothing more. For us Christmas Day is a solemn day to be spent in quiet reflection and prayer. We do gather to celebrate the season with others beforehand and after. We go visiting and enjoy parties. The children certainly inspire us with their hard work on their Christmas program. I guess you could say it is their gift to us."

"I was going to cut a tree for you. Good to know that won't be necessary. Okay, Annabeth, what is your favorite subject? Don't say recess."

Annabeth frowned at him. "Recess isn't a subject. I like reading. Teacher has lots of books that she brought to our school. I'm going to read them all someday."

"A worthy goal. Becca, what was your favorite subject in high school, and don't say boys."

"Boys aren't a subject, either," Annabeth said with a shake of her head.

He chuckled. "They will be when you get a little older. Well, Becca?"

She glanced his way and saw he was waiting for her answer. "I did not go to high school. Amish children only attend school through the eighth grade."

"No kidding? High school was mandatory where I'm from."

"The Amish were granted a religious exemption by the Supreme Court in 1972."

"Okay then, what was your favorite subject in grade school?"

That he took the information in stride without any of the usual *Englisch* comments about the benefits of higher education surprised her. "Why do you want to know?"

"Because I'm a curious fellow. I want to know more about you." He turned slightly and stretched his arm along the back of the seat.

His hand was resting behind her shoulder. If she leaned back a little, they would be touching. She straightened her posture to prevent any contact. "About me or about the Amish?"

"Both."

"*Mamm* liked reading the best, same as me," Annabeth said.

"I can believe that. You were going to recite your lines for the Christmas program for me."

Annabeth grinned and nodded. "'I'm a little shepherd girl, and no one will help me find the Christ child.'" She sat up and gazed straight ahead. "'Where is the new king? I want to see him, too. I heard the angels say he is in Bethlehem. Can you tell me where to find him?'"

"That's very good," Tully said.

"That's not all. I go to many houses and ask for him. 'Is the new king here? Where is the new king?'"

Tully grew solemn. "Doesn't anyone tell you?"

"The innkeeper's daughter tells me there is a baby in the stable. That's my friend Maddie. When I go to the stable, I can't see him because all the other shepherds are gathered around him. I try to get close, but I keep getting pushed aside."

Tully shook his head. "That's not right. Someone has to let the littlest shepherd girl see the baby. Who will help her?"

Annabeth grinned. "A very kind man. Joseph. He lifts me up to see the new king, and I say, 'He is so beautiful.' Then everyone sings 'Silent Night.'"

"That sounds like a great program. I wish I could see it, though I don't imagine you allow *Englisch* folks in the audience."

"We do, don't we, *Mamm*? Tully can come."

"Our *Englisch* friends are always welcome, but Tully may not be here then, Annabeth. He has other friends he will want to see for Christmas."

"But I want him to be there. Can't you stay, Tully?"

"I reckon I can stick around until after your program, Annabeth. Consider it my Christmas present to you. I sure look forward to seeing it."

"That will be *wunderbar*, won't it, *Mamm*?" Annabeth turned to Becca with a beaming smile on her face.

"*Ja*, it will be *wunderbar*." Becca caught Tully's gaze and nodded in gratitude. He seemed to truly care about her daughter's happiness. Her respect and affection for him grew.

It took a little over twenty minutes to cover the three miles into New Covenant. It wasn't a town in the sense of the ones she had grown up around. It was more a collection of Amish homes and businesses along a one-mile stretch of the county road.

"The farms along here appear prosperous," he said.

"What makes you say that?"

"The barns are painted, and the fences are, too. Where I'm from, you see a lot of barns covered in rusty tin. Our fences are mainly barbed wire and steel posts. What do they raise this far north?"

"Potatoes, mostly. This county is the largest producer of potatoes in the state. Our growing season is short, but the days are very long this far north."

"Now that you say potatoes, I remember that's what Arnie talked about. He hated harvesting potatoes."

"I get to work in the potato fields next year maybe," Annabeth said.

Becca smiled down at her but shook her head. "I think maybe the year after that."

"We get a whole two weeks off from school during the potato harvest," Annabeth said. "Otto told me he made lots of money last summer."

"A lot of the labor of gathering and sorting potatoes has to be done by hand. Many of the public schools let the older students off for several weeks during the harvest, because the farmers need the labor. They've done it that way for more than one hundred years in this area."

"What do folks do during the winter?"

"Most of the Amish have small businesses. Michael Shetler has a clock-repair shop. Our bishop builds garden sheds and now some tiny homes, since more *Englisch* seem to want them. Gideon and I have no such problem keeping occupied in the winter. Cows must be milked twice a day, 365 days of the year."

Annabeth scooted forward on the seat and pointed. "That's our school. It's brand-new."

"It's a very nice-looking school," Tully said, smiling at her.

"I think so, too," Annabeth said. "That's my friend Maddie." She pointed to where several children were playing on a swing set. "Her brother Willis is the blacksmith. He's going to marry my teacher, and then she won't be my teacher anymore. That makes me sad."

"Danny is going to be your new teacher," Becca reminded her. "You like Danny."

"I like him, but I like Teacher Eva better. She brings treats, and she always finds the best stories to read to us."

"I'm sure Danny will find good stories, too," Tully said with a slight smirk on his face. Becca shot him a behave-yourself look.

"I hope so." Annabeth sounded anything but hopeful. Tully chuckled softly.

Becca could only hope that Annabeth's friends didn't embarrass Tully with their questions. Eva would handle the situation with grace, but she wasn't quite so sure about Danny. He had made it plain he didn't care for Tully.

Becca turned the horse into the schoolyard and stopped beside the hitching rail out front with the other buggies. "We should let Eva know you have come with us, and then you can go meet Maddie."

She led Tully up the steps into the school as Annabeth ran off to join her friend on the swing set. Becca cast a covert glance at Tully's face. What would he think of their simple one-room school?

Eva came forward to greet them with a smile. "Annabeth insisted she was going to bring you to show-

and-tell, but I told her it would be best to ask you first. I'm glad she convinced you. I'm sure the children will have many questions for you."

Tully whipped off his hat. Becca noticed he turned it around nervously in his hands.

"I'm not good at speaking in front of folks. I'm just here to meet a little girl named Maddie."

Eva looked disappointed, but she nodded. "I understand. I used to be terrified of getting up in front of the children, but since I'm the teacher, I persevered and now it's only a little intimidating."

Tully stopped spinning his hat. "I'm relieved you understand."

"I'll take you outside and introduce you to Maddie," Becca said.

Tully put his hat on, tipped it to Eva and followed Becca out the door. She stopped on the school steps. A dozen or more parents and their children were waiting in the schoolyard. She saw Danny at the back of the crowd.

Michael Shetler stepped forward. "Remember me?" he asked Tully.

"Sure. You were the blocker for our little cattle drive. What's going on?"

"Danny invited us to see a demonstration of your cowboy skills."

"Oh, he did?" Becca scowled at Danny. What was he up to?

Danny stepped forward with a coiled rope in his hand and held it toward Tully. "Annabeth has told us so much about you. I hope you don't mind showing us a few of your tricks."

Chapter Nine

Tully took the rope from Danny with a hand that was surprisingly steady considering there had to be close to three dozen people watching him. He hadn't held a lariat in ten years. Not since his uncle had sold Tully's horse, saddle and almost everything else his grandfather had given him before putting him on a bus and sending him to a boarding school in New Orleans. His uncle had claimed that Tully needed a more rounded education, when what he really needed was a home. It was an arrangement that hadn't worked for Tully. He took off on his own two months later.

He glanced at Becca. She looked worried. Was she concerned that he was going to make a fool of himself? Because he was pretty sure that's what Danny was hoping to see. He held on to the tail of the rope and tossed it out in front of him.

"Do you trip cattle with the rope?" Danny asked and chuckled.

"I'm sure there's more to the skill than that," Becca said.

Tully looked at her. If she was so eager to defend him, he couldn't let her down. He hoped.

"A lariat, or lasso as it is sometimes called, has to be coiled properly before a fellow can throw it." Tully began gathering the rope into even-size rings, flipping it to make it lie flat in his grip.

"I told you he was a real cowboy," he heard Annabeth whisper to another little girl beside her. He looked over the schoolboys.

"Which one of you is Otto?"

One boy of about ten or so took a step forward. "I am."

He had the same defiant gleam in his eyes that Tully had worn like a badge through his childhood. Tully pulled in the last of the rope and started to shake out a loop. "The eye that the rope goes through is called a hondo. You don't hold it. You want to make a loop and hold on to the rope about an arm's length away from the hondo. We call this length the shaft or spoke. See how I've got my index finger pointing down the shaft where I'm holding both sections together? That is the key to controlling where the rope will go. And just so you know, Otto, there are cowboys in every state, including Maine. Bull riders, bronc riders, calf ropers—they're everywhere. Of course, the best cowboys are from Oklahoma, if you ask me. You want to step out there about ten feet?"

The boy crossed his arms over his chest. "Not really."

Tully chuckled. "Okay. How about you, Danny? Do you want to be my target?"

Danny shook his head. "I don't think so."

Becca walked out in front of the group with her chin held high. "Is this far enough?"

Bless her heart. It seemed one person had faith in him, and that was enough. "Cover your face with your hands so the rope doesn't scratch you."

"I will do it," Danny said suddenly.

Tully shook his head. "Nope. You had your chance. The lady is willing, and I'm gonna oblige her." He shook a bigger loop, and after whirling it above his head a few times, he let it fly. The rope settled around Becca's shoulders. He pulled it tight.

"A working cowboy usually has a horse that knows how to keep the rope taut." He handed the end to Annabeth. "Don't let her get away."

"I won't." The child grinned from ear to ear.

"The cowboy gets off his horse and goes hand over hand down on the rope all the way to his prize," he said as he demonstrated on his way to Becca.

When he reached her, he rested his hands lightly on her shoulders before lifting the rope off. "Did I hurt you?" he asked quietly.

She pulled her hands away from her face. Her grin was as big as Annabeth's. "Not at all, but I didn't get to see you throw it."

He adored the sparkle in her eyes when she smiled. He pretty much adored everything about her.

"Do it again," someone called out. He had forgotten for a moment that they had a crowd watching them.

Becca's smile disappeared. She looked down and hurried to stand behind Eva.

Tully raised his hat to the onlookers and prayed his sore, stiff muscles would remember what they were supposed to do. He wasn't seventeen anymore. "Danny wants to see some of my tricks. Annabeth, you can let go now."

Tully coiled the line and shook out another loop. Instead of whirling it over his head, he held it out to his side, making it larger and larger. When it was big enough and spinning at the right speed, he hopped through it and back. He felt it clip his heel, but it didn't catch. Okay, once was enough for that stunt. He heard gasps of appreciation from some of the children.

He kept the rope spinning and raised it over his head, where he was able to make it drop down to circle his knees and rise again. Feeling more confident, he began spinning a butterfly loop. He went through a half dozen more tricks then decided he had done enough and should stop before he messed up in a big way.

He motioned to Otto. "Want to learn to throw a lasso?"

The boy came forward eagerly this time. Tully showed him how to coil the rope, how to make a loop and how to twirl it. When the kid had the hang of it, Tully looked around for a target. "Aim for the seat of the teeter-totter."

To his surprise, Otto's loop fell exactly where he wanted it. "Good job. Now you can teach the other kids how to do it. But remember, a rope is a tool—it isn't a toy. It can hurt someone if you aren't careful. Don't go home and try roping your papa's milk cow. She might not take it too kindly. Understand?"

Otto nodded. "I do."

Tully was pleased to see the defiance had faded from the kid's eyes.

"Tell them the story about how you roped a wild coyote," Annabeth said.

Tully shook his head. "I'll leave that for another day.

I'm think your teacher is ready to start school." He glanced at Eva, and she nodded.

"Nice work. Next time our cattle get out, I'll know who to send for," Michael said and walked away with a woman holding a baby.

Tully coiled the rope again and handed it back to Danny. "I hope I was able to lay your doubts to rest."

"You did that and more. I'm sorry I put you on the spot. Annabeth likes to share the stories you've told her. You appear larger-than-life in them. I'm ashamed to say I was hoping to show her you aren't."

"Don't put too much stock in the stories the kid repeats. One thing you'll find is true about most cowboys. Telling stories is a lot like our boots—they look fine the way they are, but putting some polish on them sure makes 'em shine."

"Did you truly rope a wild coyote?"

"I did, and it was a dumb thing to do. Getting a lasso on an angry coyote is a whole lot easier than getting it off one."

Danny chuckled. "I'll remember that. How long will you be staying with the Beachy family?"

"Until Gideon is up and around, or until Becca stops feeding me. Whichever comes first. She is a fine cook."

"Your help is deeply appreciated," Danny said, looking toward Becca, who was getting in her buggy.

"They are *goot* people," Tully said, following Danny's gaze.

Danny turned to Tully. "I think you are *goot* people, too."

"Me? I don't know about that. If I am it's because Becca makes a fellow want to live up to her expectations."

"She does. I didn't think I would like you, *Englisch*, but I have been wrong before."

"It takes a big man to admit it. It appears Becca is ready to go. It was a pleasure talking to you."

"Likewise, partner," Danny drawled in a poor attempt at a Western accent.

Tully grinned as he walked away and got in the buggy with Becca. He settled back and looked at her. "What did you think of my show?"

She backed the horse away from the hitching rail and turned him around. "It was interesting. What were you and Danny talking about so intently?"

"You," he teased, hoping to see her smile.

Becca scowled at Tully. He had no business discussing her with Danny. "What is that supposed to mean?"

He held up both hands. "Sorry, I was kidding. We agreed you and Gideon are good people and that you are a fine cook. I mean, a so-so, plain cook. I keep forgetting that flattery is not your way."

"Oh." That served her right, assuming she was the main topic of conversation between the two men.

Tully flexed his fingers. "I couldn't believe I could still do some of those tricks. I haven't had a lasso in my hands in years."

"How did you learn such things?" Although it was considered rude to ask about a person's past, she couldn't contain her curiosity about him.

"There was a ranch hand who worked for my grandfather named Carl Littlehorse. Carl had been on the rodeo circuit as a trick roper. He was far better than I could ever hope to be. He used to perform while standing on the back of his horse. He taught me the basics and some tricks. The rest I picked up on my own. A kid has to do something for entertainment."

"Weren't there other children to play with? You must have had schoolmates?"

"We lived a long way from other families. My grandparents didn't mix much. I had a pair of cousins who lived on the ranch when I was in grade school. They were a few years older than me. My uncle and my grandfather didn't see eye to eye. When my uncle and his family left the ranch, I was pretty much on my own." He turned to stare out the window beside him. "I was always something of a loner, anyway."

Not by choice, she thought. His mother left him, his uncle and cousins left, his grandparents died. It was no wonder Tully reminded her of a lonely little boy who made jokes instead of letting others see his pain.

"Is it difficult to learn roping? I saw Otto do it, so it can't be too hard."

"Some people have a knack for it."

"Could you teach me how to spin a lasso?"

He turned to her with a look of surprise on his face. "Would that be permitted?"

"We are allowed to do some things just for fun."

"Name one besides checkers."

"Horseshoes. Volleyball. Singing. Visiting. At Christmas we go caroling. We have cookie exchange parties. We will even go to the Christmas parade in Presque Isle. In the summer we have picnics and attend the county fair. We women hold quilting bees."

He drew back in mock amazement. "Quilting bees, I do declare. I had no idea the Amish were such a frivolous bunch."

Becca cast him a sidelong glance. "Are you making fun of me?"

"Yes."

She giggled. "I thought so."

"Do you mind?"

She had trouble keeping a smile off her face. "If I say I do, will you stop?"

"No. It's too much fun to tease you."

"Are you ever serious?"

He looked away again. "There have been times in my life when I have been extremely serious. Now isn't one of them."

"What made you serious?"

"Getting shot at, for one."

She turned her startled gaze on him. "Someone was shooting at you? Why?"

"I was a soldier in a place where folks thought a bullet or a bomb was the best way to get rid of me and my buddies. Some of us didn't make it out alive. I saw friends die. I often wonder why I was spared."

Horrified, she struggled to find the right thing to say. "I'm sorry you lost friends."

"Thanks. They were good men and women. So any day I'm not being shot at is a good day for me."

He was trying to turn aside his grief with another joke, but she didn't find it funny. Tully's life had been filled with sadness. She prayed he would know joy from now on. How could she help? There had to be some way to show him life was good and that God meant for His children to enjoy their time on earth. Even if they suffered sorrows as Tully had and as she had, there was still goodness in life. She prayed He would show her the answer.

* * *

Tully stared out the window with his lips pressed tightly together. He could've cheerfully bitten his tongue. What was the matter with him? He never talked about losing his friends in the war or feeling left out as a child. If he opened his mouth again, he was likely to tell Becca that he was an alcoholic struggling to stay sober. Like she needed to know that about him. If only she wasn't so sympathetic and easy to talk to, he might have been able to stay silent. She had a way about her that made him want to open up.

In spite of being angry with himself, he realized he didn't mind sharing the unhappy bits of his life with Becca. She had seen her own share of sorrow. She had coped with the sadness in her life much better than he had handled the bad times in his. He turned his head to study her. Maybe it was her faith that gave her such strength. Or perhaps she was simply a strong woman because of the way she had been raised. He had never met anyone quite like her. It was a shame he couldn't take her to a movie or to dinner. She probably wouldn't go out with him even if she wasn't Amish. She was much too smart to fall for a guy like him.

He had never given much thought to starting a family. Becca and Annabeth made him realize how much he was missing out on. If he couldn't ask her out on a date, he might as well entertain her in another fashion.

"I will teach you how to spin a rope if you really want to learn."

"I do. It looks like fun."

If he could bring a little fun into her life with his cowboy antics, then he could prove to be useful after all. "First question. Do you have a rope?"

"Of course we do. We have horses and cows that sometimes need to be restrained. We use a rope for pulling any number of things."

"Okay, that was a silly question. When would you like to start?"

"Tomorrow. It is Saturday. I won't have to take Annabeth to school, so I can make some free time in the morning."

"Okeydoke. It's a date," he said wishing it could be more than a simple lesson. "In exchange I'd like you to teach me to drive a horse. I've ridden a lot of miles on horseback, but we never used driving horses or teams on our ranch. Grandpa owned tractors. I've always wanted to learn."

She held the lines where he could take them. "We don't have to wait until tomorrow for this."

He took the leather straps in his hands. "You trust me enough to give me the reins?"

"I do, but they are called lines. Reins are on the bridle of a riding horse." She scooted closer to show him how to hold them. His heart kicked up a notch at her nearness, but he forced himself to concentrate on what she was saying.

"To make Cider go, you say his name and then 'step walk' or 'step trot.' To make him stop, you say 'whoa,' or you can pull back on the lines. Our corner is just ahead. You might want to slow him down before you try to make the turn."

Tully pulled back, and the horse responded. "Is there a command for turning?"

"'Gee' and 'haw' for left or right. Make sure you say his name first. Use the lines to keep him moving straight on the roadway. He likes to drift out into the center."

"Don't you use Amish words?"

"Most of our horses are already trained by the *Englisch* when we buy them. Many of them are former racehorses. There's no point in teaching a horse Amish words because you might want to sell him or her back to the *Englisch* someday. Always say 'good boy' when he does the right thing."

Tully suspected Cider would've turned into his own drive without any prompting, but he dutifully spoke the commands. They didn't end up in the ditch, but he came close enough to make Becca draw a quick breath.

When he drew Cider to a stop in front of the barn, Becca smiled at him. "Not bad."

"Not good."

"We shall see how I do with my first roping lesson tomorrow."

He got out and helped her down, happy for the excuse to hold her hand. He allowed his grip to linger a little longer than was necessary. She didn't pull away.

They stood together silently for long moment with the snow falling gently around them. She kept her gaze down. Her face was partially obscured by the large black bonnet she wore. He wished they weren't wearing gloves. He wanted the warmth of her touch. He longed to cup her chin and lift her face so that she was looking at him. So that he could press his lips to hers.

She squeezed his fingers gently. How could he make time stand still?

He couldn't, and he had no right to think about kissing her. She wasn't a woman he could kiss and walk away from. He knew that in the depths of his soul.

And just as surely he knew that he would have to walk away. He didn't belong in her little slice of paradise. He wanted her to remember him fondly, not as a pushy outsider who thought her kindness was an invitation to trifle with her affections.

She looked up at him. He made himself let go of her hand. The loss brought a physical ache in his chest. "I'll put Cider up. You go in and get warm."

He turned away before he could take her in his arms and prove just how weak a man he really was.

"Tully."

He stopped at the sound of her voice but didn't look back. "What?"

"Thank you for telling me about your family and your friends. I understand how difficult it is to talk about loss. I am honored that you shared your feelings with me."

"The thing you need to remember about cowboys is that we like to spin tall tales."

"I think this cowboy doesn't want people to know he carries sadness and guilt in his heart. He covers up what he feels with jokes. Our burdens never truly leave us, but they are made lighter when we share them with someone who cares. I care, Tully. Never forget that. I count you as a dear friend."

He couldn't think of anything funny to say. He swallowed hard against the lump in his throat and led Cider toward the barn.

Chapter Ten

The snow turned into a driving blizzard, and by morning the world outside was a swirling curtain of white. Becca was thankful she didn't have to drive Annabeth to school, but the inclement weather meant her roping lesson would have to wait for a better day. When Tully came into the kitchen, he joined her at the window. "I didn't see this in the forecast," he said.

They depended on the daily newspaper and reports from their *Englisch* neighbors if bad weather was expected. "I don't think it was supposed to get this bad."

"What's with all the clothesline?" He nodded to the five-gallon bucket of it sitting on the counter with the blue line coiled almost to the top inside. Her mind had been so full of thoughts about Tully, worry about Gideon and all that was going on that she had neglected an important task. During a blizzard was not the time to carry it out, but now she had no choice.

"When Bishop Schultz and my grandfather came to welcome us to the community, they brought along a hundred and fifty yards of clothesline and told us how to use it. I should have put it out before now."

"You aren't going to hang out the wash today?"

She bit her lip as she looked at him. "It is so we can find our way to the barn and back in weather like this. In my defense, I spent last winter in Florida. I wasn't expecting winter to come on so soon. I should have had it out before now."

"Oh, I get you. We need to rig up a safety line. Okay, I guess I'll get my coat on."

She shook her head. "I am more familiar with the farm, and this is my fault."

He picked up the bucket. "Stay here. I'll go. You have people depending on you. If this old cowpoke gets lost in a blizzard, he won't be missed by many."

"Oh, Tully, that isn't true." She couldn't bear the thought of him putting himself in danger.

"It's mostly true, so end of discussion. I'll need something to cover my head and my mouth. I don't want my hat to end up in Canada."

Becca gave in. "I have stocking caps and wool scarves here."

She opened a drawer and pulled out several. He took a hunter-orange hat and a thick, wide black scarf. He put the hat on, wrapped the scarf over his face, then slipped into Gideon's heavy overcoat and gloves.

She handed him the bucket and put on her own coat and bonnet. "*Gott* will protect you. The line has knots in it every ten yards. If you go past ten of them, you have missed the barn. I will give you three jerks on the line so you will know to walk to your left and then to the right until you find the fence or the building. Whatever you do, Tully, don't let go of the rope."

"Not a chance. Me and ropes are old friends." He

tied a small loop in the end and slipped it over his arm so he couldn't drop it. "See?"

"All right." Becca stepped out onto the porch with Tully beside her. They made a pass around the porch post, and Becca got ready to feed the line out of the bucket. "Be careful." She shouted to be heard over the wind.

"This is not a day for funny stuff," he said and stepped out into the blizzard.

He was gone from sight within ten feet of the house. Her heart rose in her throat. He was risking his life for her and her family's safety. Did he realize that?

Keep him safe, Lord.

She played out the line as he walked, making sure it was still taut. He would be okay. She knew it. She had faith. She could feel jerks along the sturdy rope as he moved farther away. She thought he was still headed in the right general direction then realized that was because the line went through the front gate. Once he was beyond that point, she had no way of knowing for sure.

She tried to judge how long he had been gone, but time seemed to drag to a standstill. She counted the knots as they came up out of the bucket and squinted to see into the blowing snow. She couldn't even make out the gate, which she knew was only twenty feet in front of her. When the tenth knot slipped through her gloves, she knew he had missed the barn. She gripped the line and tugged on it three times. He tugged back the same number. Was he left or right of the building?

He was in God's hands, but she couldn't stop the worry that wiggled into her mind. Then the line went slack. What was wrong? Had he lost his hold on it? He would be blind without it. The urge to go out and search until she found him was overwhelming. Only the knowledge that she could be pulling the line farther out of his reach kept her from jerking on it again. Even if she reached the end of the rope, she could bypass by him without knowing it.

Keep him safe, Lord. Bring him back to me.

Just when she thought she couldn't bear it another moment, the line went tight again, and her knees sagged with relief. She held on to it, relishing the tiny movements that meant he was moving. Three hard jerks on the line signaled he was on his way back. When he loomed out of the snow, she grabbed hold of him, pulled him up the steps and into the kitchen. His stocking hat and scarf were crusted with snow, as were his eyelashes. She shook him. "I told you not to let go of the line. What happened?"

He blinked hard as he stared at her. "I didn't let go."

"But the line went slack. I almost headed out to find you."

"I missed the barn, but then I found the corral. I must've let the line sag when I followed the fence to the corner of the barn. Then I tied it off and followed it back. Some of the drifts I struggled through were three feet deep. I couldn't see my hand in front of my face."

She kept her tight grip on his arm as her panic-induced anger faded and her wildly beating heart calmed down. "You gave me a terrible fright. I don't know what I would have done if anything had happened to you."

He patted her hand and pulled the scarf away from his face to reveal his adorable grin. "I'm sorry I scared you, but I'm fine. What's for breakfast?"

She shook her head. "You and your stomach. We have to milk first, but we won't take it to the collection station until this blows over. It will freeze, but that can't be helped. We can still sell it."

"I hope the Fisher brothers don't try to get here in this."

"They are not foolish men. They know we can manage, even if it will take us longer without them."

His expression changed as he stared at her. "Were you truly concerned about me?"

She laid a hand on his cold cheek. "Of course I was. You could have easily been lost."

His gaze softened. "I'm not worth the worry, Becca."

She wanted to move away, but his eyes held her captive. What was he thinking? She longed to ask him. She wanted to know everything about him. Why did he value himself so poorly? She pulled her hand away. "You are worth far more than you think. That was a brave thing you did."

His eyes darkened. The ice on his lashes began melting and ran down his face like tears. He rubbed them away and walked to the sink, where she had four of the milk pails waiting. He leaned on the counter with both arms and bowed his head. "If I had known how hard this was going to be, I don't think I would've stayed."

She knew he wasn't talking about the work. The last thing she wanted was to heap more sorrow on him. Yet that was exactly what she was doing. She was woman enough to know that Tully was attracted to her. While she faced her own growing affection for him, there couldn't be anything but friendship between them. All else was forbidden. "Tully, I'm sorry—"

"I get it," he said, cutting off her explanation. "The cows are waiting." He turned to face her, holding out the pails. She gathered her scattered wits and took two of the buckets from him and then followed him out the door.

Tully had never been in this position before. Attracted to a woman who was so far out of his reach that he would've been better off trying to pluck the stars out of the sky. A beautiful, kind, caring woman who was not for the likes of him, a man who'd made a wreck of his life. She still mourned her husband.

Telling himself that she couldn't possibly find him attractive wasn't doing the trick. Because when she looked at him with such kindness in her eyes, he could almost imagine it was affection. He'd thought he was done deluding himself when he checked into rehab. He'd had to accept the harsh reality of his addiction. Now he had to face the fact that he was falling hard for a woman who deserved a much better man. He needed to keep those feelings in check.

He followed behind her on the guideline. Twice he had to help her back to her feet when she stumbled in the deep snow and fell. He would need to shovel a path to the barn when the snow stopped blowing so walking wasn't so treacherous. How deep would the snow be by the end of the winter? He hated to think of Gideon out shoveling this even after his injury was healed.

When they reached the barn and stepped inside, it was wonderfully peaceful compared to the storm raging outside. He drew a deep breath, inhaling the smells of old wood, fresh hay and animals. The cows mooed at the sight of them, happy to have their humans arrive to milk and feed them. He stopped to pat Diamond as she poked her head between the slats of the gate. She was getting cuter by the day, with long eyelashes framing her huge dark eyes on either side of her white patch. Becca walked past him to start milking on the farthest cow. She didn't say anything.

He leaned down to Diamond. "I have to learn to keep my mouth shut. Every time I speak to her, I end up saying something I shouldn't."

He and Becca finished milking in awkward silence.

Gideon and Annabeth were in the kitchen when Tully and Becca came in. If the old man was in much pain, it didn't show. He smiled at Tully. "How are my cows?"

"No signs of illness or infection. The blizzard is making them nervous. They didn't give quite as much milk, but everyone was eating when we put out the silage."

"Can I go see Diamond after breakfast?" Annabeth asked.

"No," Tully and Becca said together. "It's snowing too hard," Becca added. "We will all stay in today."

"Are you coming to church with us tomorrow?" Annabeth asked Tully.

"I hadn't thought about it. I guess tomorrow is Sunday." He glanced toward Becca, who was busy at the stove. Going to church with her seemed preferable to staying home by himself. "If the weather improves, maybe I'll ride along with you folks."

"I advise against it," Gideon said abruptly, surprising Tully.

"Why?" Annabeth looked puzzled. Tully wondered the same thing.

"Tully will not understand the preaching or the singing. He will feel out of place. There is an *Englisch* church not far from Michael Shetler's home in New Covenant where our service is being held tomorrow.

If you wish to worship, you will be more comfortable there. I'm told Pastor Frank Pearson is a fine preacher."

Tully hadn't been inside a church in a long time, but he suspected Becca would think better of him if he made the effort to go. He wanted her approval. "I can do that."

"I still think Tully would like to come with us." Annabeth glanced at her grandfather with a small pout to her lips.

"Tully is welcome to join us for the meal after the service," Becca said softly with a pointed glance in his direction.

Gideon nodded. "That would be acceptable."

"Sounds fine to me," Tully said. His heart grew lighter at the sight of her little smile. He wanted things to go back to the way they had been between them. Friendly.

Annabeth beamed. "Then he can show us more rope tricks."

"No, sweetheart, I'm done with rope tricks," he said. "Once was enough. I don't want folks to think I'm a show-off."

Her expression fell, but she nodded. "We must be humble and not put ourselves above others. Everyone is equal in the eyes of *Gott*." She looked to her grandfather, who nodded in approval.

"How is the rehearsal for your Christmas play going?" Gideon asked.

"Jenny wants her new nephew to be the baby Jesus, but Teacher doesn't think we should have a real baby in the play." Annabeth rolled her eyes. "She's afraid he'll cry through the whole thing. I told her babies cry sometimes. No one will care."

Tully caught Becca's eyes and struggled not to laugh. She carried a platter of French toast and sausages to the table and sat down. "Since she is getting married and giving up her position, your teacher wants her first and only Christmas play to be a success. I think using a doll would be better than having everyone shout their lines over the noise of a crying *bobbli*."

Their times together at the table had become one of the things he liked best about this family. It was how he always thought family time should be. There wasn't a lot of idle chatter. Plans for the day were made, duties laid out, but there was an underlying connection between Becca, Annabeth and Gideon that didn't need words. It was a bond he wished he could share.

They all bowed their heads to say a silent blessing. He would ask Gideon later what he said when he prayed. Tully wanted to be able to pray as they did.

After breakfast he went to his room. He took out his phone, sat on the edge of his bed and dialed Arnie's number. His buddy picked up on the fifth ring. "Cowboy, do you have any idea what time it is?"

"It's morning."

"It's Saturday morning, and it isn't even eight o'clock yet."

Tully pulled the phone away from his ear to look at the display. It read 7:55. "Sorry, I've been up for hours. Do you want me to call back later?"

"No, I'm awake now. Where are you?"

"I'm still on an Amish dairy farm near a place called New Covenant."

"You made it a whole week. I didn't think you would last two days. How do you survive without electricity?"

"I go to bed when it gets dark or I light a lamp." He

didn't bother to explain that he still reached for a light switch every time he entered a room. Some habits were hard to break.

"How are you keeping your phone charged?"

"I have a car charger."

"Are you still sober?"

"I'm happy to say that I am. It feels good."

"I'm proud of you, man. How is the pretty Amish widow?"

Tully couldn't think of a way to answer that.

"Did we get cut off?" Arnie asked.

"I'm still here. Her name is Becca Beachy. She is an amazing woman."

"Wow. That didn't take long. She must be something special if she caught your eye."

"Something special doesn't begin to describe her." She was everything good and kind. A wonderful mother and so much more.

"How does she feel about you?" Arnie asked.

Tully rubbed the palm of his free hand on his thigh. "She considers me a friend. A dear friend."

"That sounds promising. Have you asked her out?"

"I've thought about it, but what would be the point? Friendship or matrimony are the only two options a woman like her would accept. I'm not husband material. You know that as well as I do, so I don't see any point in pursuing a relationship."

"That's a bunch of malarkey. I'm not saying you should marry someone you just met. In fact I'm saying *don't* marry someone you've only known a week, but you will make a great husband when the time comes. You have a lot of heart, Tully. I hate to see you letting it go to waste."

"Thanks, but don't flatter me. That is not the Amish way. Becca needs a friend, not a suitor. I'll be content being her friend, although she deserves better."

"If you think you're not good enough for this woman…then become the kind of friend she deserves."

"What do you mean?"

"Exactly what I said. The first thing you need is to believe in yourself. You're the best of all possible friends. You'd do anything for her and her family. You fake it until you make it."

"If only it was that easy."

"I'm sorry if I sound flippant, Tully. It's too early to dispense advice to the lovelorn. So other than a crush on Becca, how is it living in the Stone Age?"

"Don't make fun of them. You don't know what these people are like. They are genuinely happy living the simplest of lives. Did you know they only go to school until the eighth grade?"

"What I know about the Amish you couldn't spread on a cracker. What I know about you, on the other hand, is that you don't believe you deserve happiness. You need to work on your self-esteem."

"I wouldn't know where to start."

"The Amish are religious, so start going to church. I hear all good things about the experience. Not that I go much myself. Start looking for a job so when the old geezer is back on his feet you'll have something lined up. I know there are a lot of farms down that way. You should fit right in. What did she say when you told her that you are an alcoholic in recovery?"

"It hasn't come up." Tully braced for his friend's explosion.

Arnie sighed heavily. "You've only known her a

week, so I'm going to let that slide, but if you want to become the kind of friend she deserves, then you need to be honest with her."

"Thanks, Arnie. I'll let you get back to sleep."

"Okay. You'll still be here for Christmas, won't you?"

"I'm staying to see Annabeth's school program on Christmas Eve, but I'll be at your place Christmas morning. That's the plan."

"Good. See you then."

Tully hung up, but Arnie's advice still rang in his ears. *Become the kind of friend she deserves.* He had stayed because he wanted to be the hero of the moment for Becca and her family. It hadn't quite turned out that way. How could he open up about his biggest failure and his biggest regret—that his addiction had led to the death of his closest friend and others?

Arnie was wrong. Tully didn't need to share that part of who he was with Becca. He would be leaving in a few weeks. He wanted her to remember him as the cowboy who rode in to save the day. Even if he hadn't.

Chapter Eleven

The storm blew itself out during the evening. By morning there wasn't a cloud in the sky to obscure the stars that were still out when Becca and Tully went to the barn. A half-moon hanging above the horizon left the snow-covered landscape almost as bright as day. He tramped a path through the snow that was thigh-deep in places and helped her along. Tully was careful to keep the conversation casual. If she noticed he was quieter than usual, she didn't comment on it.

The sun was just rising when they finished. Tully followed Becca along the narrow path toward the house. He stopped and cocked his head to the side. Did he hear sleigh bells?

The sound grew louder. He looked toward the lane and saw four magnificent high-stepping Belgian draft horses hitched abreast come charging into sight. Snow flew up from their hooves. Their breath made clouds of white around their heads as the sun glinted off their shiny caramel-colored backs and brass harness bells. An Amish man he didn't know stood on a wedge-shaped road grader behind them, a mountain of a man who looked as if he could handle the massive team easily.

He pulled to a stop in front of the house. The horses tossed their heads and snorted, seeming eager to be off again. "*Guder mariye*, Becca," he called out. "You shouldn't have any trouble getting to church service now. You are the last home on my route."

"*Danki*, Jesse. I was wondering if we would have to take the sleigh."

"My boys can break through most any drift as long as it's not higher than their heads." He nodded to her and spoke softly to his team. They lunged into their collars, pulling the grader easily and leaving a cleared path nearly ten feet wide with snow piled high on either side behind them.

"That man gives new meaning to the word *horsepower*." Tully watched in amazement as they made one more pass around the yard and went out the lane.

Becca chuckled. "Jesse Crump has a fine team. He and his wife farm on the other side of New Covenant, and he works for the bishop building garden sheds."

"How much does it cost to have your driveway plowed by four giant horses?"

She looked perplexed. "There is no charge. Jesse does it because it is needed."

"For everyone in your Amish community?" How many hours had the man been up clearing roads?

"And for some of our *Englisch* neighbors. We take care of each other."

She went into the house. He followed her after one last glance at the open lane. Tully could still hear the jingle of harness bells in the distance. "The mountain man gives new meaning to the word *neighborly*, too," he muttered to himself. He found more to admire about the Amish every day he was among them.

The next half hour was a flurry of activity as everyone got ready for church. Tully cleaned and shined his boots and put on his best pair of jeans along with a blue-and-white-striped Western shirt adorned with pearl snaps.

When he came into the kitchen, he saw Gideon dressed in a black suit with a vest. Becca wore a dark blue dress with a snow-white apron and a freshly starched *kapp* on her head. Annabeth sat in a chair while her mother fixed her hair. Tully watched in amazement as she combed, folded and pinned Annabeth's thick auburn tresses into a type of flat bun on the back of her head. Becca settled her daughter's *kapp* over the bun and pinned it into place.

"That's amazing."

"What is?" Becca asked, adding a bobby pin to her own *kapp*.

"That you can get so much hair under those things."

"It's easy." She turned around. Her mouth dropped open in surprise.

He looked down at his shirt and jeans. "Is something wrong?"

Annabeth gave a big nod. "You are not plain enough, Tully. But your buttons are very pretty."

"They're snaps." He demonstrated by popping them open and closed on his cuff. He looked from Becca to Gideon, who were both still staring at him.

Gideon cleared his throat. "You look *goot* for an *Englischer*."

"But much too fancy to be an Amish fellow," Annabeth added.

Becca had recovered her composure. "You look okay. Are we ready?" She collected a large box from the table and headed for the door. Tully jumped to open it for her. Annabeth followed her mother. Gideon came slowly on his crutches with his injured leg held stiffly out in front of him. Tully grabbed his jean jacket and stayed close behind the old man until he was safely settled in the front seat of the buggy.

"I'm going to follow you in my car."

Becca nodded. "All right."

The trip to New Covenant took about twenty-five minutes on the snowy road. He stayed behind them with his amber lights flashing to warn people coming up behind him that there was a slow-moving vehicle ahead. Almost everybody slowed down. Only two cars shot around them. One was a red sports car whose driver felt it was necessary to blast his horn in the process.

They passed Annabeth's school and turned into a farm not far beyond it. There were already a dozen buggies lined up beside the barn. He recognized Michael Shetler leading a horse, still wearing his harness, away from one of the buggies toward the open barn door. Otto met him and took the horse inside.

Michael came to Tully's car door. Tully rolled down the window. "Have you come to worship with us?" Michael asked.

"Gideon didn't think it would be a good idea. He suggested I go to an English church not far from here. Can you give me directions?"

"To Pastor Frank's church? Sure. Go back out on the highway and go left to the first intersection. Follow the road toward Fort Craig. You will see the church on the left side of the road just after you get into town. Tell Frank I'll be late for our regular meeting this week."

"I'll do that. Becca said I should come back for the meal. About what time would that be?"

"Our meetings last about three and a half hours, so if you return close to noon, there should be something left for you to eat."

"Thanks a lot." Tully watched Becca help Gideon out of their buggy. He started to get out of the car to assist her but quickly saw she had more than enough help as numerous men, including the mountainous Jesse, came to her aid. She glanced his way and lifted her hand in a small wave. He did the same. A moment later she was surrounded by a group of women, and they all went inside the house.

A familiar sense of loneliness took hold of him, although he tried to ignore it. Becca and Gideon had made him feel so much at home that seeing them surrounded by other Amish while he sat in a car made him aware of just how far apart they truly were. He put the car in gear and followed Michael's directions.

Near the outskirts of the town, a small building caught his eye. The sign above it said Lumberjack Bar. The parking lot was empty, but that wasn't unusual for any bar at this time of day. He drove on, glad he didn't have to face that temptation when he was already feeling ill at ease.

Finally he saw the small white church he'd been told about. He turned into the paved parking lot that had been cleared of snow. A beat-up orange truck with a snowplow on the front was parked at the far end of the lot. It might do the trick, but it sure wasn't as pretty as Jesse's big horses.

Tully got out of his car. Either he was among the first to arrive, or Pastor Frank had a really small congregation. He met the preacher just inside the door. The middle-aged man dressed in black looked Tully up and down. "An unfamiliar face. Welcome to the Lord's Community Church. Are you here to attend worship, or do you need directions to somewhere else?"

"I've been told that you're a good preacher. I thought I should come see for myself."

"Then you are doubly welcome. Would you happen to be the cowboy that's staying with Gideon Beachy and his family?"

His question took Tully aback. "How could you know that?"

"The Amish children around here used to attend our public school. Many have remained friends with their former classmates. The story of your ability with a rope spread quickly, including to my next-door neighbor's children, who hurried over to tell me about it."

"For people who don't use telephones, the Amish don't have trouble spreading news."

Pastor Frank chuckled. "That is the truth." He glanced at his watch. "It's almost time to begin. Please find a seat."

"Before I forget, Michael Shetler said he would be late to his regular meeting with you."

"Thank you for the reminder. I have had a change of plans. I'll have to let Michael know."

"I can give him the message."

"Great. The new days and times for our meetings are in the bulletin." He took one from the bookshelf behind him and gave it to Tully.

There were more people coming in now. Tully moved

to a pew at the back. While he waited for the service to begin, he scanned the paper Pastor Frank had given him. He saw the note about time changes for several meetings. One in particular caught his attention. The regular AA meeting had been moved from Friday to Saturday evening at six. The other meetings were for bereavement and survivors. He wondered which one of the three Michael attended.

Tully rolled up the paper. It was good to know there was an AA meeting available to him if he needed it while he was staying with the Beachys. Would he be able to remain anonymous in such a small, tight-knit community, or would word of his addiction get back to Becca before he got home from the meeting? It made him hesitate to attend. So far he hadn't needed the support the way he had when he was back in the city, but that was only because he fell into bed every night too tired to even think about driving out to find a drink.

He took note of the well-dressed families around him. A few members wore jeans with nice shirts or sweaters, although none wore the Western style he favored. He gathered more than a few inquisitive glances, making him feel like an outsider in a group where everyone knew each other. Several young children moved along the pews, climbing over their parents and fussing. Some of the teenagers looked bored. They checked their phones frequently. Older people sat quietly with their heads bowed.

A woman with a pink streak in her blond hair began playing the organ up front. Around him folks lifted their hymnals and flipped through the pages. What the congregation lacked in harmonious voices they made up for with their enthusiasm. Tully didn't bother trying to sing. He could twirl a rope, but when he tried to sing in a group like this, he sounded like a frog with a sore throat. Singing to the cows was a different story. They didn't care what he sounded like, so he was able to carry half a tune.

Pastor Frank turned out to be an interesting speaker. Tully heard his message of a child's anticipation for the arrival of Christmas and hoped-for presents under the tree. The pastor used it to show the world's anticipation for the arrival of God's only son on earth. Tully believed in God—he just wasn't sure God believed in or cared about him.

He didn't stick around after the service was over. It had only been little more than an hour, but he was already missing Becca.

He drove back to Michael Shetler's place, intending to sit in his car until the Amish service was over. The sound of singing reached him when he shut off the engine. He rolled down his window.

The song wasn't like the hymns at Pastor Frank's church. There wasn't any music, just voices raised together in slow, almost mournful undulation. They were singing in German—he recognized some of the lyrics. He got out of his car and moved onto the porch to hear better. The front door opened. A small boy of about three or four darted out quickly, followed by an older boy, who scooped him up. As they turned back, Tully recognized the kid as one from Annabeth's school.

The boy grinned. "Hello, Cowboy. Do you have your rope handy? My little *brudder* is having trouble sitting still this morning."

"Sorry, I don't."

"I'm joking. Come in."

"Are you sure it's okay?"

The boy nodded and went in, carrying his brother. Tully followed slowly. Inside he saw benches set up in rows with a narrow center aisle. The women sat on one side. Men sat on the other. He saw Gideon sitting near the front on a kitchen chair with his leg propped up with a pillow on a low stool. Tully quickly picked out Becca across the room with Annabeth beside her, and something in his chest eased. Simply seeing her made him feel better, happier.

The man preaching in Amish at the front of the room paid no attention to Tully. Off to his side Tully saw the younger boys occupied the last row of benches. Otto sat on the end beside the boy with the runaway toddler. Otto scooted over and patted the bench beside him. Tully smiled his thanks and sat down.

"Do you want me to tell you what the preacher is saying?" Otto asked in a low whisper.

"If it's okay, sure."

For the next hour, Tully listened to Otto relay what the minister and then the bishop spoke about. Some of it he was able to gather for himself when the bishop read from the German Bible he held. It was Matthew, chapter one. The messages preached were about remaining humble and keeping the true meaning of Christmas in hearts and minds during the season. The bishop asked his congregation not to be distracted by the colorful decorations and fancy gifts their *Englisch* neighbors used to celebrate the season but rather to remember it was a babe born in a lowly stable who quietly brought salvation to mankind.

When the next hymn started, Otto handed Tully a large black book and opened it for him. There weren't any musical notes, just the lyrics written in German on one side of the page with the English translation beside it. Tully listened to the worshipers singing and realized Gideon had been wrong. Tully didn't feel uncomfortable. The deep faith of those around him was as warm as if a blanket had been laid about his shoulders.

"Is it strange having an *Englisch* fellow live with you?" Becca's friend Gemma Crump asked as they set out food on the tables following the preaching.

"It was a little strange at first, but I'm getting used to Tully. He certainly keeps Gideon from fussing." His presence also decreased her loneliness, but she didn't share that with her friends.

Gemma glanced at Becca from under lowered brows. "What does Danny think about the arrangement?"

"I'm not aware of how Danny feels about Tully, and I'm not sure I'd care. He did voice some concerns about Tully's influence on Annabeth, but other than her fascination with his storytelling and rope tricks, I don't see that she is being harmed by knowing him." Annabeth was playing outside with her friends.

"I wish I could've seen his demonstration with his lasso," Gemma's mother, Dinah, said, setting out coffee cups.

"I saw it," Bethany, Michael's wife, said. "It was impressive."

It had also been a glaring reminder that he wasn't one of them. As had been the clothes he had on that morning. She had only seen him wearing his chambray shirts and dark jeans. They weren't so very different from the clothing worn by other young men in the community, except Tully wore a belt with a large buckle. Amish men only wore suspenders.

"He sat in on the last of our service," Dinah said looking out the window.

"I saw him." Becca tried to sound as if it didn't matter, but her heart had given a happy little leap knowing he was near again. It was amazing and frightening to know how much she had come to want his presence.

"I overheard Gideon telling Leroy that Tully has a wonderful sense of humor," Dinah said. "My Leroy only thinks he is funny," she added with a wry smile.

Gemma giggled. "I may tell *Daed* you said that."

Becca looked at her friends. Should she say anything? She was troubled by the unhappiness Tully tried to hide with his jokes and stories. She focused on cutting the apple pies she had in front of her. "He tells wonderful tales, but he uses humor to hide his pain. From what I have gathered, his life has been filled with sorrow and unhappy memories. I want to change that."

When no one said anything, Becca looked up. They were staring at her with shocked expressions on their faces. "What?"

"It sounds as though you have come to care for this young man," Dinah said.

"As a friend," Becca said quickly. The younger women looked relieved, but Dinah retained her look of concern.

"He feels bad about injuring our calf." Becca tried to explain what she wanted. "I'm sure that's part of why he offered to stay on and help when Gideon was hurt, but there is more to it. Tully has no family, no home to go to, not even a job to support himself, and yet he spends his time making us laugh and offering his help for nothing except food and a place to sleep. He has said he will stay until after the school program as his gift to Annabeth. I want to give Tully a Christmas season that he will remember fondly when he leaves us. As our gift to him. That's what I mean."

Gemma glanced at the other women in the room. "We give our *Englisch* neighbors candy or breads for them to enjoy. We sing carols to spread the joy of the season. Giving is something we all must practice."

"That's what I would like to do for Tully. I want us to share our gift of a plain Christmas season. I want him to feel included, not simply tolerated. Do you think that's wrong?"

"I don't," Bethany said. "I'm sure we can come up with a dozen ways to make his stay with us special."

Dinah grinned and nodded. "It is charity to a stranger. Are we not instructed by the words of Jesus to be good Samaritans? The bishop has met Tully and agreed that it was acceptable for him to stay with you. I think he will like this idea of including Tully in our celebrations."

The outside door opened, and Bishop Schultz, along with Leroy Lapp and Tully, came in together. The bishop and Leroy were laughing heartily. "That's a fine story, Tully," Leroy said.

The bishop slapped Tully's back. "I will share it in the Christmas cards to my brothers and sisters who live in Ohio. A rooster riding a pig all the way through Arthurville. I would've liked to see that."

The bishop sobered when he realized the women were staring at him. "Shall I call the community into eat?"

"We are ready," Dinah said with a smile. She leaned

closer to Becca. "I have a feeling this is going to be a wonderful Christmas season."

Becca smiled at Tully. "I couldn't agree more."

The men went through the line first and took their places at the backless benches that had been stacked to make tables. Tully came at the end of the line. Becca added a large piece of cherry pie to a plate that was already loaded with thick slices of bread, cold cuts, cheese spreads and pickled beets. He smiled at her. "You looked like the cat that swallowed the canary when I walked in. What gives?"

"My friends and I were simply making plans for the Christmas season."

"And?"

"And nothing else. Go sit and eat. There are others waiting for a place at the tables."

"I thought I might sit with you."

"Oh *nee*," Dinah said at Becca's elbow. "Men and women eat at separate tables, just as we sit on opposite sides during our worship."

"That would explain why the young people outside don't seem to be in a hurry to eat."

"They know there is plenty, and their turn will come after the older members are finished," Dinah said.

"And in the meantime, the boys and the girls can visit and make eyes at each other," Tully added.

Dinah frowned. "Who is making eyes at what girl?"

"The tall girl with glasses is making eyes at Moses Fisher," he said.

"My niece?" Dinah squeaked and moved to the window to look out.

Becca exchanged a glance with Gemma and smothered a laugh. Tully crossed the room and sat at a table where he could see her. While he wasn't exactly making eyes at her, she soon grew uncomfortable under his scrutiny. She left her serving table and went around to fill coffee cups.

"Please stop staring at me," she said softly as she handed him a cup of piping-hot liquid. She hissed as some of it splashed on her fingers when she set it down.

"Then don't stand in my line of vision. Why are all the women looking at me and smiling like they know something I don't?"

"Are you done eating?"

"If you're that eager to get rid of me, I am." He pulled a handkerchief from his pocket, dipped it in his glass of water and handed it to her. "Wrap this around your hand."

She looked around to see who might be watching, but no one was looking their way. She took it from him, wound it around her stinging fingers and nodded her thanks before moving on to the next table.

After Tully left the room, Becca was able to concentrate on her tasks. Although she would normally stay and visit with her friends, she went to Gideon to see if he was ready to leave. His cough was much better, but she noticed his leg was swelling above his shoe.

"I'd like to visit longer, but I'm ready to go home. Where is Annabeth?"

"Playing outside. I'll get her. Where is Tully?"

"I heard him say there is a game of horseshoes being thrown in the barn. It's a game he enjoys almost as much as checkers. I'm sure you'll find him there."

Becca walked down to the barn. There was a competition going on, but Tully wasn't one of the players. He was watching the game. When he caught sight of her, he nodded toward the door, got up and left the building. Curious, she followed him outside and saw him walk around the side of the building.

When she turned the corner, he was waiting for her. "Let me see your hand."

She still had his damp handkerchief wrapped around it. "It's fine. Just a little scald."

"Does it hurt?"

"Nee."

"The only burn that doesn't hurt is a third-degree burn, and that is serious. Am I going to have to arm wrestle you to get a look at it?"

She relinquished her hand but turned her face away from him. He gently unwound the bandage and turned her hand over. "It's blistered. Don't tell me it doesn't sting."

"Only a little," she admitted.

"Shall I kiss it and make it better?" he asked softly.

Did he think that's what she wanted? He didn't seem to understand how impossible such a thing was. How could she turn his affections aside without hurting him? "Please don't make fun of me."

"Okay, I'm sorry." He looked contrite as he packed a little snow into the handkerchief and wrapped it around her hand again. He didn't release her fingers. Nor did she pull away.

He sighed softly. "I need you to tell me the truth, Becca."

What was he going to ask? If he wanted to know the reason for her racing pulse, could she say it was because of him? She slipped her hand away from his.

Chapter Twelve

"What are you and your friends up to?"

Tully saw Becca relax and was glad he had defused the moment. He also realized how close he had come to kissing her. Would she have let him? Before he took that step, he would have to tell her about his addiction if there was even a chance of something between them.

She moved back. The troubled look in her eyes vanished, and a small smile appeared. "I have no idea what you're talking about. I have told you we were making Christmas plans and nothing else."

"If you say so." He wasn't convinced.

"Gideon is ready to go home. You are welcome to stay and visit with the people here. Gideon says you enjoy playing horseshoes."

"Another time, maybe. I'll follow you home."

"Don't hurry. We do only necessary work on Sunday."

Annabeth came rushing around the corner of the barn. "There you are. *Daadi* is in the buggy and ready to go. Can I ride home with Tully in his car?"

Becca shook her head. "It is not permitted to ride

to or from our prayer meetings in a car. The horse and buggy are our identity. It is the way we show our adherence to the ways of our forefathers, particularly on a day of worship."

Annabeth looked disappointed but nodded in understanding. Tully took her hand and began walking toward the buggy. "I was about to suggest we all go for a Sunday drive later. I'll change that to another day. You can have a ride in my car soon, I promise."

"Maybe you could take me to school tomorrow?" she asked hopefully.

He glanced at Becca. She didn't appear upset by the idea. "Your mother and I will discuss it just as soon as she tells me what she's planning that she doesn't want me to know about."

Annabeth cocked her head to the side. "What?"

They reached the buggy. "Tully is making a joke," Becca said, giving him a saucy grin. She opened the door and got in.

Tully lifted Annabeth and put her in the back seat. "You find out what she's up to and report back to me."

"There's nothing to tell," Becca said over her shoulder. "Cider, step walk."

Tully stood back as they rolled away. Jesse walked up to him. "I hear you are a horseshoe player. Care for a match?"

Tully looked the big man up and down. "Do you take the shoes off the horse or do you throw all four at once?"

Jesse's face split into a wide grin. "Ha. I throw them all at once. It's not hard. The tough part is training the horse to keep his feet together when he lands on the stake."

Tully laughed. "I don't have a comeback for that. One game, then I have to go."

It was easier said than done. He ended up playing Jesse and being soundly beaten. He was able to best Michael twice but lost to Danny. When the bishop stepped up to play him, Tully wondered if he should let the head of the church win. He didn't need to worry. The bishop whomped him. Tully hadn't enjoyed himself so much in a long time.

When he arrived at Becca's home later, Annabeth met him at the door. "*Mamm* won't tell me what she's planning."

He patted the child's head. "Thanks for trying." He met Becca's eyes across the kitchen and managed a smile. "Annabeth, do you want to hear about the time I jumped out of the barn loft with my grandma's best umbrella for a parachute?"

"Sure. I love your stories, Tully." She reached up and took his hand.

He winked at her. "I love sharing them with you, but your mother can't hear this one unless she tells me what she has planned."

Becca pointed to the other room. "Out of my kitchen, both of you. There's nothing to tell."

He couldn't get Becca to admit she was planning something that evening or again the next morning as they entered the barn.

"I wish you would quit asking me." She scowled at him, and he decided not to annoy the cook.

The Fisher brothers didn't show up to help, so he knew they must have gone to their weddings. Tully was gratified they thought he was enough help for Becca and Gideon and hadn't arranged for anyone else to give him a hand. Becca suggested they let Rosie out into the corral for a while to give her a break from her baby. Tully held the calf while Becca led Mama out. He gave the calf a thorough checking over. She was outgrowing her cast. Her leg still had good circulation, so he knew it could wait another day. The vet would be out to see her tomorrow.

He got busy with the milking and realized how much he was starting to enjoy his time with Gideon's big cows. It was still hard work, but his muscles were adjusting.

He had his head pressed to the flank of Maude as he listened to Becca milking the cow behind him. He was almost keeping up with the splashes of milk into her pail. Working together the way they did gave him a sense of rightness. He had a lot of things he wanted to know about her, but he wasn't sure if she would be offended by his questions. He decided to risk it.

"Becca, can I ask you something?"

"I'm making pancakes for breakfast, if that's what you want to know."

He could hear the smile in her voice even though he couldn't see her. "My stomach appreciates the information, but that's not what I was going to ask. Why haven't you remarried?"

He could tell she had quit milking. After a few long moments of silence, she started up again. "There isn't any single reason why I haven't other than I'm not ready."

"Because of your grief for your husband."

"That is part of it. Another reason is not wanting Annabeth to think of someone else as her father. Perhaps that's selfish of me. Then Gideon has lost so much. I want him to feel that we need him. Perhaps *Gott* has not sent the right person to me yet."

"But if the right person came along, you would consider it?" He was far from the right person, but he knew there was something between them. He just wasn't sure what it was.

"Maybe, but it is hard to imagine. Can I ask you a question, Tully?"

She hadn't given him an outright no. "Sure. Anything."

"Did you enjoy yourself yesterday?"

He didn't even have to think that one over. "I did. I liked meeting Pastor Frank. I appreciate what I could understand of your service. Everyone made me feel welcome. I haven't been to church much recently, but I believe I'll start attending again. You and Gideon have so much faith that I would like to find some of that for myself."

"That's wonderful. I'm so glad for you. The Lord uses us all to His purpose."

Her words were encouraging. "I suppose that's true."

Diamond began bawling in her stall. She was tired of being by herself. He chuckled. "He certainly used an odd way to get me to stop here."

"The calf might have made you stop, but I think it was the desire to serve that *Gott* put in your heart that made you stay. You have brightened what could've been a very difficult time for my family."

"I'm happy to oblige." And he was. Maybe happier than he had been in a long time. He was starting to feel useful and not like a burden. Not since leaving the ranch had he felt like he belonged somewhere the way he was starting to feel that he could belong here.

It was a wild idea. There was no reason to think Becca wanted him, but what if she did? They hadn't known each other very long, but they seemed to fit together. He was afraid to discover if time would prove him right or if this would be one more failed mission.

Becca wondered if this was what the Lord had planned for Tully all along, a happy time with a family who cared about him. He seemed more cheerful today. She had heard all about his horseshoe games last evening, and she was glad she had told Gemma and Bethany to ask their husbands to invite him to play. Some of the women from the community would be coming over on Sunday to bake cookies to take in gift boxes to the local nursing home. They would discuss other activities to include Tully when he was occupied. She nearly giggled at the thought of planning his entertainment practically under his nose. She quickly sobered. He might not appreciate that she had made him a charity case for the community.

She stood up with her full bucket. "This is the last one. Were you serious about driving Annabeth to school?"

"In the car? Sure. Do you think her teacher will mind?"

She knew Eva wouldn't care. "Many of the children went to the public school on a bus before New Covenant opened its own school this year. I don't see that it will be a problem. It's not like we will make a habit of it," she added sternly so he would know Annabeth wasn't to wheedle future rides out of him.

"Okay, I'll take her after breakfast. You did say pancakes, didn't you? And maybe some of those little sausage patties and fried potatoes with onions. How about some of those light fluffy biscuits of yours, if that isn't too much trouble?"

"You will have toast and no complaints. I must get you a pair of suspenders for Christmas, because by then you won't be able to buckle your belt."

He stood up with his bucket and grinned at her over the back of his cow. "It's all your fault. If you weren't such a good cook—I mean, such a plain cook."

"Go get the milk cans ready. I'll take them to the collection station while you are gone."

"Do you have help there to empty them?"

"I do. Get busy and stop asking so many questions, or you won't get any breakfast."

"Yes, ma'am. My lips are sealed now. Not another question. No siree. Quiet as a mouse from now until you're done cooking." He drew his thumb and forefinger across his lips.

She shook her head at his foolishness and went to the house. If she was quick, she could make the biscuits he liked so well. It was fun cooking for a man who enjoyed what she made as much as Tully did. He never left the table without giving her a compliment.

She was pulling the pan of biscuits out of the oven when he came in. His eyes lit up like those of a child getting a lollipop. He walked over and snatched one from her pan. He stepped back, tossing it from hand to hand. "Hot, hot, hot."

"Serves you right. Wash up and then see if Gideon needs any help."

He dropped the biscuit on his plate and did as she asked. When he came back with Gideon at his side and Annabeth riding piggyback, Becca smiled to herself.

He was a good and kind man. What he needed was a family of his own.

He pulled out Gideon's chair and then swung Annabeth around and planted her on the floor by the table. She looked at Becca with wide eyes. "*Mamm*, Tully is going to take me to school. *Daadi* said that was okay. Is it?"

"It is, but you will not make a habit of it."

"I know. Tully said he could take us into Fort Craig to do some shopping if you want to go later this week."

Becca considered the offer. "I do need to pick up baking supplies and fabric. Gideon, do you need anything?"

"Razor blades. I have three left, so there is no rush."

Tully sat down beside Gideon. "You go to all the trouble of shaving your mustache and cheeks but keep your chin whiskers. Why? If you don't mind my asking."

Gideon rubbed his knuckles over his cheek. "Because this is our way. This was how my father and grandfather did it. That is reason enough."

"Got it. I was thinking it might mean something special."

"Eva may know, for she has studied books about our past," Becca said. "An Amish man grows a beard only after he marries. In our church he may trim his beard after his first child is born. All married Amish men have beards, but not all churches allow them to be trimmed."

Tully folded his hands together and closed his eyes. "For such plain folks, you sure have some complicated traditions."

She peeked at him twice before Gideon signaled the prayer was done by asking for his eggs. Tully never looked up. He wore a faint frown as if he were concentrating on doing something difficult. Maybe praying was difficult for him, but she was pleased to see he was trying. Perhaps Pastor Frank would be able to help Tully find his way back to God.

The following days fell into the same pattern. She started to forget he wasn't part of her family. They did their chores together; he teased her. He kept Gideon entertained with games of checkers or stories. The days were short but comfortable as he became familiar with her routine. He brought in wood before she had to ask. He even scrubbed the milk pails in the mornings before she was up, and he never forgot to thank her for a delicious meal.

On Thursday evening Michael and Bethany stopped in for a visit along with baby Eli, Bethany's younger brother Ivan and her sister Jenny. At fifteen, Ivan was a gangly youth with a dry wit and a sharp mind. He had lots of questions for Tully about ranching and admitted he had thought of settling in Montana in one of the new Amish communities there.

The bishop arrived a short time later to check on Gideon. Michael announced he wanted a chance to even the score with Tully over their game of horseshoes and suggested a game of checkers. Tully grinned and turned to the bishop. "What about it? Are you up for a match or two, as well?"

Bishop Schultz hooked his thumbs through his suspenders and rocked back on his heels. "I like a good game now and then."

Gideon laughingly brought out the set.

Jenny, Bethany and Becca retreated to the kitchen to visit while Annabeth played with the baby on a quilt on the floor. Bethany cast a glance down the hall. "Tully seems to be enjoying the evening."

She heard a shout of laughter from the living room and smiled. "It sounds like he's having a very *goot* time tonight. He certainly enjoyed himself on Sunday thanks to Michael and Jesse."

"What are you planning for him next?"

"I'm hoping more of our friends will come to visit Gideon and Tully this next week. Please pass that along. The cookie exchange party is at the Lapp home next Saturday. The following Tuesday is our caroling. You're coming, right?"

"Of course," Bethany assured her.

"Is Pastor Frank taking a group to the parade in Presque Isle again?" Becca asked.

"He is. That's on Wednesday the twenty-third."

"We will join him if there is room for us. If not, Tully can drive his car. That leaves the school Christmas program for last. Annabeth is dying to have Tully see her in the play."

"That should make a wonderful Christmas holiday for anyone."

"I hope so." Becca glanced down the hall to where the men were laughing again. She wanted Tully to feel welcome in her community. Her friends were making that happen.

Tully beat Michael and the bishop soundly at checkers. He moved aside to let Michael take on Gideon in the next game as the bishop gathered up his things. "Walk me out, Tully."

"Sure." They passed through the kitchen, where the bishop bid Becca good-night, and the two men stepped out onto the porch. It was a cold, crisp night. The stars glittering overhead gave enough light to see by.

"It was a good game," Tully said. He struggled for a moment to put into words how the Sunday service had affected him. "I wanted you to know I enjoyed the part of your preaching and the service I caught the other morning. It was moving. I don't know much about the Amish, but I can see your faith is deep. I envy the serenity you all seem to have."

"*Gott*'s love knows no bounds. Faith and peacefulness are available to every man who seeks Him. Not just the Amish."

Tully let the bishop's words sink in. Could he find the same kind of relationship with God? Was he ready to seek that? Maybe he was.

The bishop looked at him for a long moment. "How are you getting along with Gideon and Becca?"

Tully grinned. "They are wonderful people. *Kind* doesn't begin to describe them. However, I didn't expect the work to be so hard. I don't know how the two of them have managed alone."

"It's true that Gideon has struggled with his health. It would be best if Becca married again."

Was that a hint? Tully wasn't sure where the man was going. "She would make any fellow a fine wife."

"Any Amish man," the bishop said with a pointed look at Tully. "Becca can't marry outside our faith. It is forbidden. If she were to do such a thing, she would be shunned by all the faithful who know and love her."

Tully kept his face expressionless. It was a hint, just not the kind he'd expected. "I wasn't aware of that rule. I can assure you Becca has shown me only kindness."

"I never doubted that, but kindness can sometimes be mistaken for affection of a different nature."

Tully shoved his hands in the pockets of his coat. "I get your drift. You don't have to worry. I will be moving on soon enough."

"My aim isn't to drive you away, Tully Lange. You are welcome in this community and have made many *goot* friends already. It is an unusual thing for an *Englisch* fellow to accomplish, but I have seen how you look at her. You care for her. My purpose in speaking thus is to prevent needless pain for you and for Becca."

Tully pressed his lips together tightly and mustered as much dignity as he could. "I appreciate that, sir. I do."

The bishop left, taking with him any faint hopes that Tully harbored about building a relationship with Becca.

So what now? What should he do? If the bishop could read Tully's feelings for her so easily, maybe others could, too.

The answer was painfully obvious. He would do nothing. Her family and her faith were everything to Becca. He could never ask her to give them up.

He would remain friends with her and her family until he left, but he would never forget the way she made him feel.

On the following day, Becca noticed Tully was quieter than usual, but he offered to drive Annabeth to school again and she agreed. That evening after the chores were done and both Gideon and Annabeth had gone to bed, Becca noticed a light coming from beneath the door to the living room. Thinking that Gideon must have left it on, she went in to turn it off and saw Tully reading in Gideon's favorite chair. He looked up when she came in.

He gestured to the propane lamp above his head. "This is much brighter than the one in my room. I hope you don't mind."

"Of course not. What are you reading?"

"A book Annabeth's teacher loaned me today. It's about the beginnings of the Amish church. Those early Amish sure had it rough."

"They did. Their martyrdom still inspires us to remain true to our faith in spite of any obstacle."

"I can see why you're a peace-loving bunch."

"Because violence only begets violence. We must turn the other cheek and forgive those that would harm us."

"From a soldier's point of view, I always thought the threat of force was the best way to keep the peace. There are things worth fighting for. I would've dealt harshly with the men who persecuted your ancestors."

"Vengeance belongs to *Gott*. Only He knows what is in a man's heart. Good men can do evil things, and evil men can do good things. It is not for us to judge which is which."

"Doesn't it bother you that someone can get away with cruel deeds and even murder?"

"*Gott* can mete out a punishment that is everlasting. Just because the scales are not balanced in our sight does not mean they are not balanced."

"Food for thought. Oh, I found out why Amish men don't have mustaches. Apparently the mustache was a symbol of the military in bygone days. Rather than be associated with that, the Amish chose to shave their mustaches but leave their beards."

"I did not know that. It is just something that has always been done."

He stared down at the book in his hands. "I learned that an Amish person can't marry outside the faith. Are there any exceptions?"

Her heart dropped. He hadn't known why she couldn't return his affection. Now he would understand, and perhaps things could be easier between them. "There are no exceptions."

His lips twisted into a wry smile. "It's good to know it wasn't just me."

She heard the catch in his voice. He had hoped for another answer. She clenched her hands together to keep from reaching for him. "You are a fine man, Tully, but you are not Amish. The Lord has someone in mind for you. I'm sure of it."

His gaze slid away from her back to his book. "Thanks. *Guten naucht*, Becca."

She left the room and closed the door softly. She entered her bedroom and sat on the edge of her bed. She liked him tremendously. She could easily find herself falling for him if she wasn't careful. He wasn't a little boy in need of a bright Christmas season, he was an outsider. An *Englischer* who would leave soon. She couldn't lose sight of that fact, no matter how much she came to care for him.

After a restless night, she resolved to treat Tully as she would any other visitor to her home. She bade him good morning and set about getting ready to do the chores. He seemed subdued, as well. Neither of them spoke much as they took care of the cattle and returned to the house. They washed up side by side at the sink. Finally she couldn't stand the silence from her usually talkative friend. She glanced his way. "Is something wrong?"

"I was about to ask you the same thing."

She couldn't lie to him, but she didn't have to tell him the whole truth. "I didn't sleep well last night."

"Me neither." Their eyes met, and he looked away.

"Is something troubling you?" Why did she ask when she wasn't sure she wanted to hear the answer?

"Nothing specific. I'm going to need to find a paying job after Christmas, and a place to live. I hate to rely on my friend until I can start making ends meet." He shrugged. "All little stuff. At least no one is shooting at me."

Why did he have to start joking when he was talking about leaving? Her intention to treat him like any other visitor evaporated into thin air. Sadness brought the sting of tears to the back of her eyes. "I will miss you when you leave, Tully Lange."

The smile on his face slowly faded as he gazed at her. "Will you?"

He took a step closer. The air in the kitchen seemed to thicken around her, bringing a strange warmth to her skin as she stared into his dark eyes. "So very much," she whispered.

He reached out and drew his fingers along the curve of her jaw. She closed her eyes and leaned into his gentle touch.

Chapter Thirteen

Tully wanted to kiss Becca's sweet lips but knew he couldn't. His pounding heart said *go for it*, but his conscience shouted that it would be wrong. She was a vulnerable woman dealing with a host of worries. He was here to help, not to add to her troubles. No drink had ever been this hard to pass up. Learning that she couldn't marry an outsider had left him tossing and turning for the past two nights. He longed to be a part of her life, but that was forbidden to her. She would never be his.

He bent and pressed his lips to her forehead.

Her eyes flew open. He saw confusion and then shame. She pressed her hands to her cheeks as they blossomed bright red.

She turned away from him. "What you must think of me."

"Only good things. Too good for the likes of me."

"I'm so ashamed."

"Don't be. We are both tired. Our emotions got carried away. You have nothing to be sorry for."

She heard Gideon coming down the hall. She turned toward the window so he couldn't see her face. Tully busied himself finding a clean pair of gloves from the drawer near the front door.

Gideon paused in the doorway. "Do you know how to drive a horse, Cowboy?"

Tully looked up. "Becca gave me a lesson the other day, but I'm hardly an expert. I think the horse knew what he was doing more than I did."

"Why don't you go with Becca to the milk collection station so you can take over that chore while you are here?"

"Okay." Tully glanced at Becca. She wouldn't look at him.

Becca wiped her hands on her apron. "There is *kaffee* on the stove. Do you want a cup before I leave, Gideon?"

"*Danki.* How are my cows?"

She pulled a white mug from the cupboard and filled it. "Fine. Eating well and giving between two and a half and three gallons of milk each."

"So much? No wonder Tully's arms could use a rest."

Tully rubbed his forearms and managed a half-hearted grin. "That ain't no lie."

Gideon accepted the cup from Becca. "You will toughen up in a few more days. You have done well. Much better than I expected when you first offered to stay. He has made a *goot* dairyman, hasn't he, Becca?"

"Very *goot*." Becca went toward the door. "We need to get going."

"Right." Tully settled his hat on his head and followed her outside.

She kept her gaze averted as they trudged through the snow to the barn. He didn't like the tenseness between them, but he wasn't sure how to overcome it. He'd messed up again big-time. How was he going to fix this?

When they had Cupcake, the big gray mare, hitched to the wagon, Tully offered his hand to help Becca up to the high seat. She ignored it and scrambled up by herself. He joined her, all the while wishing he hadn't put them in such an awkward position. Becca picked up the driving lines, and Cupcake headed for the highway with a word from her.

They rode in silence through the snow-covered countryside dotted with pine forests, open fields and farms with red barns trimmed in white. "It's pretty country," he said when the silence dragged on too long.

She didn't reply. After a few more minutes, he couldn't take it anymore. "You're going to have to speak to me sometime."

"Not if I can help it."

It wasn't much, but it was a start. "I stepped over the line back there, and I'm sorry. It won't happen again."

"It can't, Tully. You know why."

"Sure. Because I'm not one of you."

She looked at him then. "I care about you, Tully, but I can never act on those feelings. You must understand. I'm sorry if anything I did led you to believe otherwise."

He wanted to make a joke about it, get her to smile at him, but he couldn't find the humor in his heartache. "I made the mistake, Becca. You didn't do anything wrong. You, Annabeth and Gideon, you have become the closest thing to a family that I've known since I was a boy. I don't want to lose your friendship, but I'll understand if you want me to leave."

Becca cast a sidelong glance at Tully as she bit her lower lip. It might be for the best, but she didn't want him to go. He would be leaving soon enough. He had become so dear to her. She wanted to cherish every minute of his company. The memories would have to last a lifetime. "You may stay as you had planned. We do need your help."

"Does this mean you and I can be friends again? Are we okay?"

"Our friendship was never in jeopardy." That was true. It was her heart that worried her. And his.

"I'm so relieved to hear you say that." He nudged her shoulder with his. She looked his way and saw he was grinning. "You have no idea how much I would miss your cooking."

He was always ready with a joke. She shook her head, but she couldn't hold back a smile. "You and your stomach."

He gestured ahead of them. "If you'd missed as many meals as I have, you'd understand. Is that big barn up ahead where we're going?"

"It is. You will have to drive straight into the barn on the south end. Usually the doors are open. If they aren't, there is a telephone on the wall you can use to call the main house."

"How many cows do they milk?"

"About a hundred."

"I'm going to guess they have electric milking machines. Do you think they would rent us a couple? I could figure out how to run an extension cord from one of your English neighbors. It could cut our workload in half."

She knew he was trying to lighten the mood and put them back on their old footing. "Hard work never hurt anyone, Tully."

"Says the woman who doesn't know how easy electricity makes everything. You know, I still try to turn on the light switch when I walk into my bedroom, only there is no light switch. How long do you think before I learn not to do that?"

"We stayed at a motel in Florida for a month, and I never once turned on the light."

"And that in a nutshell is the difference between us," he said softly, making her look his way. "I need lights to see what is in front of my face. You don't. Looks like the barn doors are closed. Where is the phone?"

Tully's knees were shaking when he got down from the wagon. He stumbled a little on his first step. He wasn't sure that he had repaired his relationship with Becca, but at least she was speaking to him and hadn't told him to leave. She blamed herself for his behavior. She couldn't be more wrong. It had been his mistake. The need to have a drink and forget his stupidity hit him like a hammer. He licked his dry lips and told himself it wouldn't help. He'd still be a fool where she was concerned.

After they unloaded the milk, Becca handed Tully the lines when he climbed aboard. The big horse ambled toward home at his command.

Becca sat quietly beside him, occasionally giving him small pointers about his driving. He couldn't keep his mind on what he was doing. The more he tried to push the idea of having a drink out of his mind, the bigger it became.

Once they reached home, he put Cupcake away and went to split wood until he had a stack as high as he could reach in the woodshed. When Becca called him in for lunch, he forced himself to smile and joke with her and Gideon. He could see in her eyes that things still were not right between them, but they were both making an effort to appear normal. Fake it until you make it, as Arnie had said.

"Do you think you can drive me into Fort Craig this afternoon?" Becca asked.

He nodded. "Sure. I know Annabeth would like to go along."

Becca smiled tentatively. "I was about to suggest it."

Tully looked to Gideon. "Do you want to come?"

"Becca knows what brand of razor blades I use. I see no need to go with you. Becca, give the man his salary. He has earned it."

Becca went to the cupboard and brought down a mason jar where she deposited their payments from the milk bank. She pulled out several bills and held them toward Tully.

Shocked, he put both hands up. "No, that was not the arrangement. I work for room and board. I probably should pay you because of how much I eat."

"A worker is worthy of his hire," Gideon said. "We can't afford much, but we share what we have. Take it and be done."

Tully could tell by the man's set features that he wasn't going to take no for an answer. "Thank you. I appreciate it. Now I can put gas in the car, and Becca won't have to push it home from town."

Gideon snorted. "A horse doesn't run out of gas. You should take the buggy."

"My car has a good heater. Hot bricks under your feet are okay, but the inside of a buggy is pretty cold when it is only twenty degrees outside."

"The *Englisch* are a soft bunch," Gideon said. "Becca, is there *kaffee*?"

With the outing to look forward to, thoughts of finding a drink somewhere decreased in Tully's mind. He was going to town with a little money in his pocket. The day was beginning to look up.

Annabeth came out of the house and gave a shout of joy when she saw Tully's car parked in front of the gate. "Are we going to Fort Craig?"

He held open the back door for her. "Yes, we are. Your mother has shopping she needs to do."

Annabeth jumped up and down in front of him. "I love going to town. Do you think they will have the Christmas lights up?"

"Christmas is only two weeks away, so I'm sure they will. But you won't get to see them unless you get in the car."

She scurried in, and he closed the door behind her. He got in, as well. Becca turned around in her seat to look at Annabeth. "We can't stay late. We have to get back in time to milk."

"I know that it will be fun anyway. I'm going to tell everybody the story of our trip at school on Monday."

Tully caught Becca's gaze. She arched one eyebrow at him. "My daughter is becoming another storyteller in the family. This is your fault."

"I will take credit for that. Tell me all the things you see along the way, Annabeth, and then you will remember them when you get to school next week."

As Annabeth chattered happily from the back seat with her face glued to the passenger-side window, Tully drove slowly, glad that he was able to give the child a special outing. He was glad, too, that her mother was along. If he behaved, he and Becca could stay friends. He wanted that more than anything. It hurt that their relationship could never grow into anything more, but he would cherish the time he had left with her.

On his way through town, his eyes were drawn to the Lumberjack Bar. It was Saturday. People were off work for the weekend. The parking lot was already half-full of cars. There would be friends sharing a few beers, others drinking alone.

"Tully, look out!"

Becca's cry jerked his attention back to the road, where a truck was stopped at the light in front of them. He hit the brakes and managed to avoid rear-ending the vehicle. "Sorry. I guess I've gotten rusty at driving."

"Eyes on the road at all times," Annabeth said. "I learned that in school."

He looked in the rearview mirror. "Are you taking driver's education?"

"*Nee*, I'm too little, but Otto and the twins are."

He cocked his head toward Becca. "Seriously?"

"We share the road with all kinds of traffic. We obey the same rules. Our children must learn to be safe drivers in their buggies and wagons. Unlike an *Englisch* cowboy that I know. The light is green."

He drove on and parked in front of the grocery store at her direction. "Shouldn't we get groceries last? You don't want anything to spoil."

She pointed to a local bank sign. The time, followed by "22 degrees," scrolled across it. "It's the middle of December in northern Maine. The inside of your car will be colder than my refrigerator by the time we finish."

"Right. What was I thinking?"

Becca produced a list. "I will need two carts. I have a lot of baking to do."

She wasn't kidding. They left the building with enough flour, sugar and whatnot to fill his trunk. They gathered a few stares along the way. He wasn't sure if it was because of her Amish clothing or because she was with a man who wasn't Amish. As they walked down the sidewalk to the fabric store, he began to get annoyed with the number of people gawking at them while Annabeth and Becca were pointing out the lights and window displays they liked.

"Why do these people think it's okay to stare at you?" he asked.

"We are an oddity here. It's not like Pennsylvania, where the Amish are everywhere."

"It's rude. I'd like to tell some of them to mind their manners."

"Then you would be the impolite one. We pay them no mind."

It was good advice, but he couldn't shake the feeling that people were judging them for their lifestyle. It was a familiar feeling that he didn't like. He used to try to blur out the faces of the people looking down on him when he was homeless and panhandling for enough cash to get a few drinks. "It isn't right."

Becca didn't understand why Tully was angry with the onlookers. She and Annabeth had learned to ignore stares from an early age. "Tully, it's fine."

"It isn't." He glared at two shoppers in the fabric store. They moved away.

She decided the material for a new dress could wait until another time. "I'm ready to go home."

"Buy what you came for. Don't let these people ruin your outing."

At the sound of his raised voice, Annabeth pressed close to Becca's side. She put her arm around her daughter. "They aren't the ones making us uncomfortable, Tully."

He looked at her with a puzzled expression. "I am?"

"Please, let's go."

He seemed confused. "Sure. I'm sorry. I wanted you to have a nice time with me this afternoon."

"We have had a *goot* time, haven't we, Annabeth? We got to see lots of Christmas decorations and the pretty window displays, but it's time to get back."

"I'll go get the car." He walked away without waiting for her answer.

"What's Tully upset about, *Mamm*?"

"I'm not sure, honey, but he isn't upset with you. Okay?"

"Is he mad because we're Amish?"

"*Nee*. He doesn't understand our ways, that's all."

"I wish he did."

"So do I." Something was troubling him. She didn't think it was their conversation from earlier. Would he confide in her? Should she ask?

He arrived with the car. They got in, and he headed out of town. When he stopped at the traffic light, she noticed he was staring at a business just off the highway. She took a second look and realized it was a bar. A place that served alcohol. What was his interest in a place like that? She turned her face away from it. "The light is green, Tully."

"What? Oh yeah. Thanks."

He remained silent until they reached the house, but

his mood did improve as he helped her carry in her groceries. "This can't all be for me. I know I don't eat that much."

"It's for my Christmas baking."

"I hope I get to sample some."

She smiled to reassure him. "You will."

Afterward, they finished the chores, and she made a light supper. Tully was unusually quiet during the meal. Gideon seemed to notice. He raised his brow at her. She gave a slight shake of her head. As soon as the table was cleared, Tully disappeared into his room and came out twenty minutes later dressed in the Western shirt and jeans he had worn to church. He had polished his boots.

He took his coat and hat off the peg and put them on. "I'm going out for a while. Don't wait up for me."

"All right." She stared at the door as it closed behind him, wondering where he was going and why she was suddenly afraid he wouldn't come back.

Tully drove into Fort Craig again, pulled into the familiar parking lot and got out. He drew a deep breath of the cold air. He walked to the rear of the building and went down the steps leading to a basement. Above the door of what looked like a classroom was a hand-lettered sign that said Welcome to a Safe Place. Pastor Frank stood beside the door with a kindly smile on his face. "Are you here for the meeting?"

Tully held out his hand. "Hello. My name is Tully and I'm an alcoholic in recovery. I've been sober for four months and nineteen days."

"Welcome, Tully. Come in and meet our other members."

Tully followed Frank into the classroom. Four men

and two women were seated on folding chairs in a circle. He was relieved to see Michael wasn't among them. One of the men got up and added another chair to the circle for Tully. He sat down and rubbed his sweaty palms on his jeans.

Pastor Frank added another chair and sat down. "Let's get started. I'm Frank, and I'm an alcoholic. I've been sober for twenty-two years and nine months."

"Welcome, Frank," everyone said.

The anxiety that plagued Tully slowly seeped away. He needed to be here. He listened in amazement to the stories of the other members, some of whom, like Frank, had been sober for more than two decades. One young woman had been sober for six days. Her hands were still trembling. The understanding and compassion of those around him buoyed his spirits and strengthened his resolve to stay sober.

When the meeting was over, Pastor Frank came over and offered his hand. "It was good of you to join us. If you need to talk to someone, I'm always available."

"Thanks, that means a lot."

Later, when Tully quietly let himself into Becca's house, he was shocked to see her still up. She looked relieved to see him. He didn't understand why. He had given her one rough day. "I thought I told you not to wait up."

It warmed his heart that she had.

She gestured toward a pile of gray cloth on the table. "I had some sewing to finish. Annabeth's shepherdess costume. They're having dress rehearsals this week. Did you have a nice time tonight?"

She might be angling for information about where he had been, but she was being polite about it. He wasn't ready to reveal his addiction to her. Their conversation that morning and their trip into town had made him painfully aware that he had a lot of work to do on handling difficult situations. If only he could learn her calm acceptance. "I met with some new friends. I don't think you would know them. They aren't Amish."

"You must have a lot of friends who aren't Amish."

He hung up his hat and coat and then crossed the room to stand beside her. "I don't have many friends at all, but the one I value most does happen to be Amish." He leaned close without touching her. "I'm fortunate that she has a forgiving nature along with being a wonderful cook."

She drew back to stare at him. "Are you trying to flatter me again?"

"Nope. I know that is not your way. I'm being truthful. I'm sorry for ruining the trip to town for you and Annabeth." He longed to caress her face, but he knew it would only lead to more awkwardness between them.

A little smile tipped up the corner of her mouth right where he wanted to plant a kiss. "It wasn't ruined. Only a tiny bit raveled at the edges."

"Are you trying to be funny?"

"I am. How am I doing?"

"Needs work."

"Speaking of work, Gabe will be here in the morning to help you milk. I have things in the house to do."

"Does it involve cooking?" he asked hopefully.

"Cooking and baking."

"In that case, you should get to bed. You need your rest."

She grew serious as a frown creased her brow. "I was afraid you weren't coming back."

He pushed his hands deep in his pockets. "I'm sorry you thought that."

"Promise you won't leave without saying goodbye."

"I promise."

Her expression cleared. "All right. *Guten naucht*, Cowboy."

He smiled softly at her. She was so easy to love. "*Guten naucht, Frau* Beachy."

He watched her walk out of the kitchen and raked one hand through his hair. He wasn't Amish, but was there any way to remain a part of her life? What if he stayed in the area? They could still be friends. He could see her now and again, but he knew it wouldn't work.

He would be doomed to love her from afar, because he was in love with her. How could he bear that?

Chapter Fourteen

Becca grew concerned about Tully. Although she couldn't say that he had been secretive about his trip into Fort Craig, she knew he hadn't told her everything. She didn't have a right to pry into his private life, but that didn't keep her from wanting to know where he had gone.

When he came into breakfast the next morning, he seemed like his old self, cheerful and smiling. He apologized to Annabeth and promised he would take her to town again soon. Her daughter seemed satisfied with that and chatted happily with him. Tully had a way of making her little girl adore him.

Becca glanced at the clock on the wall. "Gabe should be here soon. Annabeth, I have a chore for you. I want you to help your grandfather shell pecans. We are baking our gift boxes to give to the nursing homes this morning." It was the off Sunday, and her friends would be over to help with the baking. None of them viewed it as extra work on the day of rest. It would be a fun-filled day, with visiting, laughter and perhaps even singing.

"But I wanted to make Christmas cards today," Annabeth said.

"I won't have time to help you. We can do that on Monday after school."

"I can help her," Tully offered.

"All right. After the chores are done, the two of you can set up a table in the living room and make cards there."

She heard the arrival of the first buggy and looked out. It was Dinah and Gemma. She turned to Tully. "Will you stable the horses for our company? It's too cold to leave them standing outside."

"I'll take care of them." He went out the door with the milking pails.

As more women showed up, Becca became immersed in measuring, mixing and baking, and enjoying the company of her friends. The kitchen became so warm they were forced to open the window. When Tully returned from the milk delivery, he stopped in the open doorway with a stunned expression on his face. "When you said you had a little baking to do, you weren't kidding. It smells great in here."

All eight women turned to greet him and began offering him samples of what had been made. Becca paid close attention to what he liked the best so she could make more for him later. Everything today was going into gift boxes to be delivered to the three nursing homes in the county.

Gideon pushed two large bowls of shelled pecans toward Dinah. "That's the last of them. I'll be in the living room if you need me."

Tully, who was sampling a thumbprint cookie,

walked to Becca's side. "I'll crack nuts if you bring me cookies to sample."

She gave him a gentle push toward the hallway. "Get out of my kitchen and out of my way. Annabeth is waiting for you in the living room."

"That's just cruel. There are at least five types of cookies I haven't tried yet."

"I'll save you some of mine," Gemma said.

"Did you make the chocolate chip–oatmeal ones?" He looked hopefully at the box she was packing.

"I made the snickerdoodles." She handed him one.

"Thanks." He took a bite and moaned. "Becca, you have a rival. Gemma, you wouldn't by chance need a hired man who works for room and board, would you? I think I'm free after Christmas."

Becca pointed to the hall. "You will find yourself free before that if you don't get out of the way."

He held up both hands and ambled out of the room. Gemma chuckled. "He's such a fun fellow. Is there any chance he will stay in our community?"

Becca sighed. "I don't think so. He hasn't mentioned any such plan." Caring for him the way she did and not being able to share those feelings would be hard if he stayed, but she didn't want him to leave.

An hour later she went to check on Annabeth's progress with her Christmas cards. She found Tully and her daughter sprawled on the wood floor with scraps of ribbon, paper cutouts and construction paper spread all around them. Gideon was dozing in his chair. Tully laid two scraps of ribbon on a piece of paper that was already adorned with the picture of a lamb. "What do you think? The green or the blue?"

Annabeth studied his composition. "I think the green."

"Glue." He held out his hand. She placed a bottle in it. He applied one drop carefully and handed it back. "Who does this card go to?"

"Teacher Eva."

He wrote the name on the envelope and added it to a small stack near his elbow. "Now what?"

"Can you draw a camel?" she asked.

"Maybe. Who are you sending this one to?"

"To Otto."

"In that case, I think my camel will be good enough." He glanced up at Becca. "May we help you?"

"I have made sandwiches for lunch. Come and have some when you get hungry."

He scrambled to his feet. "I'm always hungry."

"Would you bring me one, Tully?" Annabeth asked.

"Sure." He stopped beside Becca. "How goes the monster bake?"

"We're almost done. You're good to spend time with her."

"You have a great kid, in case no one has told you that."

"Danki."

"But then, she has a wonderful mother, so it shouldn't be any surprise." He curled his fingers around her hand and gave a brief squeeze before he left the room.

Becca kept her composure with difficulty. Theirs was a hopeless situation, but she cherished the tenderness of his touch.

"I like him, *Mamm*," Annabeth said.

"So do I."

She would miss Tully when he left, but she suspected

her daughter would miss him just as much, if not more. She straightened. Her goal was to give Tully a Christmas season to remember them by, but she would always treasure their time together.

After the baking party left and the chores were done that evening, she sat listening to Gideon read to them from the Bible as Annabeth and Tully finished her daughter's cards. She glanced Tully's way and caught him watching her with such sadness in his eyes that she longed to comfort him. But she couldn't. Because she wanted to be held in his arms and be comforted, too. Somehow, she had to make it until Christmas without giving in to that desire. For if he held her, she wasn't sure she could let him go.

Tully wasn't going to be able to walk away from Becca and her family. He knew it deep in his heart. He took a long, hard look at the path before him and wondered if it was even possible. On Monday morning when Becca took Annabeth to school, he joined Gideon in the living room.

Tully sat in the chair across from him and drew a deep breath. "Gideon, how does someone become Amish? I mean, if you're not born to Amish parents, is there an entrance exam of some kind?"

Gideon was silent for several long seconds. "We do not seek converts from outside our church. We accept that our way is not for everyone. Very few people have converted to the Amish faith. I personally do not know of anyone who has done so."

"But it is possible?"

"Possible, but I would think very difficult. To be Amish is something you are raised with. Why we dress and speak the way we do. Our rejection of higher education, even the meaning behind the songs we sing at our church service. Those are things most outsiders can't understand. Why do you ask?"

"Your people seem so content with their lives. That's a rare thing."

"Is it? Why?"

"I don't know. I guess most folks want to get ahead. They want to have more for themselves and for their children. They want a better job or to make more money, have a bigger house or own a fancier car. If they can't make that happen, they feel cheated."

"Are you one of those people? Are you discontent with your life?"

"There are a lot of things I don't like about my life." The fact that he had wasted two long years in a nearly continuous alcoholic stupor was one of them. The fact that his addiction had gotten his best friend killed was another.

"If you don't like something, can't you change it?"

"I'm working on that, but some things can't be changed." What would Gideon think if he told the man he was an alcoholic? Would he even understand what that meant?

"All things are possible with God. Perhaps you should ask for His help."

"I'm pretty sure He has better things to do than help a down-and-out cowboy."

"God does not love one of his children more than another. He has compassion for all. We Amish believe worship is important and that we are following the path He has laid out for us, but we are not more beloved in

His sight than anyone else. To assume that we are would be the worst form of *hohchmoot*."

"That means arrogance or conceit, right?"

"*Ja*, pride. *Gelassenheit*, humility, must be present in all aspects of our lives. We must be humble, quiet, submissive to the will of *Gott*. The *Englisch* admire our way of living, but very few can follow in our footsteps."

"But if someone wanted to live as you do, they could become Amish, right?"

"It would be better to live as we do and remain *Englisch*. This is about your feelings for Becca, isn't it? I'm old, but I'm not blind."

Tully felt the heat rush to his face and had to admit the truth. "I'm in love with her, Gideon." A weight lifted from his shoulders at being able to say it out loud.

"Have you told her this?"

"No. She may suspect, but I haven't said anything. I didn't know a relationship with her wasn't possible until the night the bishop came to play checkers. He's also older but not blind."

"Tully, Becca can't be the reason you look to join our faith. It must be because *Gott* has led you to that point, otherwise it is a meaningless gesture."

"It's about more than my feelings for her. I love it here. I have never felt as much at home as I do with you, Becca, Annabeth and the friends I've made here. I want to keep all of you in my life. This isn't a whim. I've been studying some books Eva gave me. Tell me how to take the next step. If God wants me on this path, He will guide me the rest of the way."

Tully was a little shocked by how much he believed what he just said. There was no denying that God had brought him here.

Gideon was silent for a long moment. "Talk to Bishop Schultz about this, but do not speak to Becca of your feelings. You are forbidden to her. It breaks my heart to say this, for I like you, Tully, and I see that she cares about you, too, but this is the way it must be."

"Okay. I'd like to attend services with you this coming Sunday."

"You are welcome to do so. If the bishop agrees, perhaps he will allow you to start instructions."

If God had a plan for him, Tully was going to open his heart and listen.

Becca joined Tully in the barn that evening, and they fell into their old rhythm of working alongside each other without saying much. It was comfortable in the barn. The troubles of the outside world were left behind as they cared for the cattle, horses and little Diamond. In their secluded world, they didn't have to worry about doing or saying the wrong thing in front of Gideon or Annabeth. Tully was quieter, but he seemed content. She was happy just to be with him. The awkwardness between them had vanished.

Over the course of the week, many of their friends came to visit in the evenings, as she had hoped, leaving less time for her and Tully to be alone. It was a good thing. She was able to keep a lid on her growing feelings for him. She enjoyed watching his interactions with Danny, Jesse, Michael and the Fisher brothers. They all liked his company. He was endearing, not just to her but to everyone he met. If it sometimes felt like Tully was withdrawing from her, she accepted that he needed the distance as much as she did.

When they didn't have company, Tully and Gideon

spent time discussing the Bible and talking about the foundations of the Amish church. Tully was truly interested in learning about their faith. Sometimes she joined the discussion. It provided a balm to her aching heart knowing Tully was seeking to understand God's word.

The cookie exchange party on Saturday turned out to be the highlight of a bittersweet week for her as she watched him laughing and interacting with everyone in the community. Annabeth was never far from his side.

Tully carried her sleeping daughter against his shoulder when they finally got home. Gideon bade them good-night and went to his room. She went ahead of Tully down the hall to Annabeth's room, opened the door and turned down the bed. He laid her child down gently without waking her. Together they took off her coat and her shoes.

Tully stepped back as Becca unpinned Annabeth's hair and pulled the quilt over her shoulders.

"Thank you, Becca."

She looked up. "For what?"

"For this. For a chance to feel like I'm part of a real family again. It's been wonderful. *Wunderbar*, as you say."

"I'm glad." It was what she had wanted for him, so why did it make her want to cry?

"I'm coming to the church service with you tomorrow."

"I thought you would be going to Pastor Frank's church again."

"I don't think that's where I'm meant to be. I know it's not where I want to be. I plan to speak to the bishop about joining the church. I know he must agree before I can take instructions."

She pressed a hand to the sudden ache in her chest. Tully was willing to become Amish?

She wouldn't get her hopes up. It was a difficult undertaking. She'd only heard of a few people who had come into the church from the outside. "If that is what God wants for you, I will be glad."

"I told Gideon I hadn't said anything, but I think you know how I feel about you."

She held a hand to his lips. "Don't. Please."

What if Tully couldn't do it? What if the newness of these weeks wore off and he said goodbye anyway? It didn't bear thinking about. Knowing she could never be his was better than believing she could be and having that dream crushed.

He pulled her hand away and kissed her palm. "I won't until I have the right to speak what's in my heart. Good night, Becca." He turned and walked out of the room.

The next morning Tully took his place on the back row of benches beside Otto, hoping the boy would help him out again when he couldn't understand the preaching. To his surprise, Gabe and Danny sat down on either side of him as Otto made room for them.

"What are you doing here, Cowboy?" Danny asked.

"I've come to worship. You?" He glanced between both men.

"The same, but we belong here," Gabe said.

"You are fortunate men. I'm still looking for the place where I belong." He gazed at Becca sitting near the front.

"And you think it might be with us?" Danny asked, rubbing his chin thoughtfully.

"It seems to me the Lord went to a lot of trouble to get me here. I'm going to give Him a chance to show me why."

"He could be right," Gabe said, looking across Tully to Danny. "We cannot know the mind of *Gott*."

Tully had learned to ask for help with his addiction. This was every bit as important to him. "I admit I'm a fish out of water here. Any advice you fellas can give me will be deeply appreciated."

"Are you sure this is what you want?" Gabe asked.

"Yes."

"Okay," Danny said. "You'll need to learn the language. I can help with that."

Tully rubbed his palms on his pant legs. "First I need to speak with the bishop. He has to agree."

"He isn't here today," Danny said. "Bishop Bontrager from Whitefield is taking his place."

That wasn't what Tully wanted to hear. "When will Bishop Schultz be back?"

Gabe clapped a hand on Tully's shoulder. "Tomorrow. He plans to go caroling with us. You can speak to him then."

They sat straighter as the bishop and ministers came in. Gabe handed Tully a songbook. He opened it and followed along, adding his voice to those raised in praise. The peace he had sensed the first time settled over him again. He realized it was the presence of God.

The day for caroling arrived with a light snowfall in the morning that tapered off by noon, leaving a fresh coat of white on the countryside. Annabeth could barely contain her excitement when she got home from school.

"Tully, hurry up," she called from her place on the

back seat of the sleigh. She and Gideon were bundled under a thick robe. Becca had placed hot bricks on the floorboard to help keep them warm.

"Hold your horses, Annabeth. I need to find a bucket," he called from the inside of the shed, where he had parked his car when he first arrived.

"What do you need a bucket for?" Gideon shouted. "We are going caroling, not milking."

Tully came out of the shed holding a rusty pail in one hand. "I need a bucket, because that's the only way I can carry a tune."

Gideon threw back his head and laughed. "You are the funniest man. Is there anything you won't turn into a joke?"

Speaking to the bishop.

Tully put the bucket aside and got into the sleigh beside Becca. "You think I'm kidding. I cannot sing."

"The Lord only asks us to make joyful noise," she said dryly.

"Oh, I can do that."

"Make a joyful noise unto the Lord, all the earth: make a loud noise, and rejoice, and sing praise. Psalm ninety-eight, verse four," Gideon said. "Oh, come all ye faithful," he began in his rich baritone.

Annabeth and Becca joined in as she urged Cupcake to get moving. She nudged Tully with her elbow. He started singing but so softly. She nudged him again. He sat up straight and began to belt out the words.

She cringed. "Are you doing that on purpose?"

"You asked for it." He began the next verse with Annabeth and Gideon.

Becca laughed. "You do have a terrible singing voice.

Wait. You sang in the barn for Dotty. You weren't this bad."

"That was different. I didn't have an audience except for you and the cow, so it didn't matter."

"How flattering," she drawled.

"Flattery is not our way," he said, folding his arms over his chest.

"Our way?" she asked quietly.

"I'm glad you caught that. Here's hoping the bishop gives me a chance to make it the truth."

They traveled quickly through the snowy countryside to the Fisher home. A half dozen buggies and other sleighs were lined up beside the barn when they arrived.

Gabe stepped out of the barn and took hold of Cupcake's bridle. "I will take care of her. Go on into the house. I think everyone is here now."

Seth came out with Asher to help carry Gideon inside so he didn't have to struggle through the snow on his crutches. Becca allowed Tully to help her out of the sleigh. He held her hand as she stepped down. She looked up into his eyes. Could she see the love he had for her in their depths? A love that had to remain unspoken for now. Maybe forever. She looked down and pulled her hand away from him. He followed her inside.

The first thing that struck Tully as he entered the home of the Fisher family was the noise. The house was filled with happy chatter and laughter as Amish and *Englisch* friends waited for the start of the caroling. The warmth in the house had as much to do with the camaraderie among the occupants as with the roaring fire in the fireplace.

This was what he wanted for his life. This feeling of belonging to a group of people who truly cared for one another. He saw the bishop standing beside Gideon's chair and made his way over to him. "Bishop Schultz, may I have a moment of your time. Somewhere private?"

The bishop and Gideon exchanged pointed glances. Bishop Schultz nodded. "Come with me."

Tully followed him to one of the downstairs bedrooms. The bishop closed the door behind them. "What can I help you with?"

"I feel in my heart that I want to join your faith. I want to learn what I must do to become Amish."

"I assume Becca is the cause of this desire to become one of us?"

"I would be lying if I said she wasn't the reason I first thought about it. She has forbidden me to speak of my feelings until I have the right to address her."

"Very wise of her."

"But I want you to know there is more to my desire to know God than hoping Becca will one day be my wife. I have never felt as close to God as I do when I am among your people. I can't even say what it is that makes me feel that way. I have never met such caring folks."

"There are caring people everywhere. We are not that unique."

"You feel that this is a whim of mine."

"Is it?"

"No. Even if Becca refuses me, I want to live among you, worship as you do. Care for each other as you do. Am I making sense?"

"This is what I will say. You must live among us as one of us for a year. If after six months you still feel as you do now, I will allow you to take instructions. If you are unmoved in your determination at the end of the year, I will agree to baptize you. However, the entire church must agree, as well. You may spend a year with us and not be admitted. Are you prepared for that?"

A year with no guarantees. He didn't have a job or a place to live. If he did this, it was going to be on faith alone. Arnie was going to be shocked. Tully nodded. "I am."

"You will have to hang up your cowboy hat for good and wear proper Amish clothes. Including suspenders. I pray the Lord blesses your decision and your journey."

Tully wanted to shout for joy. He was being given a chance. He was eager to tell Becca, but it would have to wait until after they finished caroling and were alone again. He would tell her everything, about his addiction and his struggle to stay sober. He would start the relationship with a clean slate. Maybe then he could finally take her in his arms.

As he and the bishop left the bedroom, Tully looked for Becca but couldn't find her. He soon discovered she was already outside on the large sled the Fishers would use to carry them from house to house. She had Annabeth on her lap. Gideon was seated beside her. Tully didn't think he'd ever seen a more beautiful sight than Becca with her child on her lap under the stars, her face lit by the lanterns on the sides of the sleigh. She was everything he had ever wanted.

He looked for a place to sit near her and didn't see one.

"Over here, Cowboy," Gabe called out, waving him toward another, smaller sled. This one held only young men.

Tully climbed up with their help, and he was soon

surrounded with a boisterous bunch. He didn't realize until the sleighs began moving that he and Becca were going in different directions. He settled back to enjoy the night and the company. He would give Becca the news on their way home.

Becca had seen Tully leave the room with the bishop, but she had been ushered outside before he returned. She'd had only a glimpse of his face before they got underway without him. What had the bishop said to him?

"Smile, Becca, this is fun," Gemma said.

"Okay, I'm smiling." She kept the grin on her face for most of the next two hours as they traveled from house to house along the snow-covered road that led south out of New Covenant. It was fun. She and Annabeth sang until they were becoming hoarse. When Mr. Fisher finally brought them home, Annabeth was almost asleep on Becca's lap. She climbed in the back seat with her child in her arms and snuggled under a quilt. Gabe brought Tully's group in a few minutes later. He jumped off the sled and got up in front with Gideon, who then handed Tully the lines. He looked back at Becca. "I have something I need to tell you."

Annabeth sat up. "Are we home yet?"

Tully smiled at her. "Not yet, sleepyhead, but we will be soon." He spoke to Cupcake, and the big horse stepped forward eagerly. Out on the highway, they saw Gabe returning the empty sled. His horse was limping badly. He stopped and pulled over to the side of the road. Tully went past him and stopped a few feet in front. "Can I give you a hand?"

"No, thanks, Cowboy. I'll unhitch and take Chester home and come back with another horse."

Tully waved and went on his way. A few seconds later, a huge bang shattered the stillness of the night. Becca looked back. The wreckage of the sled was scattered across the road. A red car had spun off into the ditch.

It was so much like the scene of her husband's death that she got out of the sleigh and ran toward the wreckage, screaming, "Aaron! Aaron!"

Tully handed the lines to Gideon. "Who is Aaron?"

"Her husband. Go to her. I fear she is in shock."

Tully hopped down and ran to her. He grasped her by the shoulders and held her tight. "It's okay. Aaron isn't here."

She moaned and held on to him. He looked around and saw Gabe standing beside his horse a few dozen yards away. "Gabe, are you okay?"

"By the grace of God."

Tully held Becca away from him. "I have to go see about the driver."

She seemed to have regained her senses. "He may be hurt. Do you have your phone?"

"I don't."

It wasn't needed. A second car came along and stopped. That driver got out with his phone in hand. As they looked on, the door of the red car opened and a young man staggered out. He marched over to Tully. "Did you see what idiot left a wagon in the middle of my lane?"

He reeked of alcohol. Tully looked at Becca. Her eyes were wide with disbelief. "This isn't your lane. This is a highway, and that sled was on the shoulder. What's wrong with you?"

"It is too my lane. I live right over…" He spun in a wobbly circle and threw his arm to the left. "Over there."

It was an empty field. The second driver took the man's arm. "You're drunk, buddy. Come sit in my car till the cops get here."

"I'm not going to jail again," he muttered as he was led away.

"He's drunk! Just like the man that killed Aaron, his brother and his mother. How can they do it? How can they get in a car and disregard the life of everyone else? The man is disgusting." She pressed a hand to her head. "That's not right. I have to forgive him. I have to forgive them both."

Tully led her to the sleigh and helped her in. "Take her home, Gideon."

She grasped Tully's arm. "You said you had something to tell me."

He opened his mouth and closed it. What could he say in the face of her revulsion? She would look at him that way when he told her. He couldn't bear that.

"I'm leaving New Covenant. Tonight. You have been amazing people, but I can't give up my English life. Goodbye. I'll have someone take me to get my car and someone to help you with the chores."

He turned around and walked toward Gabe in a body that had gone numb.

Chapter Fifteen

"So you bailed on her. Instead of telling her the truth, you just took off with your tail between your legs and didn't look back."

Tully sat on the sofa in Arnie's small one-bedroom apartment in downtown Caribou. He had told his friend the entire story of his relationship with Becca and how he had no choice but to leave. He expected a little sympathy, but that was not what Arnie was dishing out. "You didn't see her face. You didn't see how upset she was."

"I knew you were a drunk, but I never knew you were a coward."

"I thought the two went hand in hand." That was exactly how he was feeling. Failure one and failure two.

"So you left the woman you love behind and you stopped for a drink or six on your way here."

Tully looked up. "No. I promise you, I haven't touched a drop."

"Why not? Sounds like you had a pretty good reason to me."

Tully rubbed his hands on his jeans. Even if he never

saw her again, Becca would always be his lodestone. The compass he used to guide the course of his life. He would never do anything to dishonor her memory. "Do I want a drink? Of course I do. Will I take a drink? No."

"Then I guess we have established that you are not a drunk."

"Just a coward. I knew what I would see in her eyes when I told her I was an alcoholic. I couldn't bear to see her turn away from me." Leaving was less painful than having her tell him to get out of her life.

"So what now?"

"I was hoping I could bunk with you for a while until I can get a job."

"That's a little bit of a plan. What kind of job?"

"I don't care. I don't care about much of anything anymore."

"You are lying to yourself, man. You do care. Not about what job to get, but about the people you ran out on. That little girl is going to be heartbroken if you don't go to her Christmas program."

Becca and Gideon would accept his leaving and understand that he didn't belong in their world, but how was a seven-year-old girl going to understand that he didn't want to stay with her anymore? "She'll get over it."

"Like you got over not having a mother and I got over a father that walked out on me when I was ten. Sure, she'll get over it, on the outside, just like we have, but what about on the inside? Do you think she's gonna feel that she wasn't good enough for you?"

Tully got to his feet. "I think coming here was a mistake."

Arnie held up one hand. "Don't go. I'm sorry. It's just

that when I talked to you last week, you were certain you had found what was missing in your life. You had found a woman who made you feel complete. A child who wanted you as her father. Even a community of people who made you feel welcome and valued. You found your way back to God. Do you know how many people never find half of what you had in your hands and tossed away?"

Tully raked his hands through his hair. He wasn't a good enough man for Becca. She would see that. "I can't change what I am."

"Really? Because you used to be a stumbling drunk living out of his car in a run-down neighborhood where even the rats thought twice about taking up residence. I think you've changed a lot."

"On the outside."

"No, Cowboy, you've changed on the inside. What is the one thing you wanted when you got out of rehab?"

"A drink."

"Oh, funny, ha-ha. What did you tell me when I asked if you were looking for a job?"

"I don't remember."

"You said you just needed to find one person to have faith in you and believe you would stay sober."

"Okay, I may have said that."

Arnie rose to his feet and put a hand on Tully's shoulder. "How can you ask others to have faith in you when you refuse to have faith in them? Let me rephrase that. When you refuse to have faith in her."

Tully had no answer for him.

"You couldn't take a chance that she would reject you. You would've been crushed, I get that. You would've been miserable. You know what I see?"

"Don't hold back, tell me what you really think."

"You're still crushed and miserable. How is this any better? It's late. I'm going to bed. The couch is yours. I would say sleep well, but I suspect you won't. And just so you know, if you don't go back to her, you're a whopping fool."

Tully sat down on the sofa after Arnie left the room. What did Arnie know? He didn't have a drinking problem. He didn't know what it was like to have people look down their noses at him. To know they were judging him and finding him less of a man.

He pulled his boots off and stretched out with his arms behind his head. Sleep was the furthest thing from his mind. He kept seeing the tears that had glistened in Becca's beautiful eyes when he told her he was leaving.

He wanted to believe that she could accept the flawed man that he was, but what if she couldn't? What if she turned away from him? What if he saw disgust in her eyes instead of tears? How could he bear it if every time she looked at him, she saw the man that killed her husband?

If he didn't have faith in her, how could he expect her to have faith in him? He did have faith in her. It was himself he doubted.

What's the plan, God? I'm lost. I'm tired. I thought I knew what I wanted, but what do You want from me?

Through the thin walls of Arnie's apartment, he heard Christmas music playing, or maybe it was coming from outside. He got up, went to the window and pulled the curtain aside. The streets of the city were decorated with lights and giant ornaments. There was a Christmas tree in the courtyard below. A group of carolers stood around it singing "Silent Night."

Tomorrow night Annabeth and her classmates would be singing the same song for their family and friends, and he wouldn't be there to hear it.

The song ended, and a man's voice began a new hymn. "Love came down at Christmas, love all lovely, love divine, love was born at Christmas, star and angels gave the sign."

Tully let the curtain fall back and returned to the couch. He sat with his elbows propped on his knees and his head in his hands.

If you don't go back to her, you're a whopping fool.

Arnie's words echoed through Tully's mind. *How is this any better?*

It wasn't. It never would be. Life without Becca, Annabeth, Gideon and all the people of New Covenant would only be half a life. Hadn't he already lost enough of himself to his alcoholism? Did he have to lose the rest to his fears? There was no place left to run and hide unless he went back into a bottle, and he would not do that.

Somewhere in the back of his mind, he would always wonder what Becca would have said if he had told her the truth. Knowing had to be better than never knowing. His hands grew icy as he faced what he had to do.

Tomorrow he would go back. If he was going to lose Becca, it would have to be her choice. If he hadn't lost her already.

"*Mamm*, where is my shepherd's crook?" Annabeth hollered from her room.

"It's here in the kitchen by the front door where you put it so you wouldn't forget it."

Annabeth came running into the room. She grabbed

up the crook Gideon had made for her. "I'm ready. Is it time to go yet?"

"Not yet. We have an hour before you're supposed to be there."

"Do you think Tully will change his mind and come see me?"

Becca's chest contracted with pain. Why couldn't he have waited until after Christmas? It would've been easier for Annabeth, but not for her. She had tried to prepare herself for the inevitable, but it hadn't done any good. After thinking she would never love another, Tully—an *Englischer* and beyond her reach unless she was willing to forsake her faith—had proven her wrong. Her heart was in tatters.

"I hear a car! It's Tully, I know it is." Annabeth raced to look out the window.

Becca felt her heart leap and then drop. She couldn't get her hopes up.

Annabeth turned away from the window with tears glistening in her eyes. Her lower lip quivered. "It's not his car." She ran down the hall to her room and closed the door.

Becca forced herself to go see who it was. She opened the door and looked out. It was a small white pickup. She didn't recognize the man behind the steering wheel, but she saw an Amish fellow get out of the passenger seat. He leaned down and spoke to the driver, who then pulled away, leaving the man standing a few paces beyond her gate. In the same spot where she had first seen Tully holding an injured newborn calf. The memory brought tears to her eyes.

The man walked closer. She blinked back her tears when she realized it was Tully. She held on to the door to keep upright. Or maybe so she wouldn't race down the steps and throw herself into his arms. Why was he here? Why was he dressed like an Amish fellow instead of like a cowboy? Where did he get the clothes?

She heard Gideon and Annabeth talking as they came down the hall. She grabbed her coat and turned to them as they entered the kitchen. "I'm going to check on Diamond before we leave."

She stepped out, closed the door behind her and pointed to the barn. She marched past him without speaking. Whatever his reason was for being here, she didn't want him to upset Annabeth and Gideon if they happened to look out and catch sight of him. She hardened her resolve against the turmoil seeing him again caused. He had vanished with barely a word of goodbye, leaving her and her child brokenhearted. If he could do it once, he could do it again. Only this time she would be prepared.

Inside the barn she lit a lamp and braced herself as she turned to face him with her arms clasped tightly across her chest. She looked his clothing up and down. "What is this? Some new show like your rope tricks?"

"Hello, Becca." He took off his hat and started turning it in his hands. "Michael supplied me with a proper outfit."

Tears sprang to her eyes at the tenderness in his voice. She turned away and braced her arms on the gate of Diamond's stall. "What are you doing here?"

"I'm taking the biggest risk of my life."

"What is that supposed to mean?" Her voice broke on the last word, and she struggled to breathe against the tightness in her throat.

He stepped up beside her, leaning on the gate, too.

Diamond hobbled over to nuzzle his knee through the wooden slats. He scratched her head. "It means I have something to tell you, but I am scared to death to open my mouth."

Her hands were shaking, but she managed to clasp them tightly together. Her fingers were like ice. "Do you think coming dressed as one of us will make what you have to say more acceptable to me? Clothing has nothing to do with belonging here. You said it yourself. You couldn't give up your English ways."

"I was lying about that."

Shocked, she turned to face him. "Why would you lie to me?"

"Because I thought that lie would be less painful than the truth about me. I know that I hurt you, and I'm deeply sorry. You may not believe it, but I was trying to protect you. No, that isn't the whole truth. I was trying to protect myself."

She still couldn't make sense of what he was saying. "What is this terrible truth that made you leave and now makes you come back?" Did he know he was breaking her heart all over again?

"Becca... I am an alcoholic. Just like the man who ran a stop sign and killed your husband, your brother-in-law and Gideon's wife. Just like the man we saw staggering away from the wreckage of Gabe's sled."

"I can't believe that." Of all the things she had expected to hear, this was not one of them.

"I should've told you before you let me stay with you and your family. You had a right to know the kind of man that was living in your home."

This was the secret she had seen in his eyes. The thing he'd kept from her. She tried to hold down the anger rising inside her. What did knowing this change? He'd found it easier to walk away from her love than to trust her.

He cleared his throat. "I hope you can forgive me."

Part of her wanted to throw her arms around him and tell him it was okay. The other part of her wanted to scream, *why?* What hold did alcohol have over him that was more powerful than a family's love or the value of a human life?

As she looked at his tense, pale features, her anger drained away. Her heart filled with pity. "I'm sorry you have this burden to bear. You have told me. Is that all?"

"Except to say that I'm sorry for the hurt that I have caused you and that people like me have caused you. I was plastered when I let a friend drive drunk. He killed himself and two other people."

"You are not responsible for the sins of others. You are not the man who took my husband's life."

"Thank you." He put his hat on his head. "I guess that's it." He started to walk away.

She couldn't let him go with so much unsaid. "What do you plan to do now?"

"I turned in my Stetson for a flat-topped black Amish hat, and I sold my car. I will find an Amish community and live as they do. In time I hope to bury my *Englisch* past completely. I want to thank you for showing me the way to a place where I think God wants me to belong."

She swallowed hard against the faint hope that started to rise from the depths of her pain. "Why can't you stay among us? Did the bishop disapprove?"

His smile was sad. "No, but it would be too hard to live near you and not be a part of your life. I know I would be a constant reminder of your husband's untimely death. I care about you too much to subject you to that."

He cared enough to leave, but did he care enough to stay? "When you were here with us, were you drinking?"

"No. I had been out of rehab for only a few months when I bumped into Diamond on the road. I have not had a drink since I went into rehab. I have been sober for five months. I know that doesn't sound like much to you, but for me it's huge. I had planned to tell you that night, but after learning how your husband died, I got scared. I didn't want you to look at me the way you looked at that man, so I left."

"You have given up drinking?"

"Yup. I know it will be a lifelong struggle, but I can't go back to what I was. You helped me see that—among other things."

She took a step toward him. Something in his voice told her she hadn't heard the whole truth yet. "What other things?"

A tiny smile pulled at the corner of his mouth. "That kindness exists. That a house can be a real home if the people in it care about each other. That a community can love and nurture all its members. That God loves me and has a plan for me." He looked into her eyes. "I had stopped believing before I met you."

He was in love with her, and he was about to walk away again. She saw it in the depths of despair in his eyes. Why couldn't he tell her? Was he afraid she would cast his love aside? Had she given him a reason to think otherwise? "You have shown me something important, too, Tully Lange."

He looked away. "How to spin a rope?"

"*Nee*, you will not distract me with your humor. You will listen to what I have to tell you. The rules of my faith control every part of my life, from what I wear on my head to what prayers I say at night. Despite knowing it was wrong and trying very hard not to do so… I still fell in love with you."

Tully's gaze flew to her face—he wasn't sure that he had heard correctly. His heart began hammering in his chest. He was afraid he was dreaming. "What did you say?"

"I think you heard me."

"Maybe I did, but I would sure like to hear you say that again."

"I said I'm in love with you. Even if it doesn't make a difference, I wanted you to know."

He took a step toward her. "That is the most beautiful thing I have ever heard in my life. Spoken by the most beautiful woman I've ever seen. The dairy barn setting isn't so spectacular, but I can live with it. As long as you mean it."

A smile curved her lips. "We have spent so much time together in this barn that it seemed like the perfect setting."

He had never known such joy. "Becca, I love you. If you don't mind, I'd like to spend the next sixty or seventy years working beside you in this barn." He held out his arms. When she stepped into his embrace, he knew he had found his own paradise.

He held her close as tears of happiness slipped down his cheeks. "I thought I had lost you. I thought you'd never be able to look at me again when you knew what I was."

She gazed up at him and cupped his cheeks with her hands. "I always knew you were a cowboy, and I love you in spite of it."

"I'm the one that makes the jokes."

"I am not joking. Why couldn't you tell me that you loved me just now?"

"Because I didn't believe that I deserved to have something so wonderful in my life." He pulled her into a fierce hug. "I still don't deserve you, but I'm never going to let you go."

"Oh, Tully, I love you so much. I can't believe how happy I am, but if you are going to kiss me you had better do it now, because we have to get Annabeth to her Christmas program."

"I love the way you boss me around." He bent toward her upturned face and tenderly pressed his lips to hers.

The outside door banged open, and Annabeth came in. "*Mamm*, we are going to be late! Tully!" She threw herself into his arms. "I knew you would come. I knew it."

"I wouldn't miss your play for anything." He held out his hand to Becca. "Shall we go?"

"With you? Everywhere and for always."

"It will be a year before I can be baptized."

"Then the wedding will be in one year and one day."

He tipped his head to the side. "Did you just propose to me?"

"I did. You were dragging your feet."

"I accept."

"Goot." She made shooing motions with her hands. "Let's go. We have to celebrate Christmas with our friends and family."

Tully lifted Annabeth up and set her on his shoulder.

"And some little shepherd girl has to find the Christ child."

"We are blessed, Tully Lange," Becca said stepping to his side.

He dropped a quick kiss on her lips. "Don't I know it."

Annabeth squeaked. "Did you just kiss my mother?"

"Yup. Want to see me do it again?"

She grinned. "Yup."

* * * * *

AN AMISH HOLIDAY
COURTSHIP

Emma Miller

Can two walk together, except they be agreed?
—*Amos* 3:3

Chapter One

Ginger Stutzman followed her mother down the baking aisle of Byler's store pushing a grocery cart. They'd come midday because her sister wanted to make *rosina kuchen*. Tara made the best raisin pie in Kent County, hands down. She'd been halfway through the recipe when she realized she was short a full cup of raisins, and their mother had offered to run to Byler's as she already had a list of items to pick up. Ginger had volunteered to accompany their mother because she genuinely enjoyed grocery shopping, but also because she knew the young man she was sweet on, Joe Verkler, frequented Byler's at that time of day. Not only did the store sell groceries and kitchen goods, and even woodstoves, but they also had a deli where sandwiches were made. Amish work crews often stopped there for lunch, and Joe had mentioned after church the previous Sunday that he was overseeing a work crew nearby. She hoped that she might *accidentally* bump into him.

"Let's see, dark brown sugar and white whole wheat

flour," Ginger's mother, Rosemary, read off a list from the back of an envelope. "Anything else you can think of that we need baking-wise?" She glanced up, her new reading glasses perched on the end of her nose. She'd resisted buying the eyeglasses, hating to admit that she was at an age that she needed them, but she was finding they made her life easier.

"*Ne*, nothing that I can think of," Ginger replied, searching for Joe, but trying hard not to appear to be looking for anyone. To her delight, as she reached the end of the aisle, sure enough, she spotted him.

Joe Verkler was standing near the deli counter, waiting to place an order, a white numbered ticket in his hand. She smiled the moment she saw him and was pleased that she was wearing her favorite dress, a rose-colored one that he'd remarked on the first time they met. It had been three weeks ago, at a barn raising in nearby Seven Poplars. Joe had only just arrived from Lancaster County, Pennsylvania, and had struck up a bold conversation with her, saying he was new in town and wanted to get to know all the pretty, single girls.

Joe was what Ginger's mother called *a man too handsome for his own good*. He was tall and broad shouldered, with golden hair that tumbled almost to his shoulders and a dimple on his square chin. He was clean-shaven, of course, meaning he was unmarried. And though he wore the typical Amish male clothing of homemade denim trousers and a colored shirt under his denim coat, his suspenders were a fancy braided leather. Today he was sporting a pair of black Nike running shoes. It was something not seen among the Amish in Kent County and a bit of scandal, according to her friend Martha Gruber's mother, Eunice. Apparently, all of the mothers in Hickory Grove were in a tizzy over Joe's flashy looks and his choice of footwear. Most Amish men wore sturdy work boots or rubber boots if the weather was poor. No one wore name-brand items for fear of appearing too much like an Englisher. But the Amish church districts of Lancaster County were less strict than locally; that's what Martha said. Martha was practically engaged to be married to a boy from Lancaster, so if anyone knew such things, she would.

"Oh dear, the raisins!" Ginger's mother chuckled. "We can't forget the raisins, can we? Now where did they get to? The next aisle, maybe?" she asked, walking past Ginger.

Ginger waited for her mother to go down the next aisle and then eased the cart that was already half-full off to the side so other shoppers could get by. Even a midweek grocery run for their family was a full cart. It took a lot of food to feed the sixteen adults and children who ate at her mother and stepfather's two kitchen tables. Pinching her cheeks to give them color, Ginger pretended to be interested in a display of iced gingerbread cookies at the endcap. She took a quick peek in Joe's direction, and then when he turned his head, she quickly reached for one.

"Ginger!" Joe called.

When she didn't answer right away, she saw him, out of the corner of her eye, walk toward her. "Ginger Stutzman?"

She turned to him, pretending to be surprised. Then she smiled her prettiest smile. "Joe."

"I thought that was you," he exclaimed, hooking his thumbs beneath his suspenders.

"What a surprise, seeing you here." She returned the

cookies to the shelf. They didn't buy packaged sweets, not when Tara was such a good baker.

"I'm ordering a sandwich." He pointed in the direction of the deli counter. "Waiting my turn."

One of the clerks called out the next number and a tall, thin English woman carrying a baby on her back hurried toward the counter. "Do you have smoked turkey?" she asked, seeming quite harried.

Ginger looked back at Joe. He had big, gorgeous hazel eyes. "What kind of sandwich?" she asked, tucking her hands behind her back.

He was grinning at her and she felt her cheeks flush. She knew that *hochmut* was something frowned upon by the Amish. Especially pride in one's looks. After all, that was just a matter of who your parents were, but Martha said that she and Joe made a fetching couple—him being so handsome and Ginger being the prettiest girl in the county.

At twenty-four, Ginger had been walking out with boys for years. She had been in no hurry to get serious, though, and had enjoyed the liberty given by her mother and stepfather to get to know as many young men as possible. She knew she was blessed that they had given her the freedom to figure out what kind of man she wanted to marry. She'd gone to church suppers and picnics and more singings than she could count. But now, with her twenty-fifth birthday approaching, she was beginning to think about settling down. Like every Amish girl, she dreamed of having a husband and children. And handsome Joe Verkler was just the kind of man she thought she ought to marry.

"I ordered a spicy Italian sub," Joe responded, holding her gaze. He wore a pair of sunglasses perched on his forehead, below his navy knit beanie. The glasses looked expensive, not like the ones her brothers bought at Spence's Bazaar, two pairs for ten dollars. "With lettuce, tomato and hot peppers," he added. "I love hot peppers."

"You didn't pack your lunch?" Ginger teased. "My *mam* says buying out can be expensive. My brothers pack when they work away from home."

He shrugged his broad shoulders. "I hate to trouble my aunt Edna. She and my uncle Ader have been kind enough to let me stay with them. She's got a houseful of little ones and enough work without me adding tasks to her morning." He made a face. "Besides, she makes terrible sandwiches. Too much mayonnaise."

It was on the tip of Ginger's tongue to suggest he could make his own sandwich for lunch, but she held back the comment. She didn't want to seem shrewish. Maybe men didn't make their own lunches in Lancaster. While the kitchen was certainly a woman's domain in her mother's house, her stepfather wasn't above making his own peanut butter and honey sandwich, and her stepbrothers all knew how to make their own coffee and sweep a floor.

"So… You here alone?" Joe asked. He was practically out-and-out flirting with her right there in the middle of the store for anyone to see.

The place was busy as always with English and Amish alike. It was a good store to catch a bargain. And maybe a good place to catch a husband, Ginger thought.

"Alone? Of course not." Ginger smiled and rolled her eyes as if Joe had just said the silliest thing. "I'm here with my *mam*. My sister Tara is making *rosina kuchen* and we ran out of raisins."

"Too bad." Joe knitted his thick brows. "About you not being here alone. Not about the raisins. Because if you were here on your own, I'd offer you a ride home. I've got my rig here." He pointed in the direction of the side parking lot where folks could safely leave a horse and buggy. "A two-seater. Built it myself in two weeks. You know, after work and chores."

Ginger's stepfather had built several buggies in his shop, so she knew how much time went into such a project. It was hardly something one could build in a few weeks. A few months was more like it, but she just smiled up at him, nodding. If Joe wanted to impress her, who was she to correct him on such a small detail?

"*Atch*, there you are." Ginger's mother appeared from around the corner. "I found the raisins and lost you, *Dochtah*." A box of raisins in one hand and the list in the other, she took in Joe, measuring him up.

Ginger could tell right away by the purse of her mother's mouth that she didn't approve. "Um, you remember Joe Verkler," she introduced. "You met him at Rufus Yoder's barn raising? He's staying with his aunt and uncle, Ader and Edna Verkler. Joe's from Lancaster County," she added.

"Good to see you again, Rosemary." Joe fiddled with the numbered ticket he held in his hand.

"And you, Joe." Without a smile, her mother returned her attention to the list on the envelope. "I forgot lettuce, Ginger. Could you fetch it? Three heads of romaine."

Just then, their neighbor Eli Kutz came walking their way carrying a handbasket. Ginger couldn't help but notice that it was filled with individual servings of pre-made pudding and Jell-O, as well as store-bought cookies and snack cakes. Two red packages of iced ginger cookies teetered on the top.

"Rosemary, Ginger," he exclaimed, his face lighting up with genuine pleasure.

Eli was a widower and older than Ginger, maybe in his midthirties. He wasn't an ugly man, but he wasn't what a girl would call handsome, either. Not like Joe. But she liked Eli, as did everyone in her family. He had been the first neighbor to extend his hand in friendship when they moved from New York to Delaware almost three years ago. His kindness had particularly touched Ginger. His wife had only recently passed, yet he had appeared at their door bearing honey from his own combs and a smile that was always on his face, despite his trials.

"Eli, have you met Joe Verkler?" Ginger went through the introductions again and then explained to Joe where Eli lived. Eli hadn't been at the barn raising, as his daughter was ill, and Joe didn't belong to their same church district, so she doubted the two men had crossed paths.

"Forty-nine!" the clerk at the deli counter called loudly, sounding annoyed. "Last time. Forty-nine!"

"That's me." Joe held up his ticket as if it were a prize. "Be right back."

Rosemary offered a quick smile, but her lips were pressed tightly together as if it pained her. She rolled their cart closer and dropped in the raisins.

"I'll wait right here," Ginger told Joe, watching him as he hurried toward the deli counter. He was a fine-looking man, broad shouldered and tall.

"How is Lizzy?" Rosemary asked, giving Eli her full attention. "Eunice said Lizzy was due for a pediatrician's visit this morning." She didn't have to explain which Eunice she meant, though there were two in Hickory Grove. She meant Eunice Gruber, her friend Martha's mother. Eunice knew everything that went on in their little town, sometimes things that weren't meant to be known.

"She's doing better. Much better." Eli set the red plastic basket of goodies at his feet. "The doctor says she expects a full recovery, but Lizzy's still on bed rest. She's only to get up a few times a day yet, her being so weak."

"Our prayers were answered," Rosemary murmured. "I know you must be relieved she's recovering."

"We all are, my boys and, of course, my sister and her family." Eli looked to Ginger. "I haven't had a chance to thank you for the little doll you made for Lizzy that you sent with the chicken soup last week. Lizzy won't let it out of her sight."

"I'm glad she liked it," Ginger said. "And so glad she's going to be okay."

The little girl had suffered complications from the chicken pox and had been hospitalized two weeks previously for several days due to dehydration. Lizzy, almost four years old, was a sweet little girl, and Ginger felt so sorry for her. When she was sick as a child, she remembered how she had wanted no one but her *mam*. She couldn't imagine what it was like to be motherless at such a young age.

"I'm thankful, indeed, for her improvement." Eli adjusted the wide-brimmed wool hat perched on his head. Unlike the younger men like Joe and her brothers, he wore more conservative attire to town. "I'm in a bit of a bind now, though, with Mary Yoder married and moving to Kentucky." He was referring to the twenty-one-year-old who used to babysit for him. With four little ones, Eli cared for his children most of the time on his own, but that meant grocery shopping and doing the laundry on top of barn and field work. Ginger couldn't imagine how he did it all without full-time help.

Joe joined the group again. "I got the big sub. A man my size needs a healthy-sized sandwich to keep up his strength. But they are out of hot peppers, and I'm sorely disappointed. I had a mind for hot peppers on my sandwich."

Rosemary stared at Joe, her face expressionless. Then she turned back to Eli. "You were saying you have a problem?"

Ginger rolled her eyes. What her mother was suggesting with that look was that Joe didn't know what real problems were. Thankfully, he didn't notice, didn't understand or didn't care.

"*Ya*, I'm not sure what to do." Eli pressed his hand to his forehead. "Ader Verkler—I'm guessing that's your uncle." Eli looked at Joe and then back to the women. "He hired me to build the wood paneling on a fireplace. His client wants it all handmade." He motioned with both hands. "Built-ins on two sides. All custom plans. It's a good eight to ten weeks of work. Put me right through to Christmas."

"Such beautiful work you do, Eli," Rosemary said. "Properly *Plain*, but still so beautiful. A talent like that is God-given."

"It doesn't even have to be *Plain*," Eli explained. "The clients are Englishers. Moved here from New Jersey and have their heart set on Amish builders. Anyway, trouble is, now with Mary gone, I've no one to watch the little ones while I go off to work. I can bring one or two of the bigger boys along at a time, but Lizzy's still in bed." He chuckled. "And to tell the truth, I'm afraid Phillip's not well behaved enough to set loose on a job site. I can't imagine what he might get into."

Ginger and her mother both smiled. Five-year-old Phillip wasn't a bad child, but he could be naughty. At a fundraiser supper recently, Phillip had been caught fishing cherries out of a dozen cherry pies meant to be served for dessert. And not long before that, he filled his aunt Claudia's rubber boots with milk fresh from the morning milking. To make matters worse, the milk had sat all day, curdled and made quite a stink not only to the mudroom but also to his aunt's stockings.

"I thought your sister was helping out," Ginger said, filled with concern for Eli and his family. She imagined the additional income was important. He farmed, of course, but like most Amish men in the community, he supplemented that income with outside work.

"*Ya*, she helps out. She was a blessing when Lizzy was at her sickest. But Claudia has a family of her own, her own house to attend to." He shook his head. "I hate to turn down the work. Like I said, it would only be until Christmas, but I'm at a loss as to what to do."

Ginger's mother glanced at Ginger. Her mother didn't have to say anything; Ginger knew what she was thinking and nodded.

Her mother looked back at Eli. "What would you think of Ginger lending a hand? She's good with children, and I know she'd be happy to help, wouldn't you?"

"*Ya*, I could watch Lizzy," Ginger said, excited by the prospect. "And the boys, too," she added, thinking it might be good for Eli to spend some time without his children rather than taking them to work with him.

Every parent needed a break. She had learned that from her mother. "As long as *Mam* and Benjamin can spare me." She was old enough not to have to ask permission to do something, but because she had plenty of chores at home and also worked at her stepfather's harness shop, she wanted to be sure it wouldn't cause too much upset in the family. In order for her to work for Eli, others would have to do her jobs at home.

"Spare you?" Her mother chuckled. "I've got too many cooks in my kitchen as is. And I'm sure Benjamin can find someone to cover your shifts." She eyed Eli. "Always underfoot, my girls. I keep hoping they'll start marrying, but they don't seem in any great hurry."

"Mam!" Ginger laughed nervously. She stole a quick look in Joe's direction. He grinned.

Eli turned to Ginger, his blue eyes twinkling. "Would you consider watching my children? Lizzy adores you, you know. I think she'd heal all the quicker having you there at the house. And I'd pay you, of course," he added quickly.

Ginger pressed her lips together, touched that Eli thought she could assist in Lizzy's recuperation. "I'd be happy to come, Eli. I'd have to talk to Benjamin about using a buggy, though. It's a little cold to be walking home or taking my scooter from your house after dark. Seems like winter has come early this year."

It was true. Even though it was only early October, they'd already had several frosts. The *Farmer's Almanac* was predicting snow before Christmas and colder than usual temperatures, her stepfather, Benjamin, had told them just the other night at the supper table.

"Not to worry. I'm sure we can figure out a way to

get her to and from your place," Ginger's mother assured Eli.

"A good thing to do, Ginger," Joe put in. "Helping a neighbor in need. You catch a ride in the morning or walk to Eli's, and I could give you a ride home most nights."

Ginger felt a little shiver of excitement. "You would, Joe?" She looked from him to her mother. "Isn't that nice of Joe to offer?"

"I wouldn't want to put Joe out," her mother answered, her tone cool.

Ginger frowned. She didn't know what had gotten into her mother, being almost rude to Joe.

"You wouldn't be putting me out," Joe contended. "I go right down your road most days. My uncle's put me in charge of looking in on crews, so I'm here and there all day. Not many he trusts to see the job gets done."

"It's kind of you to offer, Ginger." There was emotion in Eli's voice. "And also kind of you, Joe." He looked back at Ginger. "And if you're sure you'd like to help me, I'll accept. My children will be so excited."

"Then it's decided." Ginger's mother clasped her hands together, settling the matter. "Monday morning you say, Eli?"

"*Ya.* I have to be on the job by eight, but it's less than half an hour to the work site by buggy," Eli answered. "I'd offer to take Ginger home each night, but Lizzy can't be out and about yet, and I can't leave the children at home. I know some folks think a boy of eight is old enough to leave home alone with brothers or sisters, but I don't do it. I'd worry too much."

"You're a good father, Eli," Ginger's mother told him. "And don't you fret. We'll figure out how to get Ginger to and from." She produced her shopping list. "Well, we best be on our way. Tara's waiting on raisins."

"*Ya*, and I need to get home. Claudia's with the children, but I promised her I wouldn't be long." Eli picked up his shopping basket from the floor. "Just needed to pick up a prescription at the drugstore for Lizzy and stop for a few groceries. I've got a driver waiting. Hired a van to take Lizzy to the doctor this morning, then home, then back into town."

"Forty-nine!" a different clerk called from the deli counter. "Forty-nine!"

"Guess I'd best go get my sub before someone else does." Joe boldly met Ginger's gaze. "You going to the Fishers' Saturday night? I hear there's going to be a bonfire."

"I think so," she said, trying not to sound too excited. But if they were both there, Joe would surely offer to take her home, wouldn't he? It was the way young men and women dated among the Old Order Amish. They attended chaperoned events separately and then a boy was free to ask a girl if he could give her a ride home.

"We'll have to see," Ginger's mother responded, then turned to Eli. "Ginger will be there at seven-fifteen on Monday."

"Excellent." Eli nodded his head again and again, gripping the shopping basket in one hand. "Wonderful." He looked at Ginger. "Goodbye. Thank you again."

"You're welcome," Ginger told Eli, but her eyes were all for Joe Verkler as he walked away.

Eli entered his cozy kitchen in his stocking feet. They had an unusual rule for an Amish family—no boots or shoes in the house. They wore socks or slippers beyond the mudroom. He had made the rule after his wife, Elizabeth, died three years ago. It was the only way he had found to keep clean the hardwood floors he had so lovingly laid for her. "Guess who's home?" he sang, carrying a paper sack of groceries in each arm.

"*Dat*!"

"*Dat*!"

"*Dat*!" his three sons cried, one after the other.

The youngest, five-year-old Phillip, threw himself at his father, wrapping his arms around Eli's knees. "What did you bring us?"

"Phillip." Eli's sister, Claudia, spoke from where she stood at the stove, stirring something in a cast-iron kettle. Something that smelled deliciously of chicken and vegetables and herbs. "Don't ask such things. Offer to help your *fadder* with his bags."

"I'll get one," Eli's oldest son, eight-year-old Simon, said, taking a bag from his father's arms.

"I'll help," seven-year-old Andrew piped up.

When Andrew took the second bag from Eli, Phillip immediately grabbed it, practically knocking both of them off their feet.

"Whoa," Eli said, taking the bag from his boys and righting Andrew.

"I want to help," Phillip complained.

Andrew crossed his arms over his chest in annoyance. "You're not big enough."

"Am too!" Phillip, who looked just like Eli had as a child—bright red hair and all—gazed up at his father. "Andrew says I'm not big. But this morning you said I was big now."

Eli rumpled his son's coarse hair as he walked past him, taking the grocery sack to the table. "I *said* you're bigger than Lizzy. Which means you're responsible for her and also means you shouldn't tease her."

"I see you bought cookies." Claudia left her place at the stove and began to unload the first bag. "Plenty of cookies." She stacked the packages of them on the table. "Did you remember the rosemary?"

"*Ya*. It's in one of the bags. They didn't have fresh, but you said dry would do." Eli walked to the stove. "I don't know what you've made but it smells wonderful." He picked up a wooden spoon from the walnut countertop he'd built and stirred the thick, creamy stew in the pot.

"Chicken potpie," Claudia told him. "I just turned it off. Piecrust is already made and on the counter under the damp towel. Pour the stew into the piecrust, cover it with the second crust and be sure to vent it or you'll have a mess to clean up. Bake for forty-five minutes at three-fifty degrees. The oven is already preheating." She held a pack of Oreos in one hand and peanut butter sandwich cookies in the other. "Really, Eli," she said gently. "The children don't need all of these sweets."

"Maybe they're for me," he teased as he set down the spoon.

"Then you don't need them, either."

He laughed at the stern look on his sister's face. "They eat healthy enough. We all do. How's Lizzy?"

"Tired but good," she said, putting the packages of cookies in the pie safe that had been a gift to Eli and Elizabeth when they'd married. It had been his great-grandmother's. "I think the trip to the doctor wore her out. She should stay in bed for the rest of the day. If she wants to eat with the family, maybe carry her out to the kitchen?"

"I'll see what she wants to do. Some nights we eat with her in her room." He looked to Simon, Andrew and Phillip. "Don't we, boys?"

"Sometimes," Phillip agreed, biting on the end of a package of cookies, trying to open it with his teeth.

Simon took the bag from his little brother. "None before supper."

"*Dat!*" Phillip cried in protest.

"He's right. You shouldn't be eating cookies, Phillip." Eli turned to his sister. "Thank you so much for staying with them while I went back into town. You should go home. John will be wanting his supper soon."

"You sure?" Claudia closed the pie safe. "I can get the potpie in the oven for you."

"I can manage the potpie," Eli assured her. "Guess what?" Suddenly he couldn't hide his excitement. "I found someone to watch the children while I work that job. The one Ader Verkler wants to hire me to do."

"You did? That's wonderful news." She removed her apron and hung it on a peg on the wall. "Who?"

"Ginger Stutzman," he announced, unable to stop grinning. There was something about Ginger that made him smile every time he saw her. Yes, she could be silly and coquettish at times, but he admired her enthusiasm for life. She always had a light in her eyes that he sensed came from deep within her.

"*Ginger?*" Claudia made a face that left no room for interpretation. Obviously she didn't approve.

He lowered his voice, walking near to his sister so the children wouldn't hear. "What's wrong with Ginger? The children adore her."

His sister looked at him in a way that immediately made him feel a little bit as if they were back on their parents' farm in Wisconsin, and he was ten, and she was fifteen again. Their mother had died when he was eight, and at thirteen, Claudia had taken on most of the household chores so their father could continue to work their dairy farm. Her duties, among others, had been to care for Eli and their other siblings. She had not quite taken on the role of mother but embraced her new responsibilities as an older sister. Eli and Claudia had remained close, and after he lost his wife, she had become his best friend.

Claudia took a deep breath. "I'm sorry to be cross. It's just been a long day. There's nothing wrong with Ginger. She'll make an excellent sitter."

He followed her to the mudroom. "My same thought."

"I just think you need to be careful," she went on as she took her heavy wool cloak from a peg and threw it over her shoulders.

"Careful of what?"

Claudia glanced in the direction of the boys as she reached for her heavy black bonnet. Phillip had managed to get into the cookies and each boy had one stuffed in his mouth. She looked back at Eli. "She's a flirt," she said quietly.

"And?" Eli pressed. Because he knew she was a flirt. Everyone in Hickory Grove knew it. She always had been. But she was also a good person, a woman of faith, and he had never heard anyone ever speak of her behaving improperly. More importantly, he knew he could trust her with his children, who were more precious to him than anything he had on this earth.

"And I wouldn't want you to…misinterpret anything she might say or do."

He tipped back his head and laughed. Nothing could

dampen his mood today. Because his problem was solved with childcare, and the money he would make would not only be enough to pay all of Lizzy's medical bills but also to buy a pony for Christmas for the children. *"Misinterpret?"*

Claudia met his gaze with green eyes. "You know very well what I'm talking about. I understand you want to marry again. I just wouldn't want you to—" She let the sentence go unfinished.

"Wouldn't want me to *what*?" he pressed.

"Fall in love with her," she said.

Eli laughed. "I'm not a boy just out of school." He opened his arms wide. "I'm practically an old man. A woman like Ginger wouldn't be interested in me."

"That said…" Her tone softened. "You have such a big heart, Eli." She exhaled and went on. "I wouldn't want to see it broken. And Ginger Stutzman—" she tapped his chest "—will break it if you let her."

Chapter Two

Eli stood on the steps of the back porch, watching as his sister went down the driveway on her push scooter, her black cloak whipping behind her. He smiled to himself, silently giving thanks for her dedication to him and his children, and to her willingness to speak up. Even when he didn't agree with her. He wasn't offended by what she had said about Ginger or him. Her heart was in the right place.

He chuckled to himself as he entered the warm house again. Did Claudia really think he would pursue Ginger Stutzman, the prettiest, most eligible young woman in Hickory Grove? And probably eight years younger than him? Did his sister believe he would think Ginger would ever be interested in him? Women like Ginger would never give a man his age a second glance. They went for flashy young men like that Joe Verkler from Lancaster.

In the kitchen, Eli put an end to the cookie snack, asked his boys to set the table for supper and then padded down the hallway. He quietly entered the parlor in case Lizzy was sleeping. Ordinarily, they all slept upstairs, but he'd moved her downstairs so he would be closer to her during the day. He slept on the sofa on the far side of the room, just in case she needed him during the night. His boys continued to sleep upstairs, though occasionally he woke in the morning to find Phillip either sleeping at the foot of his sister's bed or snuggled in Eli's arms.

Eli's gaze settled on his daughter. She was sitting propped up on pillows in her bed, a log cabin quilt tucked around her. She was playing with the little faceless doll Ginger had made for her and a wooden horse he'd carved to go with other wooden animals his children shared.

"*Dat*!"

"Lizzy." Eli went to her and sat on the edge of her bed. "Your aunt says you're feeling pretty good?"

She nodded. Her blond hair was pulled back and covered with a white handkerchief that matched her white sleeping gown.

He smoothed the hair that had escaped from her headcovering. "But a little tired maybe?" he asked in Pennsylvania *Deitsch*.

"*Ya.*" She looked up at him with her mother's big, brown, expressive eyes.

Eli swallowed hard, wrapping his arms around his daughter. She hugged him tight. "Guess what," he whispered in her ear.

"What?" she whispered back with a little giggle. "Did you bring cookies, *Dat*?"

"I did," he told her, easing her back onto her pillow. "And Jell-O and pudding. But this is better than treats. Ginger is going to be keeping an eye on you while I go to work."

The little girl grinned. "I *wike* Ginger." Then she knitted her brows. "But why do you have to go to work, *Dat*? I'll *mish* you."

He drew the quilt up to her chin and smoothed it. "Because that's what *fadders* do. They go to work so they can buy cookies." He tickled her belly and she giggled again. "And I'll come home to you every night by dinnertime. *Ya*?"

"*Ya*," she echoed, looking up at him from beneath long lashes.

Eli had always known he would become a father someday. And he had known he would be good at it because he had helped Claudia take care of their five younger siblings after their mother's death. His childhood experiences had prepared him for the crying babies, the dirty faces and the mischievous antics of little boys. What he had not been prepared for was this sweet ache he felt deep in his chest, an ache of love for his children that was like no other feeling in the world. He would do anything for his Lizzy, for his boys. *Anything* to keep them safe and warm and cared for.

He sighed as Lizzy relaxed and closed her eyes. It hadn't been an easy row to hoe, being a single father with little ones. He constantly felt as if he was being pulled in so many directions at once. There were cows to be milked, animals to be fed, dishes to be washed and beds to be made. And then there were his responsibilities in his children's religious education. Some days it was too much for one man. That was why God joined Adam and Eve together, so that they could go about their tasks together. He truly believed that.

Eli stroked Lizzy's forehead, thankful she was no

longer burning with the fever that had plagued her on and off for weeks. She was falling asleep.

He didn't agree with what Claudia had been saying about Ginger, but she had been right in saying he wanted a wife. And he wanted a mother for his children. His children needed a mother.

Watching Lizzy's rosebud lips part as she exhaled slowly, he clasped his hands and prayed a quick, silent thank-you for God's mercy in saving his daughter from her illness. And then he prayed, as he prayed every day, for God to provide him a wife.

"I suppose we'd best get home," Ginger's twin sister, Bay, said, drying her hands on her apron. They had just pulled four loaves of fresh bread from Eli's oven, and the entire house smelled delightful. "Unless you want me to wait for you and give you a ride home." She glanced at the clock. It was five-fifteen. "I imagine Eli will be home soon."

Bay wasn't the cook Tara was, but she had the touch when it came to yeast breads. She'd come for the afternoon to help Ginger make loaves of honey-wheat sandwich bread. It had been Ginger's idea to make it, thinking the bread would serve well for the sandwiches Eli took to work every day. Usually, he just ate his sandwiches on inexpensive white bread from the grocery store. However, earlier in the week he'd gone on so much about how good the homemade sandwich bread her mother had sent for him was that she thought he ought to have a few loaves of his own. She planned to slice the bread after it cooled and freeze it on cookie sheets before putting it in plastic bags in the freezer. That way, he could quickly grab what he needed in the morning and not worry about the bread going moldy in the pie safe because, without preservatives, the home-made bread had a short shelf life.

Ginger was finishing up her second week caring for Eli's children, and so far, it had gone well. The children liked her, Lizzy was improving every day and Eli seemed thrilled to have her. The idea that she could ease another's burden, especially a man so good-hearted as Eli, made Ginger feel good in a way she'd never felt before. And Eli was so appreciative of anything she did. He always made a point of telling her how delicious the meals she left for him were and reminded her every day that he didn't expect her to cook, and certainly not clean. He kept repeating that he had hired her to care for his children. But it was no burden for Ginger. She liked cooking on her own without Tara or her mother overseeing her every move, and she was discovering she was actually a decent cook in her own right. And she enjoyed the cleaning. It gave her time to pray, and also to daydream.

These days, she was spending a lot of time day-dreaming.

After years of flirtations, Ginger was feeling more and more as if she was ready to marry, settle down and run her own household. The time she spent with Lizzy, Phillip, Andrew and Simon made her think about the possibility of having her own children. Was that why God had put Joe in her path? Because He was ready to see her as a wife and a mother? Ginger knew it wasn't wise to guess at God's intentions, but it just made sense, didn't it?

Bay's voice penetrated Ginger's thoughts, sounding

impatient. Ginger had an idea her sister was repeating her question. "Do you want me to wait or no?"

Ginger looked to Bay. She was a redhead, not a blonde like Ginger was, tall, like their older sister Lovage, and willowy to Ginger's curves. They did have the same color green eyes, though.

"No need to wait," Ginger said quickly. Using the hem of her apron as a hot mitt, she slid one of the hot loaves of bread away from the edge of the stove. All it would take was one curious boy to send the bread tumbling to the floor.

"You sure?" Bay caught the hand of one of their little brothers as he ran by. "Give me that," she said. "No more cookies, Josiah. *Mam* won't be happy with us if you two have any more cookies before supper."

Josiah solemnly handed over the store-bought sweet, a bite missing from it.

Bay had brought their twin brothers with her, two-year-olds Josiah and James. Technically, they were only their half brothers. Their mother and stepfather's sons, though neither of them felt any differently about these two than their brother Jesse, who shared the same father with them.

"Where do they keep finding these cookies?" Bay asked.

Ginger laughed. "I don't know. Eli buys them. The boys squirrel them away around the house. Yesterday I found a box of animal crackers in the linen closet." She reached down and wiped the chocolate crumbs from the corner of her little brother's mouth. "Where's James?" she asked, leaning over him. "Go find James. It's time to go home."

The two sisters watched as their little brother, dressed

in denim pants, shirts and suspenders, toddled out of the kitchen, calling his twin's name in a cherubic voice.

"I don't need a ride home," Ginger repeated, giving the beef stew on the back of the stove a stir. "I have one."

Bay frowned. "I suppose *he's* bringing you home again?"

Ginger felt her cheeks grow warm. "*He* has a name." She turned down the flame beneath the cast-iron pot of stew. "Joe Verkler."

Bay made a sour face, resting one hand on her hip. "I'm sorry, but I don't care for Joe."

Ginger tried not to let her feelings be hurt. "Why not? He's handsome and fun and…and he likes me."

"Everyone likes you," Bay quipped. "You can do better, Ginger. You *deserve* better."

Ginger wanted to ask Bay what she knew about young men. She'd never even had a beau. But she bit back the comment. "Why don't you like him?"

Bay arched her eyebrows as if it was a foolish question. "Because he's conceited. He thinks he's good-looking."

"You don't think he is?"

"I think there are more important things. I've seen him around. All he does is talk about himself and his accomplishments. He's got every single woman in Hickory Grove gazing up at him with starry eyes. They all listen to whatever nonsense he weaves. The other day he told Tara that he owned a farm and a hundred acres in Lancaster County. If that's true," she scoffed, "what's he doing here living here in Delaware with his aunt and uncle?"

Ginger defended him. "He's helping his uncle with

his business. That's why he came. His uncle needed him. Joe is managing construction crews all over the county."

Bay crossed her arms over her chest. "You see what you want to see, Ginger. You always have. From where I stand, there's no substance behind that boy's fancy sunglasses and shoes…" She exhaled, letting her thought go unfinished.

"You sound like *Mam*," Ginger countered, refusing to be upset by her sister's words. She knew Bay was only trying to look out for her, and that mattered more than her sister being wrong. "*Mam* doesn't like him, either." She walked to the refrigerator to get butter. "Well, the both of you are going to have to get used to him because I like him. Maybe even more than like him," she added with her own stubbornness. "We've really gotten to know each other since he started giving me a ride home." She pressed her lips together, suddenly brimming with excitement. "I think he's going to ask me to walk out with him. We're practically already walking out together."

Bay rolled her eyes. "You and half the girls in the county think that."

Deciding not to respond, Ginger turned the flame on under a small cast-iron pan. She thought her sister was being ridiculous, but she didn't want to quarrel with her. What was the point? She knew Joe was sincere in his attention to her. What better way to prove it than to let Bay see it? Their *mam*, as well.

Ginger was silent as she dropped a couple of tablespoons of butter into the hot frying pan. It made a satisfying sizzle, and she grabbed a wooden spoon to stir the butter to prevent it from burning. A little flour and a few minutes of browning it, and the roux would make the perfect thickening for the stew that was made from thick chunks of beef, potatoes, onions, carrots and peas.

"Josiah! James!" Bay called in the direction of the living room, where the boys were all playing. When she got no response, she called louder, "Simon, could you bring the boys? We have to go." She returned her gaze to Ginger. "Guess we'll be on our way. If you're sure you don't want us to wait."

"No need to wait." Ginger smiled. "I'll see you in an hour."

Eli's oldest son entered the kitchen, leading a boy in each hand. It was clear James and Josiah weren't ready to go home.

"Thank you, Simon," Ginger said, whisking the flour into the butter in the frying pan. "Could you check on Lizzy? See if she's awake."

When Bay and the boys first arrived, Lizzy had joined them in the living room. Ginger had settled her on the couch with a quilt over her lap and she had played with Josiah and James for almost an hour. Lizzy had set up a barnyard of wooden animals and pieces of fencing on the couch beside her and entertained the toddlers by making animal sounds. When she had started to look tired, Ginger had carried her back to her makeshift bedroom, and the child had been asleep in minutes.

Bay led their little brothers into the mudroom off the kitchen. She took one little denim coat and handed Ginger the other, and both set to dressing the boys for the chilly, wet ride home.

"Thank you for coming over to help me with the bread," Ginger said, trying to button a wiggling James into his coat. Both boys looked like their father, like Benjamin's older sons with brown hair and doe-brown eyes.

"You didn't need any help, but you're welcome." Josiah's coat secure, Bay pulled his knit cap over his head, covering his eyes. "I'm impressed with how well you're running Eli's house in just two weeks. You remind me of *Mam* in the kitchen. You've always got a bunch of things going at the same time—stew simmering, bread baking, mending at the table and children well fed and content. And so many children. Everyone wanting something at the same time. You're so calm. And capable." She shook her head. "I could never do it." She threw up her hands. "I can't imagine having my own children. My own home. It would be a disaster."

"It *wouldn't* be a disaster," Ginger chided, handing her sister her cloak. "You're going to make a wonderful wife and mother someday. You're practically running the garden shop, what with Joshua busy making plans to build his and Phoebe's new house. Running a house and a garden shop are more alike than you think." She leaned on the doorjamb. "Do you want to take a loaf of bread home?"

"*Ne*, they're for Eli. The man needs a little meat on his bones." Her eyes twinkled. "I'm beginning to think you might just be the one to put it there."

Ginger laughed, knitting her brows. There was something in her sister's tone of voice that she couldn't quite interpret. "And what's that supposed to mean?"

Bay shrugged. "I don't know. All afternoon I heard Eli this and Eli that. I think you might like him."

"Of course I like him." She gave her sister a little push. "But not *that* way."

The sisters were grinning at each other when Simon

walked back into the mudroom. "Lizzy wants you," he announced, looking up at Ginger. He didn't look as much like Eli as Phillip did. He and Lizzy both resembled their mother more, but he was just like his father, such a caregiver. And so easygoing with his younger siblings. At least most of the time.

"See you at home," Ginger told her sister. "And you two, as well." She kissed the top of each of their little brothers' heads and made her way toward the back of the house to check on her charge. "Coming, Lizzy!"

Eli stood in the downstairs bathroom drying his face with a hand towel that was freshly washed and smelled of fabric softener. Ginger had declared Fridays washday and, despite his protests, had done all of his laundry two weeks in a row. She wouldn't listen to him when he assured her he could wash his and the children's clothes on Saturday mornings.

Before Ginger had started working for him, he'd managed the laundry. The children had always had clean clothes for the Sabbath at least, and the bedsheets and towels got washed at some point each month. Though his towels had never smelled this good or been this soft. He smiled to himself in the mirror, then leaned over the sink, taking a closer look. When had signs of his aging appeared, he wondered, looking at the man he barely recognized. Last time he looked in the mirror, he didn't recall the gray at his temples.

He looked older than thirty-three.

But how long had it been since he'd scrutinized his appearance beyond checking to be sure he was tidy? Not since Elizabeth died, he guessed. Where had those fine lines around his mouth come from? The ones at the corners of his eyes? He would be thirty-four come spring. It seemed too young to be going gray, he thought wistfully.

He wondered what Ginger thought of his looks. Did she see the gray, too? The wrinkles?

He dismissed the thought. Vanity wasn't a positive attribute in a man his age, with his responsibilities. And as he had told his sister, a woman like Ginger, years younger than him, would never so much as look his way.

He hung the sweet-smelling towel on the hook beside the sink, took up a brush and tidied his hair. And smiled again.

Things were going so well these days that all he did was smile. Ader Verkler was well pleased with the work Eli was doing on the job site, and more importantly, life was running more smoothly at home. Mary Yoder, who had watched the children for him before she'd left the state to be wed, had certainly done a fine enough job, but Ginger was impressive. Particularly for her age. He would have thought a young girl like her would have struggled, with four little ones to keep, with just getting something together for the noonday meal, but every night, she not only had tasks around the house done, but she made him supper. Every night he came into the house to a warm kitchen smelling of biscuits or bread or homemade cupcakes. And there was always a soup or a stew or a ham ready to go on the table.

He walked out of the bathroom, still smiling. Tonight, not only had he come home to the heavenly scent of bubbling spaghetti sauce, but his little Lizzy had been sitting at the table buttering slices of bread to go into the broiler. In just two weeks' time, his daughter's strength had greatly improved, and he was certain it was in good part due to Ginger's mothering skills and practicality. She was so good at coddling Lizzy when she needed to be coddled but also pushing her to help her gain her strength back. It had never occurred to Eli to have her do a chore at the table.

"There you are," Ginger said as he walked into the kitchen. She dried her hands on her apron. "I have to go. When you're ready to eat, throw the noodles into boiling water and cook them for ten minutes or so. And don't overcook them, Eli," she warned, pointing her finger at him.

He smiled, walking over to the table where Lizzy was still working on buttering the bread. He kissed the top of her head. "You know," he teased Ginger, "I *have* made noodles before."

Ginger flashed him a smile that lit up her entire face.

"*Ya,*" she agreed. "And overcooked them, I hear." She whipped her apron off. "Most people do. It should still have a bit of a snap to it in the middle," she explained, tucking tendrils of blond hair beneath the dark green scarf she wore to cover her hair. Like many young Amish women, she preferred a scarf to her prayer *kapp* when doing household chores. "Simon is outside gathering eggs, and the other two rascals are in the attic getting their clothes. With the rain, I had to hang some things up there to dry. Towels and sheets are done. I used the propane dryer. I hope that's okay."

"Of course." Eli followed her to the mudroom, hating to see her go so soon. All day he looked forward to the few minutes he would spend with Ginger before she headed home. He told himself that he was simply seeking adult conversation, but he talked to other men on the job site during the day. If he was honest with himself, it was Ginger he wanted to talk to. He'd always liked her, but since he had seen what she was capable of, how well she handled the children, he liked her even more. "You don't want to stay for supper?" he asked. "I promise I'll cook the noodles right. Al dente, I think the English call it."

She laughed. "Sorry. I have to go. Joe's waiting for me."

As if on cue, a male voice hollered her name from outside. The family dog, Molly, began to bark.

Eli made an effort not to frown, though just the thought of the young man brought a sourness to his mouth. He'd seen Joe at the house where he was working and had observed that the man didn't really know what he was doing. He talked a lot, threw orders around, but when it came down to it, he didn't know anything about laying bricks, putting on a roof or managing men. "Joe's outside, is he?"

"*Ya*," Ginger said cheerfully, throwing her black cloak over her shoulders.

Eli's brow creased. "Why doesn't he come inside when he picks you up?"

"Ginger! You coming?" Joe shouted.

Molly continued to bark. The dog Eli had raised from a pup usually liked most people. But the black-and-white shaggy mixed breed didn't like Joe Verkler. She barked like crazy every time he came up the driveway with his fancy rig. A rig Eli was certain had some kind of music player inside. He'd passed a buggy the other night on Route 8 and heard Englisher music blasting from inside. He was sure the driver had been Joe. He was also fairly certain he'd seen a young Amish woman with him. He hadn't been able to identify the woman in the dark, but the one thing he did know was that it hadn't been Ginger.

Ginger offered a quick smile as she yanked her bonnet over her head. "Joe wants to get home after a long day at work. You understand." She tied the bonnet on tightly. "I'll see you Monday morning, *ya*?"

Eli nodded as he watched her step out of the slippers she now kept at his door and into a pair of black rubber boots. It was on the tip of his tongue to ask her again to stay and have supper with them. After they ate, maybe they could play a board game, then he could load up all of the children, and they would take her home.

But that wasn't practical, of course. Lizzy didn't need to be outside at night. And why would Ginger want to sit and have a boring family dinner and talk about the dogwood flowers he was carving into a piece of wood, or what kind of spider his boys had found, when she could spend time with an exciting man like Joe.

Joe's voice came through the door as she opened it. "Ginger! I'm leaving with or without you!"

"Coming!" Ginger shouted.

Eli held open the door to the back porch. "*Ya*, I'll see you Monday," he agreed. Then he watched Ginger cut across the wet porch and tried to keep from counting the hours until he saw her again.

Chapter Three

Ginger sat on the top step of Eli's porch a week later tossing a stick for the family's black-and-white dog to fetch. Molly took off across the grass that had gone brown with the cooler weather, and Ginger's gaze strayed to the county road in the distance. A red pickup truck flew past Eli's mailbox, but there was no sign of the two-seated buggy she was looking for.

She sighed. Joe was late to pick her up and take her home.

Molly ran to the steps and dropped the stick at Ginger's feet. When Ginger didn't pick it up, the dog gave a subdued woof.

Ginger scratched the shaggy black-and-white dog's head. "Go away. I don't want to play anymore."

The dog put one paw and then the other on the bottom step, pushing the stick closer. Ginger remembered when Eli had found the dog as a puppy in a cardboard box in the parking lot of Byler's store. Abandoned. Eli had brought it home, bottle-fed the pup goat's milk and named her Molly when he knew she was going to make it. She was such a well-behaved dog that Ginger wondered if Molly sensed what a good life she had on the Kutz farm and wanted to express her appreciation.

Molly whined and pushed the stick at Ginger again.

Ginger laughed. "All right. Just once more." She tossed the stick, and the dog took off as the screen door opened and closed behind her.

It was Andrew, Eli's middle son. He was a sweet, thoughtful boy with a mop of reddish-blond hair and a pair of round wire-frame glasses that made him look older than his seven-going-on-eight years. "*Dat* says you should come back inside," he said in Pennsylvania *Deitsch*.

"I'm waiting for my ride home," she explained.

Molly raced up to the steps again, stick in her mouth, and Andrew accepted it from her and threw it hard. It landed on the far side of the driveway, and the dog took off after it.

"Getting cold out," Andrew said, shoving his hands deep into his pockets, something his father often did. "It's warm in the kitchen."

Ginger smiled up at him from her perch on the top step. "I'm fine. I'm sure Joe will be here any minute. He's in charge of a lot of men. He can't just quit at four like your *dat*." This was the second time Joe had been late that week. When he'd been late last time, he'd spent the entire ride home explaining to her how central he was to his uncle's entire construction business. Still, she felt as if she was making an excuse for Joe when she said it aloud.

The boy wandered back into the house. A minute later, the screen door opened and closed shut again.

"I sent Andrew out to get you."

Ginger looked up to see Eli. He had washed his face

as he did every day after he returned home from work, and she could see that his hair was damp at the temples. It was an auburn color, darker than her sister Bay's or Tara's red hair, and he kept it well trimmed. She liked that. "Joe's running late. A problem at one of the job sites, I'm sure," she said.

Eli slid his hands into his pants pockets and gazed out at the barnyard.

It was a small farm, maybe twenty-five acres, with a neat little two-story square bungalow with a wide porch along the driveway side. The yard comprised a series of standard Amish outbuildings: a dairy barn, a lean-to shed for farm equipment, a windmill, a chicken house and a woodshed. Everything was painted, neat and orderly. What was interesting to Ginger about the property was that unlike most Amish houses, which were painted white, his was a spruce green. Not *Plain*, but not too fancy, either.

Ginger pressed her lips together. She didn't often wish for Englisher conveniences, but it was times like this that she almost wished she had a cell phone. Then Joe could have let her know he was going to be late. That he'd gotten held up. Most Amish families in Hickory Grove had a cell phone these days. However, they were only used for emergencies, or when someone worked for Englishers and had to check in with their boss. Her mother and stepfather didn't have a cell at their house because there was a phone in the harness shop.

"Starting to rain again," Eli remarked. "Might turn to sleet. Why don't you wait inside with us?"

She tightened her heavy cloak around her. She *was* getting cold. And she was disappointed that Joe was late again. It would be dark soon. She watched Molly for a moment. The dog had grown bored with the game of fetch and was now digging at the base of a big silver maple tree that, in the summer, shaded the porch. She gazed up at Eli.

He tipped his head in the direction of the back door. "Come on," he coaxed. "You can wait inside for him where it's warm as easily as you can sit out here in the cold."

He had a gentle way about him. A calmness that made Ginger feel like… Like everything was going to be all right. Always.

"Lizzy just woke up and she was disappointed you were gone," Eli continued. "She'd be tickled to see you."

Ginger rose, looked in the direction of the road once more, then followed Eli into the house. The fragrant smell of the roast beef she'd left in the oven hit her the moment she stepped into the mudroom. She removed her coat and bonnet, stepped out of her rubber boots and into the spare slippers she kept there now. At first, she had thought it odd that Eli didn't allow shoes inside his house, but now she liked the idea. It kept the floors so much cleaner that she was thinking maybe once she and Joe were married, she'd establish the same rule in her home. She'd set a bench in the mudroom just like Eli had, and when Joe came home from work, he could sit on the bench, remove his barn boots and slip into a pair of cozy slippers she would make for him.

The daydream made her smile.

"Ginger!" Lizzy cried the moment Ginger stepped into the kitchen. "I thought you was gone." The little girl was seated at one end of the kitchen table with a basket of fabric scraps and buttons. She was sewing little bits of fabric together the way Ginger had shown her, the same way Ginger's mother had taught her a very long time ago. "Look, *it'sh* me." She held up a rectangle of fabric two inches tall with a yellow button sewn on for a head.

"It is!" Ginger agreed.

On the far end of the kitchen table was a brightly colored tin Chinese checkers board, all set for two players. Andrew was leaning against the table, playing with an old hinge he'd found outside.

"You want to play?" Ginger asked him, pointing at the game.

Andrew made a face. "Nah."

"You like Chinese checkers?" Eli asked Ginger, looking surprised.

"I love it."

"I'll play you then. I love the game, too. I know it's simple. More of a child's game, but—" He shrugged. He was standing at the stove, stirring the succotash Ginger had put on. "I played it with my *dat* many a night, even when I was no longer a boy."

"I used to play with my *dat* all the time, too." The memory made her smile. He'd been gone five years now. "We took turns playing him, my sisters and me. No one could beat him but me. Though that didn't happen often," she admitted.

"I was always pretty good myself." He walked toward the table, drying his hands on a dish towel. "Let's see if I can beat you."

She glanced at the stove. "The roast should be ready in half an hour or so. The potatoes should—"

"Just turned them on," he said, sliding into the chair at the head of the table where the board was set up. He tapped the chair to his right. "Come on. It'll be fun."

Eli smiled at Ginger across the round, colorful tin board that looked old and well loved. Bought new, the game board sometimes contained pegs instead of marbles. This one was marbles— red and green—set up in triangles across from each other. "You go first."

She took the chair. She had been on the verge of falling into a sour mood due to Joe's tardiness, but now she was smiling. "You sure you want to play me? You won't be embarrassed in front of your daughter, will you?" She indicated Lizzy, who was engrossed with her sewing.

He made a face at Ginger. "Why would I be embarrassed?"

She laughed. "When I beat you." And then she took her turn.

Ginger didn't beat Eli on the first game, but she did the second. They laughed and chatted while playing, taking turns getting up to check the potatoes and the succotash bubbling on the stove. Eli told her a funny story about one of the boys, sixteen years old and new to the building crew, who had played a practical joke on the father, who was also on the crew. The boy had opened their lunch boxes and passed his father a sandwich made with chocolate chip cookies between the slices of bread instead of meat and cheese. The joke had been on the boy because his father had eaten every bite, remarking how good the sandwich was. And Ginger had told Eli about her twin sister, Bay's growing greenhouse and garden shop business. Bay had started it with Benjamin's son Joshua, and even though there were other greenhouses in the area, their customers were increasing each week. They were planning to have a Christmas shop this year selling fresh-picked greenery and homemade wreaths and garlands, and were even going to give a workshop on how to make a fresh wreath.

"We should play again," Eli dared when they finished the second game and were tied.

"Supper is ready." She pointed to the stove. The roast was resting on the stovetop. They'd prepared the potatoes together between turns at the game board. Eli had mashed; she had added just the right amount of buttermilk and salt.

"Supper can wait," Eli told Ginger. He glanced at Lizzy, still sitting at the other end of the table, busy with her scraps of fabric.

"The children are hungry," Ginger argued.

"They're not hungry. I bet they ate cookies all day." He looked at his daughter. "Lizzy, you're not hungry, are you?"

The three-year-old looked up from her project. "*Ya.* I want *potatoesh.* I'm tired of *shoup.*"

Ginger raised her brows at Eli as if to say "I told you so."

"Then you should eat with us, Ginger." He got up from the table, taking the checkerboard with him. "And I won't take no for an answer. You made enough roast beef for two suppers."

"The extra is for you to pack for lunch tomorrow."

"Still too much," he noted. "I can't eat an entire roast for lunch. I'd be napping away the afternoon instead of working."

Ginger chuckled as she checked the clock on the wall. Joe was almost two hours late. She glanced out the window. And it was dark now. She wasn't sure what to do: start walking home, have something to eat and wait or—

The unmistakable sound of hoofbeats and buggy wheels came from outside and was immediately joined by the sound of Molly barking.

"He's here! I best go." Ginger leaped up from the chair and hurried to put on her boots and cloak. "It was fun to play checkers," she called over her shoulder.

Eli offered a quick smile and then turned to the stove. "*Ya.* See you tomorrow."

Something in the sound of his voice made her turn back to look at him. His gaze met hers, and he held it for a moment. The way he was looking at her made her feel strange. Strange but not uncomfortable. There was…a warmth in his gaze. "See you tomorrow," she repeated. Then she hurried outside, putting a bright smile on her face. "Joe!" she called to him. Feeling somehow upended, she didn't look back at the house, even though she knew Eli was standing in the doorway, watching her go.

On a Thursday just after noon, Ginger put the finishing touches on the wedding table called the *eck*, where her newly married friends Mary Lewis and Caleb Gruber would share their first meal as man and wife. It was the Amish tradition for a woman to marry in her parents' home, but there were so many wedding guests, Mary's family had transformed the family's barn into a beautiful dining room. They had swept and scrubbed the cement floor until it was as clean as a kitchen floor. Then they had hung white bedsheets to hide the barn walls and stalls and they'd set up more than a dozen tables and covered them with fine tablecloths. Benches and chairs had been added to seat a hundred and fifty guests, and then the whole makeshift room had been transformed with white china and colored glass dishware, bales of straw, pumpkins and vases of fall grasses and leaves. Ginger and the other single girls had adorned the *eck* not just with miniature white and orange pumpkins and mums and marigolds, but also with paper hearts as well as vases of celery, which was an Amish tradition. And now that the wedding ceremony was over and Mary and Caleb were wed, the traditional dinner would be served.

The ceremony had been typical for Kent County Old Order Amish with a three-hour morning church service. Preacher Barnabas, Caleb's father, had given a long sermon based on the book of Tobit, which had always been one of Ginger's favorite books of the Bible. The sermon was followed by hymns sung by wedding guests while Mary and Caleb met alone with the bishop for last-minute scriptural and personal words of wisdom. Then the couple had joined the congregation and made their vows, before friends and family, to care for each other and remain faithful until death parted them. The wedding ceremony ended with the couple and the guests kneeling for a final prayer led by Mary's bishop. And now everyone was ready to celebrate with the wedding dinner, which would be followed by more singing, visiting, matchmaking and the bride and groom opening their gifts. The day would wrap up with a wedding supper for a smaller crowd.

It was a big wedding with not only family and friends attending from Hickory Grove and Rose Valley, but from as far away as Kansas and Kentucky. With the ceremony complete, the women were now preparing to put on the midday meal. There would be roast chicken and beef, mashed potatoes and gravy, cabbage, dinner rolls, canned pears, canned peaches and Jell-O salads. And of course no Amish wedding dinner was complete without the traditional creamed celery dish.

As Ginger put a finishing touch on a garland of wheat sheaves draped across the front of the *eck*, she spotted Joe. He was standing in a knot of young, unmarried men, all in their twenties. Her stepbrother Levi was among them. Levi, who was home visiting from Lancaster County, where he was serving an apprenticeship as a buggy maker, had stood up with Caleb during the wedding ceremony. He and Mary's friend Alma, who also stood up with the couple, would join the newlyweds at the *eck*.

Like all of the weddings Ginger had attended, the ceremony had been solemn and beautiful in its simplicity. In his final comments, the bishop had emphasized the unbreakable holy bond created by marriage and the importance of this bond, not only to the couple but to the entire church community.

Ginger stood there at the bride and groom's table for a moment, hoping Joe would notice her. When he didn't, she waved at him, trying inconspicuously to get his attention.

Levi caught Ginger's eye and knitted his eyebrows questioningly. It was apparent he didn't approve of her behavior.

Ginger returned her attention to the table, straightening the silverware and wondering what he knew about her and Joe. The previous night, when Levi had arrived home, their sister Tara had chewed his ear off, telling him all of the news in Hickory Grove, and Ginger was certain she had heard her name spoken. She hoped she would get a chance to talk to Levi alone before he returned to Lancaster on Saturday. Levi had dated quite a bit since he moved to Pennsylvania, so she was hoping he might have some advice to give her as to how to navigate her relationship with Joe. She didn't want to be forward, but she also wanted to make it clear to Joe that she was a good girl and that her intention in dating him was to look toward a public courtship and then marriage.

Ginger's gaze fell on Joe, and she waved again. This time he saw her. She smiled the way she knew boys liked to be smiled at. Then she looked around to be sure her mother wasn't watching her, because if she was, she'd have something to say about Ginger being too flirty. The day before, while baking noodle casseroles to bring to the wedding, her mother had made an offhand remark about how if a girl had to chase a boy, chances were, he didn't want to be caught. She hadn't said it directly to Ginger, but Ginger had known the comment was meant for her.

Luckily, her mother was nowhere in sight. She was probably up at the house, helping Mary's aunts prepare the wedding dinner. Ginger had offered to help in the kitchen, but the aunts had sent her and several other unmarried girls away, telling them this was the time to socialize with wedding guests. "Never know when there might be another groom in the crowd," Mary's aunt Dorcas had said with a giggle.

At last, Joe acknowledged Ginger with a nod. He said something to the other men in the group and then slowly made his way around two tables to where she was standing at the *eck*. He was dressed similarly to the other male wedding guests: black pants and shirt-waist; white, long sleeve shirt; and clean black shoes.

But he was so handsome that he stood out among the Kent County boys like a glittering diamond in a sack of acorns.

Standing in front of the *eck*, watching Joe walk toward her, Ginger thought dreamily of her own wedding and *eck*. She imagined sitting at the table beside Joe, sharing dinner, laughing with her guests and holding Joe's hand under the table. Everyone would comment on how perfect they were for each other and what a handsome couple they made. She wondered how big a wedding it would be. Would they invite a lot of guests, or would they make it a quieter affair? Would they go straight to Lancaster to set up housekeeping at Joe's house, or would they hire a van and go visiting, as many newlyweds did before setting up their home, staying with friends and relatives as far away as California or Canada?

"Nice service," Ginger said to Joe. "A hundred and fifty guests."

"*Ya.*" Joe took a toothpick from a tiny crock on the *eck* and thrust it between his teeth.

Her first impulse was to chastise him. He wasn't supposed to be taking things from the *eck*. It was bad manners. But she held her tongue, reminding herself that rules were different in Lancaster.

Rather than looking at her, Joe's gaze wandered over the crowd as he spoke. "Not as big as the weddings we have in Lancaster. Last year, we had four hundred for my sister Trudy's wedding. We put up a kitchen tent to make all of the food."

"So you like a big wedding?" she asked, gazing up at him with a smile. He was freshly shaven, and if she didn't know better, she would have thought she smelled cologne on him. Amish men and women didn't wear colognes or perfumes. But that didn't mean a young man, thinking himself still in his *rumspringa*, didn't cross such a small line—especially one who hadn't been baptized, like Joe. During a young man's or woman's *rumspringa,* parents and elders allowed a certain amount of freedom.

"We roasted two pigs in a pit in our yard," he told her, his gaze still drifting to the crowd. "I stayed up all night, keeping the fire going. My *mam* said she couldn't have done it without me. Folks said it was the best wedding dinner they'd ever attended, on account of those pigs."

"Pigs in a hole in the ground?" Ginger asked, half thinking he was pulling her leg. "I've never heard of such a thing. Your *mam* cooked them that way?"

Joe looked down at her. "Dug a big hole, lined it with rocks and put the pigs in the hole and covered it up with rocks and dirt. The fire over it heated the rocks, which cooked the pork."

She laughed at the idea of it. "Did it take a long time?"

Again, his gaze strayed, this time fixing on something or someone over her right shoulder. "Like I said, all night. I don't know what time we put them on. Probably roasted those hogs eighteen hours or so."

Wondering what he was looking at, she glanced over her shoulder. Two rows of tables behind her stood a group of unmarried young women. Girls Ginger didn't know, probably the Grubers' relatives from elsewhere. Weddings were always a good way for unmarried young men and women to meet potential husbands and wives.

Ginger looked back at Joe, shifting her stance so she blocked his view of the young women who were now giggling openly in his direction. "You think you'll be able to give me a ride home tomorrow?" she asked. "From Eli's? I know you said you might—"

"Not sure where my uncle needs me," he interrupted. "I might be at our building site closer to Hartly."

She pressed her lips together. "So… I should wait for you or what?" Against her will, her tone turned a bit sharp.

Joe looked down at her.

Ginger couldn't read his face, and she suddenly wondered why she was pursuing him at all. Did he really have feelings for her, or did he just like being seen with her? Shouldn't *he* have been the one to initiate conversation today? Shouldn't *he* have been looking for her amongst the guests instead of the other way around? "Joe." She lowered her voice for fear someone might hear her. "I thought you said you liked me," she said boldly.

"I do, Ginger. I do."

He met her gaze, his hazel eyes for her alone at last. And she felt like she was melting.

She pressed her lips together, not sure she wanted to go on now. "You said I was the girl for you. You told me we make the perfect couple."

"We do."

He winked at her and she felt her face flush.

"Hey, Joe," one of the young men in the group called to him. "Want to head out to the fence?" He tilted his head meaningfully in the direction of the open barn doors.

Though it was late October, they had been blessed with a sunny day in the high fifties. The air was crisp but comfortable, and thankfully the clouds were light and fluffy with no sign of rain. As soon as the ceremony was over, most of the men and many of the children had moved into the barnyard to give the women room to set up the meal.

"Gotta go," Joe told Ginger, a boyish smirk on his face. "The guys need me to uh…help them out with something."

She chuckled and nodded, knowing very well what Joe and his friends were up to. It was an old tradition that young men liked to chase down the new groom and throw him over a fence. It was all in good fun and symbolized that the groom had gone from being a part of the single men to the married men. Sometimes these days, even the bride might be tossed over the fence, as well.

"I'll see you later?" she called after Joe.

He raised his hand but didn't look back at her.

Ginger watched Joe go, her gaze lingering on his broad back and golden hair. He joined the other men, and together, they all made their way toward the barnyard. She was just about to return to the *eck* when she saw Eli. He was standing on the far side of the barn at the buffet table, a covered casserole dish in his arms. Usually, dinner was served family style, but Mary, seeing herself as a modern bride, had insisted on a buffet table. Her mother, wanting her daughter's wedding day to be right in every way, had agreed.

Eli waved at her, motioning her toward him, and smiled. She waved back. Beside him stood Lizzy. It was her first social outing since her illness.

When Lizzy waved, bouncing on her feet, Ginger felt an enormous sense of relief. Lizzy was going to be okay. Ginger couldn't imagine what Eli had gone through worrying about his daughter, feeling the weight of responsibility for an ill child while still doing all of the other tasks he had to do to care for his other children.

"Ginger!" Lizzy called.

Ginger gave the *eck* one last look, deemed it beautiful and made her way around the tables and people.

Lizzy threw her arms out, and Ginger gave her a hug. Some families weren't demonstrative in their love for their children, but from what Ginger had witnessed in Eli's home, she knew he saw nothing wrong with physical signs of affection. The little girl clung to her for a long moment, and a feeling of joy enveloped Ginger.

"You didn't come and make us *breakfasht*," Lizzy said as Ginger lowered her to the floor.

"Because today we came here to celebrate Mary and Caleb's wedding."

"I know," Lizzy said, frowning. "But I *wash* hungry, Ginger."

Ginger chuckled and looked to Eli. "I imagine you still had breakfast. What did your *dat* make you?"

Again, the frown. "He made *eggsh* but I don't like *eggsh*. I like *pancakesh*. *Boo-berry*. I like your *pancakesh*, Ginger."

Eli shook his head ever so slightly. "I made scrambled eggs and cheese. And bacon and toast," he defended.

"I like *pancakesh* with *boo-berriesh*," Lizzy repeated.

"Well, maybe I'll make blueberry pancakes tomorrow," Ginger told her. "And if you feel up to it, maybe you could even help me." She gave Lizzy's prayer *kapp* string a little tug. The little girl was dressed in a rose-colored dress and white cape, with a white prayer *kapp* that was identical to Ginger's. Ginger wondered if Eli starched her *kapp,* or if that was something his sister did for him. "How would that be?" she asked.

Lizzy's smile was enormous. "I would like that."

Ginger turned to see Eli looking down at the buffet table, which went on for twenty feet. "Is there a dessert table, or should I just put this here?" he asked.

"What did you bring?" Ginger took a look and thought, *How kind of him. No other single man brought a dish.* "You know you didn't have to."

Eli shrugged.

"Ginger," Lizzy giggled. "We made worm pudding."

Ginger opened her eyes wide. "Worm pudding?" she declared with great exaggeration.

Lizzy giggled behind her hand. "Not real *wormsh.*" She walked to her father. "They're candy *wormsh.*" She pointed, almost poking her finger into the pudding. *"Shee?"*

"Candy worms?" Ginger raised her brows, looking to Eli.

He shrugged with a smile. "A tradition in our family." He pulled off the tinfoil from the pretty cut glass dish. Instead of the fruit salad or marshmallow salad one would have expected in such a delicate serving dish, the bowl was full of chocolate pudding covered in something that looked remarkably like dirt. Colored candy worms poked out of the "dirt."

"Are those real worms?" Ginger exclaimed, pretending she was afraid.

"Ne." Lizzy was still giggling. "I told you. Gummy *wormsh*!"

"Gummy worms?" Ginger glanced at Eli. His blue eyes were dancing. She returned her gaze to his daughter. "And real dirt?"

"*Ne. Cookiesh. Dat* crumbled *cookiesh* with a rolling pin. He let me help."

"Oh," Ginger said, still being silly. "I'm so glad, because I don't like dirt in my pudding."

Just then, one of Mary Gruber's younger sisters approached them. "Want to play with us, Lizzy?" ten-year-old Ann asked in Pennsylvania *Deitsch*.

Lizzy looked to her father for permission.

Eli hesitated, studying his daughter carefully. "You don't want to have a little rest? We can go inside. I'm sure Eunice won't mind if you lay down upstairs for a few minutes."

"I don't want to *shleep*," Lizzy pouted. "I want to play."

Eli hesitated, then gave a nod. "Okay. Go play, but if you get cold or tired or—"

"I won't," Lizzy said, accepting Ann's hand.

"I'll watch her," Ann told Eli solemnly. She was a thin girl, tall for her age, who wore round wire-frame glasses just like Eli's son Andrew.

Eli and Ginger stood side by side, watching Ann Gruber lead Lizzy to a corner of the barn where several little girls were playing with faceless cloth dolls on a bale of straw covered in fabric, which was meant to serve as extra seating.

Ginger looked at Eli and then the pretty glass bowl he had brought. "Worm pudding?"

He smiled. "Like I said. A tradition in our family. And fun. Right?" He turned back to the table. "I think I'll put it here with the salads. A person shouldn't have to wait for worm pudding until dessert."

She smiled. Practical jokes were often part of Amish weddings: a mousetrap in a salad, coffee that's been colored blue with food dye. "Oreo cookies for the dirt?" she asked.

"*Ya.* I just scrape the cream out of the middle."

"Ah, smart," Ginger told him. Then she turned, her arms crossed in front of her, to gaze out at the room. Joe hadn't come back into the barn.

"You going to join Joe for dinner?" Eli asked, shifting salads on the table to make room for his bowl.

She glanced at him. "Um... I don't know." While men and women tended to eat separately at large meals, especially if there was more than one seating, it was tradition that unmarried men and women paired off for the afternoon. Often the bride and groom got involved in the matchmaking. The couples ate together and then spent time visiting, getting to know each other. "Maybe."

Eli scowled. "Joe hasn't asked you?"

Chapter Four

The moment the words came out of Eli's mouth, he wished he could have taken them back. What did he care if Ginger ate with Joe Verkler? Everyone knew that a wedding was the perfect place for young, unmarried men and women to get to know each other within the guidelines established by the church. There were chaperones everywhere: parents, grandparents, children. Even a bishop or two. It was common practice for families with sons and daughters of marrying age to attend out-of-town weddings in the hopes they might meet the right young man or woman. Eli and his Elizabeth had met at a wedding in Lancaster. He had been a friend of the groom and she a friend of the bride. They had both been servers as they were called there and had sat together at the *eck*. They'd talked all day and into the night. It was love at first sight for Eli. And a few months later, he and Elizabeth had been sitting at their own *eck*.

Eli's gaze met Ginger's, bringing him back to the present, leaving the past behind. He knew very well why he cared if Ginger was eating with Joe. Because he didn't want to see her heartbroken. Because Ginger deserved better than Joe. That thought had been going through his head for weeks now. In Eli's opinion, Joe didn't show Ginger the respect a man ought to show a woman he supposedly cared for. And it wasn't just that he didn't pick her up from work on time.

Ginger was under the impression that she was the only woman Joe was walking out with, but Eli had heard Joe talking with other single men on the job. Joe was a popular man among the unmarried women of Kent County. He was so popular that some of the fathers Eli worked beside were complaining about him, saying he was nothing but a flirt and that they didn't trust him with their daughters. From what Eli gathered, the older men believed Joe was too flashy, too boastful and possibly not as honest as he should be.

Eli didn't know the boy well enough to make those observations, and he tried hard not to make judgments. What he *did* know, based on what he saw with his own eyes, was that Joe wasn't reliable. He'd tell Ginger he'd pick her up at five o'clock and then he'd be late. He'd begun arriving late to pick up Ginger after work so regularly that most evenings, she and Eli had time to play a game or two of Chinese checkers while supper cooked on the stove. It had become a ritual of sorts with them. Eli would arrive home from work, wash and instead of going outside to start feeding his livestock, he'd spend a little time with Ginger. And the children, of course. Most days, though, his little ones said hello and then wandered off to do whatever they'd been doing before he came home. Since Ginger had been caring for his children, they had become more independent, less clingy, particularly Lizzy. Before Ginger started working for him, some days it had been hard for him to get any work done at all because Lizzy wanted him beside her every waking moment. Perhaps some of that had to do with her illness, but he'd been seeing that behavior before she became sick.

Not only did the children enjoy Ginger's company, but so did Eli. That time he spent with Ginger each day had become one of his favorite parts of his weekday routine. It was time when he could talk a bit about his day with another adult and just relax before he started the endless list of chores that would take him straight through until bedtime.

Eli fussed with the serving bowl of pudding on the buffet, feeling awkward. He shouldn't have mentioned Joe to Ginger. It wasn't his business.

Ginger hesitated, then said under her breath, "You saw me trying to get his attention? Did anyone else see me?"

He shook his head. "I don't think so." He hesitated. He wanted to tell her what he thought. That she was too smart for Joe Verkler. Too mature. In so many ways, Joe seemed like a boy, and Ginger was a woman. Had Eli been in Joe's shoes, he'd have never been late to pick her up. He'd spend time with her every chance he got. And he certainly wouldn't be seeing other women.

Ginger held his gaze. She had green eyes with specks of brown and a sprinkling of freckles across her nose and cheeks. She was a beautiful woman for sure; she had a reputation for being one of the prettiest girls in Kent County with her blond hair and pert nose. But to Eli, her beauty went beyond the physical. It was her spirit he found even more beautiful. It was easy to speak of one's faith, but far more challenging to live it, and Ginger lived it so well that she brought joy to others.

To him.

It crossed Eli's mind to ask her if she'd like to join *him* for the wedding dinner. Instead of sitting with the married men as he usually did, he and Ginger could sit together at one of the singles' tables. With so many people, he doubted most people would even notice. Of course, most of the single folks were younger than he was, but his community expected him to remarry, which technically meant the same freedoms allowed to younger singles applied to him as a widower.

It was just on the tip of Eli's tongue to ask Ginger to join him for the meal when her sister hurried toward the table, her *kapp* strings flying.

"There you are!" Tara bustled toward them, carrying a cast-iron Dutch oven. Like all of the Stutzman girls, nineteen-year-old Tara was pretty. She had Ginger's green eyes, but her hair was redder than her big sister's. "*Mam*'s looking for you. Something about the blue baking dish of noodle *kuchen* missing?"

Ginger knit her brows. "Oh dear. I asked Jacob to carry it to the buggy before we left home this morning. I hope we didn't leave it. It was packed in one of *Mam*'s baskets."

"I don't know anything about that, *Schweschder*," Tara said. "Our mother asked me to tell you she was looking for you if I saw you. I guess she found the green dish, but not the blue."

"Here, let me make room for you." Knowing the pot had to be heavy, Eli started moving serving dishes around on the table to make room for the Dutch oven Tara was holding.

Tara offered a quick smile of thanks.

Eli had liked the Miller/Stutzman family the first day they had come to Hickory Grove. Benjamin and Rosemary had done something few families ever did so well, and he admired them greatly for it. Having lost their spouses of many years, they had married and somehow figured out a way to successfully blend their families. Besides Rosemary's youngest, Jesse, their ten children still living at home hadn't been little ones when they'd married. Eli knew it couldn't have been easy. But despite the many personalities and wants and needs of the household, Benjamin and Rosemary had managed to create a happy family that lived and thrived harmoniously. Not that everything always ran perfectly smoothly, but that was life, wasn't it? What mattered was that Benjamin and Rosemary were dedicated to their family, just as God meant them to be, and it showed not just in their words, but in how they carried themselves. They were some of the best role models he knew in Hickory Grove.

Ginger glanced in the direction of the doors that opened into the barnyard. "I guess I best go see what *Mam* needs," she said. She looked back at Eli. "See you tomorrow?"

"Tomorrow. But it's just a half a day. I'll be home by one. The boss is giving everyone part of the day off because of the wedding. I guess there's a bonfire or something tomorrow."

A smile lit up her face, a smile that made him warm inside. "There is," Ginger said. "I thought I'd just have to go late. There's going to be a couple of games of *eck balle* before the meal if the weather cooperates."

"*Eck* ball, you say?" He'd heard of the game, but not

seen it. It was something like dodgeball, only a small leather ball was used. The game field was a square covered in straw to cushion the players' falls, which inevitably took place.

"Levi said they play it all the time in Fivepointville, where he lives in Lancaster County."

"I'm surprised you and your friends would agree to such a thing. Girls don't usually play, do they?"

"That's why we're playing softball after the *eck balle* game," she explained. "Boys against girls. And then there's a bonfire and picnic supper. I think Mary's mother spent so much time working on the barn, they want us to use it."

"Ah. Well, if you need a ride over here." He shrugged. "I probably need to run to Byler's for groceries, anyway."

"Let me talk to *Mam*. I'm sure Tara and Nettie are going. Maybe Bay. We might just take one of the buggies." She began to back up, still talking. "I best go—" she opened her eyes wide "—and solve the mystery of the missing noodle *kuchen*."

A moment later, the Stutzman sisters were gone, and Eli stood at the buffet table, his tinfoil still in his hand, feeling foolish. Cowardly. He should have asked her. Then he thought about what he had seen from across the room—the way Ginger had looked at Joe. More importantly, the way Joe had *not* looked at her. He wondered if maybe he should pull Joe aside and tell him that if he was honestly interested in Ginger, he ought to act like it. And if he wasn't interested in her, he ought to be man enough to speak up and tell her so.

It was a ridiculous idea, of course. Eli knew that.

Who was he to say such a thing to Joe? It wasn't his place.

He scanned the beautifully decorated room that was barely recognizable as a barn unless one looked up to see the rafters. It was a wonder what the women had done with pumpkins and wheat sheaves and such for decorations. The place didn't even smell like a barn, thanks to the small dishes of ground cinnamon, nutmeg, cloves and dried orange peel scattered on the tables. And the corner table where the bride and groom would soon sit was as pretty as any he had ever seen. He had the feeling that Ginger had played a part in making the *eck* so beautiful with such simple objects as colored glass dishes and jelly jars of celery.

The barn was beginning to fill with guests in anticipation of the meal that would soon be served. Amish men and women, as well as a few English folks, laughed and talked while children darted around, playing games. He thought maybe he would take a walk outside, see if he could catch a glimpse of his boys who were, hopefully, not up to no good, and then maybe join the men standing at the fence talking about what men talked about—crops and weather.

"Not the worm pudding again, Eli?"

Eli startled and turned around to see his sister behind him. Had she seen him talking to Ginger? "The children like it, Claudia," he explained. "We made two dishes. One to bring and one for home."

"You spoil them," she told him, crossing her arms. She was tall for a woman, and slender, even though she'd given birth to seven children. But Claudia was still pretty, he thought. With every passing year, she looked more like their mother, who had been just Claudia's age now when they had lost her.

"I saw you talking with Ginger."

Caught. He didn't say anything.

She sighed, gazing out over the room. He could hear her disapproval in her exhalation of breath. "I want you to meet someone. Her name is Elsie Swartzentruber. Widowed a year now. With only one child," she added, as if that would make Elsie more appealing to him. She was always trying to set him up with women. Women who didn't interest him.

Eli lowered his head. *"Claudia."* He drew out her name.

"Eli." She spoke his name the way he had spoken hers. "She's nice. And a faithful woman. And…*nice,*" she repeated as if she could think of nothing else to say.

"I don't need my sister to introduce me to women," he said, walking away from her to add the foil to a pile at the end of the table so it could be reused.

"I think you do." She followed him, whispering so no one else would hear them. "Elsie is a suitable match. Only thirty-six her last birthday. Old enough to have some sense but still young enough to have more children. She's here with Josiah Yoder, from Seven Poplars. He's her brother. Come say hello. She has a nice farm in Ohio. Big, I hear."

"Claudia, I have a farm of my own. I'm not moving to Ohio."

"I'm sure Elsie would be willing to move to Delaware. Then she'd be closer to her brother and his family."

"Elsie doesn't need to move here because I'm not marrying her. I'm not walking out with her." He added the folded piece of tinfoil to the pile and turned to his sister. "I'm not even going to meet her. I'm going to go outside—" he pointed toward the open doors "—and seek the company of men. Men who won't be trying to marry me off to Elsie Yoder."

"Swartzentruber," Claudia corrected.

Eli walked past his sister and out into the cool autumn air. He wished Claudia would stop trying to set him up. He also wished he'd had the courage to ask Ginger to sit with him. Or the good sense to know his attraction to her wasn't going to go anywhere.

"A perfect match, Mary and Caleb," Atarah remarked to Ginger as she pulled hot dogs out of a package and placed them on a platter. She was one of Mary's cousins from Kentucky, chubby and towheaded, with thick glasses, a pointed chin and a sweet disposition. "And such a fun wedding supper last night. I laughed and laughed when Mary had Caleb open the wedding gift from our uncle, and the plastic spider popped out." She began to chuckle. "I've never seen Caleb move so fast!"

Ginger smiled as she busied herself beside Atarah at the kitchen counter. The Amish loved practical jokes, but apparently, Mary's family *really* loved them. There had also been a gift of a mixing bowl full of felt mice.

A group of friends and family were gathered in Mary's mother's kitchen, preparing snacks and supper for the bonfire frolic. Mary's parents had gone visiting for the day to allow the young people to enjoy themselves without an older member of the community dampening their fun. The bride and groom were expected anytime after going to visit an ailing aunt in Seven Poplars.

"It was even more fun when the older folks went home," Atarah's sister, Tamar, piped up. "I loved the singing."

"We don't get to sing fast hymns very often back in Kentucky," Atarah explained. "Our bishop thinks they'll lead us astray." She rolled her eyes.

Atarah and Tamar were identical twins and dressed, acted and sounded alike. They had heavy Kentucky accents when they spoke English. Their accents were so thick that at first, Ginger had had a hard time understanding what they were saying. Introduced to them the previous day at the wedding, Ginger could tell the two apart only by the dark mole on Atarah's cheek. Ginger had taken to the sisters immediately and ended up sitting with them for dinner and supper after the wedding because Joe hadn't asked her.

That afternoon there was a mixed crowd at Mary's house, though it was mostly folks in their twenties. Some of the women there were married, some walking out with prospective husbands, and others, like Atarah and Tamar, hoping to find someone special.

Ginger listened as she took two containers of leftover stuffed eggs from the wedding supper and combined them into one. It bothered her that she didn't know which group she was in. Was she spoken for or not? She thought that she and Joe had an agreement, even if he hadn't come straight out and said so. During the week, he gave her a ride home from Eli's most nights, and on weekends, they attended the same frolics, and he always took her home afterward. He'd even tried to kiss her one night, though she'd set him straight on that matter pretty quickly. That meant they were courting, didn't it? But then he'd basically ignored her at the wedding yesterday. She was confused and a little disheartened. And her mother's disapproval nagged at her. What if her mother was right? What if Joe wasn't a good match for her?

"*Hymns* are going to lead you astray?" Ellie, a friend of the bride's from Seven Poplars, slapped the kitchen counter with her hand from her perch on a stool and laughed. Ellie was a little person who, like Ginger's brother Ethan, was a schoolteacher. Ginger had heard that summer that now that Ellie was married to the farrier, Jakob, she would be resigning from her position to focus on her duties as a wife. So far, however, Ellie was still teaching. Ellie was in her late twenties, about four feet tall and quite attractive, with her neat figure, blond hair and blue eyes. Ellie's freckled face was as fair as any young woman's in Kent County, and she was always smiling and laughing.

With so many in town for Caleb and Mary's wedding, a whole weekend of festivities had been planned. That night the men were going to play a couple of rounds of *eck balle*, then there would be a bonfire supper followed by singing. There were hot dogs and sausages to roast to go along with the leftover macaroni and potato salads and creamed celery, among other dishes. And Mary's mother had bought four boxes of graham crackers, four bags of marshmallows and dozens of chocolate bars so everyone could make s'mores for dessert. The following afternoon, weather permitting, they had plans to have a spaghetti supper. The best part of the evening would be that the men would cook the noodles to go with the sauce already made and then serve the women.

"I don't think it's the hymns the bishop has a problem with, it's how rowdy the boys get," Tamar told her sister.

"*Ne*," Atarah disagreed. "I think he heard—"

"That there *was clapping*," Tamar finished.

The twin sisters looked at each other and giggled, making Ginger smile. She and Bay were fraternal twins and were close, but these two girls almost seemed more like one person than two. They even completed each other's sentences.

"Nothing like a good ole Amish scandal," Ellie remarked, shaking her head with a smile as she covered a casserole of hot baked beans and ground hamburger with foil.

"I thought Kent County never had scandals," a young woman with inky black hair covered with a black prayer kapp said. Ginger couldn't remember her name.

"I don't know about that. I heard Mary's mother talking to her sister about that handsome one," Tamar said conspiratorially. She began cutting a pan of lemon bars into squares.

"Joe Verkler," Atarah put in with a giggle. "He's—"

"*Trouble*," her sister said.

The moment Joe's name was mentioned, Ginger stiffened. Her first impulse was to defend Joe, but her curiosity won her over, and she concentrated on moving the last of the creamy eggs into their container as she listened. She imagined this was about Joe's sneakers with the Swoosh, and possibly the expensive sunglasses.

Older folks could get themselves worked up about things like that. To them, even a fancy pair of black sneakers represented change in their way of life, and it was important to their faith that they remain separate from the world. That they never become dependent upon it. It was a constant issue in Hickory Grove, in most Amish communities, really. It had been the same way in upstate New York, where Ginger had grown up. The churches constantly had to reassess their *Ordung,* which was the guide to community standards and the doctrine that defined sin. Sometimes the changes were forced upon them due to the shift from farm to nonfarm employment for men, like the necessity of cell phones. Other times, it was the younger men and women who pushed for simple changes like what board games were acceptable to play. Many men and women Ginger's age believed a simple board game wouldn't cause a misstep in faith. They believed their elders needed to have more trust in them than that.

"*Ya,*" Atarah went on. "That one with his long hair and fancy—"

"Sneakers," Tamar finished for her again.

Several of the unmarried girls giggled, and Ginger pressed her lips together. Maybe Joe's hair was a little longer than most men wore theirs, but it wasn't as if it was as long as a woman's. In her opinion, anyone worried about Joe's sneakers was making a mountain out of a molehill.

"*Ach.* Sneakers does not a man make." Ellie climbed down off her stool and, using hot mitts, carried the casserole dish of beans to the kitchen table. The plan was to gather all of the food for supper and then have the men carry it out to the picnic tables that had already been taken out to the field where they would have the bonfire.

At Ellie's gentle scolding, the giggling girls went quiet, busying themselves with their food preparation.

"And a man's footwear does not a scandal make," Ellie advised. "'The Lord seeth not as man seeth, for man looketh on the outward appearance, but the Lord looketh on the heart.'"

"It's not his shoes," the girl Ginger didn't know said in a hushed tone. "It's his *flirting.*" She whispered the last word. "He was talking up my sister yesterday at the wedding, and she's just seventeen. *Unfitting*, my *mam* says."

"I heard someone saw him buying beer," one of the Fisher girls whispered loudly. She pointed a mayonnaise-covered spoon, motioning with it to emphasize her words. "In one of those *liquor stores.*"

Atarah leaned forward, her eyes wide. "But how would anyone know that unless *they* were in the store?"

Alcoholic beverages were not allowed to be consumed among the Old Order Amish. That said, it was not unheard of for young men, not yet baptized, to dabble in beer consumption and even cigarette smoking. While the church districts in Kent County did not recognize *rumspringa*, Ginger knew from her brother living in Lancaster County, Pennsylvania, that it was accepted there. That was no excuse for Joe. But it might not even be true. What was more disturbing to Ginger was the possibility that Joe had been flirting with this girl's sister. Ginger assumed she and Joe were dating exclusively.

"I don't know," Tamar said. "Maybe one of the elders—"

A door off the kitchen opened and the tread of heavy footsteps sounded. It was one of the men.

"*Hist*," Ellie warned. "No one likes a gossip, men looking for wives least of all."

Everyone in the kitchen went quiet, returning to their tasks.

"Wow, you all sure are quiet." Caleb, the groom, walked into the kitchen and halted, hands on his hips.

"Fire's going. We've got some boys outside who are hungry enough to eat a pork shoulder on their own. Think we can get some of those hot dogs? Just to hold us over? Maybe eat a little something and get this *eck balle* game going before it starts to get dark?"

Atarah reached for the platter of hot dogs she'd been preparing, but Ginger spoke before the girl could. "I'll bring them out," she volunteered, turning to face Caleb and blocking his view of Atarah.

"Oh." Caleb shrugged. "Okay, well…" He gazed around the room. "Mary will be inside in a minute. She got waylaid in the driveway by one of the neighbors."

The moment Caleb walked out of the kitchen, Ginger slid the serving plate of hot dogs off the counter. "I'll carry these out. Best make another plate," she told Atarah, grabbing a big bag of rolls off the kitchen table as she went by. "You don't know the men in Kent County. They can eat a lot."

Before Atarah or any of the other girls offered to take the hot dogs outside themselves, Ginger headed for the back door. She threw her jacket on and hurried outside.

Sidestepping a little spotted dog at the bottom of the porch steps, Ginger walked quickly across the barnyard, the dog following. They went through an open gate into the field. She was halfway to the blazing bonfire when she spotted Joe standing near her brother Levi, who was busy cutting wood. Levi was chopping and stacking. Joe was talking to someone else.

As Ginger set the plate and bag of rolls down on the nearest picnic table, Joe moved, and she spotted who he was talking to. It was Annie Swartzentruber. Ginger knew her from Spence's Bazaar. Her family sold baked goods and the most amazing cinnamon rolls. The rolls, which were the size of a dessert plate, were always sold out on Fridays by 11:00 a.m., no matter how many they made.

Joe said something to Annie that made her giggle, and Ginger felt her face grow hot with annoyance. Was he flirting with her? He was! Without a second thought, Ginger marched over to where the two were standing between the pile of wood to be burned and the fire. The sound of Levi's ax striking wood reverberated in the cool afternoon air.

"Hello, Annie," Ginger said, her voice tight.

Annie met Ginger's gaze with surprise, then embarrassment. As if she'd been caught doing something she knew she shouldn't be. So Joe *had* been flirting with her.

"Ginger." Annie nodded without making eye contact this time. "Guess I best go see if anyone needs help in the kitchen."

Ginger folded her arms over her chest. "I'm sure they could use your help."

Levi took one look at his stepsister, hearing the tone of her voice, and his eyes widened. He turned back to the pile of wood, lifted the ax and let it fall on a piece of thick wood with a loud crack.

Joe looked at Levi, then back at Ginger. He gave her a big smile, and she felt herself melting inside. "I was just looking for you," he said.

She set her jaw. She wasn't going to let him get away with it this time. "No, you were not. You were flirting with Annie." She pointed in the direction the girl had just gone.

"Flirting?" He slid his hands into his pockets, making a face that suggested Ginger was mistaken. "I was just talking."

"Talking, my eye," she sputtered. "I heard her giggling!" She crossed her arms again and turned toward the blazing fire. There was a pile of small branches, and she picked one up to add to the fire.

Joe touched her arm and moved up beside her. "Ginger, I can't help it if she laughed. I don't even know her." He gestured in the direction Annie had gone. "I was just being polite."

Ginger eyed Joe, then turned to her stepbrother. "Levi, you think Joe was flirting with Annie?"

"Don't get me involved in this. I'm just chopping wood for the bonfire." Levi sank the ax into a log that was the size of a peck basket, grabbed several pieces of freshly cut wood and walked around to the other side of the bonfire.

It was on the tip of Ginger's tongue to straight-out ask Joe if they were walking out together or not, but then she suddenly grew worried that this was all her fault. What if she wasn't a good girlfriend? What if Joe was seeking out another girl's company because she was too boring or…or… Whatever.

Ginger moved closer to the bonfire and poked at it with the branch. The fire cracked and popped and sent sparks flying. One stung her on the back of her hand, and she flung the branch. "Ouch!" She looked at her hand, and by the bright light of the flames, she could see a red welt already bubbling up. "I burned myself," she said.

He stepped closer. "Ginger," he said sweetly. "I hope you're not upset about Annie. It was completely innocent."

She pressed the back of her hand to her mouth. It was already blistering up. She needed to get some salve for it and maybe a Band-Aid.

"I already told you, you're the girl for me." He gazed into her eyes with his big blue eyes. "So stop worrying your pretty head. Let's have some fun."

The way he was smiling at her, she couldn't help but smile back. He was right, of course. They *were* here to have fun. So she put on her sweetest smile and let him tell her about his *eck balle* strategy.

Chapter Five

"Don't worry."

It had sounded easy enough when Joe had said it, but the following morning, Ginger was still worrying. She kept going over in her head what she could do differently so Joe wouldn't want to flirt with other girls like Annie. She didn't know what to do to keep him interested in her. Because they were a good match. He'd said so himself. Everyone in Hickory Grove thought they looked like the perfect couple. Perfect for each other.

Well…except her mother. And her twin sister.

Ginger needed to talk to someone about Joe, but who? Her mother certainly wouldn't be receptive. Nor Bay. And her younger sisters wouldn't understand. While they were attending frolics now, neither had gotten serious with anyone yet. Ginger had thought about visiting her older sister, Lovey. She lived close enough to walk, but Lovey and Marshall's little one, Elijah, had taken sick with a bad cold the morning of the wedding, and Ginger didn't want to bother her.

Of course, Ginger did have a few girlfriends she might be able to talk with, but lately, it was Eli who was her confidant. Not that they talked about Joe exactly, but Eli was always easy to talk to. And such a good listener. He seemed to know when she just wanted him to listen while she worked something out or when she wanted advice. When she talked, he gave her his full attention. And he managed to beat her at Chinese checkers at the same time.

The thought made her smile.

She wondered if Eli would be a good person to talk to about Joe. Eli was, after all, a man. Maybe he could offer some insight.

Ginger went through her weekend morning routine as she mulled over the situation. She washed her face, brushed her teeth, dressed in an everyday dress and apron and tied a scarf on her head. She made breakfast with her mother and sisters: scrambled eggs and scrapple, apple cinnamon muffins fresh out of the oven and buttered sourdough toast. After the morning meal, she did dishes and took the scraps out to the chickens. As she was coming back into the house, she ran into her mother. Actually bumped into her, because she wasn't paying attention to where she was going.

Her mother caught her by the shoulders and looked into Ginger's eyes, her own eyes twinkling with amusement. "Woolgathering, *Dochtah*?"

"*Ne*…" Ginger moved the scraps pail from one hand to the other. The back of her hand, covered by a Band-Aid, was still tender from where she had burned it the previous day. "*Ya*, I suppose I was."

Her mother narrowed her gaze, studying Ginger. "I recognize that look. A woman your age can't help but think about husbands and babies after attending a wedding."

Ginger felt herself blush, embarrassed by the mention of babies. Of course she wanted children, but she wasn't ready to think of Joe and babies in the same thought.

"Plenty of nice young men visiting Hickory Grove this weekend," her mother went on. She was wearing an everyday dress that was rose-colored. Her hair was covered with a blue scarf, and she wore her reading glasses dangling from a piece of ribbon around her neck. Though her stepson Joshua and his wife, Phoebe, would make her a grandmother again in the spring, she certainly didn't look old enough to be one. "And some *goot* choices living right here."

Ginger didn't say anything. She already knew her mother didn't approve of Joe. She wasn't going to remind her that she'd already made her choice. And that it was Ginger's choice to make.

Her mother was quiet for what seemed like a very long time. She just stood there in the mudroom, looking at Ginger, somehow making her feel unsettled. Then at last, her mother said, "What are your plans for the day? Are you joining the girls at Mary's house to see the wedding gifts?"

Caleb and Mary had opened their gifts at the wedding, but there had been so many that her mother had invited all of Mary's friends over for gingerbread and hot cocoa to see what she'd been given.

"*Ya*, I think I will, but that's not until two." She met her mother's gaze. She trusted Eli, and she knew nothing she said would go beyond the two of them.

"If you don't need me for anything, I was thinking I'd run over to Eli's."

"Oh?" Her mother raised her eyebrows.

Ginger's mother broke into a smile. "Eli's? On your day off? I see."

I see? What did that mean? There was something about her tone that concerned Ginger. "I… I want to take the children some of the apple muffins we made this morning." Not exactly a fib. She *had* thought that morning at breakfast that the little ones would enjoy the fresh muffins. And Lizzy had lost so much weight during her illness that her pediatrician had encouraged Eli to increase her food intake. "Eli is a pretty good cook, but his baking?" She shook her head.

"Taking muffins to the children?" her mother asked. "And you're not going for any other reason? *On your day off*," she added.

"What other reason would I have?" Ginger asked, confused by her mother's tone and demeanor. What did her *mam* know that Ginger didn't? She took a step to the side to go around her.

But her mother didn't budge. And she was still smiling.

"Is… Is it okay that I go?" Ginger asked. "I'm not scheduled to work at the harness shop today."

"Of course. I think Eli's children would love some apple muffins." Finally, she stepped aside to let her daughter pass. "And I imagine Eli would enjoy a muffin, as well."

It was clear now by her *mam*'s tone as to her meaning. That Eli *liked* her.

The idea of it scared Ginger. And intrigued her at the same time.

Ginger spent the entire ride over to Eli's on her push scooter thinking not about her problem with Joe, but about her mother's insinuation. It wasn't until the family dog greeted her at the end of the lane that she pushed aside thoughts of Eli, because it was a ridiculous idea. Eli didn't *like* her. Not *that* way. And she... She certainly didn't—well, it didn't matter what feelings she might or might not have for her employer because she already had a beau. And *that* was why she was coming to see Eli in the first place.

The dog barked and raced in a tight circle around Ginger's push scooter. "Careful!" she warned with a laugh. "You're going to—"

Suddenly, Molly cut so close in front of Ginger's scooter that she had to turn the front wheel sharply to avoid hitting the dog. As she did, she slid in some loose gravel. One second she was balanced on her push scooter, and the next, she was lying on her side, the scooter on top of her. "Ouch," she muttered, stunned momentarily. She lifted her head, then lowered it to the ground again to catch her breath.

Molly pushed her cold, wet nose against Ginger's face.

"Ew, no." She gave the dog a gentle push and then got to her feet. The backpack of muffins on her back was still there and she hadn't squished them. She carefully moved each arm and leg. She was fine, nothing broken. Her dress was dirty, but somehow wasn't torn. Her cheekbone stung and she pressed her fingertips to it. She winced. Just a scrape. The only real pain she had was at her elbow. It burned. She raised her arm to see a tear in her denim coat. She poked her fingers through the hole to her elbow and felt something wet and warm. Blood.

"Look what you've done," she told the dog, wiping

her fingers on the front of the coat. The blood could be washed out, the coat patched. She looked at the dog as she picked up her scooter. "You could have been hurt if I'd hit you," she told it.

Molly just sat in the middle of the lane, looking up at her with big brown eyes. It was the dog's eyes that had gotten under Eli's skin when he'd found her in that parking lot. That was what he had told Ginger, and she completely understood. In many ways, Eli reminded her of her stepfather, Benjamin. Benjamin wore his heart on his sleeve, and he wasn't embarrassed by it. At first, it had taken some getting used to, seeing him show his affection for her mother. Ginger had never doubted her father had loved her mother or her and her siblings, but he'd not been a demonstrative man. He hadn't been one for words or physical affection; he had shown his love for his family in his deeds. This was refreshing, though. And she liked the trait in Eli.

Molly trotted up the driveway, then stopped and turned back as if waiting for Ginger.

"I'm coming," she told Molly. She shifted her backpack. At least the muffins hadn't been ruined. She lifted the scooter's handlebars and began to push it up the lane, deciding not to get on it again.

Phillip greeted them in the barnyard. "Ginger's here!" the five-year-old shouted. He dropped the handle of a red wagon he'd been pulling and ran toward her. "*Dat!* Ginger's here!"

When the boy started to run, the dog got excited and began to bark.

All thoughts of her little mishap went out the window at the sound of Phillip's excitement to see her.

"Ginger's here!" shouted Andrew, coming out of the granary with a bucket of ears of field corn.

A moment later, Simon appeared in the doorway of the granary. "Ginger!" His face lit up and her heart melted.

While Eli's oldest boy was the most reserved, he'd quickly taken to her. In the last weeks they had formed a special bond, so special that he had begun giving her a quick hug before she left each day, and he seemed to appreciate her affection for him. Unlike the other children, he remembered his mother well, and missed her all the more for it, Ginger thought. Not that she felt she was in any way replacing his mother, but she was willing to do anything she could to help Eli's children. She'd become so attached to them in the month since she'd begun watching them that she didn't want even to consider what would happen when Eli's job was done and he didn't need her anymore.

All three boys were dressed for outdoor chores in patched denim trousers with denim coats and a knit cap pulled down over their ears. They needed haircuts, she noticed. She'd have to say something to Eli. She'd be happy to cut their hair, but she didn't want to overstep her bounds.

"What are you doing here?" Simon set down the bucket and walked toward her.

"Did you come to play?" Phillip asked in Pennsylvania *Deitsch*. His cap was too big for him and was threatening to cover his eyes, but he didn't seem to notice. "Can I ride your scooter?" He grabbed the handlebars, which were almost as tall as he was. "*Dat* says when I go to school next year, I can have a scooter like Simon and Andrew." He made a face. "But he says I have to wear an orange vest so Englishers can see me." He frowned.

"He thinks school will be fun," Andrew told her, joining them. He rolled his eyes comically at Ginger.

Ginger chuckled, and then looked down at Phillip. She pushed his cap back so she could see his eyes again. "You *can* try my scooter but it's big for you," she said in English. "I think you'd do better trying one of your brothers'."

He gripped the handlebars, testing them out. "But yours is *blau* and theirs is *schwarz*."

"*Ya*, mine is blue. And theirs are black," she said, not directly correcting his speech. Though Phillip wasn't in school yet, Eli believed that he should be speaking English as well as his native tongue.

"Blue," he repeated, and grinned. "*Ya*. Yours is blue."

"Ginger!"

She turned around to see Lizzy running out of the barn, bundled in a coat, a knit cap on her head, a scarf around her neck and gloves on her hands. "I said you was coming!" she cried in Pennsylvania *Deitsch* as she raced across the yard as fast as her little legs could carry her. Her cheeks shone bright and rosy. "*Dat* said you weren't, but I knew you were." Reaching Ginger, the little girl threw her arms around Ginger's legs. She peered up, switching to English. "I *misshed* you."

Ginger laughed and squatted down to hug Lizzy. "And I missed you."

All talking at once, the three boys gathered around Ginger's scooter and rolled it away.

"I thought I heard your voice."

Ginger glanced up as Eli strode out of the barn, and the strangest sensation went through her. He looked the same as always and yet… Somehow, he seemed different. Why? How? Was it because her mother had suggested Eli liked her—the way a boy likes a girl? Lots of boys and men found her attractive. That didn't matter to her. What she looked like was God's doing, not her own.

She watched Eli as he walked toward her, seeing him in a different light than she had seen him before.

He liked her.

And if she was completely honest with herself, she *liked* him, too.

"What brings you here?" Eli was smiling. "Not that you have to have a reason to come by. You know you're always welcome. The children were disappointed this morning that it was a Saturday and you wouldn't be here. Lizzy wanted me to bring her to your house at about six, but I didn't know that you would appreciate such an early visit."

His laugh was easy and comforting in the way that a cozy blanket or a cup of hot chocolate was on a cold evening.

Ginger slowly came to her feet, looking up at him. "You could have brought her over. I was up."

Lizzy remained where she was, holding on to Ginger's apron.

"I brought the children some muffins," Ginger explained. "We made them fresh this morning. I don't know what Nettie was thinking but she made enough for everyone in Hickory Grove."

Eli looked down at his daughter. "Did you hear that, *boppli*?" He reached out and touched Lizzy's cheek, the smile suddenly disappearing from his face. "She seems warm. Does she seem warm to you?" He touched his daughter's face again and Lizzy wiggled away. "And her cheeks are red. Lizzy, are you feeling all right?" He frowned, pushing his knit cap back on his head. "I knew I shouldn't have brought her outside," he fretted. "It's nearly fifty degrees, but the wind—"

"Eli, she's fine," Ginger assured him with a laugh. "She just looks overheated. Which is no wonder. You've just got her wrapped up too much. Are you hot, my Lizzy?" She unwound the scarf from the little girl and removed it and then unbuttoned the top button of her coat that was a soft navy corduroy. "Better?"

Lizzy bobbed her head.

Ginger removed the knit cap from Lizzy's head for good measure and straightened her headscarf. "You worry too much, Eli. She's fine," she repeated, this time softly.

He closed his eyes for a moment, then opened them. "You're right. I know you are." He opened his arms, then let them fall to his sides. "Claudia says I need to stop fussing over her. It's just that she was so sick, and I was so—" He frowned and narrowed his gaze. "Ginger, what happened to you?" His face became a mask of concern, now for her. He reached out to touch her cheek.

She ducked to avoid his hand. "I'm fine. I fell in the lane." She grinned at him, feeling silly, though not embarrassed. Everyone took a spill on their push scooter once in a while. Two weeks ago, one of the men who worked for her stepfather at the harness shop, while on his scooter, had to move over to give a pickup truck as much room as possible. He'd slid off the pavement into a ditch and broken a finger in the tumble. Ginger hadn't broken anything. Besides, she and Eli were friends. There was no need to be embarrassed with a good friend.

And he *was* a good friend. She knew that because the moment she had arrived, she'd felt as if the burden on her shoulders had lightened. Joe's flirtation with Annie at the bonfire the previous day seemed less important being here with Eli. And the children. The children, who lived each day without their mother and still managed to laugh and hide cookies, reminded her to keep her troubles with her beau in perspective. God truly was good.

"Let me see," Eli insisted, taking her arm and gently turning her so she faced him.

Ginger winced as he bent her arm at the elbow.

He turned her arm to get a look at the tear in her coat. "Do you think it needs an X-ray?" His face was lined with concern, his blue eyes piercing. "I have a cell phone for emergencies. We can call a driver."

"*Ne*, I'm fine." She pulled away, wincing again as she straightened her arm. It was already beginning to swell.

"You're *not* fine. You're bleeding and it looks like there's swelling." He glanced down at Lizzy, who was looking up at him. The red circles on her cheeks had faded. "Let's take Ginger inside and fix her boo-boo," he said.

"Eli…" Ginger rolled her eyes.

"Would you like to help your *dadi*?" Eli asked his daughter, ignoring Ginger.

The little girl bobbed her head up and down. "I'll be the *peedy-tishun*," she said.

Ginger chuckled. "The what?"

"Pediatrician," Eli translated.

"Ah." Ginger nodded. "Good word, Lizzy."

"Boys, I want you to finish your chores," Eli called to his sons. As he spoke, he eased the backpack off

Ginger's back and slung it over his shoulder. "And no fighting," he warned. "Or it will be slug stew and spider biscuits for supper tonight."

Lizzy giggled as she set off for the house, leading the way. "No *shlug shtew, Dat*. I don't like to eat *shlugs*."

"Come on. Inside with you." Eli gently prodded Ginger forward.

"Eli, I'm fine," she argued, though she was already walking to the house.

"You're not," he said. Then he stopped and looked into her eyes. "You do so much for me, Ginger," he said quietly. "Let me do this for you."

He held her gaze for a long moment and she thought about the night before when she burned the back of her hand. Joe hadn't even acknowledged the injury. Joe, who was supposed to be her sweetheart. It didn't even hurt today, but that didn't matter. What mattered was that Joe hadn't cared all that much about her well-being.

And Eli did.

Chapter Six

In the gray light of early dawn, Ginger crept from the bed she shared with Bay and hurriedly dressed. It was a church Sunday, and they would be attending service at the Grubers' house midmorning. Ginger would change into her Sunday dress after breakfast, but for now, she dressed comfortably, throwing an old knit shawl over her shoulders.

It was going to be another cold day. The wind had been bitter the evening before when she and her sisters had returned home from the frolic at Mary's parents' place. They'd had a grand time there, though, looking through Mary's wedding gifts while sharing hot chocolate and cakes and cookies.

As she dressed, Ginger could hear the wind outside their window and wondered if there would be snow flurries.

The house was quiet. Usually, even at this hour, her *mam* was bustling around downstairs, one of her sisters was snoring and someone was banging on her little brother Jesse's door, calling him to get up for milking. When Ginger went to her bedroom window and pulled back the curtain, she understood the silence that seemed to blanket the house. The ground was covered with snow, and large flakes were coming down so thickly that she could barely make out the roofline of the *grossdadi* house in the orchard.

Her oldest stepbrother, Ethan, had been building it, intending to bring his new bride, Abigail, and her son there after his marriage. But Abigail's mother had dementia, and Ethan decided it was best to move in with Abigail rather than bring his bride home. When he'd decided *not* to live on the family farm, Ginger had been so proud of him. His love for Abigail was stronger than his pull to tradition, and that had made her love him all the more for it.

For now, the small *grossdadi* house stood empty. *Watching the family*, Ginger thought. Waiting to see who would take residence. At some point, Benjamin and her mother would move into the house, once their adult children were married and gone. But with Ethan now settled down the road with his new wife, who would eventually take the big house was unknown.

Ginger squinted, looking out the window, and then smiled. Snow…

Delaware rarely saw snowfalls of more than just a dusting, and certainly not before Christmas, but the fall had been colder than usual. Eli had told her the previous day that the *Farmer's Almanac* was predicting a hard winter with several big snowstorms. He'd wondered aloud if it was due to climate change, something the farmers talked a lot about. She'd asked how often the almanac was correct in its predictions. He'd told her it was right often enough to make him move his potted herbs closer to the house and wrap them in burlap to protect them. That was when he told her the herbs had been his wife's. Then he'd apologized for bringing her up so often. Ginger had told him that she didn't mind. What she didn't say was that she liked him all the more for the fact that, though his wife was gone, he hadn't forgotten her.

Ginger padded down the hall to the bathroom in her stocking feet. Although she loved her big blended family dearly, it was nice to not have to wait to brush her teeth or get into the shower. And it was better yet to be able to think about everything that had happened the previous day and remember all the details of her visit with Eli, uninterrupted.

Ginger had gone to Eli's with the intention of asking his thoughts on Joe, hoping to get some insight. But she had soon realized she didn't want to talk to him about Joe.

Sitting in Eli's kitchen while he made up a pan of hot soapy water for her to wash her wound, she'd recognized that the real reason she had come to Eli's was to be with him. And with the children. She had wanted to talk to him, not Joe. She had wanted to hear about the mantelpiece Eli was building for Verkler Construction's client. She had wanted to hear about how his old mare Bess's leg was coming along. After cutting it on a bit of tin roof that had blown off the corncrib, Eli had been concerned the wound wasn't healing. And that he might have to put her down. But the Amish veterinarian from Seven Poplars had come the evening before, cleaned the wound and given the mare an antibiotic. She wasn't out of the woods yet, but Eli was hopeful she would come around.

Eli had fussed over Ginger's little accident as if she

had been involved in a car crash on the highway. At first, his attention had flustered her. But it had also made her feel cared for. Since then, she hadn't been able to stop comparing Joe and Eli. Friday night, Joe hadn't even acknowledged the burn on her hand. Eli, on the other hand, had treated her banged-up elbow as if it was a major injury. He had cared for her wound and treated her with such gentle kindness. Her visit to Eli's had turned out to be a wonderful morning that slipped carelessly into afternoon.

They had made a beef stew together. It had started out with him asking her how to brown the meat, and what vegetables to put in. Then it had turned into her showing him how to make it, which had turned into him pitching in. He'd peeled potatoes and cut up onions, and he'd even run outside and taken a clipping of the last of his thyme from a pot of herbs he'd moved to the south side of the house to protect it from the weather. The thyme had been his idea. It wasn't an herb her *mam* put in her stew, but Eli had been right when he'd suggested it might work in the recipe. The subtle taste had been amazing.

It had intrigued her that Eli was interested in cooking, then tickled her when she saw how easily he took to it. She'd never known an Amish man who cooked. And after they'd made the stew, she had whipped up caramel sauce with brown sugar, vanilla and canned milk. She and Eli and the children had all sat around the table eating apple slices with the warm, sticky caramel.

When Lizzy had grown fatigued, Eli had sent his boys out to play, built a fire in the fireplace in their living room and laid Lizzy down on the couch with her doll. Eli and Ginger had then sat down at a small table to play Chinese checkers while they kept Lizzy company. The little girl was soon asleep, and Eli and Ginger had chatted as they played. They talked about all sorts of things, some not so serious, like what kind of pie was their favorite. They both loved sweet potato. Other conversations were more serious, like the changes that ought to be made to the *Ordung* in their church district.

Ginger had felt as if she had only been at Eli's a short time, but suddenly, it had been half past one. She'd ended up being late to Mary's because she had to go home and hook up the buggy so she and her sisters could go together.

Finishing up in the bathroom, Ginger went downstairs to build up the fire in the woodstove. They didn't need the woodstove to heat the house. Benjamin had added propane heat to the place when he bought it. But her *mam* loved making stews and soups on it and loved the way it made the kitchen cozy on cold mornings. There would be no cooking that day because it was the Sabbath, so starting the woodstove would allow the family to have a hot breakfast rather than a cold one. The day before, her youngest sister, Tarragon, whom they called Tara, had baked two huge egg, cheese and sausage casseroles, which would reheat well in the woodstove's oven.

Once the fire was going, Ginger went to the refrigerator to remove the breakfast casseroles. To do so, she had to step over the two Chesapeake Bay retrievers sleeping sprawled out in the middle of the kitchen floor. Her stepbrother Jacob wasn't supposed to let the dogs in the house at night. Her mother didn't like animals in the house because they made such a mess. But Silas and Ada often found their way into the house at night, especially when it was cold out, and her *mam* never did anything more than fuss about them after the fact.

Ada waggled her tail as Ginger took care not to step on her. Silas never moved.

Once the casseroles were in the woodstove oven and the fire had been stoked, Ginger stood in the kitchen listening to the quiet. Even on a Sunday, there were things to be done. The whole family would be awake soon. She already heard stirrings, and she wasn't quite ready to immerse herself in the controlled chaos of a Sabbath morning. Her youngest brothers, the twins born to her mother and Benjamin, would be demanding breakfast at once and have to be appeased with coffee mugs of dry cereal while the casserole reheated. Her sisters would fill the kitchen with breakfast preparations and gossip about what had gone on the night before at Mary's house. Her little brother Jesse would come downstairs begging for someone to help him find his Sunday-best clothes before he went to the barn. And her stepbrothers would fill up the kitchen and mudroom with their big bodies and bigger voices.

On impulse, Ginger went into the mudroom, took one of the many denim barn coats off a hook and put it on.

"Come along," she called to the two dogs as she tied a wool scarf over her head. Ada and Silas jumped to their feet and raced for the door Ginger held open for them. With the dogs outside before her mother came down to her kitchen, Ginger would be sparing everyone in the family her fussing.

Outside, Ginger walked through the inch or two of snow, falling flakes hitting her on the cheeks. She looked up into the sky and wondered if the sun would come out later. It would be a pretty buggy ride to church service if it did.

Inside the barn, Ginger went where their cows were stalled. Normally it was the boys' chore to milk. Ginger hadn't had to milk a cow since her mother married Benjamin more than three years ago. Most of the time, she was thankful for that, but sometimes she became nostalgic, remembering what it had been like before her mother remarried. After their father had died, they had all been so sad, but their grief had united her sisters and their mother. The pettiness teenage girls could find so easily fell away, and they had worked together to keep the farm going. And with only a little brother not old enough to be much help, Ginger and her sisters had taken up many outside chores. One of Ginger's jobs had been milking. There was something about a cold winter morning and the warmth of a barn that always made her heart sing.

"Time for milking," she announced as a white cat rubbed against her leg, purring loudly.

Two of their cows would be calving in the spring and had about gone dry. Their young Guernsey, Petunia, however, still had plenty of milk to give. She'd had a late calf and was still producing well.

"Good girl," Ginger crooned to the fawn-and-white cow with the large brown eyes. "Nice girl. Nice, Petunia." She washed the cow's udder with warm soapy water that she got from the tap. Then she poured a measure of feed into the cow's trough and settled onto a milking stool. As she rested her head against Petunia's side and streams of milk poured into the shiny stainless steel bucket, her heart swelled with joy as she thought of all the gifts the Lord had bestowed on her rather than mulling over her problems with Joe.

She had a wonderful mother and siblings, stepfather and stepbrothers, a home that she loved and the security of the faith and community that surrounded her. She needed to stop obsessing over Joe. She had assumed God had put him in her path so she could marry him, but what if she was wrong? After all, Eli had been in Byler's that day, as well. Had God meant Eli for her all along, and had she just not seen it? She was confused about her feelings. Was Eli the man for her?

Or what if God didn't intend for her to marry either of them?

It was the Sabbath, a day to remind herself that no human could hope to understand God's ways, least of all her. What she *could* do was work each day to appreciate the bounty He had blessed her with. With that thought, she closed her eyes.

As she prayed, the level of the milk rose in the pail, smelling sweet and fresh. Among other things, she prayed for God to heal Eli's sorrow from when he had spoken of the thyme and his wife. She also prayed for patience for herself, patience to wait to hear God's will. To listen for it and not confuse her human wants with God's plan.

Ginger finished, as always, with the Lord's Prayer and a plea that God guide her mind, hands and footsteps through the day to help her serve her family and faith according to His intentions. She was about to murmur a devout "amen" when one last prayer slipped between her lips. "And please, God, could you show me the way to a husband?"

* * *

"Smells delicious, Claudia," Eli said as he walked into his sister's kitchen in his stocking feet. Every time he came into her house, she told him he needn't take his boots off, but it was a habit he couldn't break. Lizzy's shoes were in the mudroom, as well. And his boys' boots would be there as soon as they came into the house with their cousins. It just seemed like the polite thing to do—not to track dirt into his sister's clean house. The only downside was that everyone could see your socks, know if they were clean or mismatched. Today he was wearing a sock with a hole in it. He'd learned many domestic skills since his wife died, but darning wasn't one of them.

Claudia stood at the stove, her back to him. She was stirring a pot, and the whole room smelled of sauerkraut with roast pork and dumplings. Biscuits, too. When Eli and Claudia were children, their mother always served the main meal of the day at one o'clock in the afternoon and supper was cold sandwiches or leftovers from the midday meal. However, like most Amish families, Claudia's husband, John, worked off the farm during the week; he was a mason by trade. So Claudia served the biggest meal of the day in the evening when the family could gather together as one.

"New hot water heater is all hooked up," Eli told his sister.

Her husband, John, had purchased a new water heater when their old one had sprung a leak. Eli had experience installing a new propane gas hot water heater because he'd done so in his own home. "Two are better than one; because they have a good reward for their labour." That had always been one of his grandmother's favorite Bible verses.

Eli walked to the kitchen counter where a tray of biscuits was cooling and pinched a piece off one. He popped it in his mouth. It was crisp and soft and buttery all at the same time. "John is just breaking down the cardboard shipping box," he told his sister. "Said to tell you he'll be up shortly for supper."

Claudia turned around and he noticed that she was wearing a clean apron and had replaced her head scarf with a white prayer *kapp*. She was looking rather formal for a weekday supper at home. "Eli, I want you to meet Elsie." She indicated the large kitchen table behind him. "Elsie Swartzentruber." She smiled sweetly at him. "Remember, I was telling you about her?"

Startled to realize someone else was in the room, Eli turned to see a petite woman sitting at the table filling a salt shaker. She was attractive, with dark eyes and a dimpled chin. For a moment, he didn't say anything. He was annoyed that his sister had invited Elsie to supper on the same night she had invited him and his children. This was obviously a setup.

But that wasn't Elsie's fault.

He smiled and nodded. "*Guter owed*, Elsie." He suddenly felt self-conscious about the hole in his sock.

"Elsie's son, Abner, is the same age as Andrew," Claudia said. "They're here visiting from Ohio."

He cut his eyes at his sister, then looked back to Elsie, who had slid to the edge of her seat, obviously eager to meet him.

"Elsie, do you mind if I borrow my sister for a second?"

"*Ne*," Elsie murmured.

Eli pointed to the hallway that led to a living room large enough to host church for their district. Though they only lived two miles away, Claudia and John belonged to a different church district than Eli.

With an impatient sigh, Claudia followed him down the hall.

In the living room, Lizzy was playing on the floor near the woodstove with her two cousins, Mary John and Anne. The little girls were busy dressing clothespin dolls with scraps of fabric and paid the adults no mind.

Eli rested his hands on his hips. As he spoke, he tried to remind himself that Claudia only had his best interest at heart. "You invited Elsie to dinner without telling me?"

"Would you have come if I had?"

"*Ne.*"

She shrugged. "So there you have it."

"There I have *what*?" Eli let out his breath. "The children and I are going home. I won't be put in this position, and you shouldn't have put Elsie in it, either. I told you I wasn't interested in you setting me up on a date."

"It's not a date," she argued. "It's supper. On a weeknight," she added as if that made all the difference.

"But you were hoping I'd find Elsie agreeable and then ask her on a date." He pointed in the direction of the kitchen, trying to keep his voice down. "And *she* thinks that's why she's here. Why *I'm* here."

Claudia shook her finger at him as if he was a boy again and not widowed with four children. "Eli, if you're going to be contrary, she's not going to want to go anywhere with you."

He threw up his hands. "I don't want to go on a date with her!"

The girls all looked up at him, and he turned his back to them, lowering his voice. "I told you," he whispered harshly, "when you mentioned Elsie before, that I wasn't interested."

She crossed her arms. "Because of Ginger Stutzman?" she said. "Because you think she's going to fall in love with you, and you're going to marry her."

He hesitated. A few days ago, he might have disagreed, but after Ginger's visit Saturday, when she'd shown up unexpectedly… Somehow the impossible didn't seem quite so impossible anymore. Something had changed between him and Ginger, though he didn't know how or exactly when. But what he did know was that there was an attraction between them that he hadn't felt before.

And things weren't going well with Ginger and Joe. It wasn't much of a courtship, and he sensed Ginger was beginning to realize that now. She hadn't come right out and said so, but he could tell something was different in her. In how she looked at Joe. But more importantly, in how she looked at him.

After Ginger's tumble on her scooter, Eli had taken her inside and cleaned up the scrape on her elbow and put ice on it to keep down the swelling. He suspected she'd come for some reason other than to deliver the muffins. She could have brought them easily enough on Monday. Instead, she had come on a Saturday morning when she didn't have to be there for work. He guessed she had wanted to talk to him about something, maybe even about Joe, but she'd never brought him up. That was fine with him, because he'd have had to be forthright with her and tell her exactly what he thought.

She'd ended up staying for hours, which had delighted the children. And him. They'd ended up making beef stew together. It was still a fairly new experience for him because he'd never cooked with someone else before Ginger. His wife had always done the cooking, and after she had passed, either he cooked alone or was at the mercy of his sister or neighbors to provide meals.

Moving around the kitchen with Ginger had been so easy, so comfortable. Just thinking about it made him smile. He'd had a whole list of chores to do, plus he'd intended to repair a blade on his windmill. Instead, he'd whiled away hours with Ginger, talking and playing games like he had in his younger days back when he was single and courting girls.

It was while they were chatting and playing Chinese checkers that Eli had realized she was looking at him differently than before. There was something in her voice, a tenderness, and a sparkle in her eyes he hadn't seen. That was when it occurred to him that there just might be a spark of attraction there. That maybe it wasn't one-sided anymore.

Just thinking about their day together made his heart swell. Ginger had stayed so long that she'd been late going home to pick up her sisters to visit with Mary, the new bride.

"Eli."

The tone of Claudia's voice pulled him from his thoughts. His sister had said something to him that he had missed. He waited, hoping she would repeat the question and not realize he hadn't been listening.

"Is that what you honestly think?" she asked, obviously as annoyed with him as he was with her. "Because if you do, you're a fool. Girls like Ginger don't marry men like you, men nearly ten years older. With four children," she added pointedly.

Eli stood there for a moment, wiggling his big toe that poked out from his sock. "Claudia," he said quietly. "I can't help how I feel."

She sighed again, but this time it was a kinder sigh. Gentler. "I know you can't, little brother. I'm just trying to protect you from a broken heart."

He mulled that over for a moment. "I know you're probably right," he said finally. "But wouldn't it be worth a try? Just in case Ginger is the woman for me? You know, I never thought I had a chance with Elizabeth, either. She was too smart, too beautiful." He met Claudia's gaze. "But she came to love me. And look at what a wonderful life we had together, even if it was too short. And had I not taken the chance, I wouldn't have our children now."

Claudia reached out and rubbed Eli's arm. "Will you at least come back and join us for supper?"

He smiled. "Of course, I will."

"And will you promise not to get your hopes up?" she asked. "About Ginger?"

"'Hope does not put us to shame because God has poured love into our hearts,'" he paraphrased from Romans. Then he walked down the hall to talk with Elsie. And tried not to think about the fact that it was Ginger he wished was joining them for supper instead.

Chapter Seven

Ginger sat on Eli's porch steps huddled in her cloak, trying not to be angry. It was well past dark, and still, Joe hadn't shown up. Eli had been out twice: first to tell her she should wait inside and the second time to offer to drive her home. She'd been stubborn and insisted on staying put on the porch.

Now Joe was nearly two hours late. He wasn't coming. Ginger knew that. She knew Eli knew.

Slowly she stood, wrapping her wool cloak around her. Her nose was cold and numb. So were her fingers because she had forgotten her gloves that morning. She sighed, thinking it was time to either start walking home or agree to let Eli take her home. She hated to do that but—

The sound of hoofbeats and buggy wheels sounded at the end of the lane, and she looked up. It was Joe. He hadn't forgotten her. He'd just been running late again. He did so much for his uncle these days, it was a wonder he ever left home on time, she told herself, trying to lift her spirits. Trying to convince herself she didn't know what she secretly knew: that Joe was no longer interested in her. That there were too many pretty new girls around with wedding guests still in town. Pretty girls who were younger than she was.

Ginger went down the steps to get a closer look. The snow from the weekend had melted into puddles and had been freezing at night, then thawing during the day, turning all the barnyards in the county into mud mires.

She lifted on her toes to get a glimpse of Joe's buggy. The lights on the front of the buggy looked familiar, but she didn't think they were Joe's. It was required by law that all buggies have a triangular slow-moving vehicle sign and lights, but there was no standard light configuration, so all of the buggies were slightly different.

She squinted, trying to see through the dark. The buggy coming up the lane didn't sound like Joe's two-seater, either. It sounded heavier.

Ginger spotted her stepfather's new driving horse trotting up the lane. For a moment, she tried to convince herself she was mistaken, but the gelding's high-stepping gait was unique. Then she recognized the old buggy her mother had brought with her into her second marriage, and her shoulders sagged. *That* was why the lights looked familiar.

The buggy entered the barnyard and circled, coming to a stop in front of Eli's porch. The driver's door slid open. It was Bay.

"What are you doing here?" Ginger asked dismally.

"Come to pick you up," her twin responded. "*Mam* sent me."

Ginger glanced back at the house as she circled the gelding. She spotted a curtain pulled back in the mud-room. She assumed it was one of the children, but it was Eli. He dropped the curtain when he saw her looking back at him.

Ginger opened the buggy door and climbed up and inside. "How did *Mam* know I needed a ride? Did Joe call the harness shop?"

Bay looked at her sternly, the dim interior light emphasizing the knit of her brows. "*Mam* said this late, he wasn't coming for you. The plan is for one of the boys to come for you if Joe doesn't show up, but—"

"Wait," Ginger said. "*Mam* has a plan for if Joe doesn't come for me?"

"Of course she does. She's still our mother. It doesn't matter how old we are. Anyway, one of the boys was supposed to fetch you, but they were all busy down at the barn fixing a gate. One of the hogs broke his way out and was headed down the middle of the road toward Lovey's place. Marshall spotted him. *Mam* was going to come herself but decided you'd be less cross with me."

"I wouldn't be cross with *Mam*," Ginger argued.

Bay gave her sister a look that meant she didn't believe her for a minute. "She watches the clock every weeknight, Ginger." She turned off the interior light, lifted the reins and urged the gelding forward. "Waiting for you to get home. Worrying over you."

Ginger sat back in the seat and pulled a wool blanket onto her lap. "She never told me that."

"I think she's trying not to interfere." Bay halted at the end of the driveway and waited for a little red car to pass before she pulled onto the road. "I think she's afraid if she says much, she'll drive the two of you closer."

Ginger looked at Bay, not angry, but upset with their mother. "How old does she think I am? I'm not a teenage girl turning my head to every boy who smiles at me." She folded her arms over her chest. "Is that what *Mam* thinks?"

"I think she thinks you're headstrong. That you set your eye on Joe Verkler, and now you're determined not to change your mind about him. Even if he gives you reason," she said more gently.

Ginger stared out into the darkness. Her mother knew her too well. A pickup passed them, splashing water on the windshield. Bay turned on the wipers, and they rode half a mile without speaking. The inside of the buggy smelled of Bay's muddy boots and a sachet of herbs their mother kept under the dash.

"How was your day?" Ginger asked her sister, changing the subject entirely.

"It was good. You wouldn't believe the number of orders coming into the greenhouse, not just for wreaths but swags and table arrangements, too. I don't know how we're going to fill them all. We're going to have to find another supplier for fresh greenery. I can't pick it all from our property. The place would be bald." She chuckled.

At first, Bay and their stepbrother Joshua's greenhouse that they had built the spring before had just been to sell plants in the spring and summer, maybe some gardening supplies. But when Bay had started making fresh wreaths, the business had taken off. They had gotten so busy so quickly that Joshua's new wife, Phoebe, was helping out. And Bay was hiring a couple of young folks from their youth group to work Saturdays.

Bay looked at Ginger, "And now we have so many people signed up for the wreath-making class, Phoebe thinks we should offer a second session."

"*Ya*, I told Eli about making the wreaths. How you wanted to make it a family event. We thought we'd bring the children."

"*We?*" her sister asked. The controls on the dashboard dimly lit her face. English folks didn't realize it, but a buggy had a dashboard just like a car. From there, a driver controlled the lights, the windshield wipers and even a little heater sometimes.

"*Ya*, Eli and I. We thought we'd make a big wreath for the back door. Lizzy's probably young to do much, but the boys would enjoy it. And if there's cookies, hot chocolate and spiced cider being served, I imagine they'll love it. Eli said when he was growing up, they didn't do family projects like making Christmas decorations. I think because his mother died when he was young."

Bay looked at her funny.

"What?" Ginger asked.

For a moment her sister didn't say anything. There was just the sound of the gelding's rhythmic hoofbeats and the wooden wheels rolling on the pavement. A lot of Amish had rubber wheels now, but in Hickory Grove, they were still the traditional wood. Ginger had ridden in a rubber-wheeled buggy that summer while visiting friends in Lancaster County. She preferred the sound of the wooden wheels.

"What?" Ginger repeated. "Why are you looking at me like that, *Schweschder*?"

Bay had a silly little smile on her face, like a cat caught lapping cream from a milk bucket. "You talk a lot about Eli."

"I spend a lot of time with him," Ginger responded, feeling as if she had to defend herself, though why she didn't know.

"Right. More time than you do with Joe," Bay observed. "And you talk about the children as if they're yours."

"I do not." Ginger turned on the leather bench seat to face her sister. "It's just that I'm with them all day and—" She went quiet.

Bay was right. She *did* talk about Eli's children as if they were hers. But wasn't that natural with how much time she spent with them? And them not having a mother?

Ginger thought before she spoke. "It's a lot for Eli to do alone. To take them places. I figured if we took them together, especially it being a Friday night, it would be easier. We could all go together after Eli gets home from work, and I wouldn't have to worry about Joe—" She fell into silence. The plan was a good one because these days, she couldn't rely on Joe to give her a ride home, could she?

"You know he's in love with you."

"Joe?" Ginger asked, frowning.

Bay laughed. "Don't be a silly goose. Joe doesn't love anyone but himself. I'm talking about *Eli.*"

Ginger stared at her sister for a moment, glad she had leaned back on the seat so her face was in shadows. "He isn't," she heard herself say. But it came out as more of a question than an adamant denial.

"You know what I think?" Bay said. She went on without waiting for Ginger to say she was interested in her sister's opinion. Big families were like that, always ready with an opinion whether you wanted it or not. "I think if you weren't so stubborn, if you weren't so obsessed with Joe Verkler, you'd admit that, while maybe you're not in love with Eli, you're sweet on him."

"I am not—" Ginger went quiet again, crossing her arms over her chest. Leaving the door open for her sister to go on. Because even though a part of her wanted to deny it, a part of her wanted to hear what her sister had to say. Was Eli really in love with her? Could that be possible? And if it was, how did she feel about it?

"*Mam* thinks Eli is more suitable for you than Joe, and so do I," Bay went on.

"Eli?" Ginger laughed. "We've known Eli for years now."

"What does that have to do with anything?" Bay asked.

Ginger couldn't come up with a snappy answer. Instead, she stared out the window. So what if she was a little sweet on Eli? How could any young woman who knew him not be? Unmarried women were attracted to unmarried men. It was part of God's plan. That didn't mean she wanted to marry Eli.

Did it?

Ginger stood in the hallway of John and Edna Fisher's house, her arms hanging at her sides, trying not to cry. Joe had said his piece and now had gone silent.

The house was filled with friends and neighbors, all gathered to celebrate Bishop Simon's fiftieth birthday. It had been a surprise supper party his wife, Annie, had cleverly planned for weeks. When the bishop arrived at the Fishers', he hadn't been the least suspicious of all the buggies in the barnyard because he thought he was there for a birthday party for John Fisher. John had been in on the whole thing, as had everyone from their church district. It was only when Bishop Simon walked into the house, carrying a dish of his wife's *boova shenkel*, and everyone hollered "Surprise!" that the ruse was up.

A potluck buffet supper had then been served, and now all of the dishes were being *ret* up in anticipation of an entire table of desserts, including a big chocolate cake with pink frosting, decorated with maraschino cherries.

"Joe," Ginger said softly, looking up at him. "Can we talk about this? *Please?*"

He stared at the polished wood floor for a long moment. The rooms around them were filled with people laughing and talking, babies crying, children squealing. There was joy all around Ginger. But none in her.

"I don't see the point," Joe muttered. "Like I said, it's best we go our separate ways. All we do is disagree."

It annoyed her that he still looked so handsome to her. Even when she was angry with him. "We don't disagree all the time. I came to you because I'm upset with you because you didn't save me a seat beside you. Because you were flirting with that girl, because you're always flirting with other girls."

"Girls flirt with me," he countered. "Nothing I can do about that."

"Sure there is. You could tell girls you're walking out with me," she responded, trying to keep her voice down. If her mother caught wind of their argument, she'd be at Ginger's side in an instant, intervening, and that wasn't what Ginger wanted. It wasn't what she needed right now. "I didn't want to break up. I just wanted to talk."

"You say I'm not reliable."

"Joe, you're not." Mentally, she counted up how many times he'd been late to pick her up after she worked at Eli's all day. Or didn't come at all. Ginger had tried to talk to Joe about it before, but he was always tired after work and hungry and not receptive to the conversation. To any conversation about their relationship.

And then finally, it had come. The straw that broke the horse's back for her.

The men, led by Bishop Simon, had all gone through the buffet line first, made their plates then scattered to the downstairs rooms to find seats where they could. There were tables set up in every downstairs room in the Fishers' house, but there were also other places to sit like a sofa or a stairstep. The women had gotten into the food line after the men. Ginger had filled her plate and then gone into the parlor, thinking she would join Joe on a bench under the window where she'd seen him sit down. She had assumed he'd saved the place beside him for her.

She'd been wrong.

By the time she had made it to the parlor, one of Edna Fisher's nieces was sitting beside Joe. When Ginger had walked in, Joe hadn't even noticed her. He'd been too busy telling the girl, who couldn't have been eighteen years old, some story about him saving one of his uncle's big contracts. Edna's niece had been giggling and batting her eyelashes as Joe told the story. A story Ginger had heard before, one that seemed to be getting bigger and better each time he told it. Which was another niggling issue she had with him. She hadn't caught him in an out-and-out lie, but if he embellished stories, did he embellish facts as well?

Ginger had wanted to confront Joe the minute she'd seen him chatting up the girl, but out of respect for Bishop Simon on his special day, she hadn't. Instead, she'd walked out of the room and joined a group of unmarried women in the front hall seated on the staircase.

She had kept thinking while she ate that when Joe realized she hadn't joined him, that he would come looking for her. She'd been wrong. Again. After supper, she'd practically had to drag him into the hall to talk to him.

Ginger stood there in front of Joe, her arms crossed. "You said I was your girl," she said quietly.

"Your family doesn't like me," he responded, taking on the tone of a spoiled child. "Your mother barely speaks to me. Your stepbrother Jacob keeps asking me questions hoping to trip me up."

"*Trip you up?* What kind of questions?" she asked.

"About my property at home. What I do for my uncle. Why I left Lancaster. He's just jealous of me because the girls all flock to me." He slid his thumbs under his suspenders, his chest puffing out until he looked like one of her sister Lovey's peacocks. "All the single guys are jealous of me in this town."

She ignored the subject of girls flocking to him. And his hint that maybe he'd ended up in Hickory Grove for some reason other than the one he had given her when they first met—that his uncle had desperately needed him, else his business was going to fail.

"What my mother or Jacob thinks of you shouldn't matter, Joe," she told him, trying to soften her tone. She knew anger wasn't something she should bring into a discussion. That was something her mother had taught her, had taught all of her girls a long time ago. It was just so hard not to be angry with Joe. And hurt. She was more hurt than angry, she thought. And she was feeling foolish to have dated Joe this long. Because he wasn't interested in her. Not interested enough. And he clearly wasn't ready to settle down, otherwise girls *flocking* to him wouldn't be something he'd have brought up.

"I don't want to court you anymore, Ginger." He didn't look at her. "We're not well suited."

"Not well suited?" She flared. "Are we not well suited, or are you just too—" She bit back her next words, words that would not be charitable. Words she would have to pray for forgiveness for later. She crossed her arms so tightly that she was hugging herself. Suddenly she became resigned. "I think you're right, Joe."

"You do?" He looked perplexed, as if people didn't say that to him often.

"*Ya.* We're not well suited," she repeated, purposely not allowing her thoughts to drift to the time she had spent with Eli Saturday. She'd been trying to ignore for weeks the fact that Eli was far more suited to her than Joe. "And we shouldn't be courting. But we can still be friends. *Ya*?" She offered her hand to him. "We're still friends, aren't we?"

Four toddlers ran down the hallway squealing as they chased each other. One was Ginger's little brother Josiah. She pulled in her hand, letting the boys go between her and Joe. When they darted into the living room, she offered her hand to him again.

He looked at her hand, then clasped it awkwardly, giving it a squeeze before letting go.

"Well…" She clasped her hands together, awash with emotions. She knew Joe was right. They weren't a good fit. But it still stung—especially because he broke up with her before she could break up with him. Before she could make that decision. "I've got things to do." She offered a quick, less-than-heartfelt smile. "In the kitchen." She pointed in that direction. "Cleaning up."

Joe just stood there.

Ginger marched off, her chin held high. "It's for the

best," she murmured under her breath. "It's for the best." And it was, but by the time she reached the kitchen doorway, she had to stop and wipe the moisture from her eyes.

"There you are, Ginger!" One of the Fisher girls waved to her as she came down the stairs. "Did you hear—"

Ginger ducked into the kitchen, not ready to talk to anyone yet. The kitchen was a flurry of activity with leftovers being wrapped up, dishes being put away and desserts being set out. One of the counters was covered with freshly washed serving dishes. She grabbed her mother's blue baking dish they had brought *schnitz un knepp* in; there hadn't been a spoonful of the pork and dried apple casserole left. Ginger hugged the dish to her, not making eye contact with her sister Bay at the sink, or anyone else. "I'll take this to our buggy, so we don't leave it behind," she said to no one in particular.

She slipped through the back door. It was dark and cold outside, and it smelled as if it was going to rain any minute. There would be no snow tonight. On the way over to the Fishers', Benjamin had said that they were only expecting a low of forty-five degrees, so he didn't have to worry that the new waterlines that he'd run to the barn might freeze.

Ginger followed the path to the barnyard that was illuminated by solar lights. Her stepfather had them at his harness shop, too. Englishers were always amazed the Amish would use solar power. They didn't understand that things like electricity and phone landlines were about being connected to the world. They were against the *Ordung* because the Amish believed they should hold themselves apart from the non-Amish. But solar power was just like wind power, and not just accepted but encouraged among her people. At least in Hickory Grove.

As Ginger followed the path to the barnyard, she heard male voices and spotted a group of men in the distance gathered at a hitching rail. Someone was smoking a pipe, something she didn't often see. She couldn't tell from a distance who it was. It didn't matter. While smoking was technically against the *Ordung*, it was a small vice. When she was a child, her father had smoked a pipe occasionally, though she had never seen him, only smelled the sweet tobacco.

Ginger hurried toward the long row of buggies, the baking dish clutched to her chest as if it was far more precious than it actually was.

Because of the damp chill, Benjamin had unhitched his gelding and led it inside the barn. She found their buggy easily enough and opened the passenger door. But instead of just sliding the dish inside, she climbed in. She needed a moment to collect herself before she joined her friends and family. She still couldn't believe that Joe had ended their courtship... Or whatever it had been.

Boys didn't break up with her. She broke up with them. The fact that Joe was the one who had ended their relationship seemed to be what was upsetting her more than anything else. How did he not recognize what a catch she was? What a good person she was? What a good wife she would make?

Ginger fumbled in her pocket for a tissue or a handkerchief. She felt foolish to be crying.

A tap on the buggy's side window startled her.

"Ginger?" came a male voice from outside.

She gripped the seat, unsure for a moment as to what to do. Was it Joe, come to beg her to take him back?

"Ginger?" he called again.

She reached to open the passenger-side door. He beat her to it.

She sat back on the leather buggy seat. "What are you doing out here?"

Eli stuck his head inside. "I came to check on you. You all right?"

She studied him by the light of a kerosene lantern someone had hung on a pole outside the barn door. "I'm fine." She looked down at her hands in her lap and sniffed. "Why wouldn't I be?"

He glanced up into the sky, the broad brim of his wool hat casting a shadow across his face. "Starting to rain." He hesitated. "Would it be all right if I came inside?"

Though Ginger's head was down, she could feel his gaze on her. "Sure," she said. She didn't know that she wanted any company right now, but if she was going to choose someone to be there, it would be Eli.

She moved over to the driver's side. Rather than having a full front bench seat as in her mother's buggy, this new one that Benjamin had built had a split front seat, which allowed one to easily get to the rear benches that faced each other. The buggy was so large that it could accommodate six adults as well as several children.

Eli got inside and closed the door. And suddenly the buggy seemed smaller.

And more intimate.

Which made no sense because she'd been in a buggy with Eli before. Just a day earlier, she'd ridden with him and the children in his buggy to his sister's house to pick up some clothing. Claudia had been doing some sewing for Lizzy and Simon, both of whom seemed to be growing taller every day.

But the children weren't with them now, and that made it different. She'd never been alone with Eli in such a confined space. One that smelled of his clean clothes, shaving soap and something she couldn't quite put her finger on. Something very masculine.

Again, Ginger could feel Eli looking at her.

"You're fine?" he said, his tone suggesting he didn't believe her. "Because I saw you inside in the hallway talking to Joe. You looked upset." He took a breath. "Ginger…you don't have to tell me what happened if you don't want to. But I think I'm a pretty good lis—"

"He broke up with me," she blurted.

He slid back in the seat, seeming as surprised by Joe's action as she was.

"Broke up with you?" Eli repeated. As he took off his hat, raindrops fell on his denim coat. He stroked his clean-shaven chin. When she had first met him, when they had just moved to Delaware from New York, he had still had a beard. It had been a sign of his marital status, though his wife had already passed. But some time ago, he had shaved it off. And had become a single man again.

She gave the slightest nod. "*Ya.* He did. I think it's for the best," she said quietly. She looked down at her hands. "I don't think he ever liked me all that much. He just liked the idea of me."

"Then why are you upset?"

"I don't know. I guess it just…" Why *was* she upset? Hadn't she known it was coming? She opened her hands. "It stings. To be rejected." She was surprised by the words that came out of her mouth. Surprised she would admit such a thing to Eli. Ordinarily, Bay would have been the only person she would have told such a thing.

"*Ya.*" He set the black wool wide-brimmed hat on his knee. "I know exactly what you mean." His eyes twinkled with good humor. "I've been rejected a time or two. As you know." He shook his head. "Everyone in Hickory Grove knows. Everyone in the county. I think word even made it to Lancaster."

Then he smiled at her and suddenly she didn't feel so bad.

"I guess we're in the same situation." He took his time speaking. "And if I'm wrong, say so, but I think you're at the same place I am in my life. I want to marry. I want a partner. And not just to help me care for my children, but to care for me. Care *about* me. I want a partner to care for."

Eli's heartfelt words made her a little uncomfortable, but at the same time she couldn't help but admire him for his honesty. And she was touched that he would share something so personal with her. She didn't know what it was like to be married or even be in love, but she could imagine what it would be like to lose a spouse. She knew what it had been like for her mother.

She sniffed again. "*Ya.* I thought marriage was in my future. I thought Joe and I were well matched. Everyone said so."

"Not everyone," he said. "Not me."

She chuckled. She had suspected all along that Eli hadn't approved of her beau, but unlike her *mam* and sister, he'd kept it to himself.

"And why is that?" she asked boldly.

"I think you know why, but I'll say it. Because Joe didn't treat you the way a man should treat a woman he wants to marry. The way you deserve to be treated, Ginger."

She lowered her gaze. "Which is…what?" she asked, peeking up at him.

"Cherished, respected, adored." This last part he added almost bashfully.

She didn't look away from him this time. "That sounds like something Benjamin would say. He adores my *mam*."

"As a husband should."

"I don't know that every husband adores his wife." She folded her hands, thinking on the matter. "We marry for many reasons. The most important being because it's God's wish."

"*Ya*. I agree, Ginger. But I also think God wants us to be happy. And to feel loved. By Him, but also by our spouse, by our children. By our community. We don't talk enough about that."

"Can you imagine Preacher Joseph giving that sermon?" she asked, pressing her lips together to keep from smiling. Their new preacher was a good man, one of strong faith, but he was in his seventies and was the soberest soul she thought she had ever known. He tended to lean toward expounding the Old Testament God of wrath. He loved to preach from Deuteronomy, reminding his parishioners of God's threats to the Israelites if they abandoned the covenant he made with them at Sinai. Preacher Joseph also loved the story of Job, always managing to emphasize his trials: the boils, the loss of everything he owned, the death of children.

"*Ya*," Eli agreed with a conspiratorial smile. "I don't think we'll be hearing much from First Corinthians anytime soon."

Ginger wasn't the best with her Bible knowledge, but First Corinthians she knew. Benjamin often liked to read from Peter's letter during family worship before bedtimes. *Love is patient. Love is kind.* Thinking of those words made a lump rise in her throat. Her mother's husband was such a good man, a good husband, a good father, not just to his boys but to his stepchildren, as well. Ginger had loved her father, but she loved Benjamin too and she admired him for the husband he was to her mother. She wanted a husband like Benjamin. One who would cherish her. Even adore her. But that wasn't something one often saw among the Amish, so she didn't want to get her hopes too high.

Her gaze moved to Eli again. He was just sitting there, watching her by the light that came in through the windshield from the kerosene lantern.

"Well," she said, placing her hands on her knees. "I should get back inside. There are still dishes to be washed."

"*Ya*." Eli tapped his hat on his knee. "And I should get inside and see what the children are up to. If I don't keep an eye on them, they'll be putting slices of pie and slabs of cake in their pockets."

She laughed. "They do enjoy their desserts," she agreed.

"That they do." He sobered, pausing a moment before speaking again. "So, I have a question for you, Ginger. One I best ask before someone else beats me to it again."

She knitted her brows, puzzled as to his meaning. *Beat whom to what?* "What's that, Eli?"

"Ginger…" He swallowed hard, suddenly looking very determined. "May I court you?"

Chapter Eight

Ginger's eyes widened with such surprise that Eli feared he had made a terrible mistake. Had he misread her? All the hours they had spent together when she seemed as if she had enjoyed his company... Had he misinterpreted friendly behavior for one of attraction?

He searched her green eyes with their little specks of brown, trying to read her thoughts.

Why was she hesitating?

Was she trying to think of a way to let him down gently?

Eli wasn't concerned about her hurting him. That was his sister's worry, but it was unfounded. He'd grown a tough skin. He'd asked half a dozen women to walk out with him over the last two years, and not a single one had gone on more than a date or two with him. He wasn't a twenty-year-old boy trying to get a girl to ride home with him from a frolic or sit next to him at supper or a singing. He was a widowed man with a houseful of children and he was asking Ginger to court him with the intention of marrying her.

Ne, he wasn't worried about himself, he was worried about Ginger. Had he upset her? Frightened her? Did she think his request was inappropriate because he was older than she was? It was true she was nine years younger, but he had never thought age mattered. His grandmother had been twelve years older than his grandfather, and they had shared a happy marriage, a happy life together. Or was the fact that he was her employer a problem?

Claudia's words began to bounce around inside his head. A pretty young woman like Ginger would never be interested in an old widowed father of four. That's what Claudia had said. He wasn't handsome enough for the prettiest girl in Hickory Grove. He had never been, not even in his younger years. And he certainly wasn't flashy like Joe Verkler. He didn't wear fancy running shoes or expensive sunglasses. He didn't have blue lights strung on his buggy that lit up after dark.

But the companionship, the laughter, the serious conversations and lighthearted ones he and Ginger had shared had suggested she *was* interested in him. That she saw beyond the threads of gray beginning to show in his hair to who he truly was. What they could be together.

"I… I don't know what to say, Eli." She unfolded her hands and then folded them again.

Had she been staring at the floor, avoiding eye contact, he probably would have apologized for his behavior and taken his leave. But she was watching him. And he could tell she was thinking.

Eli spoke before he lost his nerve. "I know it might seem like this has come out of the blue, Ginger, but—" He hesitated, searching for the right words. He sent a quick prayer heavenward, praying to God to guide him.

Because looking into her eyes, he truly believed God meant for this beautiful, kindhearted woman whom his children adored to be his wife. "We've spent a good deal of time together, you and I, over the last… What has it been? Seven weeks since you started watching my children?"

Ginger didn't speak, but she was listening. He took that to mean she wanted to hear what he had to say, and he went on.

"In that time, I feel like I've gotten to know you pretty well and, and…" He fiddled with a sore spot on his palm—a splinter that had not yet made its way to the surface. A carpenter's hazard. "And I think you've gotten to know me pretty well, at least I hope you have." He took a breath, trying to calm his nerves. "We get along well, Ginger. We seem to be able to talk to each other about…about anything and…" He felt like he was making a mess of this, even though for weeks, he'd been rehearsing what he would say to Ginger if he ever got the chance. Practically since the first day he'd come home to find her in his kitchen, supper in the oven, his children happy. And now here the opportunity had presented itself, and he was stumbling and stammering like a boy with his first chin whiskers asking a girl to ride home from a singing for the first time.

Eli took another deep breath, forcing himself to look into her green eyes. "Have I misinterpreted our friendship, Ginger? To think it could be more?"

She wrapped her arms around herself, holding his gaze, and he held his breath, waiting for her to speak. "You've not misinterpreted," she said softly.

He let out a sigh of relief, feeling as if he'd been holding his breath for weeks. "So…would you let me court you? So we can get to know each other better the way a couple should know each other if they're considering—" He stopped, wondering if it was too soon to say it. He didn't want to scare her off. He'd half thought she would flat out turn him down. Like the others. But while he desperately wanted the chance to win her love, he knew he had to be honest with her. Because that was the kind of marriage he wanted, and not just for himself, but for Ginger, too. "If they're considering marriage," he finished, his confidence returning. "And I'll tell you right up front, that's my intention. To marry you, Ginger."

She trembled.

"Are you all right?" He reached out to her but stopped short of touching her hand. He didn't think anyone had seen him get into the buggy with Ginger, but if someone had, he didn't want any assumptions to be made. At their age, the rules of courting were a little more relaxed than if they had been twenty, but there were still rules, especially if they weren't courting.

"*Ya.*" She tightened her arms around herself. "Just chilled all of a sudden."

"I'm sorry. Of course. It's cold out here." He shucked off his coat and put it around her shoulders. "Here you are without even your cloak."

She pressed her lips together, watching him as he eased back into the passenger seat. "*Ya.*"

"*Ya?*" he asked, not sure what she was saying yes to.

"*Ya,* I'll court you, Eli, but—"

Suddenly he began to imagine evenings in front of the fire, reading to the children, playing games, coming together as a family to say evening prayers. He imagined tucking the children into bed and walking down the hallway holding Ginger's hand. He imagined not having to wake each morning to the loneliness he had endured since Elizabeth's death.

"But," Ginger repeated, closing his coat around her. "I'll be honest with you, Eli. I'm not ready to talk about marriage."

And as quickly as that, his dreams faded. He frowned. "You don't want to marry ever, or you don't want to marry me?"

She broke into a smile, chuckling. "Of course I want to marry, Eli. It's only that—"

She exhaled, seeming impatient with him, but it was a good kind of impatient, the kind a wife exhibited with her husband when he said or did something foolish. Eli felt himself begin to relax. She had said yes, that was all that mattered for the moment. "It's only what?" he asked.

"My beau just broke up with me half an hour ago, Eli. It's too soon for me to be talking about marriage to you or anyone else. I think it would be unseemly, don't you? Everyone in the county will be calling me fickle."

"I understand," he said, grinning. He couldn't stop grinning. Ginger said yes. She said she would walk out with him. That was all he wanted—the opportunity to show her how good they could be together. How good a man walking out with a woman should be to her. God was good.

"You sure?" she questioned, sounding an awful lot like his sister. "You understand what I'm saying. I'm willing to enter a courtship, but I don't want to talk about marriage. Not yet."

He nodded, still smiling. "I understand. Nary a word about marriage." He drew his finger across his mouth as if to seal it shut.

Ginger smiled back shyly at Eli, and he felt a rush of warmth run through his body. A rush of hope.

Nettie slid a tray of gingerbread cookies into the oven while Ginger continued rolling out the dough for the next batch. Her stepbrother Ethan, a schoolteacher, was having a cookie sale the first Friday night in December as a fundraiser for Hickory Grove's one-room schoolhouse. With more families moving into the area every year, their building was now barely big enough to hold all of the students. Everyone had agreed that it was time to consider building another school and hiring another teacher—that, or put an addition to the schoolhouse they had now. Either way, they needed money. The community had decided that while they contemplated the best direction to take, the fundraising should begin.

The big news in Hickory Grove was that the holiday cookie sale would be open not only to the Amish but to the Englishers, too. Midsummer, Ethan had proposed the idea of reaching out to their *entire* community for support. After much contemplation and several meetings, the bishops and elders from the different church districts in Hickory Grove had agreed to her stepbrother's proposal. His wife, Abigail, thought they could sell as many cookies as they could bake if they welcomed their English neighbors and encouraged all of the women in Hickory Grove to get out their rolling pins for a good cause. Abigail had even made a huge hand-painted sign announcing the event and planted it in front of the school. Other Amish communities had found that this was an excellent way to raise funds for their schools. One west of Dover held a farm auction every year that was quite successful because the Englishers flocked to such events. Some of the older folks in Hickory Grove had objected to the notion of including Englishers, feeling they would be putting themselves on display for the curious English. Still, in the end, the bishops in Hickory Grove had decided the good outweighed the bad.

It was Bay's idea for their family to start baking early and freeze the cookies so they could contribute plenty to their brother's school. Today, however, she was working in the greenhouse, preparing for the Christmas rush, so she wasn't able to join in. This morning, they were making gingerbread cookies, butter horns and cranberry white chocolate cookies.

"What are you and Eli doing tonight for your first date?" Nettie asked, plucking one hot mitt off and then the other. She'd been pumping Ginger with questions about Eli all morning.

"Are you going to the singing at the Fishers'?" their youngest sister, Tara, asked excitedly.

Taking her time in responding, Ginger chose a cookie cutter in the shape of a cow and began to cut out cookies and slide them onto a baking sheet. She had told everyone in the buggy on the ride home the previous night about her breakup with Joe and about agreeing to court Eli. Her sisters had broken into cheers and giggles. No one seemed to be upset about her breakup with Joe.

Ginger's *mam* had seemed particularly pleased, though she'd been careful not to say too much. She had somehow gotten it into her head that Ginger was inclined to do the opposite of what she wanted, just for the sake of doing it. Which wasn't true. At least not anymore. Dating Joe and working for Eli had changed her perspective. Maybe it was the disappointment of Joe not being what she had hoped he would be, maybe it was the responsibility of caring for Eli's children, but either way, Ginger felt as if she'd matured in the past two months.

"We're a little old to attend singings," Ginger told her younger sister. "Though we may stop by. Eli likes to chaperone the Fishers' frolics."

Edna and John Fisher were the youth leaders for Hickory Grove and did an excellent job of keeping young folks busy while also providing them an opportunity to mingle and get to know each other under proper supervision. Though some Amish around the country practiced *rumspringa*, in Hickory Grove they did not. The church districts were too strict to allow their young men and women the opportunity to possibly dabble in alcohol and smoking, premarital relations and other self-destructive behaviors. Some of the young men occasionally argued that because they weren't yet baptized, it was permissible before they made a formal commitment to live the laws of the Amish life. The bishops in Kent County disagreed. Baptized or not, those behaviors were not permitted.

"So what *are* you two doing then?" Tara pressed. She had been attending frolics for three or four years now but had just begun accepting rides home with boys. She didn't have a boyfriend yet, so she was fascinated by the whole process.

Ginger dropped another mound of dough that smelled of ginger, cinnamon and molasses on the floured board. Then, taking up the wooden rolling pin that her grandfather had made for her mother as a wedding gift, she began to roll out the dough. Tara moved in beside her at the table and began to measure out the dry ingredients and sift it with an old turn-handle sifter to make the butter horns.

Ginger smiled to herself. As she was leaving the Fishers' last night after the party, Eli had grabbed her hand and pulled her behind the bishop's buggy to whisper, "Would you like to go out on a date with me tomorrow night?" When she'd agreed, he'd asked what she wanted to do, where she wanted to go. She'd told him they didn't have to *go* anywhere. He and the children could come for supper at their house, or she could come to his, and they could play Chinese checkers after they ate.

"That's not a date!" he'd protested.

The way he had said it had made her laugh. At the same time, she'd felt a little shiver of excitement. Her hand felt good in his. Eli had surprisingly soft hands for a carpenter, big and smooth. She thought maybe it was because he used hand lotion out of a bottle he bought at Walmart. He didn't use lard like a lot of men she knew.

"I thought the point was to get to know each other better," she'd argued with him, a twinkle in her eyes. He'd still not let go of her hand. "We don't have to go anywhere to do that."

"We need time without the children," he'd insisted. "Time together alone."

"I don't mind them," she'd told him.

"I mind them," he'd responded, humor in his voice. "Don't get me wrong, you know I love them dearly. But I'm not taking my four children *courting* with me. You deserve my full attention. I'm not saying we'll never do things together with the children. Truth is, most of our courting will be with my children, with your family, with friends and neighbors, but tomorrow night, I want you all to myself. So tell me what you'd like to do." Then his brow had furrowed. "I don't even know how a man my age spends time with a woman, courting. When I courted Elizabeth, we were young." He'd shrugged. "We went to frolics and corn husking parties and—" He had met her gaze, his eyes suddenly widening. "I'm sorry. I shouldn't have done that."

"Done what?" Ginger had asked. She had heard her family loading up the two buggies they'd come in. Her stepbrothers and her brother Jesse had taken one while she and her *mam* and Benjamin and her three sisters and the twin little boys had all ridden together. Benjamin would be ready to go at any minute, and then he'd come searching for her. "What did you do wrong?"

"Mentioned Elizabeth. I shouldn't be talking to the woman I hope will be my future wife about my dead wife."

She'd exhaled, gently pulling her hand from his and tucking it inside her cloak so she wouldn't be tempted to let him hold it again. While Eli's age might give them certain allowances younger folks didn't have, a certain amount of decorum was still expected. "Eli, I don't mind when you talk about Elizabeth. I love that you loved her so much that she still lives inside you." She'd pressed her lips together, wondering what it was about Eli that made her feel comfortable to say what was on her mind.

"Ginger!" Her sister Bay's voice had come from the darkness. "Where are you? Benjamin's ready to go. The littles are falling asleep."

Ginger had looked to Eli, trying to come up with something for them to do. While she'd done plenty of dating, it was always through organized events, mostly with the youth group the Fishers ran. "I have to go home. I don't know what to do. It's not like we go to movies like the Englishers."

"*Ne*, but…" He'd thought for a minute. "We do go out to eat, though. Do you like pizza?"

She had smiled. "I love pizza. I keep telling *Mam* we should learn how to make it. It can't be too hard."

"We'll go for pizza, then. How about that? I'll come to your house to pick you up, but I think I'll get a driver. The place I want to take you to is out on Route 13. Too busy for a buggy at night."

"Ginger!" Bay had called from the darkness outside the puddle of light where Ginger and Eli stood, now sounding annoyed. "She was just here a minute ago," she said to someone.

"I really have to go," Ginger had whispered. She hadn't been able to stop smiling at Eli, because he had been smiling at her. He'd seemed so pleased with himself. He'd looked like Phillip did when the little boy thought he'd managed to snitch cookies from the cookie jar without being caught.

Eli had buttoned up his coat, and Ginger had thought about how it had felt around her shoulders when they were in the buggy earlier. The weight of it had felt like a hug and it had smelled of him.

"Five o'clock?" Eli had asked. "I'll have you home by eight."

"*Ya*," she'd agreed as she backed away from him.

"I can't wait," he'd called after her in a loud whisper.

"We're going out to eat pizza," Ginger said, returning her attention to her sister standing beside her in the kitchen. She dusted a bit of flour off Tara's chin.

"Where?" Tara asked, dumping the last of the dry ingredients into the sifter she held over a big mixing bowl.

Ginger began cutting out more gingerbread cookies. This time she chose the shape of a little house. Later, when they were completely cool, they'd be decorated with homemade orange icing made from orange juice and zest and powdered sugar. "I don't know. Somewhere in Dover."

Tara frowned. "That doesn't sound very safe to me," she said. "There are a lot of Englishers at pizza places with their big cars. You can't leave a horse and buggy in a parking lot in a place like that."

"Eli's hiring a driver," Ginger explained.

"Mam!" Tara turned to their mother as she walked into the kitchen carrying a flour sack of something. "Ginger said she's going out for pizza tonight with Eli. I don't think it's a good idea. Benjamin said that when he went to Dover, he couldn't believe how heavy the traffic was. He saw a red car hit a blue one at a stoplight. Those Englishers, they don't pay attention to where they're going."

"I trust Eli to keep our Ginger safe, *Dochtah*. Do I smell cookies burning?" their *mam* asked, sniffing the air.

"Ne." At the counter, Nettie was sliding cookies off a baking sheet onto a cooling rack. "Just a cookie I accidentally knocked off the tray into the oven. It's burning on the bottom. I couldn't reach it." She slid the last warm cookie onto the rack. "I'm going to run up to the attic to get some of those old cookie tins. We can freeze the cookies in them. Anything else we need?"

Ginger shook her head and Nettie walked out of the kitchen.

"I didn't find any more dried cranberries in the pantry," their mother said. "We'll have to make the white chocolate and cranberry cookies later in the week after I can get to Byler's. I *did* find some walnuts Lovey gave us, though. We could make snowballs." She held up the cloth bag in her hand. "But someone will have to crack them."

"I can crack nuts when I'm done here," Ginger offered. She loved snowball cookies, which were made with a shortbread recipe and the walnuts. The dough was rolled into balls and baked that way, then rolled in powdered sugar while they were still warm.

"*Ne*, your little brother can do it," her mother answered. "He's been hiding out all morning, avoiding chores."

"Why don't you just come to the singing with us?" Tara's green eyes fixed on Ginger, her pretty face fraught with concern. She'd always been a worrier since she was very young. Their *mam* said everyone in the family had a job to do; Tara's was to worry so no one else had to.

"I told you, we're too old for that sort of thing." Ginger carried the tray of gingerbread cows to the stove for Nettie to put in when the next batch came out. Back at the table, she began to transfer the little gingerbread houses to a clean cookie sheet. "I'm kind of feeling like I am, too."

"You weren't last week when you went to a frolic with Joe," Tara pointed out.

Ginger stiffened but didn't say anything. She continued transferring the cookies. She was still trying to square up the fact that Joe, the man she thought she might marry, had broken up with her. And that Eli had asked her to walk out with him a few minutes later. She couldn't believe she had been so quick to agree. She supposed it was because she was so hurt and disappointed by how things had gone with Joe.

"Tara, can you go find Jesse?" their *mam* asked. "I want him to start cracking these walnuts."

"But I'm mixing up the dough for the butter horns," Tara protested.

"No room in the oven for them until we finish the gingerbread, anyway," their mother responded.

Ginger's sister shrugged. "*Ya*, I can go. I saw him through the window trying to put a leash on that white cat Ethan brought home from school last year."

Tara went to the sink, washed her hands, dried them on her apron and left the kitchen. Ginger's *mam* didn't speak until Tara closed the door behind her. Ginger got the feeling their mother had sent Tara on the errand so she could be alone with Ginger.

"I want you to know that Benjamin and I are very pleased that Eli has asked you to walk out with him and you had the good sense to agree to it."

Ginger picked up the rolling pin and started rolling out another piece of dough, though she already had dough rolled out and ready to be cut into cookies.

"I know you know I didn't approve of Joe from the beginning."

"He's not such a bad person," Ginger said, not wanting to have this conversation with her mother.

"I didn't say he was, *Dochtah*."

An egg timer sitting on the counter went off and her mother opened the oven and pulled out two cookie trays. The kitchen filled with the smell of warm baked gingerbread. "These ready to go in?" She pointed to one of the cookie sheets Ginger had prepared.

"*Ya.* And these." Ginger picked up a cookie sheet of houses from the table beside the one she'd been working on. Their family was so big, with so many adults for meals, that they had two big tables that they configured in various ways, depending on how they were using them. Today they formed an L shape.

"I think you'll find Eli to be kind and patient and very truthful with you. But you already know those things about him, I suspect. And he's fun," her mother added. "Some women like a man more serious, but I think it's important for you to have a husband you can laugh with and play games. Someone who sees your playful spirit. Those times will help you get through the harder ones we all meet."

Ginger cut her eyes at her mother. "No one is talking about marriage right now, *Mam.* I told Eli I'd go out with him. I don't even know why I agreed to it in the first place. It doesn't seem right to be walking out with one man one day and another the next. I don't want people thinking I'm fast." She reached for the rolling pin again.

Her mother was standing there, dressed in a leaf-green dress, her big apron with many pockets over it. Like her daughters, she wore a scarf to cover her hair, tied at the nape of her neck. In her simple clothes with the head kerchief, she looked younger than her years. She looked like she could have been Ginger's sister instead of her mother. Ginger hoped she would age as gracefully as her mother did.

"I guess I said yes because I was upset with Joe," Ginger said as much to herself as her mother.

"Do you mean you *don't* want to walk out with Eli?"

Her *mam* took a tone with her that wasn't exactly stern, but it wasn't gentle, either. "Because if that's so, you need to go to him now and call off this date before he pays a driver and carts the children to his sister's so he can take you out."

Ginger stepped back from the table, turning to face her mother. She crossed her arms over her chest. "I'm not saying I don't want to walk out with him. I'm just…"

Her mother waited.

"It's just that…" Ginger exhaled. "I saw my life going one direction, and now it seems as if that's not the way it will go and it's…unsettling."

Her mother smiled warmly. "Life is like that, *boppli*. When I married your father, I thought we would grow old together. That wasn't God's plan for me. But God knew what He was doing, even when I didn't." She opened her arms. "And it all worked out, didn't it? I lost your father, but now he's in Heaven. And I'm happily married to Benjamin. Just because your life doesn't turn out the way you thought it would, that doesn't mean the path you've found yourself on isn't a good path. It's just different."

Ginger nodded, trying to grasp what her mother was saying. Intellectually, she understood, but she was still struggling to reconcile it all in her head and her heart.

"Tell me something," her mother said after a moment. "Do you have feelings for Eli?"

Ginger looked down at her black sneakers.

"Answer my question, *Dochtah*. If you set Joe aside in your mind, do you have room for Eli in your heart? If the answer is yes, then you should put on a clean dress and a freshly starched *kapp* and go have pizza with him. But if you don't think you can be open to the new path God has set in front of you, you have to cancel your date. For Eli's sake and your own."

Ginger stood silent in her mother's warm, sweet-smelling kitchen for a moment. "I do have feelings for Eli. I think I have for some time now." She lifted her gaze to her mother, half-fearful she would judge her for walking out with one man while lying awake at night thinking of another.

But her mother smiled, closed the distance between them and wrapped Ginger in her soft, warm embrace. "Everything is going to be all right, *Dochtah*. Just take a breath, say a prayer and see where this path takes you."

Chapter Nine

"Oh my!" Eli sat back on the bench seat of the van and pressed his hand to his stomach. "I don't think I'll be able to eat for a week. Why did you let me eat five pieces of pizza?"

Ginger slid in beside him and fastened her seat belt, laughing. "I didn't tell you to have five pieces of mushroom pizza. And two root beers. You did that to yourself."

"But no one I know likes mushroom pizza," he explained. "I never get to eat it. Andrew and Simon always want pepperoni." He counted his children off on his fingers. "Phillip likes extra cheese, no meat, no vegetables, and Lizzy only eats the crusts." He waggled his finger at her. "*So* the fact that we both like mushroom pizza is another good reason why we should be walking out. Who else am I going to share mushroom pizza with?"

Ginger smiled and gazed out the window because she had no answer for that. Why *was* she fighting this? Why was she wrestling with this sense that she and Eli were right for each other? Why was she trying to ignore these feelings she had for him? He clearly felt an attraction to her, though so far, he'd had the good sense not to say anything about it. It was just so obvious that they were well matched. Everyone she cared for thought so: her mother, Benjamin, her sisters, even her friends. So why was she being so stubborn?

So stubborn that she'd almost backed out of their date.

By the time Eli had arrived at her house in the hired van, she had been so nervous that she'd half wanted to cancel, claiming an upset stomach. Her stomach *had* been upset when Eli had come to the door. Since they moved to Hickory Grove, Eli had been coming and going in their house, but he'd never been her suitor before. Her upset stomach must have just been butterflies, though, because by the time Eli had finished chatting with Benjamin about his search for a small pony for his children for Christmas, Ginger had caught her breath and calmed down. She had told herself she was making too much of this whole thing—she was just going for pizza with Eli. Her Eli, whom she saw at least five days a week. Her Eli whom she spent hours with each week in his kitchen playing games and talking.

Still, when he'd asked her if she was ready to leave the house, she'd almost chickened out. But she made herself go because Eli was so excited about going for pizza that she didn't want to disappoint him.

And now she was glad she hadn't canceled because she'd had a wonderful time. None of the boys she had dated had ever taken her out to a restaurant before. It had been an exciting adventure. There had been music playing over loudspeakers: country music, Eli had told her. She didn't know how he knew about English music, but she filed it away in her head to ask him sometime.

They'd been seated by a sweet young woman who reminded her of her sister Tara. The girl had strawberry blond hair and dangly earrings that looked like kittens. And then another nice young woman with her black hair in long braids had served them.

Ginger and Eli ordered a large mushroom pizza and large root beers and sat across from each other in a booth. The place was busy, probably because it was a Saturday night, so it had taken a bit of time to get their pizza, but she hadn't minded. Talking with Eli was so easy. So comfortable. With Eli, she didn't have to think about what she was going to say before she said it, and she never regretted her words. With Joe, she had always worried about whether or not she was too outspoken or if he would disagree with what she thought and criticize her for it. That wasn't the case with Eli. He knew who she was, maybe because they had known each other for some time now. But it was more than that. The way he looked at her when she spoke, he seemed truly interested in what she had to say.

"Buckled up?" their driver, Lucy, asked.

Ginger knew Lucy because her family used her services, too. With the heavy traffic and long distances the Amish sometimes had to drive to get to a doctor's appointment or a store, it was common practice for them to hire a driver. It was faster and safer. Lucy, in her late sixties, was a tiny bit of a woman with a helmet of fiery red hair Ginger suspected was dyed. Lucy was a good driver, but a no-nonsense woman and she didn't tolerate tardiness. When she pulled into your driveway at the agreed time, she expected you to be standing on the porch waiting for her. Lucy also wanted to know exactly where she was taking her clients and how long they would be at each stop, and she didn't mind telling you if you broke the rules. She was a local retired schoolteacher who had taught math to seventeen- and eighteen-year-olds. She told Ginger's *mam* that she didn't have to work but that she liked keeping busy. She said that at first, she'd started giving rides to her Amish neighbors over in the Rose Valley area as favors, but transporting those in need had become a full-time job. She was even willing to make longer trips, like out of state to take families to weddings and funerals, though Ginger's family had never used her for that.

Lucy eased out of the parking lot and onto the busy highway. They had one more stop to make. Eli had told Ginger when they got in the van at her house that after they ate, he wanted to go to a local store to get a new ax handle if that was okay with her. Ginger knew the store because they sometimes cut through the parking lot to get to the big box store where they shopped in bulk once a month. The large hardware store Eli needed to go to had intrigued her. They always had rows of small equipment like lawn mowers, snowblowers and gas barbecue grills lined up out front, depending on the season. And they had a huge garden center. In the spring, there were racks and racks of blooming flowers and come fall, there were all kinds of trees and bushes displayed for sale.

"You sure you don't mind stopping?" Eli asked Ginger as if reading her thoughts. "If you're tired, we can go home. I've got an old ax I can use until I get out here again."

Ginger shook her head. "*Ne.* I don't mind stopping." She looked up at him. "Is it all right if I come inside with you?"

She couldn't see his face well in the dark, but she could tell he was smiling at her. "Of course," he said.

"I've never been in here before," she explained, excited now about it.

He rested his arm on the back of the bench seat. He wasn't touching her, but he was close enough for her to feel his warmth and to smell his shaving soap. He'd arrived at her house freshly shaved and his hair, still damp, carefully combed. He was wearing clean, unpatched clothes, his church shoes and what appeared to be a brand-new shirt the color of a robin's egg. She guessed his sister had made it for him. She wondered if Claudia knew he was wearing it out on a date with Ginger. No one had ever said anything, but she had the feeling that Claudia wouldn't approve.

"Never been here before?" he asked, drawing his head back as if shocked. "Well, you're in for a treat. I know it's not very Amish of me, but—" he lowered his voice so that only she could hear him "—this is my favorite store."

Ginger pressed her lips together, suppressing a big smile, and gazed out the window at the sparkling streetlamps and strings of Christmas lights in storefront windows.

Five minutes later, Lucy had parked her minivan and pulled out a paperback novel to read. She always had a book with her.

"Twenty minutes," Eli told Lucy as he opened the sliding door to the van. "That okay?"

Lucy reached for a big paper cup from a fast-food place and took a sip from the straw. "I'll be right here."

Eli stepped out into the dark parking lot and offered his hand to Ginger.

She hesitated. Usually the drivers they used had a step stool to get in and out.

Before she could decide whether to take Eli's hand, he grasped hers.

She stepped down out of the van, distracted by the feel of Eli's warm, strong hand. Just then, a gust of wind kicked up, and he let go of her to grab his hat. She laughed as the wind whipped at her heavy cloak.

"Ready?" he asked.

She nodded, and they walked side by side toward the glass door. When they got close, it opened automatically.

"Let me grab that ax handle, and then I have a surprise for you. Something I suspect you'll like."

She looked up at him. "What?"

He shook his head. "It wouldn't be a surprise if I told you, now, would it?" They walked past a customer service desk. At the back wall, they took a right. There was so much to see that Ginger couldn't take it all in. She saw light fixtures and sinks and flooring. The store was busy with customers, Englishers dressed in fuzzy coats and thick colorful sweaters and bright hats with pom-poms on top.

"Let's see," Eli said. "We're looking for aisle RW," he said. "Here we go. Ax handles."

Ginger followed Eli, turning her head to watch a woman in a puffy white coat walk past them, pushing a cart. In the front of the cart was a tiny white dog dressed in a puffy coat that looked remarkably like the owner's. Ginger had to press her hand to her mouth to keep from giggling. Both had short spiky white hair on top of their heads and a red barrette.

Eli caught Ginger gaping and grabbed her hand,

leading her down the aisle. As they walked, their gazes met. Eli's blue eyes were dancing. He'd seen the dog with the coat and hair barrette, too.

"Here we are," Eli said, coming to stand in front of a display of axes and ax handles. "Let's see, hickory double-bit, fiberglass, forged steel." He squeezed her hand before letting go and then began picking up the ax handles one at a time.

Ginger stood there watching him, still feeling the warmth of his hand on hers. She couldn't believe how relaxed she felt with Eli in this new role as his girlfriend. It was as if they had been a couple for weeks, months. Years. Being with him was just so easy, so comfortable. Standing beside him, watching him weigh the differences between one ax handle and another, she could see herself at his kitchen table as his wife, riding to church on Sunday mornings in his buggy. She could see herself growing old with Eli, raising a family with him.

Interestingly enough, even though she'd been determined she and Joe would marry, she had never seen those things in her mind's eye with him. It was almost as if the *idea* of Joe had been what had attracted her—his good looks, the way folks made a fuss over him.

"I think I'll go with the hickory," Eli said to her, holding it up. "What do you think?"

"I don't know a thing about ax handles."

"Maybe not, but I've found that most women have an opinion on just about everything." He smirked. "And they're usually right."

"The hickory." She pointed to the ax handle in his hand. "I'd get the hickory."

"Hickory it is, then." He reached for her hand and

took it and then looked at her. "Is this all right? My holding your hand?"

Suddenly in the busy store, Ginger felt as if she and Eli were the only ones there. She gazed into his eyes. "I don't know that Bishop Simon would approve," she said, surprised by the shyness in her voice. "But...it feels right."

His smile was gentle. "It feels right to me, too, Ginger." He held her gaze another moment longer and then tugged on her hand. "Okay, shopping done. Now your surprise. Well, it's not exactly a surprise. I'm sure you've seen such things before, but they have a nice Christmas shop here. Lizzy loves it."

She let him lead her back down the aisle they'd come. "You think Lizzy and I like the same things?"

"You both like chocolate chip cookies without walnuts," he pointed out.

She rolled her eyes at him as they walked through a doorway into the area that was the garden shop. "*Ya*, but—" She stopped where she was and gazed around her. The whole room was filled with Christmas trees twinkling with white lights and colored lights, some flashing, some blinking, some as steady as the stars. There were Christmas lights everywhere and decorations galore. She turned around slowly, not knowing where to look first. There were big Santas popping out of fake chimneys and little birds on garland strings. Around the artificial trees were buckets of ornaments that looked like foxes and shoes and candy canes and cats. The Christmas trees were big and small, most green, but one a sparkly white. And they were covered in lights and ornaments.

Still holding Ginger's hand, Eli led her through what

seemed like a forest of Christmas trees. "This is my favorite one," he told her. He stopped in front of a tree decorated with soft, unblinking white lights. The whole tree was decorated in what looked like homemade ornaments: cookie cutouts, pine cones painted with white tips to look like snow, sticks of cinnamon glued together and tied with a little red bow.

Ginger reached out and touched one of the bundles of cinnamon sticks and it spun slowly. It had a little white tag attached to it. She read the tag. "Five dollars?" she exclaimed.

An employee stacking boxes of purple lights looked at her.

She lowered her voice, turning her back to the Englisher. "They're charging five dollars for two sticks of cinnamon and a bow. Do you know what that would cost to make?" She went on before he could answer. "Bay needs to see this tree. She could sell ornaments like these in her garden shop." She looked up at Eli. "Those are just pine cones sprayed with a clear coating and a little white paint."

He was smiling at her.

She smiled back and then said suspiciously, "What?"

He shook his head. "Nothing."

"Why are you looking at me like that?"

"You always say Bay is the businesswoman of the family, but I think you have a mind for it, too."

"Me?" She drew back.

"I've seen you working the cash register at Benjamin's harness shop. You're good with the customers."

"I usually work in the back." Before she had started working for Eli, she'd often worked shifts in Benjamin's shop, repairing bridles and such. She liked doing leatherwork. It was less delicate than needlework, and she liked the smell of freshly cut leather.

"I know you do. I'm just saying you're smart, Ginger."

Smart. She didn't know if anyone had ever said that to her. In her family, she had always been the pretty one. Bay was the smart one. She liked that Eli saw that in her rather than just focusing on her looks.

"Thank you," she said.

He looked down at her. "For what?"

She looked around. "For the pizza and soda. For this. I've had a really good time with you tonight, Eli."

"A good enough time to do something again with me? There's a chicken and dumpling supper over at Seven Poplars' schoolhouse Tuesday night. A fundraiser for Abe Zucker's little one. Been in and out of the hospital for weeks. Want to go with the children and me?" He raised an eyebrow. Like his hair, they were a dark red, which seemed to make his eyes look even bluer.

"I'd like that," she whispered.

They went to a cash register to make their purchase and then out into the cold night. Walking hand in hand with Eli across the parking lot, Ginger thought to herself this might have been the best evening she'd ever had in her life.

Eli made his way slowly toward his back porch, trying to settle himself. Molly seemed to sense his mood and trotted beside him, rather than circling him and barking the way she usually did. He hadn't had a good day at work. The client had stopped by to see the progress of his house and had gotten into a long, agitated discussion with Eli about what he liked and didn't like about the custom work Eli was doing for him. Mostly it was about what he didn't like. Eli had notes and drawings, which had been preapproved before he'd started the paneled woodwork that would go over the fireplace and flank it. He'd done exactly what the client had asked, and now the client had changed his mind. The whole interaction had frustrated Eli. Though he tried hard not to be prideful, he knew he had created a beautiful fireplace. The client didn't understand wood as a medium and what could and could not be done with the type of wood he had chosen. Now Eli would have to have a talk with his boss to see what was to be done. If the client wanted the whole mantelpiece and surrounding wainscoting removed and remade, Eli would do it. But it would mean a week of additional work and he didn't believe he or Ader should be penalized for the client's fickleness.

At the back steps, Eli stopped, and Molly dropped down beside him. The dog peered up at him expectantly.

Eli tried to soothe his irritation. He'd been gone all day; his children deserved better than a cranky *dat*. And what would Ginger think if he came into the house with a sour face? He took another step and stopped.

What would she *think*?

He would hope she would think that he'd had a bad day. Everyone had one occasionally. If this was going to work, if he and Ginger were going to marry, and he hoped with his entire heart that would be the case, she had to know him as he was. Yes, he was normally a positive person, a man that reminded himself every day of God's goodness. But at times, everyone got tired, frustrated and stuck in a loop of negative thinking. Being married meant respecting, even loving, their partner for all the good things about them and the not-so-good things, as well.

Inside the mudroom, Eli removed his work boots, his coat and his hat and walked into the kitchen in his stocking feet. The room smelled of the fire in the fireplace and the delicious aroma of baking chicken and fragrant herbs.

Ginger was seated in the chair that was to the right of his chair at the kitchen table. The chair that had become hers. And she was darning socks… One of his socks.

She looked up at him and smiled. "How was your day?"

He hesitated, his emotions suddenly a jumble. There was something about seeing her with his sock in her lap that tugged at his heartstrings. Tugged at them even more than her beautiful face, her beautiful smile. He shrugged. "Not the best. Yours?"

She lowered the darning to her lap. She was wearing a dark blue wool scarf over her hair and tied at the nape of her neck rather than a prayer *kapp*. He liked seeing her in his kitchen in a scarf because it symbolized her comfort in his home.

She nodded slowly. "Sorry you didn't have a good day. Want to tell me about it?"

"Maybe later," he responded. "But right now, I'd rather hear about your day."

"All right. Hmm. Let's see," she said. "I had a nice day. We all did. After Andrew and Simon went to school, I did laundry, fixed the torn hem on Lizzy's green dress, helped Phillip make piglets out of cardboard tubes from the paper-towel roll, washed dishes and…made supper."

"And darned socks." He pointed at the darning basket.

"And darned socks."

He nodded. "Smells good in here. Chicken?"

"Turkey breast. Tara's recipe. You rub it with olive oil and sprinkle fresh chopped rosemary on it. We have baskets of rosemary. *Mam* grows it in her garden and Bay's been using it in some of her floral arrangements she's selling at the garden shop."

He walked over to the stove to see red-skinned potatoes bubbling on a back burner. He turned and leaned against the sink, sliding his hands into his pockets. In a minute, he'd go wash up, but right now, he just wanted to stand here and be with Ginger. "What time is someone coming for you? Can you stay for supper?"

She picked up her darning again and smiled teasingly. "I had supper with you last night."

"But not here." He watched her capable hands make short work of the hole in the toe of one of his socks. "That was a fundraiser, and we were surrounded by fifty other people. Including my children." He glanced around, realizing he hadn't heard a peep from one of them since he got home. "Speaking of my children, where are they? It's awfully quiet around here. You lock them in the cellar?"

She gave him a look. "I did not. Let's see. Andrew is cleaning up a mess he made in the upstairs bathroom sink, trying to wash his marbles. I sent Simon to the smokehouse to get a bit of bacon for the lima beans. I would guess he stopped to play with the kittens in the barn. I'm surprised you didn't see him when you put the horse up. And Lizzy and Phillip are doing puzzles in the living room. We made them from a cardboard box. Kitten puzzles. That's what they're supposed to be. My drawing isn't the best."

He smiled, feeling himself begin to relax. She was always doing fun things like that with the children, making puzzles from cardboard, toys from scraps. Things he would never think to do. He loved that she was here to do those little activities. "You didn't answer my question. Can you stay for supper? And maybe a quick game of Chinese checkers?"

"Bay's been teasing me. She says marriage would never work for us because all we would do was sit around and play games. She says nothing would ever get done and the children would have to live on cookies you bought at Byler's."

He laughed. That sounded like something Bay would say. "You and your sister are talking about us marrying, are you?" he dared. "She thinks you ought to marry me?"

Ginger lowered her gaze to her darning and pushed the needle through the wool sock. "I shouldn't have told you that. It will put ideas into your head."

Her tone was playful, but he also got the impression that she hadn't discounted the idea. They hadn't been walking out together for long, but if they were right together, they were right together. The amount of time they courted didn't matter. And with every passing day, he was more certain that they *were* meant for each other. He'd been praying for so long for God to send him a wife. Now he had come to believe that God had meant for him to bump into Ginger and her mother at Byler's that day so that she could be here caring for his children while he worked. While they got to know each other. And now here they were.

"I told you from the beginning that was my intention, Ginger." He took a step toward her. "I told you I wanted to marry you."

She was quiet.

"I think we're meant for each other," Eli went on. "We get along well. The children love you and…" He suddenly felt tears sting the backs of his eyes. He thought of his Elizabeth and the love they shared and realized that he loved this woman, too. What a gift from God, he thought. To love two women in a lifetime. The question was, could Ginger love *him* one day? Because he'd made up his mind long ago. Men and women married for many reasons, and not always for love, but after the love he had shared with Elizabeth, he couldn't imagine a loveless marriage.

"The children love you, Ginger, and I love you," Eli pressed on, having no idea what had made him say such a thing in the middle of his kitchen on a Wednesday evening.

Ginger rose, setting the darning in a basket on the kitchen table. She walked slowly toward him and he watched her, looking for signs that he had ruined everything by talking about marriage too soon. By making proclamations of love when they'd only been courting less than a week.

"I thought the plan was to wait awhile before we talked about this," she said.

He brushed his hand across his mouth. "You're right. That was the plan. I'm sorry. It's only that I—" He glanced away. "I didn't mean to—" He returned his gaze to her. She was standing very close in front of him. So close that he could have kissed her. So close that he wanted to kiss her. But he restrained himself. He wasn't interested in casual dating. Or kissing a woman he would not marry. He prayed silently now that he would get to kiss Ginger one day, when they were man and wife.

"It's all right, Eli," she said to him. "It's only that… that I'm not ready to talk about…love yet."

"Because of Joe?" It came out of his mouth before he had time to think. "Because you were in love with him?"

The smile she offered was so sweet, so kind, and also a smile that gave him hope. There was something about the way she was looking at him that made him think maybe she really would agree to be his wife. Maybe not today, maybe not tomorrow. But one day.

"Joe doesn't matter anymore, because I'm not walking out with Joe. I'm walking out with you, Eli. But I need more time. I want to be sure this is right. That you're the man I'm meant to marry."

"So what I'm hearing," he said, lightening the mood, "is that this old man might have a chance with you?"

She smiled up at him. "This old man just might."

Chapter Ten

By the time Ginger walked down the lane from the house to the garden shop, the parking lot was packed with buggies, cars and trucks. Despite the cold temperatures and threat of a wintry mix, it seemed as if everyone in Hickory Grove, Amish and English, had turned out for Bay's first annual Christmas wreath-making workshop.

Ginger had been sent to the kitchen to grab another big tin of peanut butter thumbprint cookies. Bay and Joshua were serving cookies, hot chocolate and hot cider after their workshop, and the turnout was higher than they'd expected. Bay was worried they would run out. Tara had fussed that they would be giving away a lot of the cookies they had made for the schoolhouse cookie sale, but Bay explained that it was good business to give away a few cookies in the hope folks would come to the sale the next weekend. She'd put up signs in the harness shop and her garden shop advertising the fundraiser, and she suspected they'd sell every cookie the women in Hickory Grove could bake for the cause.

As Ginger cut across the gravel parking lot that

served both the garden shop and the harness shop, she spotted Eli's buggy and smiled to herself. She was looking forward to seeing him and the children; she missed them on the Saturdays when they didn't get together. Ginger was amazed by how easily her life had fallen into place once she had surrendered to allowing God to guide her. With Joe, she'd been constantly trying to force her will on God and Joe, trying to convince them both that she and Joe were meant to be together. Now she knew that she was wrong. And she was thankful she had been, because she was so happy with Eli, happy in a way she doubted she could ever have been with Joe.

For the first time in her life, Ginger felt like she was a better person when she was with someone else than when she was alone. And that someone else was Eli. It was just so easy to talk with him, to be with him. He made her want to be a better person, a woman of stronger faith with more patience. And she loved the days she spent with his four little ones while he was at work. She had fallen in love with them. And now she was beginning to realize that though she didn't know what it felt like to fall in love, she suspected she had. Or was. She just hadn't taken the time to process it.

Exhaling puffs of frosty breath, Ginger hurried toward the garden shop door. Bay had decorated it with one of her generous wreaths made from boxwood branches, pine cones and a big red gingham bow. The door was outlined with white Christmas lights that were powered by one of the generators that ran the shops. There had been talk as to whether Bay was getting too fancy, adorning the shop with twinkle lights. However, because many of their customers were English, Benjamin, as the head of the family, had approved the decorations and said that if their bishop had a problem with it, he could talk to him.

Bells jingled as Ginger stepped through the doorway in the shop. The building was barely more than a shed and lit brightly with more Christmas lights. The greenhouse and garden shop were already so successful that Bay and Joshua had plans to build a new shop in the spring, one much bigger than this temporary building they were using.

Joshua's wife, Phoebe, greeted Ginger at the door. She'd been tasked with checking families in before sending them in the direction of the greenhouse, where Bay would be giving her workshop on wreath making. They'd spent the whole morning moving poinsettias and fresh table arrangements to make room for those attending the workshop. They would be using the tables that usually displayed plants as a work surface. Bay had also borrowed some chairs from the church wagon. Ordinarily, the tables and chairs were used for church events, weddings and such. However, Bay had convinced the elders to let her use them for the event with the promise to deliver the wagon to her brother Ethan's house in time for him and his wife, Abigail, to get everything set for the next church Sunday.

When Ginger walked in, Phoebe opened her eyes wide as if to say "Help me! Things are crazy here!"

Which they were. The shed, smelling of pine boughs and cinnamon and nutmeg, was packed with friends and neighbors and familiar and unfamiliar English faces. It was standing room only. Bay stood near the checkout counter, trying to usher folks past her and into the connecting greenhouse.

The doorbells jingled, and an English woman in a long skirt, leading a little girl by the hand, walked in.

"My, it's bitter out there," she remarked. The woman and child were wearing brown, fuzzy coats with red scarves around their necks that made them look like the teddy bears Ginger had seen in stores.

"Amber and Taylor Crouse," the woman said to Phoebe. "We preregistered." She glanced around. Her cheeks were bright red from the cold, and she was wearing lipstick that matched. "This is so much fun. Doing a craft at a real Amish farm. We just moved into the area. We're across the street from the schoolhouse, the old Baker farm." She pointed in the general direction.

Phoebe smiled and made a mark on her notepad. "Good to have you with us. Head that way, and someone will help you find a spot at a table in the greenhouse. We're going to get started in about fifteen minutes."

"Is there going to be a tour of the farm? I know it's dark, but we'd love a tour."

"Sorry, no tours," Phoebe said sweetly.

Ginger watched the woman and her daughter make their way toward the greenhouse. Bay had finally gotten the crowd in motion, and there was now space in the shed to move around a little. There were still folks stopping to talk to each other. Eunice Gruber was standing by the checkout counter, talking loudly about someone's trip to the dentist. Probably not one of her own family members. Eunice always knew all of the gossip in Hickory Grove. Good and bad.

"With all these preregistrations, we can only take one more walk-in," Phoebe told Ginger. "Joshua only made up frames for thirty-five wreaths."

"I just put three more together, so we can do thirty-eight, but any more than that and we won't have enough greenery anyway," Joshua said, walking toward them. He was dressed as if he had just been outside, in a heavy denim coat and a navy blue knit cap pulled down over his ears. "We're getting another shipment Monday morning." When he reached his wife, he frowned at her. "I brought you a stool so you would sit on it." He pointed at the stool next to the door. "You've been on your feet all day. You need to rest." He took her hand and led her toward the stool. "Sit, wife."

Phoebe obediently dropped to the stool.

"Joshua!" Bay called from her post at the checkout counter. "Could you grab a couple more chairs from the church wagon outside? Mrs. Carter's grandmother needs one. At the end of the first table. They're just making one wreath, but I wasn't expecting so many people to come from each family."

"Great, isn't it?" Joshua called back. "I'll take care of it, Bay. It's fine. We've got plenty more chairs, and I dug up some more floral wire and pine cones." He set his hand on the door to go outside. "Ginger, could you please make sure my wife stays put for a few minutes? She's done too much today."

Phoebe laughed. "I've not done too much. There's been a lot to do today. We had to get ready for this evening, and customers were still coming and going."

Joshua looked at Ginger as he walked out the door. "She's done too much," he repeated, then closed the door behind him, the bells jingling overhead.

Phoebe met Ginger's gaze. "I can't get him to understand that there's nothing wrong with me. I'm not sick or hurt." She rested her hand on her rounded belly. In the last few weeks, she'd really popped out. While it was poor manners among the Amish to speak publicly of pregnancy, there could be no doubt in anyone's mind that Joshua and Phoebe were expecting their first baby. "I keep telling him there's nothing more natural. I feel wonderful. You'll see when you and Eli are married," she added softly, her eyes twinkling.

Ginger was surprised by the lump of emotion that rose in her throat. She looked away. She hadn't really ever thought that much about having babies of her own. Of course she had always known she wanted children, if God was willing to so gift her and her husband. But now the idea of having a child of her own body was something she was thinking about more and more often. It wasn't something she had ever thought about with Joe, but with Eli… This was somehow different. Of course, Andrew, Simon, Phillip and Lizzy would become her children when she and Eli wed. And she was now thinking in those terms: when they wed, not if. But having their own children together seemed like something that would only add to the close knitting of their new family.

Ya, she wanted to marry Eli. But she was pushing him to be patient. And herself. Marriage was for a lifetime, a big commitment before God and their community, and Ginger knew she had to be absolutely sure that Eli was meant to be her husband and she his wife. There had been whispers among the younger unmarried women in Hickory Grove that Ginger was making a mistake considering marrying a man with children, a man so much older than she was. One of the girls had piped up with a giggle that it would be like marrying your father. Tara had told her she'd overheard several girls talking at Spence's Bazaar about it. None of them could understand how Ginger could let a boy like Joe Verkler get away.

Eli's age wasn't an issue for Ginger. He never seemed too old or fatherly in any way to her. And despite his comments about his gray hair and wrinkles, she found Eli attractive. Not in the way she had found Joe attractive. Joe was so handsome he was almost pretty. Granted, Eli had a few lines etched on his face, but to her, they were tiny lines of experience, of knowledge. And the twinkle in his eyes, the way he looked at her when he thought she wouldn't notice, made her feel weak in the knees in a way Joe's gaze never had.

The bells jingled as the door opened again, breaking Ginger's reverie. "I best get these cookies to the refreshment table. You know how Tara worries," Ginger told Phoebe. "She wants everything laid out just so. I tried to tell her we could set up the snacks while folks were making their wreaths, but she wouldn't have it."

Phoebe got up off the stool. "I'll be in to help in a few minutes. Just a few more folks to arrive."

"I think the plan is to start on time, whether everyone who's registered is here or not," Ginger said over her shoulder as she walked away. "You best sit down before your husband comes back in."

Phoebe cut her eyes at Ginger. "My husband likes to pretend he's tough, but I know better. He's soft and sweet in the middle." She smiled the smile of a woman in love with her husband, her new family and her new life. A distant cousin to Ginger on her mother's side, Phoebe had had a hard go of it in Pennsylvania where she'd grown up. She'd loved a man and nearly lost everything, including her son, but all had changed the previous year when she'd arrived on the Millers' doorstep in need of shelter and a new chance at life.

As she made her way to the greenhouse, Ginger greeted friends and neighbors, having to talk loudly to be heard above the cacophony of voices speaking English and Pennsylvania *Deitsch*. And one English man trying to talk in German to one of Ginger's stepbrothers who had taken over for Bay, trying to usher everyone to their seats so the workshop could begin.

As Ginger entered the greenhouse, she began to unfasten her cloak with one hand. It was quite a bit warmer inside; she'd have to shed her cloak. Her sweater over her dress would be enough.

"Ginger!"

Ginger saw a flash of denim and barn boots as Phillip launched himself against her, wrapping his arms around her legs.

"Easy, Phillip!" Ginger cautioned in Pennsylvania *Deitsch* as she laughed, trying to keep her balance.

"*Dat* said I could come get you. He said you were going to help us make our wreath. Are you going to help us?" The little boy bounced on his toes and hugged her again.

"Where is your *dat*?" she asked, gazing out over the crowd.

Phillip spun around. "I don't know. He's here somewhere."

Ginger laughed. "Let me put these cookies down and we'll look together." But as she headed for the refreshment table set up in the back and decorated with white and red poinsettias, Phillip took off in the opposite direction with one of the neighbor's boys.

"There you are," Tara called to Ginger in Pennsylvania *Deitsch* as she approached the table. She was busy setting out napkins. "I don't know if we have enough cups for the hot cider." She looked up. "Do you think we should serve cold cider too?"

"I think just the hot cider will be fine," Ginger said, setting down the tin of cookies.

"I don't know. Maybe we should have cold. I'll have

to get more cups. I think we have paper ones up at the house," Tara fretted.

"Here. Can you put my cloak with yours?" Ginger asked, handing it across the table to her sister.

"*Ya*." Tara took it and turned around to lay it over a chair. "Oh, I almost forgot. Someone was looking for you."

"Eli? I know. Phillip—"

Tara turned back. "*Ne*, it was Joe."

Ginger made a face. "Joe? Verkler?"

"*Ya*. He was here a little while ago asking for you." She held up some small napkins. "You think these are okay? I thought we had bigger napkins at the house, but I couldn't find them."

Ginger made a face. "What does Joe want with me?"

Tara shrugged. "I don't know. I heard he broke up with that girl from Seven Poplars." She leaned closer and whispered, "Maybe he wants to get back together with you."

Ginger dropped her hands to her hips and laughed. "Get back together with me? *That's* not going to happen."

"You might have to tell him that yourself," Tara said. She nodded in the direction over Ginger's right shoulder. "There he is," she whispered.

Eli stood talking to Lynita Byler and nodded as if he heard every word she said. As the older woman went on about how she'd chased a fox from her henhouse, his gaze fell on Ginger's back. She was standing at the refreshment table talking with Tara. Ginger was wearing a rose-colored dress and navy blue knit cardigan. Her prayer *kapp* covered her blond hair, but tiny tendrils had escaped and curled at the nape of her neck. He couldn't hear what they were saying; Lynita was getting hard of hearing, which meant she thought everyone else was, too. He smiled and nodded as he watched Ginger. Tara was directing her to look at something or someone.

Eli slid his hands into his pants pockets as he casually turned to see what Ginger was now looking at. Not what. But *whom*.

Joe Verkler.

It took Eli by surprise. To see Joe and his Ginger in the same room. To see Joe looking at her the way he was.

Eli suddenly felt sick to his stomach.

Could he really compete with a young man that handsome, a man still in his twenties who could probably chop wood all afternoon without stopping?

Eli's gaze shifted to Ginger again. Then to Lynita, who had wandered on to the subject of her grandson and his fondness for golden raisin cookies. "Where are those children?" Eli muttered, shaking his head. "I best find them." He nodded politely. "Good to talk to you, Lynita."

"*Ya*," she agreed. "You let me know if you have trouble with foxes in your henhouse," she called after him as he walked away.

He raised his hand. "Will do."

By the time Eli reached the refreshment table, Ginger was talking to Tara again. When Ginger saw him, she broke into a wide grin. "There you are."

"Here I am," he said, glad he'd taken the time to change not just his shirt but his trousers, too. Ginger was as pretty as ever. Her cheeks were pink, maybe from the cold.

She slid her arm casually through his, taking him by surprise. They held hands in private: when they were out on a date, like when they'd gone for pizza, and sometimes at the table when they were playing Chinese checkers. But only when the children weren't in the room. This was the first time he could recall them ever touching this way in front of anyone, and it made his heart swell. He was pleased that she found it natural to take his arm. He was equally pleased that she would do it in front of others. In front of Joe. He knew he shouldn't feel this way. He wasn't in a competition with Joe for Ginger's heart. He couldn't compete with a flashy young man like Joe, nor did Eli want to. But just the same, her touch made him happy. It was as if she was announcing to the world that he was her beau. That she chose him.

"I asked Phillip where you were," Ginger said. "But he couldn't remember."

"Up front, on the left." He met Tara's gaze. She was watching them. He nodded hello and she nodded back.

"Hello! Thank you for coming tonight!"

Eli glanced over his shoulder to see Bay standing in front of the room, trying to get everyone's attention.

"If everyone could find a place!" Bay practically shouted.

Several people were trying to shush their neighbors, and one of the young men, maybe even Joe Verkler, whistled between his teeth.

"Hey, listen up!" someone hollered.

Suddenly the entire group lowered their voices.

"If you could find a place, we'll get started. Each family needs to find a spot with one of these." Bay held up a round wire frame. "You're going to use this frame to form your wreath."

"Are you going to help us?" Eli asked Ginger. "The children are excited about making a wreath with you."

"Let me help Tara get these cookies out and then I'll be over." Ginger's gaze met his and he felt himself relaxing. He had nothing to worry about, least of all Joe Verkler. Ginger cared for him. He could see it in her green eyes when she looked at him.

"I'll try to keep them busy until you get there." He reluctantly released her arm. "And try not to mess up the wreath."

She flashed him a smile and Eli felt as if he was walking on clouds as he crossed the room and joined Phillip, Andrew and Lizzy at the table next to Claudia and two of her girls.

"Ginger coming to help us?" Andrew asked.

"In a minute," Eli assured him as he took a spool of floral wire from Phillip's hand. "We're going to need that in a minute, *Sohn*."

"Ginger's coming?" Andrew repeated.

"She sure is."

As Eli said it, he caught, out of the corner of his eye, his sister watching him. Her arms were crossed over her chest. As if she wanted to say something. Eli sighed. "What?" he said softly.

"I didn't say anything," she responded.

"*Ne*, but you want to." He met her gaze. They were the same height, he and Claudia. Maybe that was how she had remained so formidable in his mind, even after all these years. After their mother died, it was Claudia he'd always worried about displeasing. Not their father.

"I saw her flirting with you right in front of everyone."

Eli looked straight ahead. Bay was talking again, explaining how to choose longer pine branches to make the base of the wreath.

When Eli didn't respond to his sister, she went on.

"You know why she's doing that, don't you? That old boyfriend of hers. He's here tonight."

Eli cut his eyes at his sister. "Ginger and I are walking out together," he said softly. "Old boyfriends don't matter anymore."

Claudia sighed. "I know I've said this before, but I'll say it again. I think you're naive, Eli. She's playing with you. I don't blame her. It's what young girls do. But you, you're old enough to see through it. And if you don't, I'm afraid you're going to get hurt."

Eli took a deep breath and exhaled. Claudia went on talking, even as Bay started giving instructions again. But he didn't hear either of them because he was too busy making up his mind that tonight was the night. He was going to ask Ginger to marry him and put an end to this nonsense with his sister.

An hour later, Eli had a beautiful wreath sitting on the table in front of him. Thanks to Ginger, who had not only tied the bow and added several sprigs of holly with red berries, but had also saved the day when she managed to reattach part of the greenery that fell off when Andrew accidently cut the wrong piece of wire.

"*Dat*!" Lizzy cried. "Can I have a cookie? Ginger *shaid* there was cookies."

Looking for Ginger, who had just walked away, disappearing into the crowd, Eli clasped his daughter's hand and led her toward the refreshment table. "*Ya*, one cookie. But that's it. You had cookies at home before we left." They were almost to the table when Eli spotted Ginger. He looked around, saw Simon. "Get a cookie for your sister," he told his son. "Keep her right here. I'll just be a minute." Eli gave Lizzy a nudge toward her brother and then slowly made his way across the greenhouse to where Ginger was busy stacking half-used spools of wire.

"Thank you for helping us tonight. I think we have the prettiest wreath," he told her.

"I don't know." She looked up at him. "Did you see the one someone made with all the pink plastic dough-nuts on it?" Her mouth twitched with amusement. "I guess she brought them with her."

"I did not." He laughed, now stalling for time. He'd planned what he wanted to say, but now that the time had come, he was suddenly nervous. He knew that Claudia, though well-meaning, didn't know Ginger. She didn't know how kindhearted she was. What a good parent she was to his children. How perfect she was for him. All Claudia saw was the pretty face; she couldn't get past that.

"Ginger…" He took a breath. "Can I talk to you for a minute?"

She lifted a blond eyebrow, as she began putting the rolls in a cardboard box. "You are talking to me."

He glanced around. The greenhouse was still full of people. Everyone was visiting with friends and neighbors, having a cookie and a drink and in no hurry to go home.

"In private," he said, grabbing her hand and ducking behind a tall arrangement of poinsettias. Anyone who looked closely might be able to tell they were back there, but it would at least give them some semblance of privacy.

"What's gotten into you?" Ginger asked, laughing.

He was still holding her hand. He took a deep breath and looked into her eyes. "Ginger Stutzman, will you marry me?"

At first Ginger seemed surprised. Then her face softened. "I thought we were going to wait a little while before we talked about this," she said quietly.

"I know. I know you said that, but… I can't help myself. Making the wreath together, seeing you with the children. They all love you so much. And…" He pressed his lips together and forged on. "You already know I'm in love with you," he said softly. "So…"

She took his hand between hers. "Eli, please. I'm not ready. I still need some time to get to know you. To—"

"It's Joe Verkler, isn't it?" Eli interrupted, taking his hand from hers.

She looked up at him, her forehead wrinkling. "Eli. This has nothing to do with Joe. It has everything to do about you and me. And what marriage means. I marry you," she said, "and it's forever. Until death parts us. I want to be absolutely sure."

"So you're not saying no. You're just saying you need more time."

She nodded. "A little more time. That's all."

Eli let out a sigh of relief. He would have preferred she'd just said yes, but at least she wasn't saying no. "Can I ask how soon you'll be ready? A day from now? A year?"

She smiled. "Maybe somewhere in-between?" she teased.

"All right. Fine. I should gather my children." He turned away from her to go and then came back again. "You know I'm going to keep asking until you say yes."

"I hope so," she said.

And then she smiled at him in a way that warmed him from the tip of his toes to the top of his head, and Eli walked around the display of poinsettias to join the crowd, thinking he might be the most blessed man on Earth.

Chapter Eleven

Eli stood in the rear of the schoolroom, watching his neighbors and friends, both Amish and English, as they moved from desk to desk, sampling cookies and making purchases. Ginger's stepbrother Ethan and his wife, Abigail, had done an excellent job of organizing the Christmas cookie sale. Abigail had enlisted the help of the women, young and old, in Hickory Grove to make dozens of cookies, hundreds of dozens, to sell as a fundraiser for the school. Mothers made cookies with their daughters, grandmothers made cookies with granddaughters and adult sisters like Tara, Nettie, Ginger and Lovey made cookies together. One of Benjamin's Englisher customers, a retired schoolteacher, had even baked cookies to donate when she heard about the cause.

With more Amish families moving to Kent County each year, the schoolhouse was bursting at the seams. The original idea had been to build an addition to the structure to accommodate the extra students, but at an elders' meeting that week, it had been decided that a new school needed to be built on the other end of town, if they could raise enough money. One of the new families around the corner from Eli had even offered to donate an acre of ground. With a couple of fundraisers as successful as this one and the help of all of the tradesmen in Hickory Grove, Eli had the feeling they'd have a new schoolhouse in no time.

He nibbled on a cookie Ginger had given him as she'd passed by carrying a wooden crate of cookies from their family buggy. It was as good a piece of gingerbread as he'd ever eaten. She'd made them herself, she'd told him. His gaze moved about the room until it settled on her. Tonight she was wearing a green dress the color of summer grass that made her eyes all the greener. She wore a white prayer kapp to cover her blond hair, the string of the *kapp* a loop that brushed the nape of her neck, where tendrils of her hair curled. His hand itched to touch those little wisps, but he would never do that. He didn't think the age difference between him and Ginger mattered that much, except in the circumstances of physical intimacy. While he knew very well that young folks engaged in kissing and such while courting, at his age, and as a widower and a father, he didn't feel it would be appropriate. Ginger's parents or even someone in the community might look at such behavior as him taking advantage of the younger woman, and he would never want that. He was so set on proper behavior that he had decided he wouldn't kiss Ginger, though he wanted to, until they were properly wed before God, their bishop, friends and family.

He watched Ginger. She was standing behind her younger sister Nettie, showing her how to use a spatula to ease cookies onto a scale. The women were selling the cookies by the pound so folks could buy as many varieties as they wished. Most of the buying customers were Englishers, and they didn't even seem to blink at what Eli had feared would be too much per pound for anyone to buy cookies at all.

"*How much* a pound?" Eli had overheard an Englisher woman with her elderly mother in tow ask earlier in the evening.

Ginger's fraternal twin sister, Bay, had repeated the price, and the woman, wearing a bright red hat with a white pom-pom on top, had chuckled with glee. "Homemade cookies? We'd pay twice for that, wouldn't we, Mom?" she'd said. "I'd pay anything, so I don't have to make them."

"Twice that," her mother had agreed, pulling a fat wallet from her handbag. "No one bakes anymore."

The mother and daughter had made Eli smile as they'd moved from desk to desk, checking out the cookies and even sampling some. Bay, who had as good a head for business as anyone Eli had ever known, had come up with the clever idea of passing out samples of some of the cookies, ones that had gotten broken being transported. Eli had a feeling that trick would guarantee they would sell every cookie that had been carried into the schoolhouse that evening.

"Pretty impressive turnout," Ginger's stepfather said, walking over to stand beside Eli. Benjamin had a bit of a limp these days. A flare-up of gout, he'd told Eli earlier in the week. Eli liked Benjamin immensely. He admired him as a man of faith and the head of the family. He also admired how well Benjamin had handled the death of his first wife and his willingness to accept the gift of Rosemary and her son and daughters when God set him on their path. Rosemary's husband had been Benjamin's best friend back in upstate New York. That might have deterred a lesser man, but Benjamin was a devoted man of God, a man who had the good sense not only to pray but to listen to the answers to his prayers.

"Our wives and daughters and sisters," Benjamin went on. "They outdid themselves, didn't they?"

Eli's sister, Claudia, hadn't come to the cookie sale to volunteer because one of her girls was down with croup. However, she'd sent her oldest son over to Eli's with twelve dozen cookies for the sale and an extra dozen for Eli. She'd made one of his favorites, the candied fruit cookies that their mother had made for them as children. With assorted nuts and dried fruits like pineapple, dates and cherries, the cookies always reminded him of fruitcake. Claudia now continued their mother's tradition each year, making multiple batches for her family and Eli's.

Benjamin and Eli stood side by side, watching the ladies sell box after box of cookies. They had set up an assembly line on the school desks. The teenage girls placed cookies into boxes that the customers picked up when they came in the door. Then the older women weighed the cookies, taking money and making change from an old fishing-tackle box someone had brought to serve as a cash box. Little girls were helping at each of the stations. Lizzy was standing with Tara and talking nonstop.

Ginger had indeed brought his shy daughter out of her shell. To see his Lizzy so comfortable with Tara, someone she would have once considered a stranger, even though she knew Benjamin's family, made Eli's heart sing. After his Elizabeth had died, one of his greatest fears had been that he wouldn't be able to raise their children to be the men and woman his wife wanted them to be. Since Ginger had come into his life, that fear was gone. The blended Miller-Stutzman family had embraced his in an even tighter hug since Eli and Ginger had begun walking out together, and he saw in his mind's eye the families only getting closer with the years.

Eli's gaze naturally wandered to Ginger again. The line of customers was no longer out the door, which was a good thing because when she'd last walked past him, she'd told him she was bringing in the last of the cookies they had to sell.

"Rosemary said you and the children will be coming to our place Christmas Eve for supper and prayer," Benjamin said. "I was glad to hear it. We like to keep Christmas quietly, but it's always nice to have another family join us."

"It was kind of you to ask us. We usually join Claudia's family, but she's got her in-laws coming in from Tennessee, and the house and kitchen will be bursting. And truth be told, her mother-in-law can talk until a man's ears ache, so…" Eli's voice drifted off as Benjamin chuckled.

Several of the unmarried men of the community came into the schoolhouse in a burst of bitter cold and rowdy male voices and began moving desks back to their proper places as the women sold the last of the cookies.

"Seen a big change in Ginger these last months," Benjamin mused aloud. "Since you hired her to look after your little ones. She's set aside her girlish ways and become a young woman right in front of us."

"Ginger's truly been an answer to my prayers," Eli responded. "Here I was, worried whether or not I could even take the job Ader had offered, especially with Lizzy being so sick at the time, and Rosemary walks up to me in Byler's. The next thing I know, Ginger's coming to work for me."

"'For my thoughts are not your thoughts, neither are your ways my ways, saith the Lord. For as the heavens are higher than the earth, so are my ways higher than your ways, and my thoughts than your thoughts,'" Benjamin quoted from the book of Isaiah.

"*Ya,*" Eli agreed. He wasn't much for being able to recite scripture, but he was good at remembering their meaning when it was quoted to him. He knew this one because it was something his grandfather used to say. "The Lord works in mysterious ways."

"That he does," Benjamin agreed. Then he met Eli's gaze, taking on a serious tone. "I know I'm not supposed to get involved with our adult children's lives. Rosemary tells me that all the time. We have to accept that we've raised them right, and they'll make good decisions, but I have to ask, Eli. What's your intention with our Ginger?"

Benjamin's directness took Eli by surprise. But he wasn't insulted or embarrassed, he just hadn't anticipated the question tonight. "My *intention*?" he asked. He didn't have to think on it because it was all he'd been thinking about for weeks. "My intention is the same as any man's when he walks out with a woman. At least a man my age, with a houseful of children." He paused, unprepared for the emotion that welled in his chest. "I intend to ask Ginger to marry me. When the time's right. Now I know there's an age difference, Benjamin, but—"

"That's no concern of ours, mine and Rosemary's," Benjamin interrupted. "Had it been, we'd have said so from the start."

"My sister might not agree."

Benjamin gave a wry smile, and for a moment, they both watched an English couple arguing over what kind of chocolate chip cookies they wanted.

"Claudia's expressed the same concern to Rosemary," Benjamin said.

Eli looked at him, feeling a speck of irritation. He was a grown man. He didn't need his sister in his business. "She has?" He frowned. "Claudia should mind her own knitting."

Benjamin waved his meaty hand in dismissal. "Women's talk. Claudia meant no harm. You're her little brother. It's natural she be protective of you and your little ones."

"I know," Eli agreed. "I just worry that no one will suit her unless she chooses for me, and that's not going to happen. You know she and Elizabeth were good friends. Closer to sisters."

Benjamin nodded in commiseration. "I hear what you're saying." He cut his eyes at Eli. "I'd ask that you not tell Claudia I tattled, else I'll be in trouble with my wife."

"No fear of that." Eli exhaled. "Anyway, like I was saying. I want to marry Ginger. I think she and I are well matched. We find it easy to go about the tasks of the day together. We think along the same lines. We work well together and talking is easy." He smiled. "Ginger's so full of life that she brought life back into our home. Into me."

"I agree you're well matched. More importantly, Rosemary agrees." Benjamin tucked his thumbs beneath his suspenders and tugged at them. "So what are you waiting for?"

Eli looked at Benjamin, not sure what he meant. "What?"

"You've known Ginger since we moved to Hickory Grove, and she's been in your household for months. I think maybe it's time you ask her to marry you," Benjamin said.

"I, um… We—Ginger and I—agreed to wait awhile before we made that decision. To…take our time."

"But you *want* to ask her to marry you?" Benjamin looked Eli directly in the eye.

"*Ya, ya,*" Eli stumbled, suddenly feeling uncomfortable. "I do."

"Then I say you best ask and make it official. I don't believe in long courting or betrothal for that matter. And in this case, if it's what you both want, I think it's best you get to it. Especially with *him* prowling about." Benjamin lifted his chin in the direction of the far side of the room.

Eli saw at once who his friend was pointing out. Joe Verkler, who must have come in with the young men to clean up, was standing next to Ginger as she cleaned cookie crumbs from a school desk. They were having a private conversation and she was laughing.

The way a girl laughs with her beau.

Eli felt his heart tumble. Joe was such a handsome young man and Ginger was so gorgeous. Too pretty a girl for Eli, with his wrinkles and his gray hair. They were a good-looking couple, too. And Ginger seemed to be happy, the way she smiled up at him. Eli couldn't hear her laughter over the voices in the room, but he could hear it in his head. Had she ever looked that way when she talked to him?

Eli slid his hands into his pants pockets and swallowed hard. Suddenly he felt overheated. A voice in the back of his head made him wonder if Claudia had been right from the beginning. *Was* Ginger playing him? Had she agreed to court Eli because she wanted to make Joe jealous? Was Joe who she still wanted to marry, not him? Was that why she'd put him off last week?

Eli wondered if he *was* too old for Ginger. He'd been telling Claudia and himself that he wasn't. He'd even been trying to prove it to Ginger, but what if he was wrong? What if this had all been a mistake, these weeks of courting the prettiest girl in the county? Was he just being selfish?

Maybe Ginger deserved a younger man. One without children already, too. Ordinarily, a young woman had time to adjust to married life, then the duties of a mother came on slowly as the children came one by one. If Eli married Ginger, she would walk away from the wedding ceremony the mother of four with the responsibilities of a big farm and five to wash and cook and clean for.

Eli's mouth became dry and he could feel his heartbeat increase. Was he so lonely that his judgment had been off? Was he not really suited to be Ginger's husband?

Eli felt sick to his stomach. If it *was* a mistake, he might be ruining not only Ginger's life but that of his children.

Benjamin clamped his hand over Eli's arm. "No time like the present time, eh?"

Suddenly resigned, Eli watched as Benjamin walked away. His friend was right. If he was going to do this, there was no need to put it off.

Eli gathered his children one by one and put them into the buggy. As he did so, he kept an eye out for Ginger, glancing over his shoulder again and again.

The schoolyard was lit with kerosene lanterns and the lamps from departing buggies.

He'd caught Ginger without Joe at her side and asked her if she had a minute to talk. She was just packing up the scale and the last few bakery boxes they hadn't used. He'd told her he'd get his four little ones situated in the buggy and then be back into the school to see if anything needed to be carried out.

"Can we have a cookie, *Dat*?" Lizzy asked. She was on the front seat, bundled in a thick denim coat, a wool hat and wool mittens. Her brothers had piled into the back and were wrestling like puppies on the floor. The buggy rocked.

"*Sohns*! In your seats," Eli ordered, tucking a blanket over Lizzy's legs.

"Cookies!" Phillip shouted. "We need cookies. Did you buy us cookies, *Dat*?"

"No one *needs* cookies," Eli responded, trying not to be short with him. He wiped a cookie crumb off Lizzy's cheek, easily seen with the bright lights he'd recently installed in the buggy.

The interior lights ran off a car battery. He'd added a little heater, as well. In his day, his mother had heated bricks on the stove, wrapped them in kitchen towels, and that was what had warmed them on cold trips in the buggy. But Eli didn't have the time or energy for heating bricks on the stove, plus he worried about the danger of the children being burned by them if they were too hot.

"One cookie each," Eli conceded, opening one of the white bakery boxes at Lizzy's feet. He'd bought two boxes of cookies. Four and a half pounds in all. He gave Lizzy her cookie first. "Anyone else wanting a cookie needs to sit down," he warned his boys.

One by one, they found a place on the bench seats

that faced each other, and one by one, he gave them sugar cookies. Made by one of the older Fisher girls, they were Christmas trees that were frosted with green icing and had little bits of brown icing on them that looked like pine cones.

"I have to run inside. Stay put. All of you," Eli warned, raising his finger and speaking in his best fatherly tone. "Simon, you're in charge. That means everyone has to listen to Simon until I get back. I won't be long." Eli closed the buggy door and strode across the frosty grass toward the schoolhouse.

Ginger was suddenly a bundle of nerves. Eli had come to her a few minutes ago and asked if he could talk to her. *Privately.* She knew at once what he wanted to talk about. And to her surprise, she realized she was ready to talk about it, too. About making their courtship official. About moving on to the betrothal stage. She knew she'd been the one to tell him she wanted to take things slowly, and she had at first, but in the last couple of days, she'd realized she wanted to finalize the matter and to be able to call Eli her own publicly. Because, as she had suspected, she was in love with him. Had been for weeks, maybe since she started working for him. It had just taken her a little while to see it. To accept it. Maybe because it was nothing like what she had dreamed it would be.

In girlish expectation, Ginger had thought love would hit her hard, maybe even feel like she was falling. Like the time she'd tumbled from the hayloft when she was a girl and had felt all dizzy and light as she'd tumbled. Because that was what people said, you *fall* in love. Her love for Eli had come on slowly and quietly; it had been like a warmth that she had first just felt in her fingertips as they brushed his when she took her turn at Chinese checkers or handed him a plate for the supper table. As the days had passed, the warmth had spread in her until now she flushed from her toes to her cheeks every time she laid eyes on him. She wanted to be with Eli every minute of the day, and when they were apart, she missed him terribly. She missed his calm, steady voice, his kindness, his practicality, but mostly she missed the way he talked to her, the way he treated her. He had spoken of love, but more importantly, she saw it in his eyes every time he looked at her.

Eli had told Ginger he'd be back in to see if anything else had to be carried out of the school. But the room was already put back together just the way Ethan liked it with desks grouped rather than in rows. Joe and some of the single men had done the cleaning up and moving. She'd talked to Joe for a few minutes during the cookie sale, and she was pleased that she felt absolutely nothing for him. When he first broke up with her, she'd avoided him because her feelings had been hurt. She'd been angry and upset with him. But now, having gotten some distance from him, and with Eli in her life, she realized Joe had done her a favor. She'd told him that and they'd both had a good laugh over it.

In the cloakroom, Ginger squinted, trying to see if she could spot Eli through the frosty window. Her sisters had already walked to their buggy. They'd come in two buggies, so her mother and Benjamin had taken one home, and she and her sisters would take the other. Bay, who was driving, had asked if they should wait on Ginger or if Eli was dropping her off. It would be easy enough for him to do. Their place was on his way home. It would give Ginger and Eli a few minutes to be together, which would be nice, even with the children. It would be their first buggy ride as a betrothed couple and, for some reason, the idea of that tickled her.

Unable to see into the dark outside with the bright lights of the schoolhouse still burning, Ginger took her cloak off one of the hooks the schoolchildren used. She was just putting on her bonnet when the cloakroom door opened, and Eli walked in.

"There you are!" she said, barely able to contain her excitement. He was going to ask her to marry him; she just knew it. And she was going to say yes. While she was busy filling cookie boxes for customers, she'd decided to be bold when he asked and suggest they not wait long to marry. The fall was the usual time for weddings, but that was tradition, not *Ordung*, and they could be married when they wanted, with the bishop's permission. As she saw it, once their minds were made up, there was no need for the children to go on any longer without a woman in the house. A mother to care for them. And truthfully, now that she knew what she wanted, what God wanted for her, she didn't want to waste any time. She wanted to be Eli's wife and it couldn't happen quickly enough.

"Bay's about to leave. She asked if I was going home with them or if you were dropping me off." She smiled up at Eli. His blue eyes could change with his mood. Tonight they seemed grayish, and she couldn't recall ever seeing them that color. "Do you want to drop me off so we can have a few minutes together?"

Eli looked down at his boots. He seemed nervous. And upset. "Not sure you're going to want a ride home from me when I say what I have to say."

She frowned. What was he talking about? Did he think she was going to put him off again? Now she felt bad. And foolish. "Why wouldn't I want to ride home with you, Eli?" She took a step toward him. There were a couple of people still in the schoolhouse, including Ethan and Abigail and her son. But they were busy sweeping and collecting the lamps and lanterns they'd borrowed to light up the schoolhouse in the dark. No one was paying Ginger and Eli in the cloakroom any mind.

Eli slowly lifted his head.

Something was wrong. What, she didn't know. She waited.

"Ginger, I've been thinking, and…" He went silent.

Ginger heard the voices coming from inside the schoolroom, but she didn't hear what they were saying. The cloakroom with its fresh coat of paint seemed to shrink around them, the voices fading. Suddenly there was no one but her and Eli. And the dread she suddenly felt in the pit of her stomach.

"I think we should end this," Eli said flatly.

For a moment she didn't know what he was talking about. But then he lifted his gaze to meet hers and she knew.

She knew.

"I'm sorry," he said.

Tears sprang in Ginger's eyes. He didn't want to marry her.

"You and I, we shouldn't be…" He exhaled. "The courtship is over. I release you from any…the obligation you feel—"

"Any *obligation*?" she blurted, surprising herself. "What are you talking about, Eli?" She never lost her temper, but she lost it now. "You're breaking up with me?" she demanded. How was this possible? Eli had told her he loved her. He had— She took a shuddering breath, her heart fluttering in her chest, a lump rising in her throat.

Eli was still talking, but she barely heard him.

"Didn't mean to… Mistaken… Unfair to you to… The two of you… Better off…"

Ginger felt like she was shattering inside. Because she loved him. She loved Eli, but he didn't love her. That was what he was saying, what he obviously meant by the words she was only catching bits of.

She wanted to marry him and he didn't want to marry her. That was what it all came down to.

Ginger suddenly felt like she couldn't breathe, and she had to get outside. She had to get out into the cold and catch her breath. Get away from Eli and his betrayal. He had told her he loved her. But he hadn't meant it. He couldn't have meant it, otherwise, he wouldn't be saying these things now.

"I have to go," she managed, sidestepping to get around him.

"Ginger—"

"Bay will leave without me and…" She reached the door that led outside and she yanked it open. A cold wall of air hit her in the face.

Outside, she heard buggies making their way down the lane and out onto the paved road. Bay would leave without her, and she'd have to walk home in the cold.

"Ginger," Eli called after her as she stumbled down the steps. "You're upset. I haven't done a very good job of explaining myself." Following her, he touched her shoulder. "Ginger, please, let me explain. I don't want you to be upset with me. You'll see this is really for the best. You only have to—"

"Don't touch me, Eli, and don't speak to me," she said, her feet finding the frosty grass. She spotted their buggy. Bay had just backed up and was ready to pull into the lane.

"Ginger, wait!"

But Ginger didn't wait for him. She ran across the lane, cutting in front of the buggy, forcing Bay to pull up hard on the reins. She threw open the door and climbed up.

"Ginger, what—"

"Please don't say anything, Bay," Ginger said softly as she slid the door shut. Nettie had vacated the front passenger seat for her and she dropped down into it. "Just drive," she said, burying her face in her hands.

Ginger stood in the doorway of the Troyers' living room watching her sister Nettie flirt shyly with a boy visiting the Troyers from Michigan. The Troyers, who owned the other harness shop in Hickory Grove, had kindly offered to give the Fishers a break and host a holiday singing. With so many folks visiting from out of town, it was the perfect opportunity for the young, single men and women of the community to meet other singles.

There had been singing, and refreshments, of course. Lettice had served mini egg salad and tuna sandwiches, coconut cupcakes that looked like they were frosted with snow and gallons of hot spiced apple cider. They sang fast hymns and then they played Change Seats. Then, when everyone was out of breath, they played some word games.

Ordinarily Ginger would have enjoyed the fun and games. But tonight, everything seemed silly and superfluous. She should never have come. She'd only done it to give the impression that she was fine with Eli breaking up with her.

Which she was not. She was brokenhearted.

Ginger was there with Joe, and he was the last person she wanted to be with. Since she'd walked in the Troyers' door, she had wanted to go home. It had been wrong to ask Joe to bring her and her sisters tonight. She didn't want to be here with him. After walking out with Eli, she realized just how immature Joe was. She didn't want to be here at all. And she certainly didn't want to walk out with Joe again. It had been a mistake to think there was any way she could go back to the way things had been before she began keeping Eli's children. Back to the way she had been before she had fallen in love with him.

Now she just wanted to go home. But she couldn't, because Joe had brought her as well as Nettie and Tara and Bay, and they all seemed to be having a wonderful time. Even Bay, who didn't usually like social events, was enjoying herself. Ginger had seen her talking with Levi Troyer several times during the evening, and now they were standing off by themselves, conversing in private.

Ginger exhaled and looked out the farmhouse window into the dark, wondering if she could plead a headache and get Joe to run her home. Or better yet, catch a ride with someone going her way. Then she wouldn't have to speak to Joe. He could give her sisters a ride home when they were ready to go or catch a ride with someone else. She needed to get out of there before she burst into tears.

"Oh Eli," she breathed. Blinking back the moisture in her eyes, she pressed her hand to the cold glass, then rested her forehead against it. It was hard to believe that a week ago she had been so happy, and now it seemed as if she never would be again.

Chapter Twelve

Eli stood in his sister's driveway and watched as his children clambered into his buggy. The sky was gray, the air damp and cold. "Thank you for keeping them today, Claudia." He lifted Lizzy in and then closed the door against the wind and a few stray snowflakes. "I have a day or two of work left to do after Christmas to finish up the job. If you don't mind having them, I'd appreciate your help."

"Of course I don't mind." His sister followed him around to the driver's side. Her breath came in white puffs in the cold air. "They're my niece and nephews. They're always welcome here."

"I know, but with your in-laws here—" Eli wiped his mouth with the back of his gloved hand.

He hadn't seen Ginger or heard from her since he broke up with her. The Monday morning after the cookie sale, her sister Tara had shown up to watch the children. When Eli had seen Benjamin's buggy coming up the driveway, his heart had sung, thinking it was Ginger. Even considering that maybe she'd come to protest his decision, to tell him that she didn't care how old she was, that she loved him and not Joe.

But it hadn't been her.

And while it had been kind of Tara to come in her sister's stead, it had been too hard to have her in the house. Too hard when all he wanted was Ginger. So he'd asked his sister to watch his children for the two weeks it would take him to finish the job he'd taken. She'd been happy to do it and not said a single unkind word when he'd explained why Ginger wouldn't be coming to the house anymore. She'd been sweet and gentle and not pried for once, though it was apparent she knew what had happened. Everyone in Hickory Grove knew. The Amish telegraph.

To his amazement, dealing with Claudia had been much easier than with his children. Lizzy cried every night for Ginger, Phillip was misbehaving at every turn and Simon was so angry with his father that Eli didn't know what to do with him. And Andrew's response to the breakup was the most heartbreaking at all. He hadn't said a word when Eli told the children Ginger wouldn't be coming to the house again. Andrew didn't talk anymore. Not just to Eli but to anyone. It seemed like he'd built a little shell around himself, and Eli didn't know how to break through. Claudia suggested gently that he just needed to give Andrew time, that children were resilient and that they'd get over the change. Eli prayed she was right but feared she wasn't.

Ginger hadn't even gone to church last Sunday. He hadn't had the heart to ask her family why she wasn't there. Probably had a cold… That, or she'd gone to church with the Verklers over in Rose Valley. He'd heard she'd gone to a singing at the Troyers' with Joe Verkler. He'd been so upset when he heard, though he didn't know why. That was why he had broken up with her, so she could be with Joe… Or some other young man of her choice. A man deserving of her beauty and youth.

Eli opened the buggy door slowly, feeling as if he were slogging through mud. He had been this way since the night of the school fundraiser. No colors seemed as bright to him as they had been, no smells as good or sounds as sharp. He missed Ginger so much that his chest ached. He kept telling himself he'd done the right thing, but after two weeks without her, he was beginning to have second thoughts. Not that it mattered now. Ginger hadn't come to him, so obviously, she was over him. Over them.

If there had ever been a *them* to begin with.

Eli had *thought* she'd cared for him, but he kept telling himself over and over again that he had been mistaken. That he'd done the right thing. It was the only way he could get through the day right now. There was no way of getting through the nights. That was probably why he felt so exhausted, so defeated. A man couldn't live on two or three hours of sleep a night.

"Eli, I'm worried about you. Are you sure you don't want to come to supper tomorrow night for Christmas Eve?" Claudia rested her hand on his arm. "We're just having soup and bread, but it would be nice to have you with us."

"Thank you, but you've already got a houseful." He nodded in the direction of the barnyard, where several of her nieces and nephews on her husband's side were jumping into puddles to break the ice that had formed on them overnight and not melted on the gray day. "We're supposed to go to Benjamin and Rosemary's," Eli said, not trusting himself to speak Ginger's name aloud. Especially in front of Claudia. "Rosemary invited us weeks ago," he explained. "Wouldn't seem right not to go."

"I think they'd understand if you changed your mind," she said gently, pulling her cloak tighter around her shoulders.

Eli stepped up into the buggy. "The children are looking forward to going. To seeing——" He focused straight ahead, watching the children playing through the windshield, the backs of his eyes stinging.

Claudia was quiet for a moment. "Eli, maybe I was wrong," she said quietly.

Only half hearing her, he looked down. "What's that?"

"I hate to see you this unhappy. I… I've been doing a lot of thinking. And praying, and…maybe I was wrong about Ginger." She shuddered against the cold. "About the two of you. Maybe you're meant to be together after all."

Eli couldn't bring himself to look at her. He wasn't angry with his sister. It didn't matter what she had thought or what she had said. He was the one who had broken up with Ginger. Impulsively broken up with her without thinking it through, without talking about it with her. And now he was stuck with his decision. And now Ginger was dating Joe Verkler again—good-looking, flashy Joe. For all he knew, they'd be crying the marriage banns come next church Sunday.

"Eli." Claudia reached up and grabbed his arm, not so gently this time. "You should go talk with Ginger."

"Too late for that." He lifted the reins, his gelding stepped up and the buggy rolled forward. "See you Christmas Day, Claudia."

"It's never too late, Eli!" she called after him. "Not until one of you is married to another!"

* * *

Ginger sighed and tugged on her sewing needle, catching a loop of thread around her finger. She wasn't the best at hand sewing, but her skills were perfectly adequate. She knew full well how to hem a dress. She'd been whipstitching hems since she was seven. So why couldn't she do it today? How did she keep getting these little knots in her thread? And why were her stitches so uneven? She groaned and tugged again, this time so hard that the thread snapped.

"*Ach!*" Ginger muttered, dropping the dress to her lap as she reached for the scissors. She'd have to pull out enough stitches now to tie off the thread and then restitch the same three or four inches of hem she'd already stitched twice. "I just can't do anything right today," she muttered. Then as she lowered the scissors, she somehow managed to prick her hand with the needle. "Ouch!" she said loudly. She looked up to see her mother and her sisters Nettie and Tara staring at her. No one said a word.

Ginger narrowed her gaze at her sisters. "What?" she demanded in a not-so-pleasant tone. Then she pressed her injured hand to her mouth.

Her mother cleared her throat and looked to Tara and Nettie. "Could you girls make us some tea and maybe cut us a few slices of that banana bread? I just love the chocolate chips in it."

"I'm sorry," Ginger said to her mother and sisters. She looked away as tears filled her eyes. "I'm sorry," she repeated in a whisper.

Tara and Nettie both rose from their chairs, set their sewing down and left the sewing room without so much as a sound.

"Ginger," her mother said quietly when the girls were gone.

"I don't mean to be so cross." Ginger shook her head. She sniffed and pressed her chapped lips together. She set the needle down on the little table beside her and fumbled in her apron pocket for her handkerchief. She'd been using it a lot these days.

Her mother looked up from the sock she was knitting; it was so small that Ginger knew it had to be for one of her youngest brothers, Josiah or James. "I know you don't, *Dochtah*." Her knitting needles clicked together as her hands made the stitches from memory.

Ginger glanced around and realized, for the first time since they'd moved into the house here in Delaware, how much this sewing room resembled her mother's old sewing room back in New York.

Nearly square, with two large windows, this sewing room, like the old one, was painted a pale blue, with a blue-and-white-and-yellow rag rug in the middle of the floor. There were the two rocking chairs placed side by side where Tara and Nettie had been sitting. One wall boasted an oversize walnut cabinet rescued from a twentieth-century millinery shop, and open drawers revealed an assortment of various sizes of thread, needles, scissors and paper patterns. A small knotty pine table with turned legs stood between the windows. In the warmer months, her mother, who had the greenest thumb of anyone Ginger knew, kept fresh herbs and flowers planted in a terra-cotta planter there.

"Bay said you told her you wouldn't be walking out with Joe again," Ginger's mother said. "Would you like to talk about it?"

"About Joe?" Ginger arched her eyebrows. "There's

nothing to talk about. You were right. He was a bad choice from the beginning. We're not well suited." She looked away. "I guess that makes you happy. To know you were right."

"It never makes a mother happy to see her child in pain." Her mother's knitting needles went still and silent. "I meant, did you want to talk about what happened between you and Eli."

Ginger sniffed and wiped her nose with her handkerchief. "*Ne*, I do not."

"Then don't talk to me about it, but you and Eli need to talk. The bad air needs to be cleared. It's hanging over us all, Ginger."

Ginger stared at the dress in her lap. She needed to finish the hem. She had to be in the harness shop in an hour's time to work her shift. Since she'd stopped watching the children for Eli, she'd gone back to working for Benjamin in his harness shop. She ran the cash register when he needed her, but mostly she worked in the back, sewing leather with a heavy-duty sewing machine powered by a large foot treadle. The work had been good for her; it helped ease the ache in her chest that came from missing the little ones so much. And Eli. She missed Eli so much that she could barely think straight. The first few days after Eli broke up with her, she had mostly been angry, but now she was just sad. And lonely. Even in her mother's busy house that was always busting at the seams with people, she missed Eli.

Ginger's gaze strayed to a window, the glass white with frost. "I've nothing to say to Eli. He broke up with me."

"But you said you're not even sure why. Don't you think he owes you an explanation?"

Ginger's eyes teared up again. "It doesn't matter. He wanted to marry me and now—" Her voice caught in her throat. "And now he doesn't."

"But you're miserable, and from what I hear, Eli's more miserable than you are. If that's possible," her mother added.

Ginger didn't say anything. What was there to say? Eli didn't love her. And if he didn't love her, she didn't want to marry him. Because she loved him. It was as simple as that. She couldn't even remember what he'd said at the schoolhouse that night. She'd been so upset that she'd not heard or absorbed his explanation.

"Did you hear what I said?" her mother asked. "I said Eli's very upset. I think the two of you need to talk. You can't keep hiding from him."

"I'm not hiding."

Her mother rose, pushing her knitting down into the fabric bag that hung on her favorite chair, a recliner Benjamin had brought home for her when she was expecting the twins. "Oh you're hiding, all right. You sent your sister to watch the children. You went to church with Anne Yoder and her family last Sunday so—"

"Anne invited me," Ginger argued.

"So you wouldn't have to see Eli," her mother finished. "And I think you're behaving foolishly. If the two of you aren't right for marriage, that's one thing, but you're such good friends. You shouldn't lose a good friend, nor should he."

Ginger just sat there staring at the dress in her lap.

Her mother walked to the door. "I'm not convinced it's too late to set things right with Eli."

Ginger didn't look at her mother. "I am. He said he didn't want to court me. That's the end of it."

Her mother stopped in the doorway and exhaled. "We don't always mean the things we say, Ginger. You're old enough to know that." She hesitated. "Are you sure there isn't anything between Joe Verkler and you now?"

Ginger looked up. "*Ne*. There is not. Joe's not any more ready to marry and be the head of a family than Josiah or James. Honestly… I think I liked the *idea* of him more than I actually ever liked him." She glanced out the window again. It was a gray day and the wind was howling. The temperature was dropping fast. Benjamin had said at the breakfast table that morning that snow was in the forecast for the following day, Christmas Eve. A storm coming out of the west, he said.

"Just talk to Eli, Ginger," her mother murmured. "If nothing else than to clear the air and ease your pain and his."

"If I never talked to Eli again, it would be too soon," Ginger said, looking up defiantly at her mother.

"Well, that's going to be interesting, considering the fact that he and the children are coming for supper tomorrow night."

"What?" Ginger got to her feet. "He's still coming? Can't…can't you…*uninvite* him?"

"On Christmas Eve?" Her mother raised her eyebrows. "Certainly not. Benjamin saw him at the feed store yesterday and he said he would see us tomorrow night."

Ginger crossed her arms over her chest stubbornly. "I don't want to talk to Eli. I'm not doing it."

Her mother walked out of the room, still in good humor. "We will see about that, *Dochtah*."

* * *

Ginger stood at the stove and threw the last of the vegetables into the soup. She liked to add them at different stages, so they didn't all cook to mush.

"Could you turn the back burner on under the clam chowder?" Tara asked as she passed behind Ginger, carrying a stack of plates.

She was setting the two kitchen tables for the Christmas Eve meal. They were just having soup and sandwiches, but there were an apple crisp and blueberry buckle baking in the oven, and there would be ice cream to go with the dessert. When Benjamin bought the house in Delaware, he'd added propane tanks to the property, which allowed them to run not just the refrigerator, washer and dryer, but a freezer in the cellar. Even after being there three years, their own freezer still seemed like such a luxury.

After supper, their family and Eli's would gather together in the parlor for prayers and a short sermon that Benjamin, as the head of the household, would give. When Ginger had heard that Eli was still coming with the children, she'd been half tempted to say she was sick and go to bed for the evening. But then she wouldn't get to see Andrew, Simon, Phillip and Lizzy and she missed them so much that she feared she would shatter if she didn't hug them. And as much as she hated to admit it, her mother was right. She couldn't avoid Eli forever.

That didn't mean she had to talk to him.

That was what she had told her mother that morning. Her mother hadn't been pleased. Ginger could tell by the way she'd pursed her mouth. But her mother hadn't said a word, which was a relief because Ginger didn't want to get into an argument with her, not on Christmas

Eve. Not on any day, because her mother was a woman to be reckoned with when she got a bee in her bonnet.

"Don't the tables look so nice?" Tara chattered as she set the plates down one at a time. "I love how Bay arranged the greenery and pine cones on the center of the table. It's so pretty and smells so good."

"Whatever you've got cooking on the back of the stove smells good, too," Ginger said, trying to forget herself and her trials for a moment. Since she and Eli had broken up, she had felt very removed from her family. All her own fault, she realized, because she hadn't just been avoiding Eli, she'd been evading her family, too. Instead of leaning on them at a difficult time, she'd avoided them, making herself feel even more isolated than she had to. She'd been selfish, thinking of no one but herself. "What is it?" she asked Tara.

"Nothing to eat." Tara laughed as she put the last plate down at the head of the table where Benjamin always sat. "It's just to make the house smell good. Water with orange peels, cinnamon stick and clove."

Ginger breathed in the sweet, spicy aroma. "It smells so good, I bet you could sell it," she said, setting the wooden spoon down.

"Funny you would say that. Bay thought the same. We're going to try drying orange peels and see if we can make dried packets that can just be dumped in a pot of water. Bay thinks she can sell it in the Christmas shop next year."

Ginger smiled at her young sister. "I think that's a great idea."

"Ginger?" Their mother bustled into the room carrying a child-size chair in each hand. Though the little ones usually sat at the big table, with Eli's children coming, she'd decided at the last minute to set up a small table for them. She'd found a little table and chairs that had been brought from New York in the attic and she was now setting them up. "Could you do me a favor?"

Ginger took a teaspoon from a drawer. "What do you need? Both soups are on, but turned down." She dipped the spoon in the vegetable-beef soup and tasted it. It was the perfect balance of broth and meat and vegetables with just the right amount of salt.

"Could you go in the living room and set up some games? Maybe puzzles for the children, Chinese checkers and that game with the spinner?" She set the little chairs down. "Jacob put up two more tables."

"Sure." Ginger set the spoon in the sink and washed her hands. "We're playing games tonight? I thought we were just having family prayers and turning in early."

Her mother gave a wave. "You know Benjamin. He gets ideas in his head," she said, walking out of the kitchen. "Sometimes it's just easier to go along than to argue. You best do it now," she said as she disappeared down the hall. "I think Eli is here, so we'll eat soon."

Drying her hands, Ginger took a couple of deep breaths. Just hearing Eli's name made her heart patter in her chest. But after spending a long time in prayer that morning, she had decided that she wasn't going to behave so childishly anymore. She was a grown woman whose romance hadn't worked out. And it was time she behaved like an adult.

"Keep an eye on the soups, will you, Tara?" Ginger asked as she went down the hall.

"*Ya*," Tara called after her.

In the living room, Ginger found the two small tables Jacob had brought up from the cellar. She discovered that he had also started a fire in the fireplace, which made the big living room warm and cozy. "So we're playing games," she said to herself under her breath. That meant Eli would likely stay later.

But she could handle that, she told herself as she took three boxes of puzzles down from the bookshelf and set them on the table farthest from the fireplace. Then she went back to the shelf for the Chinese checkers game. *I'll be fine. I'll do puzzles with the children. Eli and I are adults. We can certainly be in the same room together.*

But she wasn't fine. As she started setting up the Chinese checkers board, taking the brightly colored marbles from the box, a lump rose in her throat. How many hours had she and Eli spent at his kitchen table talking and laughing and playing Chinese checkers? When she looked back now, it all seemed like a dream. A wonderful dream.

"It's in the living room," Ginger heard her mother say to someone. "Let me show you. I don't know what's wrong with it, but a three-legged table won't work, will it?"

Ginger heard someone respond, but couldn't make out what he said. The voice was male. One of her brothers, she guessed.

"It's old, but I think it still has years of use left in it." Ginger's mother walked into the living room.

Eli followed in her footsteps. He was in the living room before he saw her. Their gazes met and he froze. Ginger froze. Eli's eyes opened wide, and for a moment, he looked like one of the farm animals cornered in a barn.

Ginger's mother backed into the doorway.

Eli glanced at her. "There isn't a wobbly table in here, is there?"

"There is, but that's not why I brought you in here." Her mother rested her hands on her hips. "I brought you in here, Eli, because the two of you need to talk." She shook her head. "Honestly, I don't know which of the two of you is more stubborn. You deserve each other, I say."

"I have nothing to say to him," Ginger said, surprised by how loud and clear her voice came out, because she was trembling inside.

"Then it's going to be a long night, because no one in these families is eating until this matter is settled. One way or the other." Her mother backed out of the room, grabbing the doorknob.

"*Mam*, you're closing the door on us? What are you doing?" Ginger made for the door.

"My children…" Eli managed.

"I'm doing what I should have done two weeks ago," Ginger's mother declared. "Making you talk to each other." She looked to Eli. "Your children are fine."

"*Mam*!" Ginger protested. "You can't—I don't want to talk to him," she called after her.

"Then play a game of Chinese checkers," her mother called back.

Then the door lock clicked.

"You're locking us in?" Ginger cried, angry and horrified at the same time.

"I'll be back to check on you in a little while," she heard her mother say.

Ginger stood there for a moment staring at the locked door, hearing her mother's footsteps as she went down the hall. *She had locked them in?* Ginger couldn't believe this was happening! She turned to Eli. "I'm sorry. I didn't know anything about this."

He frowned. "Me, either."

She just stood there for a moment, looking at him. Then swallowed hard and looked away. *No tears*, she told herself. *No tears.*

After a moment, Eli cleared his throat and spoke. "Would you like to…" He exhaled. "Let's play. She'll have to let us out eventually." He gave a half-hearted chuckle. "I have to milk come morning."

Ginger pressed her lips together in indecision. She didn't want to play checkers with Eli. She didn't want to sit so close to him. She didn't want to look at him, because it would only make her sad. But she was locked in the room with him, and what other choice did she have? She could play a game with him or stand here like a scarecrow in the garden.

"Fine," she said. "I'll be green."

At the table, Ginger sat down first and moved a marble, not even waiting for Eli to take his seat. He moved and then she moved again. They each took five turns before either spoke a word. It was Eli, God bless him, who broke the impasse.

"Ginger, I want to tell you how sorry—"

"Do you realize how much you hurt me, Eli?" Ginger burst out, startling them both. "One minute we were talking about marriage and the next you're saying you're breaking up with me." She opened her arms wide. "I don't even know why."

"So you could be with a man your own age," he said as if that was obvious. "Be with Joe. Which is what I assume you wanted because you're courting again."

"Joe and I are not courting. Who told you that?"

"Eunice Gruber."

She rose from her chair and started to pace. "I'm *not*

courting Joe. I went with him to a singing, thinking maybe I could give him a second chance, but I couldn't do it. Because he's not right for me and I'm not right for him. I was just so angry with you, so hurt that I... I..." She looked at him. "I think I did it for spite and—" Her voice caught in her throat. "And I'm sorry. That's not very becoming of a woman of faith. That's not who I am."

Eli rose from his chair and came to her. "If we're making confessions, I have to say, I think half the reason I told you I didn't want to court you was because I was jealous of Joe."

She drew back in disbelief. "Jealous of Joe? Whatever for? Joe Verkler isn't half the man you are, Eli. He... He's not even a man. He's a boy!"

Eli pressed his hand to his forehead. "I just... I saw the two of you together at the cookie sale and he was so handsome, and you were so beautiful and the two of you were laughing together, and I just... I thought you two deserved each other. And I didn't deserve you," he said quietly. "I think I just got scared and... I lost my way for a moment. Not very becoming of a man of faith," he finished quietly.

Ginger stood there looking at Eli for a moment and then said softly, "But Eli, I think you're the most handsome man in the world. The kindest, the—" She hesitated, thinking she shouldn't say any more, but if she didn't say it now, she would never say it. And if she was ever going to recover from this, she had to speak the truth here and now, even if it would make no difference. "I think you're the kindest, the gentlest, most family-devoted man I've ever known. You're smart and funny and you can cook and clean and..." She was fighting tears again. "And I love that you take your boots off in the house. I love you for all of those things."

Eli started to laugh and Ginger had no idea why, but suddenly she was laughing, too.

"You love me because I take my boots off, even though I have holes in my socks?"

She was still laughing, trying not to cry. "I loved you more for the hole in your sock."

"But I'm older than you. I have gray hair and children and a dead wife and—" He stopped, his gaze meeting hers. "And you don't care about those things, do you?"

She shook her head slowly. "I don't. And I never did."

Eli stood there for a moment and then reached for her hand. When he took it, when she felt the warmth of his touch, all of the pain of the last two weeks fell away. Nothing mattered but the feel of his hand and his eyes on her.

"Ginger, I've been a fool. I asked God to find me a wife and He delivered you literally to my door. I asked and He answered my prayers and then I didn't listen. I didn't obey as I should have. I allowed myself to be undermined by self-doubt, and I am so sorry. Can you forgive me?"

She nodded, not trusting herself to speak.

"Then let me ask you another question. I have to ask. And it's fine if you say no. I'll understand if you do. Why you would." He squeezed her hand, looking down, then lifted his gaze. "Ginger, will you marry me? Will you marry this silly old fool?"

A sigh of relief escaped her lips. "*Ya*," she whispered, and then, she didn't know if he drew her into an embrace first or if she just threw her arms around him. Either way, she was in his arms.

"You will?" he asked, laughing but sounding as if he might cry at the same time.

She nodded and hugged him tight and then lifted her head from his shoulder to look into his eyes. "*Ya*, I'll marry you."

He smiled. "You know," he said softly. "I had made up my mind that I wouldn't kiss you until we were wed. It didn't seem fitting that a man my age should kiss a young woman of—"

Ginger pressed her mouth to his and, at that moment, had there been even a sliver of doubt in her mind that she and Eli were meant for each other, it was washed away in an instant. As his lips touched hers, she knew in her heart of hearts that she was kissing her husband.

"Does this mean you've mended your differences?"

Startled by her mother's voice, Ginger backed out of Eli's arms, bringing her fingers to her lips where his kiss still burned. How had her mother gotten into the living room? Ginger hadn't even heard her unlock the door!

"I think it does," Eli managed, his face turning red.

"*Goot*. The Christmas gift I was praying for." Her mother turned to go. "Let's have supper, and later we'll talk about the wedding over a cup of hot cider."

Their gazes met and they both laughed, then Eli took Ginger's hand and led her into the kitchen to begin their new life together.

Epilogue

One year later

Ginger heard the crunch of snow beneath Eli's boots as he came up the walk from the barn. "All fed and tucked in for the night. The mare's hoof is—" She heard him start up the porch steps and stop. "Wife, what are you doing?"

She glanced over her shoulder at her husband and grasped the stepladder to keep her balance. The wind was blowing and the snow had just begun to fall. Their original plan had been to go to her mother and Benjamin's for supper and family prayers, but with the snowstorm coming in, they had decided to stay safe and warm at home. In an hour's time, Ginger had cobbled together a nice meal. There was beef stew simmering on the stove, biscuits baking in the oven, and they had a cookie jar full of treats she and the children had made that morning.

"Trying to rehang the wreath we made," she explained. The wind whipped at the wool scarf, tugging it off her head. It was the wind that was the culprit in blowing the wreath off the door in the first place. "But my fingers are so cold, I can't get the string back on the nail," she explained, showing him her hands with her fingerless gloves. She'd thought it would be easier to return the wreath to its place wearing the gloves, but she hadn't anticipated the windchill factor.

"Get off that ladder before you hurt yourself," Eli said, taking the last porch steps two at a time. When he reached her, he offered his hand. "I'll put it back up. You go inside and get warm."

Ginger accepted his hand and came down the slippery ladder, but when she reached the bottom, she didn't let go. "The children are eager to open their gifts. I think maybe you're right. I should never have left them out where they would see them."

It wasn't really an Amish tradition to give gifts for Christmas, but her mother had always given each of them a gift as children, and Eli's mother had done the same, so they had agreed there would be a gift for each child, but only one. The two younger boys had gotten wooden toys Eli had made, Lizzy had gotten a doll and Simon had gotten a brand-new shiny pocketknife. Ginger had wrapped them in bits of fabric from her sewing chest and tied them with ribbon she'd gotten from Bay at the greenhouse.

"Do you think we should open them tonight or in the morning?"

Eli drew her into his arms. "I think tonight is fine. We have the candies and oranges for them for tomorrow, and the socks and scarves you knitted."

Ginger smiled up at him and then rested her head on his shoulder for a moment. Despite the bitter cold, she was immediately warmed by his embrace. Ten months into their marriage and she still marveled at how comfortable she was as a wife, as Eli's wife. How happy she was to have him as her husband and the children as her own now.

"I've a little something for you, as well," Eli whispered in her ear.

She looked at him with a smile. "You do? I thought we agreed to no gifts. All that money we spent on the trip after our wedding."

Though for practical reasons, few folks with small children followed the tradition of taking a journey together to visit relatives before setting up housekeeping, Eli had insisted they needed some time alone together. Leaving the children with Claudia, they had gone to upstate New York to visit Ginger's relatives who were still there, staying with Benjamin's daughter Mary and her husband and children. It had been a week she would remember for the rest of her days.

"It's just a little something," Eli told her, brushing her hair from her face. When her headscarf blew off, her hair had come partially undone from its knot and she could only imagine what a fright she was. But he didn't seem to mind. He kissed the top of her head. "I don't need a gift from you, Ginger. Not ever." He gazed into her eyes, his blue eyes twinkling with joy. "You are gift enough."

Ginger pressed her lips together. Actually, she *did* have a gift for him. She had thought she might wait another week before she told him, but suddenly it felt as if the right time was now. "Now that I think about it, I do have something for you, Husband. Though you'll have to wait a bit for it."

He knitted his brow. "And what is that?"

She leaned toward him and whispered in his ear.

"What?" he exclaimed, drawing back from her, but still holding her in his arms. His face was alight with joy. "Are you sure?"

She smiled up at him. "As sure as a woman can be."

"Oh Ginger." His arms around her, he lifted her off her feet. "You know you and the four *kinder* are enough for me. More than a man deserves, but I prayed… I hoped God would bless me again. Bless us." When he set her down lightly and met her gaze, his blue eyes were teary. "Thank you. For loving me. For giving the children a mother, for—" He sniffed and laughed, unembarrassed by his emotion.

Ginger couldn't stop smiling.

"And you were on a ladder!" he burst out.

She laughed. "I'm not sick. It's the most natural thing for a woman. I—"

"In the house, wife," he interrupted. "You shouldn't be out in the cold."

She took his hand. "Only if you come in with me."

"What of the wreath?" He pointed at it, lying on the porch.

She shrugged. "Put it back up tomorrow. Come on." She led him to the door. "Let's get ourselves warm and put supper on the table."

Eli brushed his lips against hers, and Ginger closed her eyes, saying a silent prayer of thanks for that happy moment and all the happy moments of their life together yet to come.

* * * * *

SPECIAL EXCERPT FROM

LOVE INSPIRED
INSPIRATIONAL ROMANCE

He needs a housekeeper. She needs a job.
This holiday season, will they join forces—
and find true love?

Read on for a sneak preview of
Her Christmas Dilemma *by Brenda Minton.*

"We need a housekeeper because I can't chase you down every other—" Tucker suddenly remembered they had an audience. "We can talk about this at home."

Nan, spritely at seventy with short silvery hair, grinned big and inclined her head toward the other woman.

"Clara needs a job," she said.

"I don't think so," Clara shot back.

"You need something to do," Nan insisted.

"She doesn't want the job." Tucker winked at the woman and watched her cheeks turn rosy.

Flirting was an art he'd learned late in life, and he still wasn't too accomplished at it. He'd never been a ladies' man.

"No, I really don't," she answered. "I'm only here temporarily."

Should he feel relieved or let down?

"You should introduce us," he told Nan.

"Tucker Church, I'd like you to meet Clara Fisher," Nan said. "She's one of my kids."

One of Nan's foster daughters. She'd had a dozen or more over the years. He held a hand out. "Clara, nice to meet you."

It was a long moment before Clara slid her hand into his. Then she stepped back, putting space between them.

"Nice to meet you, too. But I'm afraid I'm not interested in a job." She gave his niece a genuine smile, then her gaze lifted to meet his. "I think that we probably met in school, but you were a senior and I was just a freshman."

He couldn't imagine forgetting Clara Fisher, with her dark brown eyes that held secrets and a smile that was captivating. He found himself wishing he could make her smile again.

Shay elbowed him. "She doesn't want the job," she whispered. "Can we go home now?"

"Of course she doesn't want to work for us. She's probably heard the stories about you running off two housekeepers." He gave Clara a pleading look.

"Would you take my number? In case you change your mind?"

"I won't change my mind," she insisted.

He had no right to feel disappointed. She was a stranger. And yet, he was.

"Well, we should go," he said as he walked Shay toward the door.

"I bet she can't even clean," Shay said under her breath.

He didn't disagree. But Clara looked like a woman who was trying to put herself back together. He needed someone strong who could stand up to Shay.

The woman who replaced Mrs. Jenkins couldn't have soulful brown eyes and a smile that made him want to take chances.

Don't miss
Her Christmas Dilemma *by Brenda Minton,*
available December 2021 wherever
Love Inspired books and ebooks are sold.

LoveInspired.com

LIEXP1121

LOVE INSPIRED

Stories to uplift and inspire

Fall in love with Love Inspired—
inspirational and uplifting stories of faith
and hope. Find strength and comfort in
the bonds of friendship and community.
Revel in the warmth of possibility and the
promise of new beginnings.

Sign up for the Love Inspired newsletter
at **LoveInspired.com** to be the first
to find out about upcoming titles,
special promotions and exclusive content.

CONNECT WITH US AT:

LISOCIAL2021

Get 4 FREE REWARDS!

We'll send you 2 FREE Books plus 2 FREE Mystery Gifts.

Love Inspired books feature uplifting stories where faith helps guide you through life's challenges and discover the promise of a new beginning.

FREE Value Over **$20**